WRITTEN BY

BRADY J. SADLER

www.bradyjsadler.com

Cover Art by Jordan Smajstrla
Cover Layout & Graphic Design by Chris Doughman
Logo by Evan Simonet
Additional Graphic Design by Brady J. Sadler

ISBN: 978-0-9853679-8-5 (Hardcover)
ISBN: 978-0-9853679-9-2 (Paperback)
ISBN: 979-8-9910250-0-3 (eBook)
ISBN: 978-0-9853679-9-2 (Paperback, IngramSpark)
ISBN: 979-8-3314416-8-5 (Hardcover, Barnes & Noble Press)
ISBN: 979-8-3314416-0-9 (Paperback, Barnes & Noble Press)

Also by Brady J. Sadler

www.bradyjsadler.com

The Days of Astasia

Eve of Corruption (2012)

The Malice of Light

The Acrid Sky (2023)

The Withered Roots (2024)

The Smoldering Vein (Forthcoming)

Emerald Decay (2025)

In Short Order (2025)

Relic Meyers

Relic Meyers & The Rhythms of Ruin (2024)

Relic Meyers & The Harmony of Hexes (2025)

For my twin brother, Adam.

We dumped a lot of time and money into our heavy metal dreams, and it didn't go as planned.

But I would never have written this story if we hadn't given it a shot.

I don't think I'd do a damn thing differently.

Also, I think we rocked.

Prologue

Twenty miles outside Indianapolis, Indiana. 1987.

Steven "Stick" Meyers reached for the phone, but stopped short.

His eyes were fixed on the silver buttons that each displayed a dark, grimy number. Those keys would—if pushed in the right sequence—connect him with his wife. She would answer in a panic, asking if he were alright, where he went. He would calm her, like he always did, using his casual charm and dark humor to make her forget all the fights that had led up to this point.

But then he would have to answer the questions.

He sighed and lowered his hand.

There were few things in the world that Steven wanted more than to tell Dina the truth, but he knew he couldn't. There wasn't enough time to explain everything, and he would only get one shot at this.

Outside the phone booth, Steven heard the rest of Unknown Oath coming out of the gas station. Gate—Steven's bassist and best friend—was laughing at something Ricky said, but when Steven locked eyes with him through the phone booth's cracked glass, the gap-toothed smile quickly faded from Gate's face. Ricky and Jeff kept on chuckling as they continued to the band's van, but Gate broke off toward the phone booth as if he were going to the gallows.

"No dice, Stick?"

Steven stepped out of the booth, jiggling the broken door that wouldn't fold back closed, kicking it in frustration. He jammed his hands into his pockets to keep himself from punching it as well. Yet it didn't calm the violent tension rising within him there in that parking lot.

Gate sighed, reaching up to tuck his long, bushy hair behind his ears. "Well, man, maybe it's better off. Like you said...we'll only get one shot at this, and the European scene is where it's all happening. Dina would just try to stop you."

Steven let out his own sigh, leaning back to look up into the clear sky. Thousands of stars. The entire world waited for him. This was his time. He felt a cool breeze blow through his thick hair, brushing the back of his denim jacket covered in heavy metal patches.

"I know we have to do this," he said. "We've come this far...I just can't stop thinking of being *that* guy." Steven straightened, giving Gate a level gaze, looking for anything in his friend's eyes to convince him that he could stray from their course. "You know? That scumbag in the movies that bails on his family to chase some stupid dream."

Gate stepped forward. "Dude, this is not some stupid dream. You know how big this is. You, me, Ricky...hell, even Jeff, who barely does shit for the band, we all started this. No one believed us, but we did it. And now, goddammit," he stepped forward to lay his heavy hand on Steven's shoulder, "we gotta finish it, Stick. Or we'll never forgive ourselves."

Steven nodded, knowing he wouldn't find any resistance from Gate—the dude was committed. There was a time when his old friend would have been the first one to find an excuse to get out of something. Up until the 1976 Chambers High battle of the bands, the only things Gate took seriously were tabletop roleplaying games and toaster pastries.

A lot has changed since then.

The realization seemed to summon a chill breeze and an eerie howl split the night's silence. Steven felt his friend's hand pull back as if his shoulder had suddenly caught fire. Gate looked toward the black trees on the other side of the empty highway.

"That may be our cue, Stick."

Feeling a shiver creep up his spine, Steven nodded and motioned to the van. "Like you said, man. We gotta see this thing through. It's not every day your band gets invited to tour Europe."

Gate's laugh was a gentle roll of thunder. "Yeah, baby!" Steven let out his own laugh, trying not to think of Dina or their four-year-old son. Unknown Oath's rhythm section made their way back to their van as Jeff finally got the junker to start.

A rustle of leaves stopped Steven short as he raised and planted one leather boot inside the van.

"I'm telling ya, man," Ricky was saying, "she'll probably follow us to the airport."

A shadow took shape across the street from them, and Steven felt his throat tighten. Icy daggers pinned his limbs in place, and he could only watch, frozen, as the Widow took shape.

"Who are you talking about?" Steven asked Ricky, his body still and his eyes locked on the woman who stood sentinel on the edge of the woods. The mists began to gather around the Widow, but her eyes were glowing orbs of white oblivion.

"Our groupie," Ricky said between mouthfuls of chips. "That pale chick that comes to all our shows. Check it out."

Steven managed to pull his gaze away from the distant figure now obscured by the evening fog. He peered into the van, dimly lit by its only functioning interior lamp. Ricky presented a photo smeared with the same cheese powder that covered his fingers, but the image was unmistakable.

In the photo, she leaned casually against a wall covered in overlapping posters featuring a myriad of local bands. Unknown Oath's own poster from their big show at the Variance last October hung right above the Widow's head, which was easy to notice since Ricky was in the picture flashing metal horns with one hand while the other pointed to his face in the poster.

"This was from last night?" Steven asked, trying to keep the panic from his voice. He shot Gate a side-eyed look, but his friend looked just as shocked as he felt. "At the Rash Pit?"

"Shit or get off the pot, Stick!" Jeff commanded from the driver seat. "We got a plane to catch."

Steven flashed a glance back toward the woods even though he knew there'd be no sign of their biggest fan. The terror that had seized him suddenly fled as well and he climbed into the van, sliding the door shut and taking shotgun next to his lead guitarist.

As Jeff kicked the junker loudly into gear, Steven spun around in the passenger seat to face Ricky again. "You didn't tell me she was there, man. I told you to keep an eye out for her."

Ricky sucked on his cheesy fingers, his blonde curls swaying in front of his face while the van made a wide turn to get back on the road. "Oh I did, bro. Couldn't keep my eyes off them titties of hers." He returned to flipping through the stack of photos from the show. "I think we got a shot of them somewhere."

"Seriously, dude," Gate said, looking out the window in a feigned show of slight disinterest, "we told you she could fuck up this deal for us. You gotta let us know when she's around."

Jeff swerved the van suddenly, causing them all to nearly lose their seats. "I don't get it, dude. You both keep warning us about this chick—how is some Hoosier whore gonna blow up our record deal?"

"It's a long story," Steven said, hoping Jeff would lose interest in the topic as he usually did. Fortunately, he was the least focused member of the band and Ricky wasn't far behind. As long as Steven and Gate kept the shows lined up and wrote all the music, their bandmates barely asked any questions.

"Here it is," Ricky said from the back seat, reaching over the band's gear to hand Steven another cheese-flavored photo. "Not the nicest I've seen, but she's always willing to whip 'em out."

Steven took the photo, swallowing a lump in his throat before looking at it. He tried to remind himself how close they were—they just needed to get to England and sign the contract. Maybe after a year of touring he could finally come back here and make things right with his family.

As long as the Widow was following him, he would never be a good husband or father, he couldn't be anything except her disciple.

Steven finally allowed himself to look at the photo. Ricky was wrong, she had very nice tits. But that's not what drew Steven's eyes. The pale woman in the photo who was pulling up her shirt to reveal herself, letting Ricky cup one of her bared breasts, was no woman at all. Her face had faded into a ghostly mask, her true form reserved for Steven's eyes.

Over the course of the last three years, Steven had come to know the Widow's face all too well. Her almond eyes always accented with heavy black eyeliner and violet eyeshadow, and her jet black hair framing her skeletal face like funeral shrouds.

However, that face was gone. Now he stared at a demon—a demon with a killer rack, but a demon, nonetheless. The face he knew so well was shredded into strips of leathery flesh with white bone below and horns protruding from brow and jaw.

Steven could only assume he was finally seeing the Widow's true form—whatever wicked entity had stolen Cecily Moreau's body.

Steven let the photo fall from his hand, his eyes focusing on something beyond his own comprehension. "Hurry, Jeff."

"We'll get there, man. I'm not going to risk another ticket."

"Just hurry. We need to make it."

"We're gonna make it," Gate assured him from the back.

"Yeah, baby!" Ricky banged on the van's ceiling. "Unknown Oath's going to make those Euro babes squeal!"

Jeff pounded the dash in agreement, clicking on the tape deck to unleash some more Metallica.

As they continued their trek to the airport, Steven found himself hoping that—even if he wasn't around to see—his son would have a normal, boring life.

And he would never pick up a goddamn drumstick.

CHAPTER 1

LARAMIE, INDIANA. 1997

Relic spun a drumstick lazily through his fingers as he looked into the green lacquered woodgrain of his bass drum, which acted like a mirror despite the layers of dust it had gathered. While some people could look pretty cool twirling a drumstick, what stared back at Relic was less than impressive.

At fourteen, Relic hadn't grown much since eleven or twelve, except for maybe around the waist. His bare pudgy midsection was wrinkled into several chubby rolls, partly because he was hunched over and partly because he hadn't yet "stretched out his baby fat," as Dr. Weaver put it.

"I've seen it a hundred times," the old man had told him during his last checkup, "late bloomers like you hitting that sophomore year growth spurt and shooting up like a rocket. Next time you come in here, I'll be craning my neck to see your face, trust me. You're gonna be a stud, kid, just like your dad."

Relic stopped spinning the stick and slammed it back down onto the snare, once again unable to find the desire to play a single beat. He stood up to glare over his drum set, his mood even darker than when he came down to the basement. The once-brilliant emerald mist finish was now like a murky swamp, begging for someone to stir its waters once more. But the words "just like your dad" echoed in his mind.

Thinking of his dad used to inspire him, but these last couple of years, it was doing the opposite. The last letter Relic had gotten from the legendary drummer of Unknown Oath was in December of '94.

"I think I'll finally be able to come home in a couple months, buddy," his dad had said, the words still driving tiny daggers in Relic's heart even as he recalled them. "This last tour was brutal, but I think we finally put the bitch down."

The "bitch" was what his dad called the band's third and worst album, *The Rest of the Wicked*. The album was almost unanimously reviled, but it still held a special place in Relic's heart, despite the dark legacy that followed it. Not a day went by that Relic didn't either think about or listen to that album.

Thinking of it now, he turned toward the wood-paneled wall where various heavy metal legends overlooked his drum kit from dozens of posters. The album art for *The Rest of the Wicked* featured the members of Unknown Oath—Stick, Gate, Ricky, and Jeff—standing triumphantly in their torn robes, heavy metal cultists sealing away whatever dark goddess the album's lyrics were about.

As far as concept albums go, *Rest* was…well, Relic always thought the Stacky Riggs review in *Metallic Mayhem*'s September 1994 issue summed it up best.

"Many of us fans of this genre," Stacky had eloquently written, "have come to terms with enduring rehashed themes of chainmail bikini babes fighting demons in some far-flung universe just so we can headbang to four-and-a-half minutes of shredding guitars and machine-gun double bass. However, Unknown Oath brings new meaning to the *concept* of a concept album with their latest release, *The Rest of the Wicked*, dragging us through about an hour and a half of some of the most arcane, Lovecraft-esque plot drudgery ever conceived just so we can blindly grope our way through fifteen tracks in search of a single, solitary worthwhile vocal hook or guitar lick; but like a reprieve from the overwrought subject matter, none can be found. Honestly, aside from Stick's impressive drumming—especially on the album's closer 'Sealed Away'—most of us would have been far better off if the Oath just let this wickedness rest and gave us more classic power thrash, like the untouchable magic of their debut, *Lead Her Astray*."

While Relic also loved his dad's drumming on that record, he likewise shared Stacky's opinion that they could have done without the weird story, which bogged the music and lyrics down. Not even reading the liner notes helped Relic understand what the hell his dad and his bandmates were trying to convey with that nonsense.

That's probably why everyone hated it so much, Relic thought, stepping away from his kit. *People don't like to be made to feel stupid, which is why pop songs about relationships make so much money—anyone can understand that.*

"Relic!" There were three stomps from upstairs, which meant his mom thought he had his headphones on again. "Come here!" Three more stomps.

Her voice sounded stressed again, which was par for the course these days. Relic took a deep breath, wishing summer would just end. He made his way around the cramped corner of the basement, dodging the boom stands that held his cymbals and tiptoeing around the *Dungeons & Dragons* books strewn about the floor.

He spared one last glance at the Unknown Oath poster. Not for the first time, he wished he looked as awesome as his dad—tall, lean, confident. The doctor's voice echoed in his mind once more: "Just like your dad."

Looking down at his puffy, inverted nipples and the fat-roll marks on his stomach, then back up to his dad's shredded midsection peeking through the ripped robes on the poster, Relic almost laughed.

"Bullshit, doc," he said as he turned away.

Not wanting even his mom to see him without wearing a shirt, Relic slipped on the black tee that proudly displayed Metallica's *Master of Puppets* cover art and headed upstairs.

His mom's voice from the kitchen mingled with the newscaster on TV in the living room. While Relic couldn't hear what either source was saying, he could tell his mom was arguing on the phone—almost certainly about money—while pacing loudly across the kitchen's fake laminate tiles. Not in a hurry to interrupt the phone call, Relic stopped in front of the TV.

"...and in other news, a few lucky residents of Laramie might be featured on the latest docuseries coming from Constrained Media." Monica Bridges was the most gorgeous reporter Relic had ever seen, but even she was usually unable to make him care about the local news. However, Constrained Media produced some of his favorite horror movies, so his interest was piqued. "Several film crews will be set up in downtown Laramie—as well as West Laramie—to interview any residents that witnessed the events of what has since become known as the Dire Decade, or the Decade of Decay, depending on who you ask—"

"No, I don't care!" Dina shouted from the kitchen. "You can't do this; we've had that unit for over ten years! Where am I going to put all that shit, Ted? You've seen our house!"

Any excitement Relic might have felt from the news of his favorite horror studio filming in his hometown was now deflated as he turned toward the kitchen.

"Fine," Dina said, defeated. "We'll be there tomorrow to pick up what we can." She slammed the only cordless phone in the house back onto its charger. "Goddammit."

Relic slowly turned the living room corner like a man on death row walking to his final meal.

"And that's all for today," Monica said behind him from her small box resting in the Meyers' meager entertainment center. A commercial for Pizza Hut kicked in, making Relic's stomach rumble as he stepped into the kitchen.

"What's up, Mom?"

Dina pulled a rolling chair from the kitchen table and sat down, reaching for her lighter and cigarettes. She only started smoking again last year, around the time they stopped getting checks from Devon, Unknown Oath's manager.

"I'm going to need your help," she said, putting a Camel to her lips and sparking the lighter. "We gotta make some room in the basement and maybe the garage—don't ask me how, I can barely fit the car in there as it is."

"But I practice in the basement." Relic immediately regretted the words, knowing how much his drumming had become a sour point between them. He could play dumb all he wanted, but he knew perfectly well why his mom didn't want him following in his dad's footsteps.

Yet he couldn't bite his tongue. The basement was his only retreat. He pictured his haven suddenly flooded with boxes from the storage unit, turning his perfect hangout area into a giant closet. "I can't set my drums up anywhere else."

"Okay," Dina said, puffing a cloud of second-hand smoke into their small kitchen, "I'll just go buy a bigger house then, Relic, with all those tips I'm getting at Rook's." She gave him that look, the one that warned him not to push her any further; it was a look she had perfected over the last few years. "Maybe an indoor pool, yeah? Sound-proofed studio?"

Relic sighed and managed to bite back his words this time. Dina Meyers got more sarcastic as her patience ran out, and he wasn't looking for a fight. "I'll move what I can up to my room." He turned to leave.

"Thank you, Ste–Relic."

He froze for a moment, feeling a strange sense of déjà vu. But he couldn't remember a time his mom had ever accidentally called him by his dad's name. Just as he was about to turn around to ask her about it, the doorbell rang.

"If that's the turd trying to sell us new windows, tell him to get bent."

Despite the levity in her voice, Relic went to the door in a somber mood, smacking the TV off on the way. His mother's depressive state had worn him down all summer, and his home had become a suffocating vortex of worry and despair.

All that changed when he opened the door.

"Bree!"

Relic's best friend flashed him that crooked smile of hers—it was always as if she were trying to hide any semblance of joy on her face. Almost immediately upon seeing Relic, her eyes widened. "How long was I gone, dude!? Your hair is bonkers. You look homeless."

Incapable of suppressing a chuckle, Relic reached up a hand to rub the back of his head, shaking his wild, bushy hair. "Still can't tie it back, but it's getting there. How was camp?"

Before the question was out, Relic already heard his mom putting out her cigarette and scrambling out of her chair. "Red?! I thought your dad said you were coming home tomorrow!"

Relic stepped aside to let Bree in, trying hard not to notice the tank top she wore. He didn't think he had ever seen her in one. Typically, the only shirts she wore came from her dad's old collection of baggy, classic rock tees. Now she wore a form-fitting, yellow waffle top that was low cut enough for Relic to see the tops of her breasts—which he didn't even know she had until now.

There was a bizarre feeling in the pit of his stomach, but he told himself it was just the sudden shift in mood and the excitement of his friend coming home.

Dina embraced Bree; the two were almost the same height now, Relic realized.

"Nope, change of plans." Bree said. "They needed to clear us out of there before the weekend."

"We missed you here, kiddo!" Dina leaned back, her hands still on Bree's shoulders. "And holy shit, you got some sun! Double red!" She laughed as she ran a hand through Bree's curly red hair.

Relic felt himself smiling like an idiot as he watched them, but he couldn't help himself—he hadn't seen his mom so happy in...well, he couldn't even remember when. He wanted to go over and give them both a big hug, but something held him back.

"Yeah," Bree said with a laugh, "for an orchestra camp, they sure made us spend a lot of time outside. But it was cool. There was a lake nearby and a few other camps in walking distance. So we played softball and stuff with a bunch of strangers." She stepped back, displaying herself to Relic and Dina. "Got super sunburned in the process."

Relic couldn't help but avert his gaze to his feet, smoothing out the old carpet with his beat-up sneakers. He didn't like this new uncomfortable feeling around the one person he was most looking forward to seeing all summer.

"I'm so glad you had fun," his mom said, in a tone of voice Relic hadn't heard directed toward him in a long time. "You didn't miss much around here; just your buddy here moping around the house while I worked double shifts at the diner trying to keep the lights on."

Shifting on his feet, Relic nodded toward the door. "Wanna go to the Palace?"

"Sure," Bree said, moving out of Dina's grasp.

"Come back for dinner, guys. I'll order a pizza or something."

"Awesome," Bree said, "thanks, Dina."

"Thanks, Mom." Relic led Bree from the house into the sweltering summer heat. He pulled at his damp Metallica shirt, squinting up at the late Indiana sun; he was more prone to sweating these days, and wondered—not for the first time—if he should expand his wardrobe beyond black band tees.

After crossing the front yard in silence, Bree finally gave his shoulder a playful punch. "Things getting weird?"

Startled, Relic gave her a confused look. Had he been that obvious about his eyes wandering and keeping his distance. But relief washed over him when he saw Bree point a thumb over her shoulder back toward his house.

"Oh, Mom?" Relic shrugged and gave a so-so shake of his hand. "All she talks about is bills anymore. I don't know why; she just makes me feel like it's my fault."

"No, it's your dad's fault."

Relic cast her a sidelong glance, suddenly feeling like he hadn't truly escaped Dina's dark influence.

She held up her hands, rolling her eyes. "I don't mean it like that—I just mean, you're obviously not your dad, Relic. He left, and your mom depends on his money. Who knows why he stopped sending it, but there's no way she's blaming that on you."

Stepping off the curb to cross the street, Relic kicked a rock. "Yeah, I just feel like I can't even play drums anymore—like she thinks I'm following in his footsteps or something."

Bree didn't seem to have a response to that, so they walked a bit more in silence until Relic asked her more about camp.

"Surprisingly we didn't play a ton of music," Bree explained while they cut through the Davis' backyard to get to Greenbush Street. "I mean, we had a big performance on Friday, but it was stuff we'd all played last year. Honestly, I think that was the only time I really touched my viola. There was a guy there who had a guitar, and he let me play it pretty much whenever I wanted."

A strange jealousy bloomed within him as she continued on about the unnamed guitar-playing camper, who Relic imagined looked just like Jon Bon Jovi. As Bree hopped over an upended wagon on the sidewalk, Relic caught himself noticing how much of her legs were left exposed by her high shorts. He averted his gaze to the busy intersection ahead, wondering what the heck was wrong with him.

This was his closest friend in the world. They had spent nearly their whole childhood together, as well as the horrors of middle school. They slept over at each other's houses, and their parents were almost closer than they were.

Plus, Bree was a lesbian.

That stark reminder seemed to clear Relic's mind of enough dangerous thoughts—thoughts that could ruin their friendship—that he could smoothly change the subject. "Can't believe we start high school next week. Sucks you were gone all summer; I felt like I just sat around doing nothing." In truth, Relic had played a ton of great video games and got to see some killer movies, but now that Bree was back, he felt like he had been in some sort of coma.

"I told my dad this is the last time we're doing two vacations right before I have to go to camp," Bree said, sounding annoyed. "You got my postcards right?"

"Yeah."

There was an awkward pause, as if Bree expected him to say something else.

When he didn't, she gave him that tight-lipped look, like she was biting her bottom lip to avoid smiling. "Well, at least we got a weekend of freedom before Chambers High kills us. Let's go."

They crossed Greenbush Street as the traffic died down, making their way through the mostly vacant parking lot of Greenbush Plaza. The CD Palace was a little hole-in-the-wall pawnshop at the eastern end of the strip mall that specialized in old records, used video games, and other second-hand electronics, and it was Relic's main stop for cheap entertainment.

When Bree pushed the door open, the sweet stench of patchouli welcomed them to the Palace, along with that digital bell that would wake Natalie up from her afternoon nap behind the counter.

"There she is," Natalie said in her deep, raspy voice, hidden behind the metal cage-like divider that guided customers through the store's electronic surveillance gates; Relic only knew what the vertical devices were called because a clearly high Natalie once told them that they didn't actually work and were only there for show. "The prodigal girl returns."

"Hey, Nat," Bree slapped Natalie's raised hand as she crossed the shop's threshold. "What's new?"

"Same old," Natalie said. The middle-aged hippie that worked as The CD Palace's lone cashier had dreadlocks, thick-framed glasses, and the slumped shoulders of someone that didn't have much to concern themselves with. When she saw Relic, she snapped her fingers and pointed at him. "Got somethin' you might like, my man."

Natalie waved Relic to follow as she came around the counter, leading him toward the CD racks. The walls of the store were lined with thousands of old cassettes, but CDs were turned over quicker and were relegated to a few racks in the center of the store. Bree broke off toward the collection of VHS tapes, her guilty pleasure.

Natalie pushed her dreads over her shoulder and Relic got another fresh whiff of patchouli. "Remember my guy, Duncan?"

"Yeah, the guy who knows that German dude?"

She nodded and stopped near the H divider on one of the racks. "He brought this in yesterday. Figured it might be right up your alley." She flipped through a few albums and then produced one featuring an armored knight with his hands resting atop a mighty hammer which coursed with electrical magic.

"HammerFall?" Relic took the CD. He had never heard of them. The knight on the cover was standing in front of some dying trees on a stormy, crimson background. A castle could be seen in the distance, behind the withered woods, foreboding in the mists.

A familiar sense of wonder took hold of Relic, the same kind that had made him impulse-buy those *Dungeons & Dragons* books he had found in a second-hand bookstore. Something about knights and dragons always rekindled the obsession he had with medieval fantasies as a kid—the kind he didn't really tell anyone about because he was afraid it would make him more of an outcast than he already was.

He turned the album over to see the tracklist. The first song, "The Dragon Lies Bleeding," already sold him, and he cringed thinking about how big his tab had grown with Natalie. He'd probably have to settle up before she let him take any more albums, and he knew his mom wouldn't spare him any money.

"Mother of god!"

Relic turned toward the VHS section to see Bree holding up a white box featuring a dude making goofy faces.

"Relic, how have you not bought this?!"

"Ah, the holy grail," Natalie said with a laugh, moving toward Bree. "Honestly forgot that came in last month."

"What is it?" Relic joined them as they made their way to the counter. When he caught sight of what Bree held, a different kind of excitement took hold of him. "No way."

Setting it carefully on the glass counter which held all manner of watches, jewelry, and the more pricey artifacts that junkie thieves might pawn for drug money, Bree stepped behind Relic and rested her chin on his shoulder.

Despite his recent discomfort around Bree upon her return, the sight before Relic made him completely comfortable with her head next to his. The feel of Bree's casual closeness was familiar and welcome, as opposed to awkward and unnerving, and before the altar of a *Mr. Bean* VHS boxed set, he was transported to simpler times when he and Bree would watch classic episodes of their favorite show, such as "Mr. Bean Goes to Town" or "The Curse of Mr. Bean."

Relic smiled as he looked from the box of TV magic to the promise of adventure he held in the form of a shrink-wrapped jewel case. The smell of Bree mixed with Natalie's patchouli was the icing on the cake.

For the first time this summer, everything felt right.

But then the electronic chime proclaimed a new shopper had arrived, stirring Bree from his shoulder. All awkward romantic thoughts about his lesbian best friend were completely shattered as Relic saw who walked in.

He was in love.

Chapter 2

W hile Relic hadn't spent much time sitting around wondering what his "type" was, he always felt like he would know it when he saw it.

And he saw it now.

The girl that walked confidently into The CD Palace was a gothic herald of Relic's every unknown desire. Long, dark hair framed a pale face with full cheeks. Sharp black thorns extended from the corners of her eyes, giving her face a sinister quality that made her that much more appealing to Relic.

"Delilah?"

Jolted, Relic turned to Bree, who looked at the newcomer with a wide-eyed smile.

"Brianne?" The girl—Delilah—didn't return the smile. She wore a shy expression that managed to be equal parts dismissive and welcoming.

Relic snorted, much to his immediate dismay. No one called his friend Brianne except for her grandparents. Both Bree and Delilah gave him cold looks.

Bree looked back toward Delilah. "It's just Bree. The head counselor called me Brianne on the first day and I just never bothered correcting her. I thought you were from Fort Wayne—what are you doing in Laramie?"

Delilah pointed over her shoulder. "We just moved in down the street, on Tularosa." Her voice was quiet and words articulate, like she didn't want to speak but if she had to, she wouldn't muck it up. "My dad just opened the new sporting goods store where Wagner Drugs used to be in the mall."

"Your dad is Marshall Crane?" Natalie asked.

Delilah gave her a surprised look.

Moving back behind the counter, Natalie waved a hand to shake away any concern from Delilah's face. "I know the real estate agent that handles local commercial lots. She told me Crane had bought up several pieces of property." She motioned Bree to bring the Mr. Bean box over to the register. "After what happened there, I'm shocked anyone wanted that place."

Relic was still frozen in place as Bree moved past him. He pretended to inspect the HammerFall album while trying to keep Delilah in his peripheral vision. The name Marshall Crane didn't mean much to Relic, but the way in which Natalie said the name told him it might be something to look into later.

At least he knew her name now—Delilah Crane.

"Probably why he bought it," Delilah said dismissively, moving toward the CD racks. "My dad's company is constantly buying up cheap property to convert into their stores. This is like the fifth time we've moved to a new city."

Now that her back was to him, Relic watched her inspect the CDs, wondering what she was looking for. His heart sank a little bit as she picked up an album by The Cure and then another by Depeche Mode. Normally such musical tastes would be enough to deter him from getting to know someone, but he was already too deeply in love with this stranger. There was an unnatural allure he felt toward her, and he just couldn't look away.

"You want that, Relic?"

The question nearly made him gasp, visibly jerking toward Natalie and Bree. His friend was looking at the HammerFall CD in his hand.

"Oh, yeah." He almost took a step toward the register when he remembered his mom's phone call and the fact that he had zero dollars. He was too embarrassed to ask Natalie about the sizable debt he still owed The CD Palace. "But I can get it later."

"Come on," Bree said with a nod toward the register. "It's on me for the pizza—but we're watching *Mr. Bean* tonight, not listening to heavy metal." After Relic reluctantly put the CD on the counter, Bree's eyes caught the cover. Her eyes sparkled with interest. "Oh. Maybe we can listen to a little at least."

He couldn't help but grin. His new romantic interest might have some weird taste in music, but he and Bree were almost always on the same page when it came to tunes and fantasy worlds.

"Check you two later," Natalie said as she handed Bree the generic plastic bag that read "thank you" in block letters, holding it out on the other side of the sensors.

Bree looked past Relic and called out. "So, are you starting at Chambers next week, then?"

Turning around, Relic saw Delilah glance up from a black CD to give Bree a shy smile. "Yeah. Guess I'll see you guys there."

"Yeah, check you there," Relic said, opening his mouth before his brain registered what he wanted to say. *Check you there?* he thought in apocalyptic panic. *What the hell does that mean?! Like check you later had sex with see you there and accidently got pregnant?!* He ducked his head and bolted for the door before he could see her reaction to his nonsense.

The walk home was uncomfortable for Relic. There was a toxic teenage mix of embarrassment, excitement, and dread brewing within him. He desperately wanted to ask Bree about how she knew Delilah—he needed to know everything about her—but between the new Swedish metal album and the box of British comedy she purchased, Bree repeatedly dodged his inquiries.

"So you guys met at camp?"

Bree nodded, inspecting the back of the HammerFall album. "These song titles sound awesome. You ever heard of these guys? Getting kind of an Iron Maiden vibe from the cover and these track names."

"Na, looks like a debut." Relic kicked a rock, considering another approach. "What was her dad's name? Morgan Crane or something? Marshall?" He cast Bree a sideways glance, making sure she wasn't onto him. But she was now inspecting the *Mr. Bean* videos with her trademark not-a-smile. "Some rich dude. Must be famous if even Natalie knows him."

"Natalie's kind of old," Bree said as they turned down Tularosa Drive toward their neighborhood. "She knows lots of boring people. Oh! I have to tell you before I forget. There was this old lady at camp..."

Relic's mind wandered as Bree went into another story about some hysterical situation that he had almost no frame of reference for. His thoughts were fixated on Delilah's face, which most likely changed in his mind—some sort of amalgamation of Demi Moore, Jennifer Connelly, Christina Ricci, and any other celebrity crushes he had over the years. He faked a laugh as Bree finished the tale, still not sure what it was about.

The stone walls of Greenbriar Heights welcomed them home, the familiar black lanterns already kicking on even though the sun still hung fairly heavy in the sky. Several cars pulled out of the neighborhood as Relic and Bree made their way in. With windows down and music blaring, the teenagers in the cars were clear evidence that the end-of-summer anxiety had officially reached its peak.

School was looming. The thought made Relic's dread overpower the other emotions warring inside of him and he slowed his pace, falling behind Bree. As they rounded the corner of Elkton Court, Bree looked back over her shoulder.

"What's wrong?"

Relic couldn't really articulate what he was feeling, but as he looked up toward Bree, he could see his house clearly behind her—more specifically, the red Jeep Cherokee parked in the driveway—and he was oddly glad that he could at least direct his misery to something tangible.

"Dammit."

Bree raised an eyebrow, turning to see what drew Relic's attention. "What?" She looked back at him, even more confused. "Whose car is that?"

"Hey, guys!"

As they walked through the front door, they were greeted by the most forced, cornball enthusiasm that Relic had ever heard. The delicious smell of pizza was spoiled by the sight of the familiar dweeb that eagerly waved to Relic and Bree from the living room couch.

"Hey, Calvin," Relic offered under his breath, raising a couple fingers in a motion that could maybe have passed as a pleasant greeting if Relic's eyes weren't glued to the living room carpet. Even with his eyes averted, Relic could see Calvin get up from his seat. He was dressed as he always was—boring khakis, generic old man sneakers, tucked-in polo shirt—with his huge glasses amplifying his desperate eyes.

"Hi," Bree said, offering him a much warmer greeting.

Dina came out of the kitchen holding a two-liter bottle of soda. "Hey, just in time! Cal just got here with the pizza."

The words instilled Relic with a deep sense of betrayal. When his mom had said she'd get a pizza, he had excitedly imagined she would order from Pizza Hut whose main delivery guy, Trevor, the Meyers were on a first name basis with. The fact that she called Calvin over meant that she probably planned for them all to have some sort of "get to know Cal better" party. And Relic would be damned if he'd let that happen.

"Oh, you guys got *Mr. Bean*!" Calvin exclaimed with raised eyebrows. "Classic!"

"Who was stupid enough to sell that to The CD Palace?" Dina asked with a chuckle. She set the soda on the coffee table and motioned to the VCR atop the TV. "Why don't you pop it in? Dinner and a show to celebrate your return, Red?"

Bree moved toward the TV, but Relic shot her a look. She stopped and waited. "Well," Relic said, looking toward his mom, "we were actually going to watch it downstairs. Can we take a pizza down?"

Calvin put his hands in his pockets, keeping that phony smile on his face as he looked at Dina and gave her a nod of his head—as if he made the decisions in the house.

Dina's own smile faded a bit, but she nodded as well. "Sure, you guys have a lot of catching up to do, I'm sure." She motioned to Bree as she told Calvin, "Bree just got back from camp today, so I doubt she wants to spend her first night home hanging out with a couple geezers like us."

Calvin replied with his patented dopey laugh. "Totally get it, no problem at all. I brought over a couple movies anyway that might not be totally family friendly. We'll have our own slasher-theme pizza party up here."

"I might want invited to that," Bree said with a laugh. "But yeah, we can catch up in the basement and let you guys watch some murders in private."

Ew, Relic thought, not wanting to imagine his mom and this twerp getting "private" together. He moved toward the kitchen to grab a pizza box, eager to be out of the cringy situation.

"Oh, speaking of catching up," Dina said as Relic inspected each of the three pizza boxes, looking for the sausage, "Why don't you stay over like the old days, Red? If your parents don't mind, I'd love some extra hands emptying the storage unit tomorrow morning if you're up for it."

"Yeah," Bree said from the living room, "I'd love to help out. Can I use the phone real quick to see if they're cool with it?"

Relic grabbed the cordless phone on the way out of the kitchen, pizza in hand.

"He's got his dinner figured out," Calvin said with a chuckle as Relic passed by him, "but what are you going to eat, Bree?"

Relic turned his head and snapped over his shoulder. "I'm not going to eat an entire pizza! I'm not that fat, man." His face hot, he kept walking toward the basement stairs, trying to stomp just loud enough that Calvin would know just how much he hated him.

There was an awkward moment of silence in Relic's wake before Calvin finally stammered an apology. "Oh...that—that's not what I meant at all. Sorry. I just meant...there's plenty more if you wanted to take another box."

Blood was rushing to Relic's ears, but he could still hear Bree behind him give a consolatory laugh saying that they'd have plenty to eat. "But thanks again for dinner," she added before following Relic downstairs.

Relic dropped the pizza box down on the card table, hoping that being down in his lair away from his mom and Calvin would improve his mood.

"Well, that was something." Bree took the phone from Relic. "Are you sure you want me to stay over? Seems like it might be crowded here tonight."

"Please," Relic said, sitting down and opening the pizza box as he glanced up at her pleadingly, "don't leave me here alone."

Bree laughed and set their purchases from the Palace on the table next to the pizza. "Alright, let me call Dad. Save me a few slices." She stepped into the basement's shadowed corner as she punched in her number. The light over the table flickered slightly.

Relic shoveled two slices of pizza down while Bree spoke to her dad—Russ Thompkins was a jolly, chatty man—and nearly threw them up when he heard footsteps coming down the stairs. His mom stepped out of the darkened stairwell holding two cups and the bottle of soda. Her face was stone.

"Figured you kids could use something to drink," she said softly, setting her offering on the old table. She looked from Bree on the phone back to Relic, leaning toward her son. "That was very rude, Relic. I think you know Calvin well enough to know that he's not cruel like that."

Relic swallowed the bite he was chewing, his gaze drifting between his mom and his father's image on the Unknown Oath poster behind her. There was a coldness growing within him in his father's absence, and it felt like his mother was pushing him to embrace it by trying to force some other man into their lives.

"I barely know him," Relic said, resenting the idea that it was up to him to know what Calvin meant when he said something stupid. "But you can tell him I said sorry. I wasn't trying to be mean."

"Maybe you could tell him," his mom replied. "Calvin is a very nice man, and he does a lot for us."

"He does a lot for *you*," Relic said, looking back at his father's frozen face, thinking about all the money he had sent them over the years, wondering if his mom appreciated that at all—wondering if she would defend Steven Meyers as much as she's defending Calvin Green. "You can tell him."

"My dad says it's okay," Bree said, stepping toward the table but stopping short when she saw Relic's face.

"Great!" Dina said, pretending everything was fine. She took the phone that Bree held out. "I'll get out of your guys' hair then. Enjoy Rowan Atkinson's brilliant buffoonery."

As his mom made her way back upstairs, Relic pulled out the first *Mr. Bean* tape and moved to the small TV that had a built-in VCR.

"So," Bree said with a mouthful of pizza, "how long has this been going on?"

Relic grabbed the TV remote off the stand and joined Bree back at the table. "Too long. Mom's car wouldn't start after work one night, and apparently Calvin spends most of his evenings at Rook's, so he jumped her car."

"Ah, saving the day."

"Yeah," Relic said, grabbing another slice as the TV displayed the obligatory FBI warning at the beginning of every VHS, "something like that. Apparently they went to school together, so they knew each other before, but ever since then he's been showing up a lot. Taking her to work, bringing her home—Mom says he's a computer engineer or something, but you'd think he was a taxi driver."

Bree laughed, but Relic wasn't sure if it was because of his comment or because Mr. Bean just fell from the sky and landed in a pool of light on a cobbled road.

"Honestly," Relic said, watching Mr. Bean comically try to copy off another person's written test, "I try not to be a dick to him, but I just get this weird feeling that he's trying to be like a dad with me."

"I can tell," Bree said, taking another bite of pizza. She had a bad habit of chewing loudly and talking while she ate, which kind of grossed Relic out. Between chews, she offered, "He does seem to come on a bit strong, but seems like he means well."

"Yeah, but he's not my dad."

Bree threw the crust of her pizza into the box. "Yeah, your dad left, dude."

Taken aback, Relic could only stare at her while the laugh track on *Mr. Bean* filled the silence that followed.

Leaning over the table, Bree looked directly into Relic's eyes. "I'm sorry, you know I think your dad's awesome. And I think it was very cool of him to support you guys while he tours Europe or whatever he's doing. But, Relic, he pretty much abandoned you guys."

Relic looked at the pizza, not wanting to hold her gaze anymore, feeling embarrassed and angry all at once. He wanted to tell her that no, his father did not *abandon* him; Steven Meyers had dreams to chase and legends to make. He wrote Relic notes. He sent them money. He sent gifts, and albums, and signed shirts from famous bands.

He was Relic's hero, even though he couldn't really remember what it was like being physically with him.

Hot tears welled up in the corners of Relic's eyes while the TV laughed at him with raucous abandon.

Bree didn't seem to notice. "Your mom's alone, and this Calvin dude seems nice and helpful. I mean…it could be worse, right? She could be dating some psycho axe murderer."

"She's not dating," Relic said a little too loudly, tears now rolling down his face. "She's married to my dad. She—" Relic's voice finally gave out.

Mr. Bean did something ridiculous again and laughter exploded as Bree got up and hurried around the table, wrapping her arms around Relic. The act made him break down and he sobbed, his blurry vision going from the image of his dad to his and Bree's favorite TV idiot. He felt a bizarre sense of sorrow and hope, slowly realizing he may never see his dad again but knowing that Bree would always be there for him.

Relic hugged her back, hard, letting himself sob for a moment.

Feeling his friend here with him now made Relic suddenly realize how long they had been apart. For the past seven years, he and Bree had been as inseparable as the closest of siblings, and now that she was back with him after being gone for months, he was both happy and profoundly sad that his father was not as real of a part of his life as Bree was.

"We could have just fast-forwarded this episode if it bummed you out this much," Bree said, still chewing on her pizza.

Relic fell out of his seat laughing, pulling a snorting Bree with him, and not because Mr. Bean was trying to change into a swimming suit on the beach without taking off his clothes. They watched the rest of the episode on the floor, forgetting about Calvin, unpaid bills, and Unknown Oath as they joked and renewed their enduring friendship.

Relic didn't even think about the new girl, Delilah, until he fell asleep later.

Chapter 3

Delilah Crane stalked through Relic's dream like some sort of upright feline, slightly hunched so her stringy hair hung like damp seaweed, swaying with each step she took toward her prey. Like many of his recurring dreams lately, Relic was bound to the floor, his limbs frozen and unresponsive.

Relic remembered vividly when, in sixth grade, Andy Houser had told the lunch table about his experiences with night terrors.

"You can't freaking move when you wake up," Andy had said, giving everyone a wide-eyed look like he was unable to move his limbs there at the lunch table. "All you can do is stare while whatever you were dreaming about keeps moving around your room...it's like your nightmares spill over into whatever you see in real life, but you can't do anything about it!"

While Relic had never experienced the phenomenon himself, he could only imagine the sensation he experienced in his current dream was the closest thing to Andy's night terrors.

However, he didn't feel scared as Delilah approached him from the shadows; on the contrary, he was eager for her to reach him, desperate even. But she took her time, circling him from the consuming shadows of the dream world. The anticipation was killing him.

There was a coldness gripping Relic's chest, moving down to his bowels, and then his waist. And then it crept even lower. A familiar stiffness settled in, and Relic shifted uncomfortably in his dream, waiting for whatever was going to happen—or not happen.

Delilah stepped close enough that he could see her face—once again, taking the form of more familiar faces that he had been attracted to throughout his life;

faces with dark, mysterious pools around their eyes—eyes that were deadly pale orbs.

"Relic," Delilah said, though her mouth didn't move. Black lipstick began to spread to reveal bright white teeth, sharper than normal. "Can you hear me?"

The icy chill that was creeping into his bones felt exhilarating and he felt his spine pulled forward, compressing his body to find some warmth, even though the coldness felt good.

"Relic?" Delilah leaned in, her face was all he could see now, blocking out the terrifying unknown behind her. "I know what you're looking for."

His mouth went dry, and whatever was brewing within him had reached its peak. He felt like his body was about to fold in on itself.

"Relic."

He awoke with a sudden overwhelming sensation. Even though his eyes were opened, he couldn't see anything. A foreign pleasure blinded him, and he almost shouted out as something released from his body. *Did I just piss the bed?*

"Hey, Relic."

He tried to gather his senses, rolling over to see Bree lying on the couch under a blanket, her face lit by the glow of the TV. "Huh?"

"You alright? Sounded like you were having a nightmare."

Relic looked down. He was in his old He-Man sleeping bag on the floor. He turned to the TV and saw credits silently rolling on a finished VHS. "Yeah," he managed, shifting uncomfortably. There was something wet in his sleeping bag, but it wasn't piss.

Realization sunk in, and he quickly shot Bree what he hoped was a casual look. "Just a weird nightmare about Calvin trying to take me to a baseball game."

Bree's body shook as she laughed silently. "Get some sleep, man. I don't want to carry all those boxes by myself tomorrow."

Unsure of what he should do, and also exhausted from what Delilah had done to him in his dream, his body went limp in the sleeping bag. He knew the dampness would dry and he could wash the sleeping bag tomorrow.

Right now he just wanted to drift off into a few hours of complete oblivion. And he did.

"Relic!"

Dina's voice woke him with a jolt, and Relic sat up with a notable cramp in his neck. It'd been a while since he slept on the floor. Nearby, Bree was stirring on the couch, her back still to him. He immediately recalled the bizarre dream he had, pulling open his sleeping bag to let the faint morning sunlight reveal the gym shorts he slept in.

The stain confirmed his fears. He had learned about wet dreams in school, both from sex ed and the misinformation spread around the boys' locker room, but he never would have imagined having his first one while falling asleep to *Mr. Bean* with Bree just a few feet from him. Regardless, he knew he had to take care of this quickly. Turning toward the laundry room just past the stairs, he was certain he had some clean clothes in there that he had been too lazy to put away.

Unfortunately, Bree was already kicking her blanket off, and he didn't want to make a scene of trying to scramble across the room in a hurry, drawing more unwanted attention to himself.

"Relic, you guys want some donuts?!" Dina's voice sounded like she was at the top of the stairs now.

"Yeah!" Relic shouted, hoping it would keep her from coming down. He did not want another female presence to deal with in his current situation. "Cake with sprinkles!"

Bree yawned loudly before adding, "Same for me! Thanks, Dina!"

"You got it! Be back in a few!" The front door slammed shut almost immediately after.

Groaning, Bree rolled back over to face the wall. Panic froze Relic in place, and his mind went back to his dream, feeling a sensation akin to what Andy

Houser had described sleep paralysis feeling like. All he could seem to do was watch Bree stretch out her limbs.

Something caught his eye and relief washed over him—a distraction!

On the seat of his orange gym shorts that Bree had borrowed to sleep in, Relic saw his salvation.

"Dude," he said, trying to sound groggy and nonchalant, "did you sit on some pizza?"

"Huh?"

As Bree got up to inspect the back of her shorts, Relic slipped out of his He-Man sleeping bag like a freaking ninja and dragged it with him toward the laundry room with the perfect excuse. "Don't worry, I'll grab you another pair."

"What the fu..."

Bree's voice trailed off as Relic's bare feet slapped against the cold concrete of the unfinished laundry room. He deftly pulled the curtain that divided the rooms closed and breathed a sigh of relief. He slipped out of his soiled underwear and tossed them in the washer along with his sleeping bag. As predicted, a collection of folded laundry sat on the bench next to the seat; he had never been so glad to have skipped a chore.

While he slipped into a clean pair of undies, he heard Bree approaching. "Hang on. I'm changing real quick."

"No, I—I need to run home real quick."

"I have plenty of spare shorts. Or you can just wear your clothes from yesterday. We got donuts coming, dude."

There was a brief, uncomfortable silence as Relic slipped into a pair of army green cargo shorts.

"I'll try to hurry back," Bree said, her voice strained. Before Relic could respond, her feet pounded up the stairs in a hurry.

Poking his head out of the curtain, Relic heard the front door slam again. He was alone.

"Weird," he said to himself. He walked over to the table with the empty pizza box, but he didn't see any pizza sauce on Bree's chair. As the realization hit him that maybe he had somehow imagined the pizza stain on Bree's shorts, his stomach heaved. Had she somehow seen the evidence of his nocturnal activities? Did she leave out of sheer embarrassment?

There were footsteps upstairs that jolted his attention from his imagined horrors. *Who the hell is here?!* He imagined some sinister form that resembled Delilah from his dream—a spindly shadow with hair like thin strands of melting wax and claws that writhed like sharp, undulating snakes.

"Relic?"

His mom's voice came down the stairs like a demonic shriek as Relic's wandering mind snapped back to reality. "Mom?!" He walked over to the stairs to see her standing at the basement door. "I thought you went to get donuts?"

"Calvin did. What's wrong with Bree? I just saw her running home."

Relic had to process those two statements. What would make Bree run home? Maybe because she saw something that disgusted her? Or she was so embarrassed that she sat on pizza that she couldn't just laugh it off with him? Did she crap her pants?

And then there was the other thing.

"Calvin stayed here?"

Dina's worried expression melted into one of disbelief. "Yeah, Relic. Your friends get to stay over and so do mine."

"Yeah, but I'm not *dating* Bree!"

His mom crossed her arms and leaned on one leg as if a lecture were coming. "And I'm not dating Calvin. He's just a friend. We fell asleep watching horror movies and now he's getting us donuts. What's the problem?"

Relic closed his eyes and ran a hand through his hair. He didn't want to relive their fight last night—he wouldn't keep letting Calvin ruin things. Anyway, he needed to go check on Bree.

As if reading his mind, Dina pointed toward the front door. "Did something happen between you and Bree? Why'd she rush out of here?"

Relic shrugged, obviously not wanting to voice all of his theories. He settled for the most likely situation. "I think she sat on some pizza or something. There was sauce all over her shorts. Maybe she was embarrassed." Of course, now he felt terrible having said that out loud. If Bree was embarrassed, she certainly wouldn't want Relic telling everyone about it. "But don't say anything about it."

Dina raised a skeptical eyebrow.

"I'll take her donuts over there. She's supposed to help us at the storage unit anyway."

"You're not leaving the house like that," she warned.

Relic observed his clean cargo shorts and his wrinkled Megadeth "Rust in Peace" tee.

"You reek. Go take a shower and get ready to head to the storage unit. I'll walk over to the Thompkins' and see if Bree's going to join us—I want to say hi to Lydia anyway, I think she just got back from Paris."

As a top executive in the Rothen Corporation, Lydia Thomkins was always traveling, which is why Bree had been gone most of the summer. Before camp, she traveled with her parents to Germany and then France, where Lydia had to remain for work.

"But first," Dina added, "before you come up, clean up all the pizza boxes—not just from last night either. I want it all in the trash before we leave."

Relic reluctantly obliged, actually eager for a shower. He collected all the trash scattered around the basement, picking up the HammerFall album as well. *Shower tunes,* he thought, his mood already brightening. After taking the trash out, he went to his room to grab a clean shirt and some socks. Like the basement, his bedroom walls were adorned with heavy metal and thrash legends, mostly whatever images he could find of Unknown Oath over the years, touring all kinds of exotic places overseas.

Never the States, Relic thought to himself, observing all the scenes of his father spinning sticks, smiling wildly, shouting to fans, being a heavy metal god. He couldn't help but think of Bree's words last night.

"He left you."

None of the photos were of his father playing catch with him, or taking him fishing, or laughing over a birthday cake. Relic swallowed back tears, refusing to cry about it again. Instead he stripped off his clothes and headed toward the shower.

One of Relic's favorite parts of personal hygiene was listening to music in the shower. Something about being locked in a steamy box, shut away from the world, while he was bombarded by heavy metal spoke to the core of his being. He had never been to therapy, but he was certain that this activity was the most effective type he could hope for.

There was an old boombox on the back of the toilet, and Relic popped open the CD player. A Rod Stewart album greeted him. He couldn't hold in the groan. He set the aberration aside and flipped open the HammerFall jewel case to see a plain black disc with the band's name displayed in big, red block letters. The album name, *Glory to the Brave*, was emblazoned on the lower part of the CD, right above the Nuclear Blast record label, which was flanked by the two nuclear symbols that Relic thought were such a perfect image of heavy metal music.

Ready to be transported from his reality, Relic put the disc in and turned on the shower. As he waited for the water to heat up, a customary cymbal choke introduced a tasty metal riff, immediately getting Relic's blood pumping. As a high-pitched singer declared "we ride" with soaring intensity, Relic stepped into the shower and was swept away to a fantasy world where "The Dragon Lies Bleeding."

Sometimes he had felt like he had heard it all when it came to metal, but after years of listening to bands growling about killing people, or snarling about their ex-girlfriends, or grunting about some form of disembowelment, Relic felt like he had just discovered an entirely new genre of music.

With shredding guitars and pounding drums, HammerFall pledged its anthems to glory, majesty, and fantasy, and Relic had no idea how desperately he had been craving all of it. His imagination was catapulted back into childhood stories of Robin Hood and King Arthur, while creating his own new adventures with warriors, wizards, and rogues from tabletop games he had played with Bree.

Randomly, during the eponymous song "HammerFall," Relic wondered if his dad had ever heard these guys. And for some reason, he hoped not.

This discovery was his.

Chapter 4

By the time HammerFall finished their fifth track—a catchy speed metal tune called "Child of the Damned" that featured plenty of double bass—Relic felt the hot water starting to give and he knew he should get out. He dried himself off, got dressed, and smeared some of his mom's leave-in conditioner into his hair before finally turning off the majestic tunes.

As he killed the fan, he could hear the muted sounds of the TV. He stepped out of the bathroom to finally find out what was up with Bree.

"Did you get my pizza shorts from Bree, Mom?"

Relic felt a rusty spear ram into his bowels—partly because he was so hungry and partly due to the sight of Calvin sitting on the couch holding up a glazed donut with a bite taken out of it.

"Hey," Calvin said, motioning to an open box of donuts on the coffee table. "Got plenty of cake with rainbow sprinkles...those the right ones?"

A war waged within Relic. He desperately wanted those donuts—his stomach begged like a dog at the sight of them—but he felt obligated to sit with Calvin if he accepted the offering. The sound of the *Saved by the Bell* theme song coming from the TV—one of Relic's favorite guilty pleasure shows—made his decision much easier.

His hunger won out. Relic grabbed a donut and took a seat on the loveseat that was kitty-corner to Calvin's seat on the sofa. He was able to enjoy a few bites in silence, watching Screech do something stupid that caused Zach Morris grief. But Calvin had to open his mouth.

"So, your mom went over to the Thompkins'?"

Relic nodded, keeping his eyes on the TV, almost ready for a second donut. He heard Calvin shift in his seat.

"Hey, Relic. I wanted to apologize for last night. I—you know, I'd never purposefully make a joke at your expense. I just have a habit of tripping over my words." He set his donut back in the box, only half-eaten. "Anyway, I shouldn't have said that, no matter what I meant. I'm sorry."

Shoving the rest of the donut in his mouth, Relic nodded, thinking about how stupid it was for him to get offended over something like that. It was almost comical to him now, as he stuffed his face with junk food.

"It's fine," Relic finally said, avoiding eye contact. Looking at the donuts Calvin brought, he felt compelled to explain himself. "I got made fun of a lot in middle school. Lots of the other guys are getting growth spurts, and I'm still short and fat. I just get defensive, I guess."

On cue, there was a roar of fake laughter from the TV.

"I get it," Calvin said, shifting again in his seat again. "Did your mom ever tell you about when we went to Sunnyside together? Back when it was on the other side of town?"

Relic finally looked at him, assuming his mom had only known him from high school. "You went to middle school together?"

"Yeah, me, your mom, your dad. We all knew each other."

The mention of his dad unsettled him, but he waited for Calvin to continue.

"Anyway, I was a big kid, around the waist that is—way bigger than you. I was certainly a late bloomer, as they call it."

Relic found that almost impossible to believe. For as much as he didn't care for Calvin, even he noticed how tall and handsome the guy was. He even looked a bit muscular, with the tight sleeves of his stupid yellow polo shirt strained against his biceps.

"I also didn't really do any sports, and loved junk food. I guess that's why I made that joke last night—to me, all guys want to eat a ton, it's just a matter of being smart enough to know how much your body can take." He chuckled, slapping his flat stomach. "That definitely took me a long time to figure out."

The studio audience on *Saved by the Bell* found that humorous as well.

Calvin chuckled. "They used to say stuff like, 'Oh, it looks like Calvin is going to need two seats,' or something about how my boobs were bigger than most girls' in our grade." Relic looked toward him to see Calvin's eyes distant, staring toward the front door. "Kids can be some of the meanest creatures in the world."

"Yeah," Relic agreed, feeling guilty for making Calvin feel bad last night. He wanted to say something that might ease the tension between them, but he had no clue what it would be. Fortunately, the front door swung open, and Dina interrupted any risk of them bonding.

"Hey," Calvin said. "We saved you some donuts."

"Oh, my hero," Dina teased, striding over to them. "And *Saved by the Bell*! Now we're talking."

"Where's Bree?" Relic asked, grabbing another donut.

"She's not feeling well," Dina replied—a little too quickly, Relic noted. "We'll wrap up her donuts until she's feeling a little better."

Relic wanted to press the matter, not believing that Bree suddenly got sick—even if she did feel sick, why wouldn't she tell him? But he just watched as his mom packed up the donuts.

"We need to get going though before Ted sets our stuff on fire. Calvin, you want to follow us there in your Jeep? We could definitely use your trunk space."

"Totally," Calvin said as he stood up. "You want to ride with me, Relic?"

No, Relic thought, *please no.*

"Actually," Dina said from the kitchen, "I need to have a word with Relic."

"Sure thing," Calvin replied, moving toward the door. "I'm going to go put my seats down then. See you guys out there."

Relic wasn't sure which was worse: riding alone with Calvin or getting a lecture from his mom about something. Seems like he didn't have a choice anyway.

Their storage unit was a few miles away, across Union Street and far enough up Kossuth Street that it gave Relic flashbacks of middle school. As they made their way down Sagamore Parkway in Dina's little black Mazda, Relic flipped through the radio stations.

"All I'm saying," Dina continued, "is that even if you don't like Calvin, you can stand to be a little more polite. I'm not dating him, and I'm certainly not marrying the guy—he's not trying to be your dad."

"I get it," Relic said, ready for the lecture to be over. Now that there were no more donuts to buy him off, he was tired of hearing about Calvin. "I'll be polite."

"Good," Dina said, turning onto Kossuth. "Now, we need to talk about Bree."

Taken aback, Relic turned toward his mom. "What about her?"

"I don't know if it's a good idea if you guys keep having sleepovers."

Relic panicked, his heart kicking into gear. "What? Did she say something?"

Dina sighed. "Look, I doubt she wants you to know—she would have told you if so. But she's a young woman now, and they go through stuff."

"She start her period?"

Dina flashed Relic a shocked look.

Relic stifled a laugh, partly out of the absurdness of the confusion and partly out of relief that there wasn't actually anything to worry about. "I thought she sat on pizza." He let out the laugh now, almost doubling over.

"Relic! It's not funny! It's a huge deal for a girl."

"Mom, I know. I'm not laughing at her, just the situation. You have to admit—it's kind of funny."

Dina's face was hard. "It's inappropriate—just like her staying over now that you guys are going into high school."

"What do you mean? Didn't you just have a guy sleep over? A guy you aren't dating, right?"

"Yeah, and I'm an adult, first off. Second, you guys aren't kids anymore. Things happen."

"Mom! She's gay! We both know that."

"That's not the point, Relic." She sighed. "Look, we'll talk about it later. Just know that people aren't one-dimensional. It's not gay or straight or bi or whatever. The way Bree talks about her time at camp, I don't think she's all that interested in girls these days anyway."

"What's that supposed to mean?" Relic asked, completely lost. He thought of the unnamed camper who loaned Bree his guitar and felt even more annoyed. "What'd she say about camp?"

"Never mind," she said under her breath as the car came to a stop and she shifted it into park. "Let's just get this over with."

Ted Packer's Packrat Storage was tucked behind a McDonald's parking lot. Hidden in the shade of several overgrown black oak trees, the meager business consisted of two rows of rusted red garage doors and a small structure that served as Ted's office. A spiky-looking iron gate surrounded the place. The main entrance had an old keypad next to a rolling gate adjacent to the tiny parking lot.

Pacing the length of the gate was the Packrat himself. Ted Packer was a lanky man, roughly the same age as Relic's parents—another survivor of Chambers High, apparently. Sometimes Relic felt like his mom knew everyone in town, and he wondered if she had ever wished they just packed up and followed Dad to Europe. Laramie felt like a prison.

"Hey, Dina," Ted said, giving an awkward wave as he placed his other hand on his potbelly. "Right on time."

"Right on time," Dina replied, with plenty of venom in her voice. Calvin's Jeep pulled up next to their car while Relic and his mom got out. While Dina went to go talk with Ted, Relic meandered toward the gate, his eyes drawn to a black van parked across the street. He was feeling annoyed again, his thoughts still on his mom trying to keep him from having sleepovers with his best friend. Why do things have to change just because Bree had a period? Unless...

"Oh, fudge," Relic whispered aloud, quoting his favorite holiday movie—a habit of cussing without really cussing that he hadn't yet broken. He looked back at his mom who was having an animated conversation with Ted as the man led her and Calvin in Relic's direction. *There's no way Mom would know about my dream,* he thought to himself—she hadn't even been down to the laundry room today, so she wouldn't have seen any of the evidence. But it made sense to him that if she knew what happened to Relic, and she suspected Bree might not actually be a lesbian…

"So you're trying to sell our stuff now?!" Dina asked loudly, interrupting Relic's panicked train of thought. "I just told you yesterday I'd come get it."

Ted put up his hands in a motion of surrender. "I'm not selling anything, Dina! I'm just letting you know, the guy offered." He gave Relic a smile and made a show of rolling his eyes as he continued to disarm Dina. "Just wanted to let you know, since it sounds like money might be a little tight."

"Not tight enough to just hawk half our possessions on a whim," Dina replied, her temper cooling. "Who is this and why do they want to buy a bunch of random stuff?"

Ted motioned to the black van across the street that had caught Relic's eye. "Some producer who works for that film crew. They're actually over at Mickey D's right now grabbing food. They wanted to film a segment here this afternoon."

"That's Constrained Media?" Relic asked excitedly.

After punching in a code on the panel, Ted raised a finger as the gate squealed open. "That's the name—forgot what channel they were with."

"That's not actually a channel," Calvin interjected, pushing his glasses up his nose, nerdy as ever. "Constrained Media is a production house that specializes in horror films and supernatural documentaries."

"Sure, whatever," Ted said, motioning for them to follow him.

"What are they filming here?" Relic asked, suddenly excited that his day might be more than just hauling boxes and ruining his wonderful basement.

Ted motioned ahead. "Well, I think that's why the fella wanted to buy your unit and everything inside. He asked about Stick's old band, having heard they used to practice here. I may have mentioned he stored some stuff here."

"Wait," Dina said, walking faster to get closer to Ted. "I thought you kept that shit confidential!"

"I didn't say you all still used it," Ted said defensively. "The guy just said he'd offer to buy whichever unit it was, along with whatever was still in it. Jesus, Dina. I'm just letting you know the offer. Not saying you have to take it."

"Sounds a bit fishy," Calvin offered. "We should probably get the important things out of there first, Dina, just in case."

"No one's going to steal it or nothin'," Ted said, a bit offended. "I won't even let him through the gate until you're all done."

"I'll back the Jeep in," Calvin said, turning to fetch his car.

"He didn't say numbers, mind you," Ted continued, "but them Hollywood boys pay top dollar for what they want. And he seemed very keen on anything your husband touched."

Relic wasn't completely ignorant of his own quasi-celebrity status, being the son of Steven Meyers. While Unknown Oath wasn't exactly a mainstream band, they rode that line between thrash and arena rock, so they appealed to a wider audience than many American bands of either genre specifically. Also, the strange events that happened in Laramie during the "Dire Decade" seemed to always get associated with Unknown Oath due to the whole "Satanic Panic" that happened in the 80s. Every bible-thumper was looking for a metalhead to blame for weird stuff happening.

Taking all that into account, Relic wasn't necessarily surprised to hear that someone wanted to buy his family's junk, but the fact that it was someone with Constrained Media and it all might have something to do with their latest production—well, his interest was piqued, that was for sure.

"Look, sorry for freaking out, Ted," Dina said, rubbing her forehead as they arrived at their storage unit. "I know you cut me a break for a while, and you need this space for someone who can pay—I appreciate it. We'll sort through what's still in there and then maybe I'll take you up on that guy's deal. You're right, I could use the money. And we don't have to tell him we picked through the good stuff already."

"Now you're talking," Ted said, hooking a thumb over his shoulder. "I need to tend to a few things on the other side of the lot. You all have at it and let me know when you want me to put the rest on sale. I'll make sure you get all the profit! Just hurry up before they get done next door—I don't want them to see you picking it clean."

"Thanks again, Ted."

Calvin's Jeep slowly backed up as Dina unlocked the rolling steel door that locked away most of the Meyers' memories. As she rolled it up, a wave of nostalgia washed over Relic. It had been at least a year or two since he had been out here, but there was a pungent smell that took him immediately back to his childhood.

"This place still reeks," Dina said, almost to spite Relic's thoughts.

Calvin got out of the car, clapping his hands and rubbing them together as he approached. "So, what's first?"

As Dina and Calvin began looting the most boring paraphernalia—boxes of photo albums, keepsakes, and holiday decorations—Relic worked his way toward the back of the unit where his dad's stuff was shoved into a corner. Pushing aside an old vacuum, a wooden toybox painted to look like a circus wagon, and a Philadelphia Eagles tin trashcan full of what looked like folded washcloths (why?), Relic finally got to the good stuff.

Steven Meyers left behind everything he owned when he and his band left for Europe, which wasn't a whole lot. His very first drum kit—a four-piece starter set that was so generic it didn't even have any manufacturer information on it—sat stacked up next to three cardboard boxes. Relic stared at what remained of his dad, wondering why he had never gone through these things. He couldn't remember exactly, but surely his mom would have prevented him from doing so. It was no secret that she feared her son might follow in his father's footsteps.

While Relic resented the idea that someone foresaw his own decisions and acted against them, he knew full well that he idolized his dad, and there really wasn't anything Dina Meyers—or anybody, for that matter—could do to stop that.

Relic opened the first box labeled "Steven" in huge, black magic marker letters. Inside were black band t-shirts, a studded leather bracelet, dozens of used drumsticks. He grabbed the bracelet and put it on; it fit perfectly. Closing the box, he pushed it aside and dug into the next one. Jackpot. His dad's cassette tapes. He imagined some might be worth keeping, but there was a whole box full! It was more than enough to settle up his tab at The CD Palace. He slid that box aside as well.

The last box was the heaviest. Opening it, he was surprised to find it full of books. Aside from the occasional video game magazine or D&D rulebook, Relic wasn't much of a reader, so sifting through the various fantasy novels that his dad had collected didn't do much for him. A beat-up copy of *The Withered Roots: Book Two of the Malice of Light* had a crumpled up piece of notebook paper tucked into it. Relic pulled it out and read the crude handwriting: "Altars and stones — Altar Stone would be a killer band name."

Relic smiled, completely agreeing. He mentally filed that away for later as he dropped the fantasy novel back in with the rest. Another book caught his eye: a small, very old-looking journal. As he was slowly reaching for it, his mom called for him, almost giving him a heart attack.

"Relic, stop playing with that stuff. We need to hurry."

Relic closed the box and grunted as he lifted it and turned toward the Jeep. He could see his mom eyeing him suspiciously, and he dared her to object to him keeping his father's things.

"Let me help you, bud," Calvin said, stepping over to grab the heavy box.

"No," Relic said, determined to carry it himself. "I can do it."

He loaded all three of his dad's boxes himself, leaving the old drum kit behind—not even sentimentality would get him to try playing that thing. By then, Calvin's Jeep was jammed full and the three of them were ready for lunch.

Relic voted for McDonald's. As they walked next door, Relic swore he saw someone in that black van watching him.

Chapter 5

A fter lunch, they returned home to unload their haul. The Mazda only had a few things in the trunk, so Dina parked out front to let Calvin back his Jeep up in the driveway to make unloading easier.

"It's actually a relief those guys wanted to buy what was left in the unit," Dina said as she carried a box of holiday decorations behind Relic. "Even just this much feels like moving and I really hate moving."

They descended the basement stairs slowly with their heavy loads, and Relic nearly slipped on the last step. He carefully set his dad's box of books down in the corner behind his drums, wanting nothing more than to sit down and sort through it all. But when Calvin called down asking where they wanted the other "Steven" boxes, Relic raced up the stairs, not wanting them to be handled by anyone but himself.

He stopped midway up the stairs though, shocked to see Bree standing next to Calvin, holding one of the boxes. "I thought you were sick or something."

Bree shook her head. "No, just had my period."

Relic saw Calvin's eyes go wide and he looked like he wanted to be anywhere but there. Relic couldn't help but snicker as he said, "You better let me carry that then."

"I got it, it's not like I'm pregnant or something."

Calvin set the other box down just inside the front door and turned to go back outside, clearly uncomfortable.

Bree watched over her shoulder as Calvin squirmed away, then turned back to Relic and flashed him a full grin—not one of her half smiles. He knew she did that for his benefit. Bree's smile quickly melted into a scowl. "Let me through, dude. This thing is heavy. What's in here?"

Relic reversed his course to let her through. She put down her box—which turned out to be his dad's tape collection—and then Relic went up and brought the last box to his incredibly shrinking lair. Together they finished helping Dina and Calvin with the rest of the unloading, with Relic cramming as much as he could into the garage to preserve some of his personal lair in the basement. Calvin had to leave—which Relic didn't mind, even though the guy didn't bother him as much as he used to—and Dina had to sort through a bunch of family photos upstairs.

Slightly lying to his mom—telling her they would clean up the stuff in the basement—Relic led Bree downstairs so they could check out his dad's buried treasures. They sat down next to the box of cassette tapes first, crossing their legs on either side of it.

"So you really want to sell these?" Bree asked.

Relic shrugged. "I have no reason to hang onto such outdated technology. I have most of these on CD anyway." He flipped through familiar albums: Metallica's *Ride the Lightning*, Megadeth's *Rust in Peace*, some Raven classics, Bon Jovi's first couple, plenty of Iron Maiden.

"What's that?" Bree asked, reaching out to touch Relic's hand.

It was far from the first time Bree had touched him, but something about the feel of her warm skin sent him right back to his dream. And unsettling things began to happen.

As if he had been burned, he jerked his hand away.

Bree gave him a concerned look.

The quickest lie that came to Relic's mind just happened to be one of his worst fears in the basement. "Did you see that spider?"

"Gross, no!" She leaned her head into the box, shifting tapes around. "How big was it?"

"Could have been a shadow or something."

Bree scoffed. "So jumpy." She dug around and produced a crude cassette, devoid of any noticeable artwork or band logo. "I was trying to show you this. What is it?"

Relic cocked his head. "Not sure. Maybe just some mixtape."

Opening the case, Bree's eyes widened and her mouth fell open.

"What?"

After a long moment of silence, she shifted her shocked gaze to his eyes. "You won't believe this."

The phone rang suddenly, jolting both of them. But they ignored it when they heard Dina's footsteps going to get it.

"Is it, like, a copy of the bootleg *Power Metal* Metallica demo tape or something? You look like you've seen a ghost."

Bree slowly flipped the tape around so that the dirty off-white label was legible to Relic. He read the words out loud, to make them more believable.

"Unknown Oath...Alternus."

"What?!" Dina shouted from upstairs. "Are you serious?!"

Relic snatched the tape out of Bree's hand, closed it, and put it in his pocket. When he saw her shocked look, he knelt close as if worried his mom might hear. "Don't say anything about this to my mom."

Before Bree could respond, Relic made his way to the stairs to see what had caused all the excitement from the phone.

"Just some family stuff," Dina was telling whoever was on the phone, but her tone sounded detached as if her mind was miles elsewhere. "Probably not anything else super valuable." Relic took a few steps up to investigate. Behind him, he heard Bree shuffle through more tapes, probably determined to find another diamond in the rough.

"Well, what'd they say?" Dina asked. "I mean, if they're looking for any secret diaries the band kept, he won't find them. They mostly just hung out in there farting into cassette tape cases."

Confused what the hell his mom was going on about, Relic continued up the stairs to find her pacing across the living room. She cast him a quick glance, her face aglow with a wide-eyed smile.

"Alright, I can come by and pick it up. Thanks again, Ted, this is so huge!" She clicked off the phone and looked at Relic. "That guy from the horror studio just paid us a huge chunk of change for our junk." She raced across the living room to wrap her arms around Relic, something that didn't happen much these days.

Relic awkwardly patted her shoulders. "What's a huge chunk?"

Dina laughed. "Enough. For a while at least." She pulled away from him but kept her hands on his shoulders. "I can stop taking all those double shifts."

Relic gave her an approving smile, glad to hear that his mom's depression might have been cured.

She raised her eyebrows. "We need to celebrate! Let's go out to dinner."

"Oh, actually," Bree shouted up, "I forgot to mention, Relic. Dad wanted me to invite you over for dinner tonight. He wanted to watch some *Mr. Bean* with us and catch up. You can come too, Dina."

"No, no," Dina said, patting Relic's shoulder before moving toward the basement stairs. "You kids have fun. I'll see if Calvin wants to go have a drink with me after I finish up at Ted's." She clapped her hands and laughed. "What a day!"

Before dinner, Relic and Bree slipped away to head back to The CD Palace, this time with a full load of old cassette tapes. About half of his dad's collection rattled around in Relic's backpack, and he was confident he would be able to knock his tab down to almost nothing with this much trade-in fodder.

Unknown Oath's most rare demo tape—probably the only remaining copy of the first song the band ever recorded—was not in the bag; it was tucked safely behind Relic's pillows on the shelf built into his bed's headboard.

As they came up on Greenbush Street, Relic couldn't hold back anymore—he had to ask Bree about her little chat with his mom. "Did you say something to my mom this morning?"

Bree looked at him, squinting against the sun. "You mean about my period?" She gave him a mocking half-smile.

He returned the look. "I just mean...on the way to the storage unit, she was telling me about how she didn't think we should have sleepovers anymore, and something about how you didn't like girls anymore."

Bree laughed. "Oh, Dina." She nodded for them to cross when the traffic died down. Once they reached the other curb, she nodded back toward the neighborhood. "My mom wasn't home when she came over to check on me, and you know how Dad is—he thought I needed a *womanly presence*." Bree made the shape of an hourglass figure with her hands.

They shared a little laugh.

"Anyway, we just talked a bit. I mentioned camp, how that guy I was telling you about—Juan—the guitar dude, he was grabbing some of our asses as some weird joke. But I didn't give your mom the specifics, just that things got a little handsy. So, one of the girls also had her period at camp without realizing it. So that night, creepy Juan grabbed a handful of..." she gave Relic a cringing look, "pizza sauce."

The conversation died then in a fit of laughter that continued as they made their way across The CD Palace's parking lot. Even though he wasn't entirely sure what to make of Bree's tale, he guessed it made sense why his mom might have interpreted it as her maybe being into guys—but that just made him feel oddly jealous, so he tried to move past it. As Relic reached to pull open the store's door, Bree stopped him with a tap on the shoulder.

"I may be crazy, but it seems like that van's been following us."

Turning, Relic saw the nondescript black van across Greenbush Street, waiting for a clearing to pull into the parking lot. He debated telling Bree about the situation at the storage unit—she was a huge fan of Constrained Media's movies just like he was—but for some reason his thoughts went back to the Unknown

Oath cassette hiding in his room and he suddenly just wanted to be inside The CD Palace, away from whoever's eyes had been peering at him at Ted's place.

"Weird," Relic said, trying to sound as dismissive as possible as he opened the door and triggered the mechanical ding that announced a customer.

Bree didn't seem to care enough to dwell on it either, slipping into the store. Relic spared one last glance as the van pulled into the parking lot.

Just a coincidence, Relic thought.

"Back again?" Natalie coughed as they crossed the entrance, waving away a puff of smoke. On the edges of the patchouli stench, Relic got a whiff of marijuana and immediately wanted to leave—drugs made him super uncomfortable, and he got enough smoke from his mom's cigarettes. "A big reunion already," Natalie added, looking into the store.

When Relic passed through the sensors, he saw what Natalie meant and his breath caught.

"Hey, Delilah," Bree said with a little laugh. "Back again too?"

Delilah smiled shyly at Bree, tucking her dark hair behind an ear as she put the CD she had been inspecting back in place. "Yeah, I sold or traded a lot of my CDs before the move." She ran a black-nailed finger across the spines of the albums under scrutiny. "Been in the mood to write some music again, but I need some inspiration."

She's a musician, Relic thought, immediately realizing how dumb the revelation was—she had been at orchestra camp with Bree, of course she was a musician. But the fact that she was a songwriter made him instantly more infatuated with her. He and Bree both played music, but neither of them were creative enough to write anything original; well, at least he wasn't.

"That's cool," Bree said, inspecting the CDs on the opposite side of the rack Delilah was focused on—the "Classic Rock" section. Bree's favorite band was Rush and she had little patience for most modern music, outside of the metal they both enjoyed. "I want to get better about writing on guitar, but viola's been taking up too much of my practice time, and I don't think I'll ever want to write anything on that."

"What's in the bag," Natalie asked, her harsh voice breaking Relic's concentration on eavesdropping. Delilah and Bree's conversation faded away as he hefted his backpack of cassettes onto the counter.

"Hopefully something that can settle my debts," Relic said. He began unloading all the curated cassettes in organized stacks, naturally sorting them into genres. His hands were less than deft, Delilah's presence wrecking his nerves. But he managed to present Natalie with three neat enough collections. The biggest collection was old metal albums (most of which Relic already had on CD), the others were random soundtracks to action and horror movies (but Relic didn't care much for instrumental stuff), and the smallest collection were random pop albums that he was actually shocked his dad ever owned. Now that he thought about it, maybe they were his mom's, but if so, she hadn't care enough to dig them out.

"Looks like you got some nice gems in here—is that a Raven album?!" Natalie picked up the *Nothing Exceeds Like Excess* tape and laughed. "Man, I'd give you like twenty bucks for this alone, I haven't seen this in years. My kid brother loved these guys."

Relic perused the video games in the glass case that served as the counter while Natalie evaluated his offerings. Most of the more common Nintendo and Sega games were kept out on the floor, but the ones that were more pristine—in their original packaging with instruction manuals—were kept locked up, along with the smaller portable games which were much easier to steal. Those were the ones that drew Relic's eye. He mostly played Gameboy since his mom couldn't afford any of the newer consoles for him. However, Bree had a PlayStation, and when Relic saw a copy of *Resident Evil*, he began secretly hoping his haul could settle him up and also cover the thirty-five bucks they were charging for Capcom's iconic survival horror game.

After a quick evaluation, Natalie knocked on the glass counter. "I think this is enough to cover your tab."

Bree leaned against the counter and Relic realized he hadn't even noticed the girls behind him had stopped conversing. *Too busy thinking about shooting zombies,* he thought. *Story of my life.*

"Are you kidding me?!" Bree reached over to the small gathering of his dad's pop albums. "You can't get rid of this." She picked up a copy of Madonna's *True Blue*, which had just about the sexiest album cover Relic had ever seen.

He gave her a doubtful look, wondering if she was joking. "Why not?"

"Dude!" Bree scowled, flipping the tape over to point to the small text near the barcode. Under "Side One" the second song down was "Open Your Heart."

Still confused, Relic shrugged.

"That's our song, man!"

Natalie laughed. "Kinda romantic, don't ya think?"

Relic blushed and tried not to look over his shoulder to see if Delilah was listening in.

"No," Bree said, unconcerned with any implications. "We used to dance to this song all the time when we were kids. Remember?"

Natalie laughed again. "Aw, that's adorable. Want me to pop it in so you guys can show us the routine?"

Relic's embarrassment was turning into white-hot rage now.

But Bree just laughed. "You can't sell this one."

"I don't want it," Relic said, not trying to keep the annoyance from his voice. He took the tape from her and slammed it back on the counter. "I want to pay off my tab and eventually get that copy of *Resident Evil*."

"I'll tell you what," Natalie said with another chuckle, "you keep *True Blue*—honestly, it's not worth much anyway, we got plenty of copies—and I'll clear your tab and throw in the game…you just need to show us your moves." Bree laughed with her.

"Whatever," Relic said, angrily snatching his backpack and walking toward the door. "Do what you want with it. Just make sure we're even." He quickly exited the store before they could reply. As much as he wanted to see if Delilah witnessed the shameful spectacle, he kept his eyes forward, feeling hot tears beginning to form. Normally, he and Bree could tease each other because they knew their limits, but if someone else ever joined in, neither of them would tolerate much.

He was mad at Bree for joining in with Natalie, but mostly he hated how Natalie would treat him like a kid. Sure, she had known him since he was a sixth grader, spending his lunch money on video games. But the way she belittled him today in front of Delilah was inexcusable to him.

"Hey there."

Relic—who had been slowly pacing the sidewalk outside of The CD Palace, fuming as he waited for Bree—turned to see a strange man standing before him. He was an older guy, with a sizable stomach and a thick mustache. His slicked-back, thinning hair was tied back in a ponytail, and he wore a suit that stuck out in Laramie like a sore thumb.

"You're Stick's kid, right?"

Relic knew the rule about not talking to strangers, but he had a habit of entertaining anyone that wanted to talk to him about his father. Part of him felt like he relished the quasi-celebrity status it afforded him, but the other part felt like he was just making up for how little his mom wanted to talk about his dad.

"Yeah..."

The man smiled and approached slowly, hands in his pockets. "Sorry, I'm not a creep or anything. I just saw you at the storage place today where we filmed, and I thought I recognized you while we were scouting the old neighborhood." He motioned to Greenbriar Heights across Greenbush Street. He put his base-ball-mitt-of-a-hand out for Relic to shake. "I'm Larry Belinsky, a producer with Constrained Media."

Relic's heart skipped a beat. Even though he didn't know this guy, it suddenly felt like he was talking to a rockstar. He nervously shook the man's hand. "I'm Relic Meyers. I'm a big fan of your movies, especially *The Aching Asylum* trilogy."

Larry smiled. "Classics," he said. "Those movies got me through all three of my divorces."

Relic wasn't sure if he should laugh or not, so he just quietly took back his hand. "I heard on the news that you were doing a documentary about the Dire Decade..."

Nodding, Larry put his hands back in his pockets and observed the mostly vacant parking lot. "That we are, that we are. It's actually what brought me to this side of town." He turned back toward Relic, nodding his head toward The CD Palace. "I heard your dad's band spent a lot of time hanging out here, back when the place was called X-Change Your Things, or something like that. Before CDs were the thing." He smiled again, but Relic thought it felt very forced now.

Relic shrugged. "I don't know, I was like six when he left."

Larry's fake smile flattened a bit. "Yeah, that's a rough one. My dad bailed on me, too; left me and my brothers to support my mom. But from what I hear, yours at least stays in touch—helps your mom out with money, right?"

Relic gave a slight nod, not really wanting to explain the details of his family's struggles with some Hollywood producer.

Larry shifted his posture and crossed his arms. "So, Relic, I was wondering if you'd be interested in being part of our piece. We'd love to interview you and your mom about some of the things that have happened here." His voice changed slightly when he added, "Particularly if you'd have anything to share about your dad and his band."

Raising a curious eyebrow, Relic rubbed the back of his neck, feeling uncomfortable. "Why would you need to know about my dad? He wasn't even around here when all that stuff was happening." *All that stuff,* he thought, *such a weird way to describe monsters and murders terrorizing an entire city.*

"Well," Larry said, dragging out the word as if he were brushing off a wild accusation, "it's about the music, isn't it? A lot of Unknown Oath's songs could be viewed as...ah, prophetic, in a sense. Take for example, 'Gnashed Teeth' on *Lead Her Astray*. One might say a song about a cannibal eating his neighbor's entire family was just a silly romp...but when it actually happens in the band's old hometown a couple years later..." Larry inclined his head, as if he expected Relic to provide an answer.

Obviously, Relic didn't have one. He was more than aware of the wild conspiracy theories and urban legends surrounding Unknown Oath and the troubles that plagued Laramie in the early nineties. However, there was nothing of true substance. Just some unanswered questions that people liked to assign their own solutions to. Despite the popular opinion, Relic's dad's band was not some demonic force that unleashed ancient evil upon the world.

Although, part of Relic wished that were true, because it sounded badass.

Larry opened his mouth, as if to speak again, but the door to The CD Palace swung outward, forcing him to step back out of its way. "Oh, Miss Crane. What a pleasant surprise."

Delilah looked from Relic to Larry. "Hi, Mr. Belinsky." She turned back to Relic to offer a small smile—and Relic melted into a puddle of goo—before adding, "Sorry to interrupt."

"Not interrupting at all," Larry said, motioning to Relic, "I was just asking this young man if he'd also like to be featured in our little production." He flashed Relic a grin. "Delilah here is giving an outsider's perspective, while her father is providing us with his expertise on the city's recently resurging property value since the early 90s."

"Yeah, looking forward to it," Delilah said, in a tone that said she was actually not looking forward to it in the least. "See ya." She moved carefully between them while carrying her sack of purchases.

"S-s-s," Relic stuttered, "see ya too." *WHAT?!* he wailed internally, wanting to die.

Larry gave him a much more genuine smile. Once Delilah was well enough out of ear shot, he leaned forward. "Tell ya what, Relic. You agree to sit down with my team, and I'll make sure it's on the same day as Miss Crane's segment. Deal?"

Before Relic could answer, the door swung open again. This time Larry held it to let Bree exit. "Good afternoon, young lady. I'm sure I'll see you around Mr. Meyers."

Bree stepped aside and gave Larry a strange look before turning her stern expression toward Relic. Without changing her demeanor, she held up the Madonna tape in one hand; the other came up holding *Resident Evil*.

Relic's face split into a painful smile, immediately forgetting the frustrations inside The CD Palace or the strange encounter outside of it.

Bree turned toward their neighborhood, holding up the Madonna tape and shaking it. "We're dancing to this before you and Dad start shooting zombies."

Relic channeled his best Madonna impersonation as he leapt off the curb after her: "Watch out!"

They sang all the lyrics to "Open Your Heart" as they danced like morons toward Bree's house.

Chapter 6

"Yeah, I'm going to have to watch you play this one," Russell Thompkins said, flipping the *Resident Evil* case over. He was a short man with just a small amount of ginger hair remaining, which he kept neatly trimmed around his ears and around the back of his shiny head. He wore thick-framed glasses and a close-cropped beard, and Relic rarely saw him without a sweater vest.

"It's supposed to be pretty creepy," Relic said, taking a long drink of his Diet Coke before setting it back on the kitchen table. He grabbed another tortilla to fill with meat and cheese. They were making taquitos, a staple at the Thompkins house when Lydia was working late—which was almost every night, including weekends. Relic rolled his carefully and added it to the tray with others.

"No!" Lydia shouted from her office near the front of the house, her voice only slightly muffled by the closed door. "We can't wait for approvals, they break ground in three weeks, Justin!"

Russ set the game case down to help Relic with dinner. "I haven't really touched the PlayStation since finally beating *Tomb Raider*, and even that game made me jump a lot. Not sure I could deal with a mansion full of ghouls."

"Zombies, Dad," Bree corrected from near the stove, checking the oil that was heating up in a shallow pan. "Ghouls are like cannibals that get mutated from eating rotting flesh or something. Zombies are dead people that come back to life to eat *fresh* meat."

Russ laughed. "I'll take a mansion of golden rings or something, like *Sonic* or *Mario*, but I definitely want to see what this one's all about. One of you guys has to drive it though."

"I will," Relic said eagerly, knowing Bree preferred to watch video games rather than play them—she was much more of a board gamer, which worked in his favor since she was always down to be Zargon in *HeroQuest*.

The oil sizzled and Bree gasped, making Russ jump. "It's ready," she said calmly.

"Here," Russ said, giving her a tray of wrapped taquitos. "Don't burn yourself. Relic, you ready for high school on Monday? Big change, man."

Relic shook his head. "Definitely not."

Laughing, Russ nodded. "Yeah, I sure wasn't either. Going into high school as the captain of the chess club, computer club, and mathletes didn't really do me any favors with the ladies. But I had some fun after finding my niche of people." He held up a finger. "That's the trick, guys. It's like prison...you gotta go in and find some people who got your back. Because teenagers are," he looked over his shoulder to make sure Lydia's office door was still closed. Lowering his voice, he added, "complete assholes."

"Damn straight, we are," Bree said, plopping a taquito into the oil.

"Watch your mouth!" Russ said in feigned anger. He got up from his chair, but snapped his fingers like he just remembered something. "What you guys need to do is finally start a band."

Relic reached for his Diet Coke again instead of answering. Bree fiddled with the taquitos, pretending like she wasn't part of the conversation.

Russell seemed to sense the tension. "I just mean, it worked well for your dad, Relic. He was one of the coolest guys I ever knew. The band thing really worked for him. And I remember him in middle school; he wasn't anywhere near as good as you are on the drums. And you, Bree—"

"Dad," she interjected, turning to give him a pointed look, "could you grab me a soda from the garage real quick. I have to watch these."

Taking the cue, he shook a finger in the air as if he just had a revelation. "You bet, hon. Need another one, Relic?"

"I'm good."

As the door to the garage shut, Bree gave Relic an apologetic look. "I tried to explain it to him—about your mom and stuff—but he doesn't get it."

Relic looked down to stare distantly into the kitchen table, remembering how Delilah had talked about writing music with Bree. He thought about the note in his dad's fantasy book—Altar Stone *was* a killer band name—and what Russell had said about his drumming, even though Bree's dad hadn't even seen them play since that seventh grade talent show. He imagined himself and Bree up on stage, playing some speed metal anthem they had written together. Something swelled within him: a desire to go home and play his drums immediately.

It had been so long since he had that desire; he couldn't ignore it.

It obviously wasn't the first time the thought of starting a band had crossed his mind. He and Bree had jammed together a lot in the past, but almost always as a goof. They both seemed to maintain an attitude that they didn't want to take themselves too seriously when it came to music, something that had been such a core part of their lives as long as either of them could remember. Relic was pretty much born with drumsticks in his hands and Bree's parents were both musical prodigies in more classical ways, passing on those natural skills to Bree, who could comfortably play over a dozen instruments already.

"Maybe he's right," Relic wondered aloud, softly as if just to himself. He slowly rotated the Diet Coke can as the hiss of frying taquitos filled the kitchen.

Bree was silent, but Relic knew she had heard him—he knew that she was waiting for him to say he was ready, because he could tell she was ready. She always made an effort to mention her new Fender that Russ had gotten her for her twelfth birthday. But ever since Relic stopped getting letters from his dad—which is when he also began taking a sabbatical from drumming—he noticed how Bree wouldn't ever mention jamming, and certainly never brought her gear over to the basement.

She knew.

The garage door swung open again. "Or," Russ said, as if he had been having a whole conversation with himself out in the garage and just thought of a counterpoint, "you guys could start up a gaming club. Not like chess club—I didn't score any babes that way," he teasingly nudged Bree with his elbow as he set her soda on the counter, "but like a D&D club or something; something *cool*."

"You think D&D is *cool* and would score us babes?" Bree asked incredulously. "We'd have better luck with chess, Dad."

They all shared a laugh, lightening the tension.

"What's so funny?" Lydia asked, entering the kitchen with the same air as if she were walking into a board room, despite wearing sweats and one of Russ' old Jethro Tull shirts. "You know what, never mind. I don't care. Bree, darling, give me a few of those. They smell incredible and I'm starving." She glanced at Relic as she moved toward Russ. "Oh, hello, Relic. Good summer?" Before he could answer, Lydia placed a hand on Russ' neck, bending over to plant a kiss on his cheek—she was almost a head taller than him. "A glass of wine, hon. A big one."

Russell nodded as Lydia pulled out a chair to sit next to Relic.

"Now," she said, exhaling whatever had been stressing her out and leaning toward Relic as if she were about to negotiate a business deal, "tell me all about your mom's new boyfriend."

Relic stopped rotating the can of Diet Coke and tried not to crush it.

After dinner, Lydia—not quite satisfied with Relic's meager gossiping skills—retreated to her luxurious bathtub upstairs, leaving the rest of them to boot up *Resident Evil* in the den, which overlooked the ravine in the Thompkins' backyard. While Relic had always been impressed with the Thompkins' two-story house—one of the few custom-built homes in Greenbriar Heights—he was always even more impressed with their backyard, where he and Bree used to act out scenes from famous action movies with toy guns and walkie-talkies.

"This isn't two player?" Bree looked annoyed as she flipped through the game's instruction booklet. "That's lame, I want to be Jill."

"You can," Relic said, pointing to the character select screen, "just not at the same time." He pressed the controller pad arrows to switch between the S.T.A.R.S. identification cards of the main characters, Chris Redfield and Jill Valentine. Stopping on Chris' card, Relic pressed the button to select him, and the game continued to a cutscene about a bizarre string of murders in the fictional Raccoon City.

"Wow," Russ said, kicking his feet up in the recliner. "Hits close to home, huh?"

Relic gave a half-hearted chuckle. "Seriously."

There were two types of Laramie residents: those who avoided talking about its recent, dark history at all costs, hoping that it would be erased from everyone's memory eventually, and those who mocked it in a way, refusing to be terrified of it. The latter were the people who preferred to face their fears. Relic—who had once been deathly afraid of tornadoes until watching *Twister* last year—liked to consider himself part of that latter group, and Russ and Bree would gladly join him in laughing at Laramie's tragedies, as long as Lydia wasn't around.

As Relic navigated the old mansion in the game, talk inevitably led to the old Moreau Manor on Wane Street.

"This is how I used to imagine it," Russ said as Relic controlled Chris Redfield through a vacant dining room, accompanied by an ominously quiet soundtrack consisting of a ticking grandfather clock and the clomp of combat boots on tile. "Before it got that big renovation and turned into a wedding venue, I actually got to walk through it."

"Really?" Bree asked, setting the instruction manual down. "You never told me that."

"Well," Russ said, "your mom doesn't like talking about it. We were actually there because of her work. The Rothen Corporation acquired that property in the 1930s or something. Back then, it was still privately owned by the only surviving Moreau, Madeline."

"That was the Widow's youngest daughter, right?" Relic asked as the game showed him a foreboding scene of a door opening on a black background.

"Yep," Russ said, "the one with the most knife wounds that somehow still survived. She—oh god…"

Russ trailed off as Relic triggered a cutscene in the game of a zombie knelt over a decapitated corpse, snacking away as blood began to pool.

"Awesome," Bree said with a laugh, proving to her dad that this kind of stuff was nothing to her. Relic smiled, knowing he did the same kind of thing, laughing at the scariest parts in movies, finding a thrill in being pushed to your limits.

"Yeah, this feels way too familiar," Russ said.

"Whatever, Dad," Bree mocked while watching Relic try to fight through his first zombie encounter with only a combat knife. "You weren't fending off zombies in Moreau Manor. Why'd Mom have to go there for work anyway?"

Russ laughed. "I mean, a lot of the guys they had working there looked like zombies." He pushed the recliner's leg rest down, leaning toward Bree who was on the couch. "Now, don't go telling Mom I told you about this, because you know she always hates talking about the murders. But Rothen was determined to turn that place into some kind of research facility—don't ask me why. It seemed like a bad publicity move to associate your brand with such a tragedy." He shrugged, "But my guess is it was because of that Nexaphane drug your mom's been working on launching."

"Nexaphane?" Relic asked, moving Chris over to investigate a discarded gun on the ground in the mansion's main hall.

"Some neurological drug my mom's team is trying to get past the FDA," Bree said, stepping over to retrieve her dad's acoustic guitar near the piano. "It's why she's been traveling so much these past couple years. I guess it's a big deal."

"Yeah," Russ added, "a very big deal. Once it clears, I told your mom she better retire!"

Bree sat down and began plucking notes to match the game's ambiance. "What's Nexaphane have to do with the Moreau place?"

Russ clicked his tongue in response, "I have no idea. But given that it's a drug intended to counteract psychotic episodes or hallucinogenic conditions, I assume the company wanted the brand name associated with one of the city's most legendary psychotic figures. I mean, the Widow of Wane Street goes far beyond just local urban legend. That was a nationwide headline back in the 19th century. And then there's your dad's song, Relic. That was pretty big—"

"So Mom actually worked there?" Bree asked, clearly trying to divert discussion from Steven Meyers while still plucking the guitar. "At the manor?"

"No," Russ said, "not really. She only went there a few times, and I only came along once because there was some formal company gathering downtown—we just had to swing by the manor beforehand because she had to drop off some paperwork. We were just dating at the time, so I didn't know much about what she was doing there—I didn't ask a lot of questions, I was just thrilled a girl agreed to go out with me."

Relic laughed, imagining he would be the same way. "What was it like in there?"

"Just about as creepy as this," he motioned toward the game. "Before that renovation, they kept the place looking as historically accurate as possible. It wasn't like an office space; it just still looked like a residence from the 1800s. Just very bizarre."

"That is weird," Bree agreed. "Who would want to remember that place for what it was?"

"I got the sense that Rothen kind of wanted its research team to constantly be reminded of what happened there," Russ suggested. "Almost like they hoped the environment would serve as inspiration for them to make the drug prevent such psychotic tragedies in the future." He reclined back in his chair again. "Certainly didn't work, that's for sure."

Relic progressed further into *Resident Evil* in relative silence, with the exception of Bree's guitar or Russ' occasional squeak of fright—including a literal squeal when zombie dogs jumped through the windows in an empty hallway, causing Relic to drop his controller. Eventually, Russ slapped his knees.

"Well, that's enough for me. I don't think your mom would want me to have a heart attack tonight—she needs me to take her to the airport tomorrow."

"Where's she going now?" Bree asked, getting up to give him a hug goodnight.

"Back to New York," Russ said, giving Bree a kiss. He moved over to Relic for his customary high five. "Give 'em hell, dude."

"Will do," Relic said, slapping Russ' hand while keeping his eyes on the TV.

When they were alone, Bree put the guitar back on its stand and sat on the floor next to Relic, her knee touching his—something he wouldn't have normally noticed, but things had continued to get progressively weirder and weirder between them since she got home.

"Is it just me, or do you really want to go over there now?"

Relic paused the game, turning toward her. "The Moreau place? Why? I've been by there plenty of times on the way to Mom's work. It's just some event hall for weddings and stuff."

She shrugged, "I don't know. I've never been inside." Nodding toward the TV, she added, "That game just makes me super curious to check it out. We'd just need to bring some weapons in case there are zombies."

Relic snorted a laugh and tossed the controller down. "Let's stop there; my eyes are getting sore."

They retreated to Bree's massive bedroom, their normal hangout. While Relic's own bedroom was too cramped to really relax—which is why he and Bree stuck to the basement—Bree's room was luxurious, with an attached bathroom complete with shower and tub. He always teased her for being spoiled, but she knew it was only half-hearted jealousy.

Instead of heavy metal and fantasy posters, Bree's room was adorned with shelves of books and board games. She read just about anything, but had a particular soft spot for Stephen King and *The Babysitter's Club*, in equal measure. Her floor was almost completely devoid of dirty clothes and random action figures, and the carpet somehow always looked like it had just been vacuumed.

Relic plopped himself down on her bed, reclining on an elbow. His present situation made him recall what his mom said that morning in the car. "My mom doesn't think I should sleep over here."

Bree had her back to him, messing with the boombox on her dresser. "You mean like on Saturdays? You guys start going to church or something?"

"No, I mean, like *at all*."

She looked over her shoulder then, disbelief clear on her face. "What? Let me guess, because of the period thing? She knows we learn about that crap in school, right?"

"Yeah," he said, not sure he wanted to mention the real reason he suspected his mom brought it up. *Things happen,* he thought. He couldn't help his gaze from drifting back to Bree who had been wearing a loose flannel shirt but was now taking it off, revealing another tight tank top. Biting his lip, he sat up, feeling suddenly uncomfortable. "Honestly, I don't know. She's been weird all summer."

"Just call her and tell her we need to practice." Bree closed the cassette loader on the boombox, giving Relic a pointed look over her shoulder. "You promised me."

"Promised you what?"

Without answering, Bree went to her closet and disappeared behind its open door. "It was a fair trade!"

"What do you mean?"

When she came out, she was wearing a familiar black leather jacket. Walking exaggeratingly toward the dresser, she hit the play button and then fell to her knees. "Watch out!" she said along to the song, while putting her chin against the dresser with her neck extended. She dropped the leather jacket down over her shoulders and mimicked the cover of Madonna's *True Blue* so well that Relic had to quickly shift his posture.

"No way," he laughed. He tried to sound genuine, but he was feeling extremely awkward now.

Bree fell back laughing as well while the music played. As she got to her feet, she motioned for him to join her, shaking her hips to the beat of the song. "Come on, dude! We have to celebrate! Tomorrow is the last day of summer." She started to shimmy toward him.

Relic was laughing for real now, because she was actually dancing extremely well, and he didn't know how else to react to it. Unfortunately, the way she moved was making him feel things that made him fear his mom wasn't totally paranoid. He did feel something happening, and it was unsettling to say the least.

She was getting closer to him, and she kept reaching out for him, her hands dangerously close to parts of his body that were severely compromised at the moment. Just when he had to roll to the side to avoid her tickling fingers, he heard a drum fill in the song that gave him an idea that could completely derail this situation.

"Hey," he sat up, looking at her. "We should learn this song."

She stopped gyrating, breathing heavy now. But she held his gaze. "What do you mean?" Her voice was thick and low. "We know this song. It's *our* song."

"Yeah, but we should play it. Together. I need to get back to drumming." While the deception felt sort of wrong to him, that part was at least very true. He hadn't felt like playing drums so badly in his entire life since meeting Delilah.

Bree smiled, nodding to her brand new Fender that her dad got her; it sat in the corner on its stand, its purple body gleaming in the room's low light. "I know it already. Don't you?"

"I haven't really played through all of it," he slipped away from her and walked to the dresser, clicking the tape off. "But now that I have a copy of it on cassette," he ejected the tape and returned it to its case, turning back to her, "I can play it without my drums skipping the CD player."

There was nothing half-assed about Bree's smile.

Feeling relieved to have come up with the perfect excuse to return home, Relic walked from Bree's house with a pep in his step. Whistling the melody for "Open Your Heart," he tossed the Madonna cassette up and caught it, repeating the act every few steps he took. His mood was lightened. He enjoyed being out when it was this late, navigating the dark neighborhood by crossing pools of streetlight amidst the sounds of crickets and distant kids chasing lightning bugs. After a somewhat miserable summer, he finally felt happy.

As he rounded the corner toward his house, a set of headlights slowly approached him. Relic squinted, wondering if the vehicle was slowing down as he neared. The soft squeal of the breaks confirmed the theory as he came to the crosswalk that led to his house.

"Hey, Relic," a familiar voice said from the passenger-side window.

"Mr. Belinsky?"

"Larry, please."

As Relic walked beyond the glare of the headlights, his vision adjusted to the overweight man looking at him from inside the black van.

"What are you doing here?"

Larry laughed. "Funnily enough, I was going to just drop this on your porch." He held up a small wrapped package. "Figured I wouldn't waste postage since we're already in town. And anyway, I wanted to get it to you ASAP." He held it out for Relic to take.

Hesitantly, Relic reached for it.

"Don't worry, it's not drugs or a bomb or anything," Larry informed him. "In case there's any chance to get you on camera, I'd love to get your thoughts on this. It's some pretty rare footage of one of your dad's shows here in downtown Laramie, a few years before you were born, I think."

Relic's heart began to race. He had only seen a few clips from early Unknown Oath shows, and there were rumors that the band had destroyed most of their old concert footage due to them not wanting people to see how bad they were in their early years. Relic found that theory pretty odd—all bands have to start somewhere—but regardless, footage of his dad playing was certainly rare.

"Thanks," Relic said, trying not to sound too eager.

"You bet," Larry said. "And here, take this too." He held out a business card between two plump fingers. "My mobile phone number is on there. Give me a call when you decide you want to be a star."

The van pulled away without Relic even getting a clear view of the driver. But he was far too distracted by the videotape. He raced to his front door feeling on top of the world, but felt the rug pulled out from under his feet as he stepped into the living room.

"Relic!"

The room was dark, but the flickering light from the TV was enough for Relic to see his mom topless, covering herself. Calvin was scrambling to his feet, his pants undone and his stupid yellow polo shirt disheveled, the collar all stretched and crooked.

"Sorry," Relic said, averting his eyes the best he could, moving past the TV and stepping quickly down the hall toward the bathroom.

"Relic," Dina said again, but he firmly shut the door—proud of himself for not slamming it—before she could finish.

Almost completely numb, Relic began brushing his teeth. The emotions roaring throughout his body were on such conflicting spectrums that he was afraid he might just literally die. He brushed faster. He almost saw his mom's boobs. Faster. She said they weren't dating. Faster.

"Tell me about your mom's new boyfriend," Lydia Thompkins asked again in his mind. Faster, faster, faster.

"Relic?" There was a soft tap on the bathroom door.

He spat into the sink. "I'm taking a dump," he lied before brushing his teeth more violently. After what felt like ten whole minutes of brushing his teeth, he had calmed his breathing enough to attempt getting to his bedroom without further incident. He opened the bathroom door and walked swiftly across the hall to his room.

"Relic?" He heard his mom move toward him from the living room. He couldn't tell if Calvin was still out there.

"Going to bed," Relic called. "Goodnight."

Dina's footsteps stopped. He heard Calvin whisper something, and a moment later, the front door opened and closed.

Relic tossed the gift from Larry onto one of the shelves on his headboard and grabbed his old portable cassette player and headphones. He fell into bed without changing out of his clothes, reaching for the Unknown Oath demo tape he'd stashed behind his pillow.

Without hesitation, he jammed the tape into his cassette player, put on the headphones, and slammed the play button.

Unexpectedly, he fell into an exhausted abyss almost immediately.

Chapter 7

S teven Meyers looked so haggard in the dream that Relic barely recognized him until the drum set materialized from the swirling mists. His father's long hair swayed in wide circles as the drummer performed in the nothingness surrounding him, a gnarly beard obscuring his facial features.

"Dad?" Relic tried to say, but his mouth didn't work. He was only a silent observer here as the music he fell asleep to in the real world started to intensify in this formless place.

The rhythm to "Alternus" felt eerily familiar to Relic, as if it were a groove he had played a hundred times. He watched, mesmerized, as his father's hands deftly worked out the song's tom-heavy intro on his phantom drum kit, which was a spectral copy of Relic's own drums in the basement—translucent emerald green drum shells flashed in and out of existence with each hit of Steven's blurring sticks. Both bass drums thundered in steady syncopation as Stick began to build up while the bass guitar came in.

No other musicians joined though; it was just Relic (if he was even really there) and his dad, together in some timeless abyss.

A voice echoed in his mind—it was Ricky's, Relic knew, Unknown Oath's high-pitched vocalist—holding out an uncharacteristically low note over the bass and drums. "The curse," he said in a haunting melody, "has come..."

Relic was jolted when his dad slammed the snare and a crash cymbal together, accenting the rising tension in the song.

"...from far beyond," Ricky warned again, without an ounce of the upbeat energy he brought to most of the Unknown Oath songs that Relic knew. "A price to be paid for the masterpiece made."

Turning his head didn't adjust his vision in this place—Relic only saw his father, drumming like a demon as the song built up to a crescendo.

"Release me from this place!" Ricky shrieked as the music kicked into a heavy guitar riff and a driving 4/4 rock beat. There was still no sign of the singer, just the drummer, playing within his ghostly lit prison. Something deep down told Relic that these lyrics were written by his father, just like all the other Unknown Oath songs. "I am trapped within by mistake!"

Something shifted in the misty air between Relic's vision and his father's supernatural presence. The air rippled, like something swimming beneath the surface of the sea. The ethereal shape looked human, with flowing platinum blonde hair—despite the color of the figure's hair, Relic was immediately reminded of Delilah's presence in that discomforting dream he had in the basement with Bree.

He felt his slumbering body react similarly, and he tried to wake himself up. But it was no use; something wanted him to see the end of this dream, and Relic couldn't shake the feeling that somehow that *something* was his father.

As if in response, the vision of Steven Meyers slowly faded as the atmosphere continued changing into rippling waters, growing more turbulent as it divided Relic from his father.

"Dad!" he tried to call again, without making a sound. Ricky belted the song's chorus.

"You dream to relieve the unanswered questions, guiding our blades toward blood to be spilled."

The last words summoned a skeletal hand from the waters, its fingers tipped in razor claws. Relic tried to scream as it reached for his neck, but again he couldn't make a sound. He tried to wake himself as he felt the icy fingers choke him, but all he could do was lie still as it dragged him from that ethereal concert.

His dad faded away, headbanging as he kept time to a song lost to the past. As blackness claimed him, Relic heard a voice that wasn't Ricky's fading vocal melody; it was a voice as ghostly and ragged as his father had looked.

"Release me!"

Relic woke up in a cold sweat. He wasn't suffering from sleep paralysis, but he did feel too exhausted to move, his eyes nervously flicking around his room to convince his racing mind that he was indeed awake. It was still dark, and he heard the low electrical buzz of the TV on out in the living room. As his breathing slowed to normal, he sat up, pulling the headphones off his head.

He looked at the cassette player in his sweaty hand. The "Alternus" tape had played all the way through, but he didn't even remember hearing the song. The last thing he recalled last night was angrily putting the tape in after almost seeing his mom's boobs when she was fooling around with Calvin on the living room sofa. He turned to look at the neon green digital clock on his headboard—2:32 A.M.

Dropping the cassette player on the floor, Relic rubbed his eyes, trying to figure out why he was so tense after only sleeping for a few hours. He didn't remember his dream, but he knew it had to have been a doozy. Looking down, he saw his cargo shorts standing up at attention, and he let out a defeated sigh, annoyed at how all those sex ed books he had to read in school seemed to be right on the money when it came to wet dreams.

"You're killing me, Delilah," he moaned.

As he waited for his body to relax, his eyes drifted to his walls, trying to think of something dull or depressing to focus on. His gaze landed on the Unknown Oath show flier that Bree had printed off for him from the internet. On the flier, his dad (probably only twenty years old at the time) stood with his hands tucked in his tight jean pockets. He wore a denim vest, a bullet belt, and huge high top sneakers—all the necessary markings of a heavy metal warrior.

It did the trick. Lately, since the letters stopped, Relic seemed to only feel sadness when he thought about his dad. He stood up, walking over to the artifact from before he was born. The image of the band—his dad embodying the "quiet, cool" look, Gate with his dopey gap-tooth grin, Jeff with his crossed-arms, I'm-too-cool-to-be-here vibe, and then flamboyant Ricky sticking out his tongue and flashing two metal horns—made Relic's heart skip a beat.

It was as if he were trying to remember something. He leaned forward, trying to see his dad's face in the image, but it was very distorted, having once been an old photograph that was then scanned into a computer and finally printed out again. *Like a game of telephone,* Relic thought, not pretending to be tech-savvy enough to know the intricacies of digital media.

The blurry photo triggered an image in his mind, of his father's face beneath rippling water.

Release me! a voice called from within.

Relic recoiled from the flier, blinking frantically as if he had missed some sort of movement. When all he saw was the motionless flier, he whipped his head around the room looking for anything that could have made the sound.

There was a click out in the living room, and he heard movement—his mom. She had shut off the TV and was now walking down the hall toward his room. Like a pudgy ninja, he crossed the short distance to his bed and slid in, not wanting to give her a chance to have the heart-to-heart she might be hoping for.

Once he was in bed, Relic heard the door creak open and he gently let his eyelids close, playing the role of peaceful sleeping teenager to perfection.

"Relic," Dina whispered, her voice only on the edge of her son's listening.

After a long moment, the door creaked shut again, and Relic knew he was safe for at least a few more hours.

As he lay there with his eyes still closed, he wondered if the voice he had heard before was just from the TV, or if it was something in his imagination. While he pondered that, weariness took over and he drifted off to sleep again.

This time Relic was absolutely certain he was dreaming, but he was slightly relieved to find that it looked to be much more mundane than whatever had gotten him worked up before. He dreamed he was back at Ted's storage facility, but it was as if he were seeing it through some sort of floating presence. He descended over the parking lot like a camera on a crane filming the soaring intro shot of a movie. Laughter came from an open window on the office building adjacent to the main gate.

Whatever cameraman controlled his view guided Relic toward the window, coming in low so he could see just over the sill.

"I know," Ted said with another howl, "these Hollywood people don't seem to want to ask any questions—just throwing their money around willy nilly."

There was a single lamp on in the office, only lighting up Ted's desk and the scant few items occupying it: a black mug with a few pens in it, a large calendar, an electric fan, and bottle of brown alcohol that Ted took a sip from while he nodded along to whatever he heard on the phone.

"Well, no," Ted said, setting his drink down and holding up a hand to emphasize something to whomever was speaking with, "I told you, I gave her a cut. I only took what I thought was fair for the unit and moving the stuff she didn't want. She had first dibs." He waited and nodded again before laughing. "Yeah, well Hollywood boy didn't seem too happy after they filmed! Seemed like Dina took all the juicy stuff home."

Whatever was in control of Relic's consciousness guided him around the other side of the building, passing through the gate's iron bars as if they weren't even there. There was another window to the office on this side of the gate, and from it Ted's voice carried out into the vacant lot.

"Now, I ain't givin' exact numbers, Jake," he laughed, taking a moment to swallow some more booze. "But I think I got enough to float us on that new business venture we discussed."

Relic lost sight of Ted as his dream escort took him down the row of numbered storage units, each rolling door lit by a light that hung above it. Eventually, he stopped at a familiar unit. A hand reached out—it certainly wasn't Relic's, but its presence and position matched where his own hand *should* be. The appendage was pale, almost incorporeal, with long and pointed fingertips. It ran those fingers down the rolling door, creating a shrieking sound that made Relic cringe.

There was a loud bang from behind Relic's vision, and he imagined it was Ted throwing the door of his office open so he could investigate the sound. Meanwhile, the hand that wasn't Relic's moved down to the padlock, one of those sharp fingers hooking through the lock to test it—solid.

"Who's there?!" Ted shouted. Footsteps approached.

Relic's vision turned to Ted. The man strode toward him with a revolver in his hand, and Relic once more turned to regard the door as if his puppet master was unbothered by an armed, drunk Ted Packer. The pool of dim light in front of his family's old storage unit seemed bright compared to the darkness that enveloped Relic.

"Someone there?" Ted asked again, coming closer. "I'm armed! I'll have no vandalism. I'm well within my rights to put a bullet in your ass!"

A strange sensation quickened Relic's breath—a macabre sort of excitement over the strange circumstances playing out. There was a palpable thrill, but one that he certainly took no comfort in. It was as if it were someone else's excitement, trying to infect him. But he fought its influence with everything he had.

Finally, Ted stepped into the nearby pool of light, his gun held ready and his eyes searching for anything. Finally, his gaze fell onto the unit's padlock, and he froze. Relic's own gaze shifted to the door, and he would have gasped if he could.

The words "release me" were scratched into the door, and they definitely weren't there a moment ago.

"What the hell?" Ted said aloud. He knelt down to inspect it, cocking his head before snapping it to the left and right, looking for any sign of intruders. "Little bastards better not have fucked with my payday." He tucked his revolver into the back of his pants and retrieved a set of keys, jamming one into the padlock and clicking it open. "Better all still be here," Ted grumbled.

Miles away, Relic's heart thundered in his chest as the nightmare played out. But back at Ted's lot, he watched as the proprietor produced a small flashlight from a pouch on his belt. Ted clicked the light on and began inspecting the contents of the storage unit. Relic's vision followed the man, lurking over his shoulder as he inspected what remained—emptied boxes, scattered knick-knacks, and tied black trash bags piled along the sides of the unit.

After his light made a few passes of the interior, Ted grumbled and spun around. But when the man's eyes met Relic's, the color ran from his face and his eyes grew as wide as cue balls. The pale skeletal hand that wasn't Relic's reached out and buried its claws into Ted's neck just under his jawline. Three thin, white spikes emerged from different parts of Ted's face—one through the eyelid just under his eye, one through his cheek, and the other looked like it came out of his ear—in several sprays of blood.

Relic screamed, and then—

—yawned as he poured himself a huge bowl of Cinnamon Toast Crunch. His neck was killing him, and he wondered what he did last night in bed that made him so sore. It seemed like sleeping had become a full contact sport for him. Adding some milk, he took his breakfast to the kitchen table and began shoveling it into his mouth, hoping to be done before his mom got up.

"Relic?"

With a sigh, Relic stopped speed-eating and began to chew slowly. "Yeah?"

Dina came into the kitchen, wearing her silk purple robe. Her hair was wild, and her eyes were heavy. "Hey, I was going to make you breakfast."

Relic continued chewing, pretending to read the back of the cereal box.

Grabbing a chair, Dina sat down and rubbed her hands together slowly atop the kitchen table. "Look, Relic, I'm sorry that happened last night. I thought you were staying at Bree's for the night."

"You told me I shouldn't," Relic said between bites, not disguising his anger.

Dina bit her lower lip and tucked her chin toward her neck, allowing him that point. "Calvin and I went out for drinks last night, to celebrate and…" She trailed off as Relic began chewing louder. "I know this is probably weird for you, hon. And I want to respect that. But I really do like Calvin—he's a great guy."

Finishing his last bite, Relic dropped his spoon loudly in his bowl. "Great," he said, rolling the chair back to get up, "let me know when the wedding is." As he went to the sink to deposit his dish, he heard his mom sob. He wanted to pretend he didn't hear it. For some reason he wanted to stay angry, as if it were all he had to hold onto in light of this strange situation.

"He left us, Relic," Dina said, trying desperately not to let her voice fully break. "What am I supposed to do? He's had every opportunity to come back, and he hasn't!" Then her voice did break, and Relic turned around to see her raise the back of her hand to her nose. She reached for a paper towel from the roll on the table. "I think when he wrote, at least, we could pretend that maybe he'd be back—maybe we could work something out." She wiped her nose with the towel. "But now, wherever he's disappeared to this time…what the hell are we supposed to do, Relic?"

He watched as his mom completely broke down, sobbing into the wadded up paper towel.

Just as he was about to make a move toward her—to maybe offer some sort of comfort, despite how much he wanted to retain his soothing anger—the doorbell rang. Dina pulled more paper towel off the roll, hurrying to make herself presentable. But Relic—after just a little hesitation—put a hand on her shoulder.

"I'll get it."

They shared a brief look of understanding before Relic moved to the living room to see who the hell was going door-to-door on a Sunday morning.

"Morning, son," a police officer said when Relic opened the door. "Your mother home?"

"I'm here," Dina called from the kitchen. Relic heard her blowing her nose and rustling around, making herself less of a wreck. She came out of the kitchen wrapping the robe tighter. Recognition washed over her face when she saw who was at the door. "Keith?"

"Hey, Dina!" the cop said in a friendly voice. "Oh," he pointed to his badge, "it's Officer Barnes now." His voice had a mocking authoritative tone to it.

"Come on in," Dina said with a laugh. "It's been years! What brings you by?"

Officer Barnes stepped in, motioning behind him. "Dina, this is my partner, Officer Hayes."

Relic hadn't noticed the other cop, a younger woman with her blonde hair tightly bound up under her hat. She moved from the front yard up to the porch. "Sorry to disturb you, ma'am," she said.

"Oh, no worries," Dina said, "come on in. What's going on?"

Officer Barnes moved aside to let Officer Hayes in, nodding to Relic as he shut the door and moved to the living room. Both officers removed their hats. "Would it be alright if we spoke to your mother privately for a moment, son?"

Relic nodded, turning to his mom. "I'll be in the basement." He went downstairs but knelt near the foot of the stairs so he could still hear. Whatever was going on, it seemed serious.

"Do you mind if we have a seat, Dina?" Officer Barnes asked.

Before Dina could answer, the phone rang.

Shit, Relic thought, knowing that would ruin his eavesdropping.

"Relic, could you grab that down there?" Dina asked.

"Yeah." He tiptoed away from the stairs so they wouldn't know he was lurking and then grabbed the phone on the second ring. "Hello?"

"Did you hear?" Bree asked excitedly.

"Hear what?"

"It's on the news," Bree said. "Someone got murdered last night."

Relic heard his mom gasp upstairs, followed by a frantic, "What?!"

Paralyzed by the information, Relic just stared at the wall—at the picture of his dad from the poster art for *The Rest of the Wicked* to be precise—unsure how to process what he had heard through the phone or through the basement ceiling.

Release me, a strangled voice said in his mind, jolting him out of his stupor.

"—I guess someone found him in a storage unit," Bree was saying. "Isn't that where your mom kept her stuff? You were just there yesterday, right?"

The quick questions combined with his current houseguests made Relic imagine Bree in a police uniform herself, pressing him for information. "What?"

"Packrat," Bree said, exasperated. "Can you not hear me? Someone killed Ted Packer last night—at Packrat Storage."

"This can't be happening again." Dina's voice carried from the stairs, even though Relic could tell she was trying to keep it low.

He heard a cop say something in response, but he couldn't tell if it was the man or the woman from the controlled way they spoke.

Bree was still talking, but Relic's brain couldn't process anything. His mind just replayed the image of "RELEASE ME" scratched into metal, the feeling of déjà vu so palpable that he felt like he was about to hurl. When he finally gathered his senses, he interrupted whatever Bree was saying.

"Hey, Bree, the cops are here talking to my mom. Let me call you back, yeah?"

"The cops?!" Bree's voice was a shocked whisper, but Relic quietly returned the phone to its base and snuck back to the foot of the stairs where he could hear better.

"—and according to his books, you were past due on several months," Officer Barnes was saying.

"Yeah, he was going to sell our unit," Dina said with a choked voice. She sniffed. "He was nice enough to let us move some stuff out of there before he sold the entire unit as is."

"To the Hollywood fella?" Officer Hayes interjected. "Who you never met, correct?"

"No," Dina insisted, "not at all."

Combined with the nauseating confusion he was feeling, Relic also felt guilt being mixed in for good measure. He felt like he should go up and admit that he met Larry Belinsky—twice now—but doing so would also force him to admit that he was currently eavesdropping on a police interrogation.

Is this an interrogation? he wondered. *Is my mom getting grilled by the cops about a murder?* It felt very surreal; but then again, this was Laramie.

Dina seemed to be following her son's train of thought. "I'm not a suspect, am I?"

There was a restrained snicker. "Dina, I've known you since middle school. I know this wasn't you—"

"But," Officer Hayes interrupted, "we need to be thorough on this, given the nature of the murder and the association."

"The association?" Dina asked.

There was a long silence.

"We know what the media is going to latch onto here, Dina," Officer Barnes said. "This was Steven Meyers' storage unit. Ted's dad ran the place when the first murder there happened—same exact spot—in 1979." A shorter silence followed, after which Barnes added, "we need to clear you right away—keep your family away from this. Do you have someone who could verify your whereabouts late last night?"

Dina was sobbing now, and Relic couldn't sit idle anymore. "Calvin Green," he said, quickly climbing the stairs. He emerged into the living room as the officers were getting to their feet. "I came home around ten or so last night and Calvin Green was here with my mom."

Through red-rimmed eyes, Dina looked gratefully toward her son and nodded. "Yeah, before that we were over at Robin's on Beck Lane having drinks. You can ask Lucy—she's always there—that was who served us."

"That should get us by," Officer Barnes said, giving Dina a tight nod. "We'll get out of your hair now." He looked at Relic. "Big day tomorrow with school starting. Hopefully, you guys can enjoy the rest of the weekend. Sorry for the intrusion."

With that, the police officers left, and Relic went to give his mom a long overdue hug.

Relic was in a funk for the rest of Sunday, his mind struggling to figure out the weird visions and voices that kept coming to him like random memories he couldn't quite interpret. Bree came over almost immediately after the cops left, and hoping to distract him, she brought her guitar and small amp so they could mess around on the Madonna song.

It was a beautiful escape while it lasted. Relic hadn't truly played drums in weeks, and he and Bree hadn't played anything together in months. It rejuvenated him and kept his mind from dwelling on the killing—though the topic came up shortly after their jam session.

"Dad said it's probably some crazy copy-cats," Bree said, as she packed her guitar back in its case, her frizzy hair plastered to her sweaty forehead. "He said Ted's dad found a body in that same exact spot back when he was in high school."

With everything else going on, Relic was surprised that his thoughts fixated on the most mundane part of that sentence—high school.

They actually started high school tomorrow.

"Man," Relic said, getting up off his drum throne and inspecting the blisters on his fingers—he'd have to work up his calluses again. "Can't believe it." Though, if he couldn't believe whether they were starting high school already or there was a copy-cat killer loose in Laramie, he wasn't quite sure. Everything felt like it was spinning out of control; though coming off such an uneventful summer, it wouldn't have taken much to rock the boat.

As Relic maneuvered around his drums to stretch his legs, he caught Bree staring at him from her seat on the ground. He stopped.

"What?"

She inclined her head slightly, giving off strong motherly vibes that he would not normally associate with his friend. "You alright?"

He gave her a puzzled look. "What do you mean?"

Rising slowly to her feet, she maintained the look that was most likely supposed to be consoling but it felt almost patronizing. "I mean, this whole thing," she motioned as if something malevolent watched them from the basement's egress window. "This is what they always talked about—you know, with your dad's band and—"

"Relic!" Dina shouted from the stairs. "You guys want some dinner? I was thinking Chinese!"

Relic turned from the stairs back to his friend, her gaze still locked on him. "Come on," he said, "we have worse things to deal with."

"Why?" Bree asked. "Calvin bringing the food?"

Groaning, Relic threw his head back. "I was talking about school tomorrow, but dammit!" He threw his arm around her and together they marched upstairs, determined to get along with Dina's new boyfriend, if only for a night.

Chapter 8

Roanoke County School Corporation bus number 17 was responsible for picking up all Chambers High passengers in the vicinity of the Apple Acres, Maple Oaks, Sanctuary, and Greenbriar Heights neighborhoods, but the stop outside the First Church of the Nazarene probably filled up half the bus by itself. It seemed that most families in the four adjoining neighborhoods decided to have kids in the same four-year window, ensuring that the high school would stay in business.

Relic and Bree paced themselves as they walked toward the sidewalk that nearly twenty other teenagers currently occupied. It was a gorgeous August morning, but Relic was so consumed with dread over yesterday's bizarre events that he and Bree barely spoke as they marched toward their cruel destiny. The words "release me" still nagged at him, presenting as hoarse whispers in his mind or visions of jagged letters cut into metal. They meant nothing to him, but he was beginning to wonder if they had something to do with that demo tape he had fallen asleep to.

As he was trying to remember any of the lyrics to the song, Bree hissed under her breath. "Shiiiiiiit."

Relic shifted his backpack (carried by a single strap over his shoulder, because using both straps was far too uncool) and cast Bree a sideways look. His friend's gaze was shifting between the sidewalk below their feet and something up at the bus stop. One look up and Relic knew what distressed her.

"You knew Miranda would be at this stop," he said softly.

Bree just gnashed her teeth and hissed another unintelligible profanity.

As they got closer, Relic was surprised by how much Miranda Cartwright had changed over the summer. Even though she only lived a couple streets over from him, they rarely saw each other—partly because Relic spent most of the summer hibernating in his basement watching movies and partly because Miranda was in so many extracurricular activities that she was barely even home.

From what he remembered of 8th grade, Miranda was a dweeby teachers' pet who would be just as likely to rat you out for breaking a rule as she would be to offer to tutor you for no other reason than she enjoyed the wretchedness of education. She had always been a girl with long, straight brown hair, crooked glasses, a small number of huge zits on her face, and a mouthful of metal braces. But now he could see that Miranda had left that person in the graveyards of Sunnyside Middle School.

The Miranda he saw now was almost a foot taller, with curled hair that fell in perfect bundles onto her tanned shoulders, which were left exposed by a simple white top with spaghetti straps. She must be wearing contacts now, because her eyes were unencumbered and there wasn't a blemish to be seen on her face. She laughed with two other girls—Tammy Beck and Valerie Moore—who had once both belonged to a totally different society than Miranda.

But when Relic saw Tyler Richardson cross the street toward the girls, he was reminded that changing schools seemed to come with a seismic shift in the social hierarchies.

"Shiiiiiit," Relic hissed, mimicking his friend.

Bree stifled a laugh as they crossed the street.

Relic observed how Bree completely avoided any eye contact with Miranda, but the latter definitely cast the occasional look their way. There was a cruel smile on the girl's face that Relic found disturbing.

"Yo, Relic," came a familiar, lazy voice from behind, "your dad back in town?"

Relic turned to see the lone husky shape of Paul Stevens whose shoulders were pinned back by a comically small backpack. His pinched face was buried between wide cheeks that sagged lazily as his mouth hung agape.

Relic glanced around, seeing many sets of eyes directed at him. "What do you mean?"

"I heard he killed somebody again," Paul said, taking a deep breath that sounded like a snore. "Over at the storage place." There were a few whispers among the other kids, but Paul just scratched his ass, his vacant eyes staring at Relic and waiting for an answer.

"His dad never killed anyone, dude," Bree replied.

Paul nodded, his expression unchanging. "Oh," he said, in a sort of a grunt. It seemed like he was totally unbothered anyway, which seemed par for the course with a guy like Paul.

Relic saw Miranda and her friends whispering as they looked his way; he didn't have the best hearing, but he thought he heard one of them say "dyke," which wouldn't have been anything new, with him being a young kid in Indiana and having a lesbian best friend, but it still managed to piss him off.

He did know Tyler Richardson well enough to read his scummy lips, so he could tell when that piece of shit leaned in toward the girls, he said something along the lines of "playing with Relic's tits." Predictable. He couldn't believe he used to be best friends with the guy.

"Do they know who did it yet?" a soft voice asked from behind Relic. When he turned, he had to fake a cough to cover up his gasp.

He hadn't seen Delilah when they were walking up to the bus stop. He even forgot—until just now—that she had mentioned living on Tularosa when he first met her at The CD Palace. If he was going to get this chick to fall in love with him, he would have to start focusing, dammit!

"Hey," Bree said with a grin, "no, I heard on the news last night that they suspect someone's just copying the old murders."

Delilah stepped toward Bree, leaning in. "The Dire Decade?"

Relic was closer to her now than he had ever been, and he smelled a distinct aroma of incense and herbs; he couldn't put his finger on the exact scents, but they conjured up images of *The Craft*—a movie he didn't remember enjoying, but for some reason could never forget.

Bree nodded. "Yeah, not sure how much you know about this place, but it was pretty fucked up, especially in the 80s."

"More so in the 70s," Relic corrected sternly, but when Delilah's eyes shifted to him, he cocked his mouth and thought he felt himself actually drool.

"Whatever," Bree said, with a shake of her head.

The squeal of brakes alerted them all that the bus was coming around the corner, and they all moved to form a staggered line to board.

It was a short bus ride to school, and Relic was both relieved and annoyed to be sitting next to Bree. While he was glad this bus driver didn't hand out seat assignments like the middle school one—she was awful—Relic had hoped to score a seat next to his soon-to-be girlfriend, the new girl in town. However, Bree pulled him into her seat immediately when it looked like Paul Stevens might claim it.

Traffic was light down Sagamore Parkway, and the bus hit every green light. However, when it had to turn down Kossuth, there was a cop out in the street directing traffic around Packrat Storage.

"Maybe we'll see the body," someone said from the back of the bus.

"Yeah right, it's at the morgue by now," some guy added, "getting all autopsied and shit."

Relic couldn't help but lean over Bree, peering out the window to see what was going on. As predicted, it looked dull and uneventful. There were several patrol cars along the curb, with a few officers conversing on the sidewalk, and yellow caution tape was blocking off the parking lot. A few more comments were shouted from the back of the bus, drawing Relic's gaze down the aisle.

A couple dudes were being rowdy, laughing at whatever was said. But his attention was on the top of Delilah's head several rows back. He couldn't see her face, but he could see her dweeb of a seat-mate's face: Sebastian Ford. He had nothing against Sebastian Ford—the quiet weirdo who sometimes wore capes in middle school—but he couldn't look at the guy now without feeling rage. Sebastian Ford took the perfect seat that could have put Relic in the perfect position to woo the new girl.

Now, he hated Sebastian Ford.

Sebastian sneezed as if allergic to Relic's pent-up fury, and Relic turned back around before someone caught him staring.

A few minutes later, the bus squealed to a stop along the western side of Chambers High School. Everyone stood up at once before the bus stopped moving, causing all occupants to lurch forward slightly once the vehicle settled. The doors were thrown open and the stampede was released. Relic and Bree were surged along in the sea of flesh, navigating their way through the parking lot, the gymnasium, and finally the area that was referred to as the "Little Chamber."

Relic remembered taking a tour of the high school with his 8th grade class, and the tour guide described the area between the cafeteria and the auditorium as the "Little Chamber," using finger quotes. Relic never seemed to forget the name, even though it was anything but little to him.

"Hey, Bree! Relic!" an eager voice called.

"It's Howie," Bree said to him in a deep voice, "the Backstreet Boy."

Howard Sloan was no Backstreet Boy—though Relic wasn't sure if that was really a good or bad thing to be. The gangly guy waving to them was the staple "back-up" guy that Bree and Relic used when they needed a third player or wanted to ride his parents' moped down Shenandoah Street. Always standing taller than anyone else in his grade, Howie was hard to miss. Especially with those trashy dragon shirts he was always wearing.

"Dude, it's How-ward!" Howie said, in mock fury. "My grandma calls me Howie and it reeeeeally bothers me," he added through his teeth.

"Where's your brother?" Relic asked, leaning against the part of the brick wall near the trophy case that hadn't been claimed by the punk rockers gathering several feet away.

Howie hooked a long thumb toward the restroom doors past the punks. "Had yogurt for breakfast like an idiot. That IBS fairy doesn't mess around."

"Gross," Bree said, even though she didn't look disgusted at all. Relic noticed her cautiously eyeing Miranda as her posse joined some other pretty people on the far side of the Little Chamber.

"You guys hear about Ted Packer?"

"Duh," Bree said, "obviously, man. You think Relic wants to keep hearing about it."

Howie gave Relic a confused look, but then realized and shut his mouth.

Looking to ease the tension, Relic tapped Howie's shoulder. "Bree's dad thinks we could score some babes here if we start a *Dungeons & Dragons* club, man."

"My dad," Bree said, inclining her head toward Relic and widening her eyes, "is a moron sometimes."

Howie beamed. "I'm down for that, man! Daugherty moved to Chicago, and you guys never come over, so I can't keep a game together."

"What?" Bree asked with an elaborate shrug. "Are we supposed to ride our bikes all the way down state road 26?"

"I told you my dad would pick you guys up! He wants to play, too."

"No offense, Hows," Bree said, lowering her voice and leaning toward him, "but your dad creeps me out. He kept walking into your game room last time in his tighty-whities."

Relic tried to suppress his laugh, remembering how red Bree's face had gotten. Sometimes, it was almost like she blended in so well with his friends that adults would mistake her for a guy. That thought suddenly made him feel bad for laughing at her situation, and his smile quickly melted. Looking around at the other kids in the Little Chamber, he couldn't help wondering if he let himself absorb too much of the mocking energy coalescing in this place.

The bell rang sharply, drawing Howie's attention to the restroom. "I'm going to go check on Alvin. Senior year and he still hasn't gotten his shit together." He held up a finger and gave them a surprised look. "Pun!"

Relic and Bree once more joined the flow of people surging toward the main-floor lockers. As they moved into the hall, Relic saw Delilah joining the throng of people alongside Sebastian and his vampire crew. *God dammit,* Relic thought defeatedly. He knew if he had sat next to her on the bus, he might have been able to be on Delilah's radar. But as he watched the other black-clad goth kids circle around their new matriarch, he knew he was watching the solidification of a clique that he would have no hope of joining.

Delilah and her flock of ravens took perch near the school's main entrance stairs, the wide half-staircase that led to the school's elegant front doors that the bus students weren't good enough to use. Relic tried not to stare as he passed, wondering if that would be where he'd find Delilah before school and between classes from now on. From what he had heard about high school cliques, it seemed very likely.

Bree split off from him to go to her locker as Relic turned down a different hall toward his own. His disappointment continued as he saw two bodies flanking his locker, one of which was Tyler Richardson.

Tall, lean, and muscular—with annoyingly impeccable hair to boot—Tyler was an all-star baseball pitcher that Relic used to catch for in little league. Back then, they were nearly as close as he and Bree (although the three of them almost never hung out in the same company because Tyler seemed to be very uncomfortable around girls who could best him at anything). However, once middle school hit and Relic fell out of love with being bossed around by coaches, Tyler had begun ruthlessly bullying Relic.

It had started off somewhat innocuous in 6th grade, with Tyler occasionally poking fun at Relic not performing adequately in gym class or joining in when someone would make a crack about his body. Even back then, Relic seemed shorter and pudgier than most of the guys in his grade. But things started accelerating in 7th grade, when Tyler and whatever goons he was trying to impress would blow snot on Relic's locker dial, or have their female friends trick Relic into thinking one of their other female friends was asking him out only to make said other female friend shriek in disgust when the secret was revealed.

All in all, Tyler Richardson was probably largely responsible for middle school being the worst three years of Relic's life.

"Hey, Meyers," Tyler said, as Relic reluctantly approached his locker.

Relic didn't grant him a reply, focusing on spinning the combination dial to its appropriate digits, grateful at least that it wasn't covered in mucus.

The other locker to Relic's left slammed shut as Tyler slowly closed his own to the right. "Looks like you spent your summer eating candy and avoiding the barber."

Once again, Relic knew better than to reply. He pulled out his notebook and hung his backpack on the hook inside his locker, grabbing his history book for first period. He consoled himself that history was the one subject he actually didn't mind—he was fascinated by medieval history particularly, as well as World War II.

Before he could shut his locker, Tyler slammed it for him, finally drawing Relic's attention. Tyler looked satisfied, but he had nothing to really say when Bree approached behind them.

"Richardson," Bree said in a fake low voice, "did you ask your daddy if you could leave the gym?"

It was Tyler's turn to ignore the mockery, pushing Relic into the lockers with his shoulder as he headed in the same direction Relic would have to go.

"What the hell is that guy's issue with you?" Bree asked. It was rhetorical, of course—both of them knew the guy had a horrible home life. His father, Barry Richardson, a football legend turned car salesman who was now shifting into local politics, was a ruthless dictator. Relic saw firsthand as early as fifth grade how Barry completely controlled his son's schedule, working him like he was an Olympian before he even started organized sports.

As Relic watched Tyler slap someone a high five before turning the corner, he considered the many reasons why he had become such a target of Tyler's aggressions. It could be simply because Barry was a proponent of "tough love," shaming his son as a way of motivation to better himself. Maybe Tyler just saw a lazy fat guy in Relic that he needed to whip into shape. Or maybe it was some intimidation tactic, threatening Relic so he would never tell their peers that they used to do embarrassingly silly stuff when they were boyhood friends, like measuring each other's erections or trapping their own farts in jars.

Whatever it was that drove Tyler to be so cruel, Relic tried to remind himself that it was due to the guy's own unhappiness. It didn't make him hate Tyler any less, necessarily, but it let him not dwell too much on him.

Relic and Bree made it to Ms. Duncan's history class on the second floor just as the bell rang. While he was glad they had at least one class together on "yellow" days—his "green" day schedule looked miserable—he was annoyed to discover the assigned seats were alphabetical, meaning they had to sit two rows apart. Relic was sandwiched between Valerie Moore behind him and Chaz McCormick in front of him; one of them smelled like pee and Relic had his money on it not being Valerie, who doused herself in body spray.

Relic avoided looking at Tyler who sat two rows over near Miranda.

After everyone was settled in their forced seating arrangements, Ms. Duncan pointed to the word "STORY" written on the chalkboard in huge block letters. She was younger than Relic would have imagined when he thought of a high school teacher, looking like she had just graduated college. But he could never tell adult ages well—people were either kids, teens, adults, or geezers to him.

"Who likes stories?" the teacher asked. She had a half-cocked grin that reminded Relic of Bree, but she had dimples on either cheek and thin-framed glasses amplifying her brown eyes.

Most of the students raised their hands.

"I should see all your hands up," she said, beckoning the stragglers with a wiggling finger. "Whether you're watching movies, reading a book, catching your favorite TV show, playing a video game—everything has some form of story going on, holding your attention. Right?" When no one answered, she asked again. "Am I right?"

Relic found himself joining most of the class in verbally agreeing.

Ms. Duncan smiled and nodded. "There you are. Oh, I almost forgot introductions." She turned to grab a piece of chalk and wrote "HI" in huge block letters right before "STORY," adding a comma in between the words and then stepping back to wave. "Hi, story, my name's Tori Duncan. You can call me Tori or Ms. Duncan, but do not call me Toucan because I am not a bird."

There was a mild wave of laughter from the student body.

She turned to face the class. "And that goes for you all as well. I'm probably not as formal as many of your other teachers, but in return I ask that you get at least half as excited about history as I do. With that said, welcome to U.S. History, where we will," she pointed to the board again, "read, study, and tell stories. So let's kick things off: who can tell me a story?"

Stunned silence. Apparently, the rest of the class was just as blindsided by Ms. Duncan's form of teaching as Relic was. It was a welcome alternative.

"Nobody has a story?"

"There was a murder last night," someone from the back of the class said. Peering over his shoulder, Relic saw an unfamiliar face that must have been someone from a different middle school.

"There was," Ms. Duncan said. "It was quite a tragedy. But beyond that, why do you think that was the first story you thought of?"

"Because it just happened?"

Mrs. Duncan rocked her head from side to side as if uncertain she could accept the answer. "Well, sure. But I think it happens to hold a bit more of a significance in this town."

"It's because it happened in the same place where Relic's dad killed someone in the 70s," Tyler offered, rousing a few chuckles and mummers.

Relic seethed, biting his lower lip. He felt hot tears flooding his eye cavities, but he kept his gaze on the floor, determined not to let them out.

"You can see me after class, Mister…" she leaned over to her desk to check the seating chart, "Mr. Richardson. In addition to being one of my favorite drummers," Tori flashed metal horns at Relic and gave him a wink, "Relic's father was no murderer—which you would know, Mr. Richardson, if you had been informed of the history you're speaking of."

Tori's interference kept Relic from crying during his first high school class, and he was extremely grateful—enough to actually pay attention as the lecturing truly began.

Ms. Duncan leaned against the front of her desk, using her hands to keep her balanced. "I believe the real reason many of you would immediately think of the recent news as an example of a story is because of this city's history, right?"

Silence again.

"I'm not from Laramie originally," she elaborated, "I moved here to get my degree from Lafayette University in '92, after the most colorful events of the Dire Decade were tabloid fodder. So as an outsider, let me say—this place has a wild history."

Several students chuckled, but Relic leaned forward in his seat.

"That's why," Ms. Duncan continued, "your first project this semester will be to tell the class a story." She pushed herself away from the desk and crossed her arms as she paced the front of the class. "Not just any story, obviously, but a story about this city's history, touching on at least one key event in the history of the United States that either occurred during the same year or had some sort of effect on the story you've chosen."

As much as Relic loved history, this project sounded complicated, and he already felt his eyelids growing heavy.

"We'll dig more into that on Wednesday when we choose topics. But for now, let's take out your books and turn to chapter one..."

Relic nearly conked out immediately at the mention of a book, already tuning Ms. Duncan out as he mindlessly opened his book and began sketching pictures of Jason and his trusty tank from *Blaster Master*—his favorite Nintendo game of all time—on the back of his notebook. By the time the teacher had finished her first lecture, Relic was barely able to keep his eyes open.

Release me.

The voice in Relic's head jerked him wide awake, his arm knocking his textbook to the floor.

"It's ok," the teacher said, amidst a few chuckles from the class, "I'm not a huge fan of the Europeans arriving either."

Relic's face felt like it was on fire as he retrieved his book, fighting his biological urge to cry at the most mundane of embarrassments. Fortunately, the bell rang.

"Real quick," Ms. Duncan said as students began closing their books and hurrying toward the door, "your homework is to think of the story you want to present to the class: something that happened in Laramie concurrently with something important in the country's history. And you stay put, Tyler. We need to chat about your classroom etiquette."

Relic thought he saw the teacher give him a look out of the corner of his eye, but he didn't want her to see him notice, so he kept his head down and joined Bree on her way out.

"Day one homework," Bree grumbled, spinning her mechanical pencil between her fingers. "You heading to chemistry?"

"Yeah," Relic said. "See you at lunch?"

"Save me a seat," Bree said with a smile.

Something caught Relic's eye then. It felt like time froze, and Bree's face became Delilah's in his mind—or Delilah appeared right behind Bree...he couldn't tell. But when he blinked, the image was gone. He was watching the back of Bree's head disappear into the throng of students, with no sign of Delilah anywhere.

Weird, Relic thought.

On the way to chemistry in the basement, Relic saw two familiar police officers speaking to a janitor. Officers Barnes and Hayes from yesterday morning were tucked into an alcove near a fire extinguisher speaking with a portly man with a mustache wearing green coveralls. There was something eerily familiar about the janitor, but Relic couldn't quite put his finger on it. He tried to overhear the conversation as he passed by, without being seen by the officers.

"You can see why it's a little weird, right?" Officer Barnes was asking.

The janitor nodded, scratching the back of his head, looking down at the ground as if trying to avoid eye contact. "I get it, man. I just wish I could help you..."

"So you haven't spoken to him at all this year then?" Officer Hayes' tone was much harder than Barnes, who had sounded like he empathized with the janitor about something.

"Wish I had," the janitor grumbled. "He was my best friend...but I'm just trying to move on now..."

Relic had to keep his pace to avoid notice, so he didn't hear the rest of what the janitor was saying. He wondered if they were talking about Ted Packer.

Thinking about Ted suddenly made Relic feel disoriented and the hallway lurched under his feet. The sounds of the other students passing by faded into a strange white noise. His vision blurred as if he were closing his eyes, and Ted's face appeared wearing a shocked expression. White spikes burst through several parts of Ted's face spraying blood, and Relic gasped, reaching for the wall.

When his vision returned, Relic saw crude writing on the beige concrete wall, black magic marker spelling out "release me" in jagged letters.

With that vision, Relic's dreams came flashing back to him, feeling like memories from another life. He groaned and fell to his knee.

"You alright, kid?"

Relic's hearing came back, and he felt a strong hand under his arm.

"Oh, Meyers," Officer Barnes said when Relic looked up. "Everything okay?"

Relic rubbed his eyes. "Yeah, sorry, just tripped I guess."

"Eavesdropping again?" Officer Hayes asked sternly.

Relic looked up at her nervously.

"Ease up, Mindy," Barnes said. "The kid's just going to class. Right?"

Relic was jolted by the bell, and he noticed then that the hall was almost empty now. *Did I black out?* he wondered.

"Better get going then," Officer Hayes said, turning around. "Where'd Gerald go?"

Turning, Relic saw the janitor was nowhere to be seen.

"Looks like you scared him off," Barnes said with a snort, patting Relic on the back as he headed in the opposite direction of Relic's class. "Doesn't matter," he added, "we got what we needed. Watch your step, Meyers." Officer Hayes gave Relic a long stare before moving to follow her partner.

Taking a deep breath, Relic spared one last look at the wall before going to class; there was nothing written on it.

Chapter 9

The next day, Relic was sitting in art class doodling in his notebook while having an argument with Howard Sloan about who was the best Robin.

"Wasn't Dick Grayson, the *original* Robin?" Howard said, gesticulating wildly with his bony hands. "How does that not make him the best?"

"Because," Relic said as calmly as he could, "Dick Grayson didn't really *want* to be Robin, it was just like a vehicle for his vengeance, or whatever—a steppingstone. He grew up, matured, and became Nightwing for a reason. He wasn't really meant to be a partner—he wants his own identity."

"So you're a Jason Todd fan?" Howard asked incredulously as more students filed into the room, each one claiming one of the four chairs at tables other than the one Relic and Howard argued at.

"Hell no," Relic said, trying to keep his voice calm—he was about to lose his mind on Howard though. "Jason Todd was a punk. Tim Drake is the ultimate Robin—he was a good enough detective to find out Batman's identity. None of the villains could do that! And he's a better partner because he knows that Batman needs a Robin."

Howard gave him a skeptical look. "Michael Keaton didn't need him."

"Can I sit here?"

Relic turned and almost vomited when he saw Delilah's dark eyes staring straight at him.

"Yeah," Howard said, "just don't bring up Batman's sidekick around Relic."

Delilah carefully pulled a chair out and put her books on the table. "Tim Drake or Barbara Gordon?"

Tasting literal bile in the back of his throat, Relic swallowed and tried to form a smile with his dried lips. *Why can't I function around this girl?* he thought miserably.

"Welcome to drawing," a boisterous voice called, saving Relic from having to actually form words in the presence of his true love. A very large man walked past their table as he made his way toward the front of the art room. "I am Mr. Lane, and I am here to take you on a journey—no!" He held up his hands as if the class had just suggested something offensive to him. "*You* are all here to take *me* on a magical journey—through your art." He posed dramatically, displaying exceptional grace for a man of his size.

Some of the class giggled. Relic caught Delilah smiling out of the corner of his eye, and then he joined in the laughter as well. *You pathetic follower,* he accused himself, feeling internal shame.

"We'll start with the boring fruits," the teacher said, his voice shifting then into an otherworldly growl as he added, "and then Relic will jam his razor-sharp ghost claws through our faces and leave us to rot!"

Relic felt his arm tense in response to those words and he looked down at his notebook where he was drawing a crude picture of Ted as those white thorns burst from his face. He gasped and quickly tore the page out of his notebook, wadding it up. He looked up and saw everyone staring at him, Mr. Lane pausing whatever he was saying.

"Everything alright over there?"

"Uh," Relic said, panicking. "Can I use the restroom?"

"If it certainly cannot wait, be my guest," Mr. Lane replied, gesturing toward the door. "As I said, fruits and still life first—the foundations, my brave pupils—then we can work on the fun stuff. Deal?"

Relic held his breath as he exited the room, not wanting to retain all the attention he had already drawn. When he got out into the empty basement hall, he exhaled loudly and walked toward the restroom with his head hanging back like some spineless zombie. He walked that way until he heard approaching footsteps from the other end of the hall.

Straightening, Relic saw a man walking toward him, the fluorescent lights on the low ceiling behind the figure flickered in his wake. From this distance, Relic couldn't make out the man's face—especially with his shaggy hair hanging over his brow and that bushy beard covering his mouth and chin—but there was a dangerous aura about him. It may have been due to his clothes: tattered blue jeans, untied black combat boots, and a grungy Nirvana t-shirt. Once again, he heard those whispered words.

Release me.

Relic sped up his pace, making it to the restroom door before the man could get any closer. As he slipped into his teal-tiled sanctuary, Relic felt ridiculous for thinking that this would be some sort of escape from any potential danger. *Get real, dude,* Relic said to himself, moving to a stall as his stomach heaved in response to his encounter with Delilah, the embarrassment in class, and the bearded stranger. *You're not in danger. You're just bored and looking for something exciting to happen.*

He locked the stall door, dropped his pants, and sat down, figuring he might as well try to poop while he was here, and he wasn't in a huge hurry to go back to class—hopefully by the time he returned everyone would have forgotten about his little outburst. As he sat there doing his business, he heard the door creak open.

It's not the grunge guy, he thought to himself, *it's definitely not the grunge guy.*

The slow, careful footsteps that followed didn't sound right on the tile. There was a strange click with each step, and it sounded like more than one person walking in. But no one spoke—what kind of weirdos went to the restroom in pairs without talking?

Relic heard the door shut and the footsteps stopped. He tried to peer through the crack between the stall door, but he only saw a row of empty sinks below a long mirror. No sign of anyone. Not sure what else to do, he tightened his stomach and pushed out a fart that had been brewing. If there was a teenage boy in here with him (or a girl with Bree's sense of humor), he would soon know.

But there was no laughter. Silence.

His heart beginning to hammer, Relic took a deep breath and slowly gathered a handful of toilet paper. He hadn't produced anything other than gas, but he wiped anyway and flushed the toilet.

Still, no other sounds.

As Relic reached down to grab his pants around his ankles, he finally heard something—it was animalistic, like a low growl building in some creature's throat. With his hands around his belt, he slowly began pulling his pants up as he lowered his head to see what he could below the stall door. Just as his view was about to be low enough, there was a slam against the stall door that threw him back between the stall and the toilet, his elbow getting damp in the bowl's fresh water.

Despite his heart feeling like it just exploded, Relic managed to straighten himself and see two hairy legs with claws just below the stall door, which now rattled on its hinges. Whatever was on the other side was pounding and scratching on the door, growling deep in its throat.

What the hell is a dog doing in here? Relic thought, but even as that question passed his mind, he knew this wasn't just some dog. It had to be bigger than him, judging from the shadow it cast and the shape Relic saw through the stall's crack.

There was another sound then—a sharp whistle—and the creature went back to all fours, turning so Relic could see what looked like a wolf's head through the gap in the stall.

"You the alpha, Jack-o?" a gruff voice asked.

He only got a low growl in reply.

"Already skinned one of you boys," the newcomer said again. "Looks like I'll be able to make a coat once I put you down." There was the sound of something wooden cracking.

The creature's growl intensified, and then it leapt off the ground. Relic heard a yelp and then a thud, like a heavy bag had just been dropped on the ground. He was still frozen in place, waiting for something else to make the first sound.

"It's alright, kid," the gruff voice said, followed by the sound of a trash bag being whipped open. "He ain't gonna hurt ya now."

Trembling, hoping his pants were still clean, Relic reached for the stall's latch and opened it. He saw his reflection in the mirror; his face was a mask of wide-eyed terror. As he stepped out of the stall, he saw the janitor from yesterday—Gerald, if he remembered correctly—knelt over a bulging black trash bag that he was currently tying. There was a broken mop on the floor, the handle that ended in a spike was now covered in blood, a pool of red nearby.

A thousand questions ran through Relic's mind, but he settled on, "What was that?"

"A dog," Gerald said, pulling a rag out of the back pocket of his coveralls and wiping the blood off his broken mop.

Relic swallowed. "That wasn't a dog."

Gerald pushed the heavy trash bag toward the wall, his janitor cart blocking the entrance. "You ever heard of the West Laramie Werewolves?" He grabbed a big bottle of chemicals from his cart, his back still turned to Relic.

Of course Relic had heard the stories about werewolves, but that was certainly never how he imagined them looking. Besides, everyone always said it was just a pack of wild, overgrown dogs that had caused all that trouble—like most of the weird events during the Dire Decade, monster sightings and supernatural occurrences could be explained away by exaggeration or simple unsolved mysteries.

"You're trying to tell me that's a werewolf?"

Gerald began dumping the clear chemicals on the blood stain. "I'm telling you that was a dog, just like the West Laramie Werewolves were just dogs. Big nasty dogs, sure, but dogs. The minute people start talking about werewolves, playing on their fears and making something out of nothing...well," he knelt down with another rag and started wiping up the puddle he created, "that there's how trouble starts."

Relic didn't know how to respond to that, so he just watched the man clean, waiting for something else that might explain what he just saw.

"You might not know," Gerald continued, "but there were stories about werewolves around these parts as far back as the 1800s. Livestock going missing from places that wolves couldn't get to, people being attacked on the roads...there's lots of werewolf legends in Laramie's past, more so than most cities." He kept scrubbing. "Makes you wonder," he peered at Relic over his shoulder, "if talkin' about werewolves is what makes people see werewolves."

Forgetting his fear for a moment, Relic scrunched up his face, wondering what the heck that meant. "So..."

"So, you better get back to class," Gerald said, returning to his cleaning. "I'll take care of this. Just don't go talking about werewolves. We don't want anyone else seeing these things, right?"

Completely confused, Relic walked out of the bathroom in a trance, somehow winding back up in art class without even realizing it.

"You alright, man?"

Relic blinked, looking toward Howard who was staring at him from across his sketchbook. "Yeah," Relic lied, wondering what would happen if he said he had just seen the janitor slay a werewolf.

"I got your sketchbook out," Howie said, returning to his own. "We're supposed to draw something we did over the summer."

Relic looked down at the sketchbook and a row of colored pencils on the shared table, not wanting to touch either. He was afraid he might draw something from his dreams again. He looked over at Delilah who was hunched over her own sketchbook, busily adding detail to her work. Relic waited for her head to shift enough to one side so he could see, but he nearly fell out of his chair in shock when that happened.

He must have gasped, because Delilah looked up, her brows slightly creased in focus. Under normal circumstances, Relic might have cared that she was looking at him, but after surviving an apparent werewolf attack and now seeing "release me" sketched in big letters once again, he was too frightened to care much about his own shame.

Delilah looked down at her work, and then back up to Relic. "What is it?"

"What are you...uh," Relic licked his lips, trying to regain his composure. "What are you drawing?"

She spun her sketchbook around to show him. It looked like an album cover, and he was not in too much shock to internally grumble when he saw Sebastian

Ford's band name scrawled across the top. Autumnal Fall had been around for a couple years, an artsy, gothic synth project that Sebastian once tried to get Bree to play viola in (Bree's laughter in response nearly made Sebastian cry). He should have known when Delilah mentioned writing music, and then sitting with Sebastian on the bus, that she was already collaborating with him.

Delilah's sketch was not necessarily impressive. Her lettering was simplistic, and the band logo did not convey goth or synth—it looked like an indie hipster band. And the image of the tattered doll was a bit much, but he guessed it fit the whole goth vibe at least.

"Cool," Relic made himself say, but he was focused on the "release me" part of the piece. "Is that the name of the album?"

Delilah spun the book back around. "I don't know. I just had a weird dream this summer about that phrase written on a picture frame in my house." She shrugged. "It was super weird, but I just remembered it."

Relic's mouth had gone dry, but he was desperately curious. "What was the...uh, what was in the picture frame? Where that was written?"

She looked up, as if she had never considered that part. "It was a picture of my dad."

It was one of the hardest things in Relic's entire life to not tell Bree about the bathroom situation. When the dream of his dad and then the one about Ted's murder came back to him yesterday, he easily managed to keep that to himself, because he didn't even know how to describe that situation to Bree—it was all cerebral and weird.

But what had happened to him that day was very real, and it was eating away at him.

Fortunately for him, Bree had plenty to say about her day as they walked home from the bus stop, so he probably wouldn't have been able to get a word in if he wanted to. After a long story about her study hall teacher awkwardly tripping and knocking the TV off the cart in class, Bree put a hand on Relic's shoulder to make sure he was paying attention.

"You know Dustin's band? Bag of Sax? They got to play that one festival last year with Blink-182 in Wisconsin? Well, apparently their guitarist moved away and their bassist, Nick—he went to Tecumseh Middle School—said he saw me play guitar when we did that 8th grade talent show—you know, when all the middle schools got together. Anyway, he was asking if I'd want to join their band."

A jealousy more powerful than Relic had ever experienced overcame him, and he couldn't even speak. He could feel Bree's eyes on him, but all he could do was stare forward as they neared her street.

"You think I should?" There was a strange yearning in her voice, as if she wanted him to object—it was more likely that he just *wanted* her to want him to.

Relic shrugged. "I mean, you're in a band already, so..."

"I am?"

Removing his backpack from his shoulder, Relic opened it and produced his sketchbook. He opened it to the first page, where he had been spitefully inspired by Delilah to sketch out his own album cover art.

"Altar Stone?" Bree's voice couldn't hide her excitement.

"Yeah," Relic said, smiling as he admired his work and completely forgot about the day's events. Altar Stone was sketched in elegant, cracked, green stone letters, and hung above a mystical, sweeping landscape—or at least Relic's best interpretation of one. A cracked gem hung in the air, and below it the album was titled *Breaking the Oath*.

Bree took the sketchbook carefully, gazing into the art as they continued walking. "What's it mean?"

"Altar Stone? Well, I looked it up in the library. Apparently, it's an altar made out of rock to hold..." he motioned with his hands as if presenting himself to a crowd, "relics."

Bree laughed, but not in a mocking way. "That's awesome. Yeah, I love it, man. What about this?" She pointed to the album name.

"I don't know…people will always talk about my dad, can't really escape it."

She nodded. "Yeah, I think this is poetic, dude. Super cool. So what do we play?" She handed the book back to him. "Aside from Madonna?"

Relic laughed. "*Not* Madonna. I think we've done enough of that."

"No offense," she said, "but I'm sick of doing Metallica and Megadeth covers. I feel like there's too much angry metal, especially the modern stuff. Too much growling and yelling."

Smiling because she was speaking his own thoughts, Relic nodded. "You remember that HammerFall album I bought?"

"Yeah," Bree said, snapping her finger, "I was trying to remember the name of that band yesterday. Any good?"

"Amazing," Relic said, putting the sketchbook back in his bag. "It's like modern Iron Maiden meets, like, black album Metallica, or something between. Just super powerful and melodic and heavy and catchy…something about it really clicked with me. Like, it's not exactly like the stuff my dad did, but it kind of still is in a way…I don't know."

"Yeah, and their cover looks like something out of *HeroQuest*, so count me in," Bree faked swinging a double-handed sword as they got to her corner. "Remember, it's Tuesday. Buffy night."

They were currently between seasons of *Buffy the Vampire Slayer*, which just started airing in the spring, but Tuesday had become their "Buffy night," when they'd pop some popcorn with Russ and watch *Buffy* in the dark. Relic loved having stuff like that to look forward to during the week, especially right after a Monday.

"Yeah, I can head over after checking in with Mom. We doing dinner?"

"I'll call you," she said, already walking toward her house.

By the time his house came into view, Relic realized that he had almost completely forgotten about the encounter in the restroom. But for some reason, seeing his house with the vacant driveway—Mom must have had to work late again—the terror he had felt returned, and he wanted to get inside as soon as possible. He ran for his front door, waving to his neighbor Frank who was spraying his garden.

"Slow down, bud, you're always in too much of a hurry!"

Relic ignored the warning and dug the key out of his pocket to unlock the front door. Predictably, the house was empty. He went to his room and was shocked to find it completely cleaned. His mom hadn't cleaned his room for him in years. He dropped his backpack on his beanbag chair and walked over to his bed. The package that Larry had given him was still on his shelf undisturbed, but his cassette player was next to it, the headphone wire wrapped up neatly in a coil.

If it had been a more normal day, he might have noticed that the "Alternus" tape was no longer in it, but as things were, he simply kicked off his shoes and began to change into more comfortable clothes before going down to play drums for a bit.

As he left his room in a hurry, he also didn't notice that his father's bassist, Gate, now wore a pair of dark green coveralls in place of a sleeveless black tee in the concert photo of Unknown Oath hanging near Relic's door.

"Release me," a whisper called out in Relic's wake.

That evening, Bree called Relic over early for dinner. A message on the answering machine told Relic that he shouldn't expect his mom home any earlier than ten, since she had taken a later shift to spend the day cleaning the house.

"Also," his mom said at the end of the message, "I have a little surprise for you, but I'll show you tomorrow! Love you, little dude."

He always hated when she called him little dude, it just reminded him that he was a fat dude. After a quick shower to wash the drum sweat off himself—and to enjoy some more HammerFall—he rode his bike over to Bree's for his favorite dinner.

"That's a lot of mac n' cheese," Relic said, as Bree kept piling it onto his plate.

"Mom doesn't do carbs," she said, slopping on a final scoop, "so we have to finish this, or she won't buy me any more."

"Shouldn't be a problem," Relic thought, grabbing a fork.

The garage door opened, and Russ came in holding three cans of soda. "You guys are starting a band?!"

Relic gave Bree a quick look, his mouth full of pasta. She raised her eyebrows guiltily. Shaking his head in mock disbelief, Relic said with a mouthful, "I heard it's the best way to score babes."

Russ and Bree both chuckled as the former handed Relic a Diet Coke. "That's rad," he said, sounding every bit his age when using the word "rad." He grabbed a seat next to Relic as Bree slid a plate of mac n' cheese to him. "What are you guys called?"

"Did you bring it?" Bree asked excitedly.

Relic shook his head, taking another bite, feeling embarrassed for some reason.

"Bring what?" Russ asked.

Bree tried to describe the sketch, ending with the reveal of the band name.

"Altar Stone sounds pretty dang cool," Russ said. "You got it from a book you said?"

They discussed the name's origins, the band's potential sound, and their lack of enough band members during the rest of dinner, and Relic was once again glad to not have to think about the janitor, the creature, or his cryptic dreams.

It wasn't until *Buffy* that it all started suffocating him again.

Leading up to season two of *Buffy The Vampire Slayer*, the network was playing reruns of season one, which Relic, Bree, and Russ had all already seen. But in an effort to keep their Tuesday night rituals alive and on track for the next season's premier in three weeks, they were determined to never miss a rerun.

As Relic and Bree sat next to each other on the couch watching Buffy and her Sunnydale classmates take a field trip to the zoo, they half-heartedly argued over which was better so far: the Kristy Swanson movie or the Sarah Michelle Gellar show.

"You can't get much better than Pee-wee Herman as a vampire," Bree said, laughing. "Besides, I'll take Kristy Swanson over this new Buffy any day."

Relic didn't have a counterpoint for either of those, also he definitely preferred Luke Perry's character, Pike, over this apparent TV version, Xander. However, he played devil's advocate. "The movie tried to make the whole thing a joke, though. At least this show is trying to make it seem somewhat real."

"Yeah," Bree said, with a mocking scoff, "all these very real vampires turning to dust when they get staked—thank the TV gods for that wonderful realism."

Russ came into the room stirring a cocktail—his third of the night if Relic had counted correctly. "You two love to argue about stuff you clearly both like." He took a seat in his recliner and kicked the footrest up, almost spilling his drink when the seat reclined. "Whoa!"

"It's Tuesday, Dad," Bree said, as the show went to commercial, "why are you drinking so much?"

He took a sip before answering, his eyes closed in ecstasy. "Long day at the office. Long day." He set the drink down on the end table. "Plus, I'm not driving anywhere," he added, giving Relic a smirk.

Relic's mom preferred wine coolers, and there were plenty of nights over the summer when he found several empty bottles of them next to the living room sofa after she had gone to bed. He had never given much thought about alcohol himself—even though lots of kids liked to brag that they tried some at parties—but he wondered if, after the last two days, he would be reaching for a drink if he could.

A commercial came on about the opening of Crane & Co Athletic Supply. "That's Delilah's dad's shop," Bree said, motioning to the TV as a huge sporting goods store was given the panoramic camera treatment.

"You know the Crane girl?" Russ asked. "She's kind of the talk of the office lately."

"What do you mean?" Relic scooched forward on the couch as Russ took another careful, slow sip of his drink. It felt as if the man was drawing out the suspense.

"Well, I'm not sure how much you know about Marshall Crane or his family, but when a Crane comes moving back to town with a mysterious adopted daughter, it causes all sorts of rumors."

"Wasn't Marshall Crane part of Mom's company?" Bree asked, only half-interested in the discussion as she bit at a nail—she was always worrying about her nails, and they always looked worse than Relic's.

"That was his grandfather, actually," Russ said, his voice starting to sound heavy as if he were very tired or out of breath. "Old Winston Crane was actually an early partner, back when the company was called Rothen & Crane. But there was a falling out when Rothen switched its focus to pharmaceuticals. The Cranes went off and became big time real estate moguls in New York."

"Sounds boring," Bree joked. "Why are people talking about Delilah?"

Russ shrugged. "Just wondering where she came from, I guess. It's not exactly common for a rich bachelor to adopt a teenage daughter, but, hey...what do we know, right?"

Adopted, Relic thought, finding the idea fascinating—the girl of his dreams suddenly had a mysterious past. As if he couldn't be more obsessed.

"What are these kids, like werewolves or something?" Russ asked, his words sloshing together as he rattled the ice in his drink. He hiccupped.

The word *werewolves* made the room fall away and Relic was once again sitting on the toilet at school instead of the couch. His heart thundered as the low growl of the creature outside the stall door intensified.

Bree brought him back, putting a hand on his shoulder to move him out of the way of the TV. "We watched this one, Dad. These are the hyena kids that eat the principal." She gave Relic a curious look when he startled under her touch, removing her hand and returning her focus to the TV. He felt bad, remembering when he had jerked away from her hand over the weekend when they were sorting tapes. However, his mind was dealing with heavier issues at the moment.

"That's right," Russ said drunkenly. Relic found himself staring at Bree's dad, who slowly took another sip of his drink; it once more felt like an intentional way to make Relic wait for some sort of revelation. He must have felt Relic staring, as his eyes slowly drifted toward him. Relic tried to look away, but the man's gaze somehow paralyzed him. "You ever heard of the West Laramie Werewolves?" Russ asked through a mischievous smile, as if reading Relic's mind.

Relic managed to swallow in response.

"You mean those giant dogs that attacked people?" Bree asked, still focusing on the show. "Those were probably rabid pit bulls or something, not teenagers possessed by the primal spirits of hyenas."

Russ put the footrest of his recliner down, peering out the window, looking for something. When he didn't find anything, he leaned forward, putting his drink on the coffee table between himself and the teens. "Your mom wouldn't want me telling you," he said, mumbling through lazy lips, "but those dogs came from Rothen's old animal labs...out on the outskirts of the city. That's what got them shut down."

Bree turned toward her dad, finally interested. "You serious?"

With raised eyebrows, Russ nodded slowly. "You see, weird stuff happened around here, even before the 80s...all the way back to the 1800s." His vision looked distant as he shook his head. "This place is cursed, Grandpa Chuck used to say."

"What were they?" Relic asked, wanting desperately to tell them about what happened to him today, but remembering the janitor's words.

Russ shrugged. "Who knows...not even your mom knows what they were doing there. There are lots of laws about what you can and can't do when it comes to testing drugs on animals, but Rothen has its ways..."

"So you think they were making werewolves?" Bree asked sarcastically.

Russ picked his drink back up, reclining again. "Eh, not werewolves. That's just a word people recognize...it holds power. That's how these sorts of urban legends take hold."

Once again, Relic thought about Gerald's warning in the bathroom: "Makes you wonder if talkin' about werewolves is what makes people see werewolves."

On *Buffy*, the principal started screaming while the possessed students ate him just as headlights flashed across the Thompkins' windows.

"There's Mom," Russ said, getting out of his chair, nearly stumbling. "Don't talk about those animal labs...she always hates when I bring that up..."

"Weird," Bree said casually. "This place is so freaking weird."

Chapter 10

That night, Relic didn't remember riding his bike home or stumbling to bed. It was almost as if he had blacked out everything after Bree's dad had brought up werewolves, playing out his encounter in the restroom over and over in his mind until he finally found himself sprawled out on his bed.

He was asleep by the time he realized he was home.

Once again, he dreamed about the foggy place where his father dwelled. The classic green monstrosity that was pictured in every photo of Steven Meyers playing drums consisted of two bass drums (each sporting the Unknown Oath band logo on the front drumhead), four rack toms, floor tom, snare, and too many cymbals. Relic watched in dreamlike wonder as his father flailed wildly behind the kit, spinning sticks and swinging his long hair in circles.

But all Relic heard was that low, guttural growl from the Chambers High basement restroom.

As his dad continued his silent drum solo, Relic turned around to make sure there were no werewolves lurking in the mists. While he didn't see any beasts, he did see a familiar door take shape. Unlike his previous dream, he was in his own body this time—no, not his body, a larger one that was awkward to move. A hand that wasn't Relic's reached out and grasped the door's latch, opening it to reveal The CD Palace.

The smell of patchouli was overpowering.

"Hey," Natalie said, "how's it hanging, man?"

"Fine," Relic said, with a voice that also wasn't his, but was still familiar. He piloted the tall, fat body through the scanners and stopped at the glass counter. "I was hoping you could help me."

"I can try," Natalie said, not sounding eager. "Looking for something?" Her face contorted then for a split second and Steven Meyers' appeared in its place to mouth the words "release me" in desperate agony. Then, it was Natalie again, looking very bored.

"As a matter of fact, I am. Given this store's location, do you happen to have any, oh, what's the word...memorabilia, perhaps, relating to the band Unknown Oath."

Relic saw Natalie's face light up. He had never seen her look so interested in something.

"Did someone tell you?" she asked.

The body that wasn't Relic's raised its hands, palms up in confusion. "What do you mean?"

Natalie leaned on the counter. "I mean, just yesterday, Di—I mean, someone who shall remain nameless, right? Someone brought in the only remaining copy of the band's very first demo tape."

"You don't say," Relic said from his unknown host. "That would be of particular interest to me. How much might this piece run?"

Natalie looked toward the window, as if someone might be peering in. Relic looked in that direction and only saw the dark, smoky oblivion of his dream. "I called around," she said slowly, considering her words. "This thing is about as rare as it comes. It's the only copy—you can be sure of that. Steven Meyers was buying copies off people before Unknown Oath really took off, making sure no copies remained. Ask anyone."

"Oh, I've heard the stories," Relic said, this time feeling like he was actually the one speaking. Because he had definitely heard the stories. People said that Unknown Oath would have huge tape burnings at their shows, encouraging fans to bring whatever copies they could find of their first demo tape, feeding the flames that would then roast s'mores and illuminate all-night parties.

"Well, all things considered," Natalie said, looking back up at her customer, "and given what I had to pay to get it, I don't think I could let it go for less than twenty-five hundred."

"Sold," Relic said with some other man's voice. Zero hesitation. His large hand reached into his suit jacket and pulled out a gold credit card; the name on it was Larry Belinsky. Relic laid the card on the glass counter.

A moment later, Natalie placed a cassette tape on the counter. On the tape's crude label was written "Unknown Oath – Alternus."

In the distance, a wolf howled.

Relic jerked awake lying face-down in his bed. Groggily, he rolled over and saw that he was still wearing his school clothes. The clock read 12:13 a.m. and he couldn't even remember what day it was. It took a moment for the evening's events to come back, but when he remembered going to Bree's, he rolled out of bed to change into some gym shorts and a sleeveless shirt. There was a sour taste in his mouth, and he realized that he hadn't even brushed his teeth when he got home.

As he walked toward the bathroom across the hall, he heard the TV on in the living room. He peeked out to see his mom asleep on the couch, a single wine cooler on the table next to her.

At least she didn't get as sloshed as Mr. Thompkins, Relic thought with a smirk. He went to the bathroom and closed the door before flicking on the light, not wanting to wake up his mom. However, he nearly screamed when he looked in the mirror.

Larry Belinsky looked back at him, smiling wickedly as he held up a cassette tape. There was lust in his eyes, as if the item were something he couldn't wait to devour. Relic saw the Unknown Oath label on the tape. Then, Larry's eyes went from the tape to Relic.

"Release me," Larry said, with a huge, wicked smile, bloody talons suddenly bursting from his face just like they had from Ted's.

Relic jolted backward, nearly falling into the tub. Gasping, he caught himself on the towel rack and managed to not scream in terror—mostly because he could barely breathe. As he regained his footing, he saw his own tired reflection in the mirror now, but the image of the "Alternus" tape was burned into his mind.

With sudden realization, he yanked the bathroom door open, flooding the hall with light. He heard his mom stir from the living room, but he was already leaping toward his bed, reaching for the tape player.

"Relic?" Dina asked groggily.

Opening the tape player, Relic found it empty. *No,* he thought, all of his dreams rushing back to him in an instant. Ted was killed again, then, a vision of Natalie's ruined face with claw marks shredding her skin.

"Mom!" Relic turned in fury, knowing that she had taken it without asking. She never would have wanted him to have it, and he should have hid it. "Where is it?!" He stormed out of his room.

"What time is it?" Dina was asking, still not fully awake.

"The tape, Mom!" Relic presented the empty tape player to Dina, his rage reaching a boiling point.

Dina opened her mouth to respond, but a slam at the window made them both gasp and jerk away. There was low, bestial growling and the sound of claws on glass as a huge shape scratched at the window, snarling and snorting as if it were starving. Out of the corner of his eye, Relic saw Dina scramble off the couch and put herself between the window and Relic.

"No no no no," she was whispering frantically. "Not again. Please, not again."

"What the hell is that?!" Relic asked, knowing perfectly well what it was—he had felt the same terror and disbelief in the basement restroom at school.

The creature gave the window another slam before it disappeared back into the darkness beyond the TV's glow. Relic made to move toward the window to investigate, but his mom held him back.

"Wait," she whispered, eyes fixed on the darkness outside. Relic couldn't see anything with the glare of the TV reflecting back at them.

"For what?"

There was a howl in the distance. He felt his mother relax slightly.

"Should we call the cops or something?" Relic asked.

Dina shook her head, still watching the window. "No," she whispered, "that's how it starts. People will talk, and then it gets worse."

"What gets worse?" Relic asked, getting angry. "What are you talking about?" Something about what she said made him think of the janitor again, warning him not to tell anyone what he saw.

She turned to look at him now, straightening herself. Her eyes were wild, but the rest of her seemed calmer than she should be. "I sold the tape," she said flatly. "I didn't feel right destroying it—I know he's your dad, and you love his music, but we can't have it here."

At a loss for words, Relic just stared at his mom, blinking.

"Did you ever wonder why your dad didn't want that music around you?" She asked him in a whisper. "Do you know why you've never heard that song?"

"No," he said angrily, "why?!"

Dina looked back toward the window, ignoring his fury. Her breathing was steady, and it bothered Relic almost more than the fact that she stole something out of his room and got rid of it—especially something of Dad's.

"I don't know," she said, "I wonder about it all the time." She looked back at her son, grabbing his shoulders. "But I do know that when that song wasn't around here, we were fine. Call it superstitious or paranoia or whatever, but I don't want to deal with what this town has to offer when its eyes are on us." She shook her head. "Now, with Ted and this…I don't know what it means, but all we can do is hope it goes away. Your father did something to stir it up, but he's gone now." Her voice was barely audible as she added, "It has to go away now."

All the rage that had been building up in Relic leaked out of him when he saw the desperation and sadness in his mom's eyes. He was old enough to realize that she was just a woman trying to protect her child, regardless of all the crap that had built up between them this past year. Any anger he had left in him was suddenly directed toward his dad, who may have known about whatever was happening and decided to leave it for Relic and his mom to deal with.

Relic dropped the tape player and hugged his mom.

"We just keep it to ourselves, kiddo," she whispered, smoothing his hair with a gentle hand. "We'll get through this."

The next morning, Dina was gone when Relic woke up. There was a note on the kitchen table on top of a present in Christmas wrapping paper.

"Sorry for last night," the note said in his mother's writing, "and sorry I couldn't wait until Christmas. But I got you this with the money from Ted and the tape. Love, yo Momma."

Relic smiled at his mom's goofy attempt at humor, setting the note aside and tearing into the package.

"No way!"

He ran his hand over the box, making sure he was reading the package's label correctly. Zildjian 13" Dyno Beats Hi-Hat Cymbals. Relic had been using his dad's hand-me-down cymbals since he started playing, and most of them were cracked or literally missing chunks out of them. His hi-hats were always the worst. He had begged his mom for new ones multiple times—for Christmases, birthdays, good grade awards—but he knew the factors at play: cymbals were expensive, and the Meyers were dead broke.

She must have gotten a lot of money from Ted, Relic thought, feeling oddly guilty for being so thrilled over the gift while the memory of Ted's gruesome murder flashed through his mind. He reached for the kitchen shears and cut the box tape open. One look at those pristine cymbals and Relic forgot all about last night's madness and Ted's bloody face.

Bree came over early to check out his new gear after he called to share the news, and together they walked to the bus stop in soaring spirits, talking about their new band and who they might recruit to Altar Stone's ranks. The thought of telling her about the night before didn't even cross his mind.

"I wonder if Nick would be up for it," Bree wondered aloud.

"Nick?" Relic didn't like the idea of a stranger joining their band, and he had no clue who Bree was talking about.

"The bassist," Bree said, not meeting Relic's gaze, "Nick Weber, from Bag of Sax. I told you about him yesterday."

Aside from bands like Offspring and maybe Green Day, Relic didn't care much for punk, so he wasn't excited about the idea of playing with someone who favored that genre. "Sounds like he's already in a band."

Bree shrugged. "Yeah, I just don't know if they'll even be a *band* anymore without a guitarist."

He couldn't put his finger on it, but Relic didn't like the sound of this Nick guy. Maybe it was some sort of bizarre jealousy he felt—not wanting Bree to be friends with another guy—but he desperately tried to think of an alternative. "What about Howie?"

Bree finally looked at Relic with a shocked face, her mouth barely holding back a laugh.

"What?" Relic said, adjusting his backpack. "Didn't he play upright bass in middle school?"

She let the laugh out. "Yeah, and he was terrible."

"Eh," Relic replied, cocking his head. "How hard could four strings be?"

Bree didn't put up much more of a fight, which told Relic that she was considering it. He counted that as a small win. With an elbow to his side, she changed the subject. "So what'd you pick for your history homework?"

Relic stopped walking. "Shit." With everything that had been going on, he forgot about his very first high school homework assignment.

"I'm just doing the Widow of Wane Street," Bree said when they were on the bus later. "I'm sure I won't be the only one doing that one, but I had an idea for the whole historical event."

"What is it?"

"Well, you know how my dad likes to talk about the Widow a lot—he's fascinated by that whole Curse of the Ninth thing," she waved a hand as if it were nonsense.

Relic hadn't heard of that before, and his face must have shown it.

"You know? The Curse of the Ninth—like, all these old composers would randomly die when working on or performing their ninth symphony. Anyway, the Widow's husband had just performed his ninth symphony before the murders, and that was the first time it happened in America—the whole Curse of the Ninth thing, I mean."

"Weird."

Bree nodded. "Yeah, and it's wild that it happened here. That's why Dad says there was this whole spiritualism movement in the 19th century, because it was a very widely-reported tragedy and got people believing in all sorts of crap."

"Well, at least you got yours figured out," Relic said.

"What about the werewolves?" Bree asked.

Relic froze as he looked out the bus window, afraid to turn toward her. The attack last night replayed in his mind, and he could almost see claws slamming against the bus window.

"Like about the animal labs," Bree urged. "I bet there's some historical stuff there, with Rothen having to shut down their testing labs after that whole thing."

Breathing a sigh of relief, Relic nodded as he turned to her. "Oh yeah." He chuckled. "Guess it pays to get your dad wasted when watching *Buffy*."

"Guess so," Bree laughed.

After presenting their ideas in history class, and Relic managing to stay awake for most of chemistry, Bree and Relic met up with Howie in the cafeteria for lunch. One of Relic's favorite parts of high school was the food selection; he could have nachos every day with a Diet Dr. Pepper from the vending machine (assuming he remembered to grab a dollar from the change bowl at home).

"You ever think about playing bass, Howie?" Relic asked, drumming a rhythm on the lunch table with his thumbs.

"Howard," he said, pushing his glasses back up the slope of his nose and not looking up from his *GamePro* magazine. "My grandma calls me Howie and it reeeaaalllly bothers me." He shook his head as he kept reading an article. "Man, *Warcraft II* looks pretty awesome."

"Bass, Howard," Relic repeated. "You want to play bass in our band?"

Bree coughed, drawing Relic's attention. She gave him a doubtful shake of her head.

"I don't play anymore," Howard said, turning a page in the magazine before looking up at them. "You guys been checking out this *Final Fantasy VII*? Can't wait for that one."

"Hey, there's Nick," Bree said, nodding in the direction behind Relic. "I could go ask him."

Relic carefully turned around so it wasn't obvious but couldn't see who Bree was talking about. All he saw were a bunch of students eating their lunch at tables, and then a guy with spiky, frost-tipped hair wearing a green football jersey with a golden seventeen on it.

"Where?" Relic whispered.

"Hey, Weber!" Bree called.

The guy in the football jersey looked her way—as did nearly half the lunchroom; *you have no shame, Bree,* Relic thought miserably—and smiled brightly as he headed their way.

"He's on the football team?!" Relic was confused on so many levels at the moment.

"Yeah, why?"

He turned back to Bree. "Does that seem punk rock to you? Playing on the high school football team?"

Bree gave him an annoyed look. "Judgmental much?"

She was obviously right, he knew, but he dug in his heels regardless. "How you going to be in a band if you have to practice all the time and go to games?"

"I don't know," she said in an exaggerated show of animated confusion, "maybe the same way we can be in a band when we play tabletop and video games all the time." She shouldered him to scoot over on the bench so they could make room for another person.

"Hey, Bree," Nick said in a voice much deeper than Relic's. "You guys mind if I join you? I thought Dustin had lunch during this period, too, but I don't see him."

Bree motioned to the seat next to her—Relic was at least glad he didn't have to sit next to Nick, but still felt uncomfortable. "Yeah," she said, "I think they shifted things around after Monday, because some people got the wrong schedules."

"You're in my gym class," Howard said, as more of a statement than a question.

"I am," Nick said, giving a small chuckle. "You did a lot of pull-ups, man. Wish I could do that many."

Howard nodded as he looked back down to his magazine. "It helps having a gastrointestinal disorder. I can't really gain weight easily, so I have less to lift."

After a short awkward silence, Nick replied with a curt, "Right on."

"This is Relic," Bree said. "He's my drummer."

All the tension building up within Relic was demolished by her wording—something about the way she said "my drummer" made him swell with pride.

"Meyers, right?" Nick asked, peering around Bree. "You're quite the legend around here, man."

"What do you mean?" Relic asked, still working out a rhythm that was stuck in his head with his thumbs—*What song is this?* he wondered.

"I mean, just your dad and all," Nick took a bite of his pizza, chewing with his mouth open. "Did he get arrested? You know, because of Ted?"

"Dude," Bree said, annoyed. "His dad didn't kill Ted."

Relic spun around on the bench and left the table, barely hearing what Bree and Nick were saying as he stormed off. He was partly just annoyed at the rumors already spreading again about his dad, and partly frustrated that he couldn't remember what this damn rhythm stuck in his head was.

He briskly walked out of the cafeteria toward the Little Chamber where he could escape into an out-of-the-way restroom. He was so angry that he didn't even notice the janitor cart outside the door.

Gerald was mopping the tiled floor in the boys' room when Relic turned the corner and dodged the wet floor sign.

"Watch your step," Gerald said without turning around. "I'll be done in a few minutes if you want to wait outside."

Whether it was what Nick said that pissed him off or what Bree said that emboldened him, Relic felt uncharacteristically confrontational. Memories of the two encounters with the mysterious creature that he wasn't supposed to talk about came flooding back, and—especially after volunteering to present about the West Laramie Werewolves in his history class—he wanted some answers.

"What did you do with that thing you killed yesterday?"

Gerald pushed the mop back and forth methodically, unbothered by the question or the topic. "I did what I always do. I took care of it."

"What do you mean: always do?"

The mop went back and forth. "I clean up, kid. It's my job."

"I don't know a lot of janitors who are also giant dog slayers," Relic said, getting a bit irritated by Gerald's calm demeanor. "What happens if I tell someone what I saw?"

That got the man to stop his work. He turned around slowly to regard Relic with a calm expression. "I think you know, kid. People around here talk, they spread stories. Now, some people think that stories," he held up a hand as if presenting a physical story, "they're just stories. But 'round here...those stories take root and fester, becoming something dark." Gerald made a fist. "You of all people should understand the power of stories."

"Me?" Relic was taken aback. *What had he done? And how would this janitor know anything about him?*

Gerald nodded, going back to mopping. "Given who your dad is, and the stories his band liked to tell..."

Relic recalled Nick's stupid comment, and then remembered Paul at the bus stop...always back to his dad. Once upon a time, Relic enjoyed living under the immense shadow that his dad's legacy had cast over Laramie, but he was starting to feel smothered by it—as if he couldn't escape from ever just being "Steven Meyers' son."

"I'm not my dad," Relic said sternly.

Gerald nodded again. "Best keep it that way. He wanted to keep you away from all of this."

"All of what?" Relic demanded. "And how would you know anything about me? Or my dad."

Then, Gerald turned to face him, the mouth under his mustache splitting into a gap-toothed smile.

No way, Relic thought, his mind flashing back to all those images of Unknown Oath that adorned his wall. Their stocky bassist with that same smile was only ever credited as "Gate Murphy," and Relic never even knew his real name.

"You grew a lot since we last hung out, bud," Gate said. "Thought maybe I wouldn't recognize ya, but yer a spittin' image of your old man when he was your age."

Chapter 11

elic couldn't focus at all for the rest of the day. Ever since Gerald—no, Gate!—told him to keep his identity a secret for now, Relic's mind was a torrent of questions and assumptions. He wondered why the hell Gate was working as a high school janitor, and how he knew so much about the creatures that were stalking Relic.

Mostly, though, Relic wondered if this meant his father in fact *was* hiding somewhere in Laramie, just like people were speculating. But if so, why wouldn't he come to Relic? He almost hoped that wasn't the case—the only thing harder for Relic to accept than his father being a killer was his father not wanting anything to do with him.

"He didn't mean anything by it."

Relic blinked away the foggy void of his thoughts, turning toward the distant voice that pulled him back to the present.

Bree was giving him an apologetic look.

Relic panicked, wondering if he had mindlessly mentioned Gate's name without realizing it. "Huh? Who?"

"Nick," Bree said. "He went to a different school, and honestly he doesn't even know much about your dad—he is just a big fan of Unknown Oath."

While Relic found it extremely unlikely for someone in Laramie—a musician, no less—to not know enough about Unknown Oath to know that Steven Meyers wasn't around, he really didn't care. He made sure Bree knew as he groaned, "Who cares?"

She looked a bit offended as she turned away from Relic. "I'm just saying—he's a nice guy. He didn't mean to piss you off or anything."

"Why does it matter?" With everything going on, Relic was actually very annoyed that Bree was bringing up this football-playing punk. He didn't want to deal with it. "I don't care what he thinks."

Bree let it go, which oddly made Relic feel even more miserable. She fiddled with her nails instead of talking his ear off, leaving Relic with nothing to do but brood. He didn't need to sit and dwell on all the things he couldn't share with Bree. He couldn't afford to lose his best friend, especially when she was just trying to get their band a bassist.

Knowing he had to revert course, Relic used the back of his hand to nudge Bree's leg. "You think he'd be able to handle some HammerFall?"

The smile she gave Relic made the rest of the bus ride not just bearable, but pleasant. Even when he was getting off at their stop and saw Delilah and Sebastian hunched over a notebook—probably working on some Autumnal Fall stuff—Relic managed to avoid worrying about Gate, dog creatures, or anything else as he joined Bree for the walk home.

"Hey," she said, "do you want to go to The CD Palace real quick?"

"What for?"

She didn't seem to want to tell him. "I just wanted to check something."

Knowing that his mom was working late, he wasn't in a hurry to go home and hang out alone, worrying about all the things he was trying not to worry about until he could talk to Gate more tomorrow. He nodded and they diverted their course toward Greenbush Street.

"I heard there's a battle of the bands in March," Bree said, talking fast. "Valerie is in my study hall and was bragging about how she's joined the pep squad—which is only supposed to be juniors and seniors, but apparently they were short-handed this year. She was talking about which events she's planning, and one is the battle of the bands."

Relic remembered hearing about the battle of the bands his dad had played back in '77, or '78...Relic always forgot which. That was the last battle of the bands that Chambers High had. It was surprising to hear they were doing one again.

"Sebastian Ford is in my study hall, too," Bree continued, "and so is Dustin from Bag of Sax, so they started asking about it. Apparently, there's going to be a big reward—you know Delilah?"

Relic felt a strange twist in his heart. *Do I know Delilah?* he thought, wanting to laugh. He nodded instead.

"Yeah, well her dad's all rich, and he's sponsoring it, offering some cash reward."

Growing excited about the prospect, Relic finally came around to the idea of having Nick maybe join Altar Stone. If he was good, that would obviously give them an advantage, and maybe pulling him away from Bag of Sax might eliminate some of their competition.

"Maybe we should see what song Nick could play with us."

"That's kind of why I wanted to go to The CD Palace," Bree said, almost guiltily. "I was going to pick up some CDs for him—kind of give him a crash course of the kind of stuff we're into."

That same strange jealousy tugged at Relic, but he was excited enough about the prospect of having an actual band soon that he managed not to express any spiteful intentions. Still, it was hard to ignore the fact that Bree had never really bought any albums for anyone besides Relic (that he knew of), but suddenly Nick comes along and she's defending him and buying him gifts.

This jealousy was starting to make Relic feel like such a scumbag. He never got jealous of Miranda when Bree used to hang out with her all those times Relic was busy with Tyler, or when he later heard about Bree and Miranda's secret relationship. Why was he so jealous now?

It wasn't like Bree was "cheating" on Relic with Nick, and Nick wasn't "her drummer." What was his problem?

"That's weird," Bree said as they crossed the street. "Who's that behind the counter?" Relic shrugged and they hurried across the parking lot.

They rang the store's digital chime as they entered, smelling the familiar patchouli. But everything felt very different when they heard a stranger call out, "Welcome to the Palace, kids. You let me know if you need help finding things, alright?"

A small older woman walked briskly behind the counter, waving a feather duster around the expensive digital devices that hung on the pegged board behind the register.

Bree walked up to the counter. "Uh...hi. Where's Natalie?"

The woman didn't turn around. "Oh, when you find out, you tell me, ok? She never come in to open the store."

Bree looked at Relic, her face changing from curiosity to concern when her gaze fell on him. She must have seen the terror that washed over him as his dream—the one where he was Larry Belinsky buying the tape—came rushing back to him. Natalie had been in that dream, and her face had become twisted.

"What's wrong?" Bree asked.

Relic turned and walked out of the store quickly. When he got outside, he jerked his head left and right, looking for any sign of wolves or dogs or something with long white claws that may have attacked Natalie. He knew it was futile...if anything obvious happened to Natalie in the parking lot, someone would have noticed. Natalie's boss would have known if something had happened to her, especially right outside the store.

"Relic, what's up?"

He turned to Bree as the door slowly closed behind her. He wanted so badly to tell her, but then he saw her face suddenly become impaled with pale white claws, spraying blood everywhere. He almost screamed, even though he knew it was just his mind messing with him.

"Do you know where Natalie lives?"

Bree nodded, still staring at him with wide, curious eyes. "She lives off 18th Street. I forget the address, but I'd remember the apartment complex if I saw it...it's right on the corner across from that Dairy Queen."

Relic waved her along. "Let's catch the bus. Come on."

Impressively, Bree didn't ask a lot of questions on the bus ride. Her concern for Natalie and her general curiosity became a perfect mix for the discretion Relic needed—as much as he wanted to unburden himself from the dreams haunting him and Gate's sudden appearance, now was certainly not the time.

"Maybe she's just sick," Bree said softly, as if to herself.

"She would have called her boss," Relic said, his dream replaying in his mind. Something about her selling the Unknown Oath tape was a bad omen.

"That's the place!" Bree said excitedly.

Relic saw a run-down apartment complex shaded by a collection of trees that lined the corner of a block. There was a small sign with a bird flying over cursive letters that spelled out "Pheasant Run."

The bus approached the stop across the street from the complex, the brakes squealing as the passengers lurched forward in their seats. As they got off, Bree went directly to the pay phone outside the Village Pantry convenience store.

"I'm going to leave a message for my dad," she called over her shoulder. "One sec."

Relic tried to steady his breath as he waited, watching the entrance to the Pheasant Run apartments. The apartment's lot appeared almost empty, and the place looked like it was mostly vacant. There were many newer apartment complexes in the area, so it wasn't that odd for it to have so many vacancies, he supposed.

As cars passed by, Relic tapped his fingers against his thumbs, mimicking the rhythm that played in the back of his mind. It was the same song he had tried to figure out during lunch when Nick sat at their table. His fingers fell into the correct pattern and the world around him faded away.

He was back in his dreams suddenly, seeing his dad wildly drumming to the song that Relic now realized was "Alternus." Although he didn't actually remember any specifics about the song, Relic *felt* its familiarity in his bones; it was part of him, connecting him and his father. As expected, the words "release me" came into Relic's mind, but the voice was different this time.

It was his father's.

Relic had heard his father's voice on recordings—a few random radio interviews from Germany that Bree's dad had tracked down on the internet at work, and a rare segment on VH1 when they were covering the European metal scene—but he liked to think that he remembered his dad's voice from when he was a baby. Because even when he had first heard the recordings, Steven Meyers' voice still felt undeniably familiar.

Now it was like a ghost whispering in his ear, sending a haunting chill down his spine. Steven Meyers was still thrashing behind his glowing drum kit, hammering out the ritualistic beats of "Alternus," summoning more visions to inflict on Relic.

The world materialized again, but it was different. Relic looked in all directions, but every feature of Laramie's north side—the hanging trees, the decrepit roads, the occasional car barreling by—were each a shadow of their true forms, twisted and moving in strange stop-motion ways. "Release me," his dad said again, his voice hoarse, desperate, and pleading.

"How?" Relic wanted to ask, but his mouth wouldn't respond to his mind's command. Suddenly his body—or just his vision—was jerked toward the Pheasant Run apartments across the street, speeding along a crooked path toward the back of the complex. He was whipped in different directions, but he followed the path almost mechanically, like he was shooting through an invisible pipe that twisted through the apartment parking lot.

When he finally stopped, he was standing in front of apartment 715. There was a pot leaf sticker next to the doorbell and, at his feet—if his feet had actually been there—was a flower doormat framed with a wreath of dead leaves. A pale white hand reached out from where Relic stood, its fingers tipped in impossibly long claws that ended in needles. It pushed open the door.

"Alternus" could be heard from within the apartment, played at a relatively low volume. It sounded like it came from the hallway. The apartment was neat, but it was still all shadowy as if it were a dark sketch of the real place. It consisted of a small living area with a couch and coffee table facing a meager entertainment center. The kitchen was just a fridge, stove, and counter in the corner of the apartment, with a small dining table and minimal cabinets.

Relic moved toward the song, carried by whatever host he occupied this time—something inside of him knew it wasn't Larry Belinsky.

"You hear that?" Natalie said from the hallway as the song's volume lowered. It was almost inaudible now, but Relic still felt the rhythm as if it were his own heartbeat. "Yeah, it's rare, man. This is actually a copy I made yesterday—I sold the original to that Constrained Media guy in town for twenty-five hundred bucks." Relic could hear a distorted voice shout something unintelligible over the phone. "Yeah, I know. Stick's old lady let it go for a grand. I could probably sell a few more copies before word gets out!"

Natalie laughed, and despite the circumstances, Relic felt anger toward the woman who was laughing about ripping off his mom. She was also trying to scam his dad's fans. His anger turned to rage.

The ground creaked below Relic.

"Hang on," Natalie said, much lower.

Silence. Relic was frozen in place.

"Let me call you back," Natalie said, "I think I heard something."

There were footsteps coming toward the hall, but Relic couldn't move.

He could see Natalie's shadow through the slightly ajar bedroom door. Something terrible was about to happen, he could feel it. The image of Ted's bloody face flashed before him again, and then the door opened, and Natalie's face replaced Ted's.

"Wha—"

Relic reached up to show his hands in a sign of surrender, not wanting to scare her. But instead of his own hand, the pale claw came up, the long index finger hooking into Natalie's gaping mouth and coming out of her nose. Relic tried to scream but the only sound was the choking noise as Natalie was dragged into the living room like a large flailing fish, pulled through Relic as he was frozen in place.

Behind him, Relic heard the sickening sounds of Natalie being torn apart, but his eyes were focused on the boombox in the bedroom that was still spinning the copy of "Alternus" in the cassette player.

"Release me," Steven Meyers said as Ricky's voice held out some high-pitched wail on the song, blending in with Natalie's death cries. Relic took a step forward, his own foot finally appearing in the dream world.

"Relic," his dad begged as he tried to take another step toward the boom box, "please, don't—"

"Relic!"

The pale claw gripped his shoulder and pulled him back into the living room that had become a slaughterhouse. He gasped as he turned around to see Bree, her hand on his shoulder.

"What are you doing?"

He looked back toward the apartment complex and saw that he was now on the curb, about to step into the street. A car blew by, sounding its horn and making Relic jolt again. He looked back to Bree who still waited for an explanation.

"We need to go," Relic said, nodding toward the apartments.

As confused as Bree looked, she didn't stop him when bolted across the street. He heard her feet pounding right behind him.

"Did you see something?" Bree asked between breaths. "Why are we running?"

Relic didn't answer, worried that if he said anything right now, he would tell Bree everything from the last few days. He ran around to the back side of the building, following the path he was dragged along during his vision.

"How do you know where Natalie lives?" Bree asked.

Before Relic could think of a lie, he had arrived at apartment 715 and he stared at the door in terror. The words were scratched onto the door, right above the doorknob.

"Release me."

There was a long moment of silence before Bree leaned close enough to whisper a question to him. "You going to knock?"

"Do you see that?" Relic pointed toward the doorknob.

He heard Bree's arms go limp against her sides after shrugging. "What about it? We both know Natalie's a huge pothead."

Relic turned to her. "Not the leaf, that!" He pointed toward the doorknob, but when he looked back the words were gone.

Ignoring him, Bree reached around and knocked on the door.

As Relic expected, there was no answer.

After a moment, Bree knocked again. "Natalie? Are you there?"

There were no windows to peer in, just a row of derelict doors that gave the impression Natalie didn't have a lot of neighbors they could question.

Relic tried the doorknob, not really wanting to open the door. To his relief, it was locked.

"You want to just break in?" Bree asked sarcastically.

As much as he wanted to give up here, he knew they had to get in. Besides wanting to check on Natalie, he also knew deep down that he had to get that tape. Ted was killed in the place Relic found that tape. Something was following that cassette, and he'd never figure out what it had to do with his dad and his dreams if he didn't have a copy.

"Let's go check the office," Relic said.

The only person working in the office was an older man in a dirty dress shirt with one of those leather cases in the front pocket that held a pair of glasses.

"You family?" the man asked.

"Yeah," said Bree, before Relic could think to answer. "We're her cousins, and she was supposed to meet us yesterday. She hasn't been to work so we're a little worried."

Satisfied with the lie, the man grabbed his keys and the three of them returned to apartment 715.

"We'll take a quick peek in," the man said, "but I can't let you in there without her permission."

"That's fine," said Bree, as she watched him fit his key in the lock. "Like I said, we just wanted to make sure she wasn't hurt or something."

Relic's heart raced as he watched the man turn the doorknob, time slowing to an absolute crawl. He heard the rhythm again, his dad begging to be released from whatever trapped him, forcing him to play "Alternus" forever. He saw the words scratched out on the door again, each letter cutting through the paint to draw drops of blood, spelling out that same plea.

When Relic felt completely suffocated by the slowing of time, everything snapped back to the present and the door swung open to reveal Natalie's remains.

Bree screamed, grabbing Relic. The old man nearly fell over in shock.

"Dear god!"

Relic was numb, unable to look away. The jolly woman who had introduced him to HammerFall and provided him with dozens of classic thrash albums that he probably wouldn't have found anywhere else, was spread out on the floor in her tiny apartment, her body in shredded ruin.

The man scrambled away. "I'll call the police, kids. Stay out here! Don't go in there!" He ran as fast as a man his age could safely move, leaving Bree burying her face in Relic's neck as she sobbed.

With the man gone, Relic's faculties returned, and he gently disentangled himself from Bree. "You need to trust me, Bree."

She looked up to him in disbelief as he moved toward the door. She kept her arms out as if he would immediately return and her mouth moved as if she wanted to object but couldn't.

"Just wait here," Relic said softly. The calmness and assertiveness in his voice surprised him. But when things got bad and people broke down, it was just easier for someone to take control. "I need to get something."

Bree shook her head, motioning with her hands for him to return. "What do you mean? Get back here. Relic!" Her voice was a choked whisper, but he could feel the desperate plea as much as he still felt his father's urgent need. Something about that strengthened him, and he was able to move past Natalie's mutilated body without throwing up. Maybe he was able to stomach it because he had seen so much death in movies, or such visceral killing in his dreams; whatever it was, he endured the foul, sweet smell of her death and stepped carefully around any blood that might capture his footprint.

"Relic, please!" Bree hissed. "What are you doing?!"

He moved to the bedroom as quickly as he could. The apartment was exactly the way it was in his dream. He didn't have time to question how that was possible. All he could do was pull up his shirt to use it as a glove, press the eject button on the boom box's cassette player, and grab the copied Unknown Oath demo tape.

Pocketing the thing, Relic returned to Bree with plenty of time before the old man returned.

Relic was able to evade Bree's questions by telling her he'd explain later, but the cops were a little more difficult to handle.

Officer Hayes sat down in the chair across from him in the apartment leasing office. Her belt creaked loudly in the silence of the office, then her radio barked and she adjusted the knob at her waist before leaning forward with her elbows on her knees.

"So you were checking on your friend?"

Relic nodded, looking over at Bree who was in the other room talking to Officer Barnes. Relic envied her—Barnes seemed to like him, but Relic was stuck answering to the woman who only ever scowled at him.

"Can you tell me what a couple of teenagers are doing hanging out with a middle-aged pot dealer?"

The shocked look Relic gave her was genuine. "We didn't know she was a pot dealer. Bree and I just know her from The CD Palace."

Hayes kept her gaze level as she evaluated him. She slowly licked her lips, turned to look at Bree and her partner, then back to Relic. "You pretty confident if we tested you two for drugs we wouldn't find anything?"

Glad that he didn't have to lie, Relic nodded his head. "We wouldn't mess with that stuff."

The cop straightened in her chair, her expression softening slightly. "I'm not looking to make this an after-school special, Mr. Meyers, but," she hooked her thumb over her shoulder, "this kind of stuff happens with drug dealers. It's not the worst I've seen."

Relic had to bite back a morbid laugh, knowing that wasn't true at all. No matter what this police officer had seen, he couldn't imagine her ever stumbling across a death worse than Natalie's. Fortunately, he maintained his composure and nodded, feigning a "scared straight" face.

The sounds of tires squealing outside drew both of their attentions. Relic saw the Thompkins' CR-V pull to an abrupt stop in the parking lot. Russ, dressed in a short-sleeve work shirt with a loosened tie, nearly fell out of the driver's side door. Despite the circumstances, Relic was shocked to see Lydia scramble out of the car as well—murder seemed like one of the few things that could pull her out of the office.

Relic rose out of his seat, and Officer Hayes didn't stop him. She did keep a light hand on his shoulder as she led him toward the leasing office's lobby.

"Breanne!" Lydia pushed past Russ as Officer Barnes greeted them. Bree hugged her mom, looking over her shoulder to make sure Relic was still there.

"...stumbled across a body, unfortunately," Barnes was telling Russ. "Some nasty business that I wish they hadn't seen."

"I made sure they were safe when I called the police," the old man said from behind his desk.

Russ went over to Relic and put a comforting hand on his shoulder, replacing the less comforting one belonging to the police. Relic kept his face down, not wanting to be here any longer than he had to.

After a series of questions and answers between Bree's parents and the police, they were led back outside. That was when Relic's mom arrived, racing from her Mazda to hug him. He had never been as glad or relieved to be held by her, finally letting himself cry on her shoulder. Both families agreed to meet with Officers Hayes and Barnes at the station tomorrow and then went their separate ways.

On the car ride home, Dina didn't ask her son anything about the murder, and Relic didn't tell her about the tape in his pocket. When they got home, Relic was even glad to see Calvin waiting there with takeout.

"Let's not tell Calvin about this right now," Dina said before they got out of the car. Calvin was walking to greet them. "We can talk tomorrow, just you and me. Okay?"

Relic smiled weakly at his mom and nodded, grateful to not have to revisit any of it at the moment. Maybe he could have a normal night...

Chapter 12

For over a week after Natalie's murder, Relic's life felt surprisingly more normal than he could remember. The distractions of high school, dealing with his mom dating a dork, and jamming with Bree and Nick kept his mind too busy to dwell on his strange dreams and crazy dog-monster attacks. It wasn't until Larry Belinsky showed up at school that Relic was drawn back into the consuming vortex of his father's absence.

It all started with the damn pep rally on Friday, the first of many for the countdown to homecoming in September. Relic sat down in the front row of the gym bleachers, not used to being this close to any sort of action at school. Relic always considered himself a life-long back-seater.

But since Nick was on the football team, he had to sit down near the front when they were called out to the gym floor. And since Nick was now Altar Stone's bassist—per Bree's insistence—it seemed appropriate that the band sit together, putting Relic and Bree smack dab in the middle of all the popular kids who liked to sit near the football team.

Relic was surprised to see Tyler wearing a football jersey displaying number 7. He didn't even know Tyler played football—Relic couldn't recall him ever being on the middle school team, but he wasn't exactly keeping track of the guy.

Leaning over Bree, who was arguing with Nick about Geddy Lee—she loved Rush and Nick loathed them with a passion—Relic tapped Nick's knee, nodding toward Tyler. "Is Tyler Richardson on the football team?"

Without looking at Tyler, Nick scoffed. "He's starting quarterback, man. He's a total prick, but the coach loves him."

Because his dad paid him to, Relic thought. He vividly remembered back in little league when he loved playing catcher, Tyler's dad would always take on the unofficial position of team manager. There wouldn't be a practice or a game where Barry wasn't leaning over the fence, bending their coach's ear about something. After Relic struck out too many times, he was replaced by Tyler's friend, C.J. Reese, who had never even worn a pair of shin guards. But he could smack the ball, which is all that really mattered.

Once Relic started riding the bench because Tyler's dad wanted to cheat the system and give his son's team the edge, Relic lost any love he had for the game. That was the start of Tyler's tormenting of Relic, unable to accept the fact that his one-time friend no longer wanted to play the game that Barry Richardson was trying to rig.

"Can I sit here?"

Relic spun around to see Delilah motioning to the empty spot next to him. Unable to form an answer, Relic just nodded.

"Oh, hey, Delilah," Bree said as the girl took a seat—the girl that still smelled of those intoxicating herbs that Relic could not identify. "Coming to sit down next to us jocks?"

"You guys don't have to sit here," Nick said defensively. "I know how much you hate that I'm on the team, but my dad says if I don't get a sports scholarship, he won't be able to put me through college."

"Relax, dude," Bree said, patting his knee. Despite Delilah sitting so close to him, Relic still managed to feel the jealousy of that touch. "You know I'm kidding."

"You excited to play MacArthur next week?" Delilah asked Nick, leaning around Bree and Relic.

Nick inclined his head. "Yeah, you going to that game?"

She nodded. "Yeah, my dad's store is sponsoring the team, helping build some new facility."

"Yeah," Nick said, pointing behind him with his thumb, "the practice field over where the old track used to be."

Delilah nodded again. "I have to go with him to the games." She motioned with her hands, their black-nailed fingers wiggling in some mock celebration. "Family appearances and all. Anyway, I like watching football."

Nick smiled and gave her a nod. "Cool."

Relic seethed, but was also fascinated to discover Delilah enjoyed football. There seemed to be no end to the ways the girl could intrigue him.

While she hadn't struck him as a sports fan, Relic was similarly flabbergasted to learn about Nick's passion for music despite being on the football team. He supposed he should stop trying to put people in boxes that were convenient for him, slapping labels on them—preppy, jock, nerd, goth, punk—so he could set them aside and not have to worry about them. It was a lazy way to think. Relic was ashamed and embarrassed by that thought, knowing he was better than that.

Turning slightly to look over his shoulder, he saw the rest of Delilah's goth crew seated on the highest row of bleachers, hidden in the shadows of the gym's upper balcony. If Bree hadn't convinced Relic to invite Nick to play for Altar Stone, they wouldn't be sitting down here with him, and Delilah wouldn't be sitting right next to him.

As if she could sense him thinking about her, Bree jerked her knee against his to get his attention. "It's that dude," Bree said when Relic turned toward her. She was motioning to the gym floor.

The principal, Lana Sinclair, was standing at the side of the raised stage in the middle of the gym floor, wearing one of her Hillary Clinton pantsuits. The pep band suddenly kicked into Blur's obnoxious "Song 2," meaning things were about to get underway. Lana leaned in closer to "that dude," clearly trying to be heard over the band.

The dude in question was Larry Belinsky, nodding along and smiling at whatever the principal was telling him.

"What the hell is he doing here?" Relic asked aloud.

"He's filming a documentary," Delilah said, leaning close so Relic could hear over the music. He hadn't realized he spoke loud enough for anyone besides Bree to hear, and his chest tightened as he felt Delilah's hair brush his shoulder when she leaned in. "About all those murders in the 80s."

"Oh," Relic shouted, feigning surprise. Obviously, he knew why Larry was in town, but telling Delilah that would end this conversation too quickly. Knowing she was new in town, he asked, "You know about all that?"

She shrugged. "Only what the rest of the world knows, I guess," she said, looking over into Relic's eyes. "I'm sure not anywhere close to what you know."

Oddly, Relic blushed and looked down at his feet, as if that were some kind of compliment. He knew she was just referring to who his dad was, but he felt a strange chill creep up his spine, as if she was saying she knew what was going on currently.

Delilah leaned in closer, and Relic could feel her breath on his neck. He had to shift in his seat to hide his biological reaction. "He wants to interview me. He's looking for an outsider's perspective on moving to Laramie and learning about its history."

"Yeah, me too," Relic looked up, remembering their encounter with Larry outside The CD Palace. "You haven't filmed yours yet?"

She shook her head, looking back toward Larry and Principal Sinclair. "I think this weekend, once they're done doing all the setup shots."

Relic remembered what Larry said when he saw how Relic looked at Delilah. *"You agree to sit down with my team, and I'll make sure it's on the same day as Miss Crane's segment."*

"I think that's when he wanted to interview me," Relic lied, giving her a smile. She smiled back as the band died down.

"Welcome, Chambers High Ravens!"

The crowd exploded into cheers, drawing Relic and Delilah's attention back to the stage. Principal Sinclair was holding a mic up, making a show of trying to amplify the student body's enthusiasm. The standard back-and-forth followed, with Principal Sinclair asking if everyone was ready for homecoming in three weeks and everyone shouting in response. Relic even clapped along with Delilah, who was someone he wouldn't have assumed would participate in this kind of stuff.

He really needed to stop with those kinds of assumptions. Looking over at Bree and Nick who were both sharing a laugh about something as they clapped along with everyone else, Relic was repeatedly learning nobody really fit perfectly into a mold.

"I want to introduce you all to a special guest," Principal Sinclair continued, "someone who has come all the way from Hollywood, California. Executive producer for Constrained Media, Larry Belinsky!"

There was another wave of applause, with many students shouting out popular Constrained slasher flicks like *Skinned & Boned*, *Heathenry*, and *Writhe & Dine*. Larry hefted himself up onto the stage, relishing the applause as he took the mic from Lana.

"You're too kind to a greaseball like me," Larry said, triggering an explosion of laughter. "I'm just here to let you all know that my crew will be hosting your homecoming dance after the game." The place went absolutely wild, and Larry let his arms fall to his sides as he waited for it to die down. Principal Sinclair was clapping as she leaned over to say something to Larry and he nodded, raising the mic. "The theme is going to be Halloween in September, and we'll be decking this place out with props from your favorite Constrained flicks."

Relic found himself worked up with the rest of the crowd, clapping and smiling stupidly to both Bree and Delilah, who shared his enthusiasm.

"We'll have some forms for everyone to fill out before leaving here," Larry continued, "because we'd love to get some footage for our documentary, both at the big game and the dance on Saturday. So be sure to fill those out if you want a chance to be featured! And we better see you all out there!"

After the raucous reception to that news died down, the football team was called up to the stage to talk about their upcoming away game. Relic had lost interest in the event by that point, his focus on Larry Belinsky who still hung out along the side of the stage chatting with the principal. As he watched, he couldn't stop thinking about the dream he had when he was Larry in The CD Palace, buying the "Alternus" tape.

His fingers tapped the rhythms on his knees again as he wondered how he would get it back from Larry.

The interview, Relic thought. He had to do the interview. As his eyes wandered to Delilah, he knew he now had more than one reason to do the interview.

He spent the rest of the pep rally watching Larry, working up the courage to approach him before going back to class.

"That dance sounds badass," Nick said afterward, as they were all getting up from the bleachers. Bree, Relic, and Delilah joined him as a group while the crowd began migrating toward the exit. "Did you want to go?"

"Me?" Bree asked, looking at Delilah and then back to Nick, making sure she heard him correctly.

"Yeah," Nick nodded, his demeanor way more casual than Relic could ever accomplish in such a situation. "Would be kind of fun, right?"

Bree swallowed, looking unsure. She turned to Relic as if looking for an escape, "Were you going?"

"Yeah, you guys should go, too," Nick said as he led the group through the sea of other students. The way he nonchalantly suggested that Relic and Delilah go on a date made Relic both hate and worship his bassist. The guy seemed completely unbothered by social complexities.

"Sure," Delilah said, as if it were absolutely nothing to her. "I want to see if they bring any props from *Planet of Corpses*."

"Oh that movie's nasty," said Nick with a laugh. "We should watch that."

Relic felt Bree's eyes on him, but he was on another planet at the moment—he was going to a dance with Delilah Crane.

As the rest of the students returned to class, Relic split off from his group to go to the restroom—as if he could ever go to the restroom again at school after nearly being eaten on the shitter. He waited in the corridor that ran below the gym's bleachers, watching for Larry to make his exit. Relic heard him before he saw him.

"No, you tell him to spend as much as he needs, we need access to the unit."

Larry stopped when he turned the corner and saw Relic waiting for him.

"Alright, alright—Cynthia, let me call you back." He clicked a button on his cellular phone and gave Relic a smile. "Meyers. Good to see you again."

"Hey, Mr. Belinsky," Relic started, looking behind the man to see if anyone else followed him.

"We're alone, kid," Larry said, tucking his phone into his jacket. "What can I do for you?"

"Did you still want to interview me for your documentary? Delilah Crane said she was filming with you this weekend. Could I do mine then as well?"

Larry gave him a smile. "Sure thing, kid. We have a studio set up at the Crosstown Suites off Capital. Can you be there by noon on Sunday?"

Relic nodded.

"See ya then," Larry said, walking toward the exit.

"Mr. Belinsky?" When the man turned around, Relic stepped toward him. "Do you still have the Unknown Oath tape that you got from The CD Palace?"

Larry tilted his head and gave him a puzzled look. "News travels fast around here. You friends with the cashier?"

Relic swallowed. "She's dead. Someone killed her."

There was a strange flicker in Larry's eye. "That was her? In the apartment?"

Relic nodded. "I think...you haven't made a copy of that tape, have you?"

Laughing, Larry shook his head. "And ruin its value? Hell no. That thing's in a safe. It's going to be a crucial piece in the documentary."

Unsure how to convince Larry of the danger, Relic just nodded. "I'll see you Sunday." He turned to walk away.

"Oh, kid, you watch that videotape yet?"

Relic had almost forgotten about the concert footage Larry had given him—too much had happened in the last week. When he shook his head, Larry pulled his phone back out.

"Watch it before Sunday." The grin he gave Relic looked sinister.

Relic had intended to join the rest of the students and report back to his study hall. But as he walked toward the stairs, he went down instead of up, his mind fixated on all the lingering questions about "Alternus," his dad, the murders. His feet took him down to the maintenance room in the basement, where the janitor's office was.

Gate was sitting with his back toward the entrance of the room, staring at a shelf that held tools, old magazines, and accordion file folders. Relic was surprised to find the man smoking.

Relic thought of his mom—he hated how she still occasionally smoked. "You allowed to do that down here?"

Taking another drag of his cigarette before putting it out on the sole of his boot, Gate slowly turned toward Relic.

"Seems like we're both breaking the rules."

Relic dropped his backpack near the door and walked into the spacious, concrete room. "I have all these questions," he said, pacing between the janitor and the entrance, "and it seems like I've been afraid of the answers, so I haven't asked you any of them. But things are getting so fucked up right now."

Gate slowly spun his chair around so he could sit and face Relic. "He's here."

Relic stopped pacing, his heart hammering in his chest. *Dad.*

"He's here," Gate said again, with a slight nod of his head. "He said he was coming back here in '94, and he didn't want me coming with him."

A thousand more questions, and Relic couldn't form any of them.

Gate leaned forward, elbows on his knees. He looked old and completely spent, his coveralls stripped off to the waist revealing a hairy, paunchy body covered only by a greasy white tank top. Relic noticed the scars on Gate's hands and arms, as if he had been in a war or something.

"It was toward the tail end of *The Rest of the Wicked* tour," Gate said, as if the story pained him to tell. "That was about four years ago. We were all getting pretty sick of each other at that point, but the trouble had stopped. Stick told me getting out of Laramie would change things, but it took a few more years after we put out *Lead Her Astray* before we were truly free of her."

"Free of who?"

Gate looked up at Relic. "The Widow."

Relic's dreams flashed through his mind again—the pale claws killing Ted and Natalie, scratching those messages to him. Suddenly the title of Unknown Oath's album made perfect sense. He never thought the "her" in *Lead Her Astray* was anyone in particular. His dad used to write letters about "shaking that bitch" or "losing that bitch." Relic always assumed it was in reference to the album, *The Rest of the Wicked*, or other abstract things that just got in the way.

He never imagined that his father was running away from the Widow of Wane Street—an urban legend that everyone in Laramie joked about.

Relic bent down slightly so his eyes were level with Gate's. "Was my dad dreaming about her?"

"We both were," Gate said. "She was at every show, killing fans or members of other bands...people thought we were a band of murderers, man." Gate shook his head. "No one really knew what was going on, until your dad figured out that it all started with that song."

"You mean 'Alternus?'" Relic asked.

Gate looked up at him, shaking his head. "Don't even say that name. Your dad went through hell to get all the copies of that tape back—made sure we never played it again. Fortunately, Ricky and Jeff forgot the damn song, but some of our fans kept calling for it."

Ignoring that for now, Relic couldn't hold off asking any longer. "You said my dad was here?"

His eyes falling to the ground, Gate nodded again. "After the tour, he told me had figured it all out. Said he could end it for good. Even though the Widow was weaker the further we got from Laramie, she was still there. Stick said he had to put her down."

Relic couldn't come to terms with the Widow of Wane Street being an actual thing, but he set that aside for now. "So, he told you he was coming back to Laramie, but why wouldn't he come home? Where is he now?"

Gate looked up at Relic again, pain in his eyes. "He's here, man." Stomping his foot on the concrete floor, Gate repeated, "He's right fucking here."

The visions of Steven Meyers playing drums in that eerie abyss flooded Relic's mind, and somehow he knew that wherever his father was, he had gotten there from this very spot.

"I didn't figure it out until I got back here," Gate said. "It all came back to Chambers, back to when we first played that goddamn song. You see, when we recorded it, it wasn't...ritualistic. Whatever power it held, it wasn't until we played it at that battle of the bands—in front of that crowd—that something happened." Gate shook her head. "Steven never told me. He said the more people knew, the more power the Widow would have...whatever that means."

Relic thought about the words he had kept seeing and hearing. *Release me.*

He felt completely out of his element with trying to figure all this out, but if Unknown Oath played "Alternus" and somehow summoned the Widow, the song would probably be crucial to undoing everything. Wherever his father was, he was stuck playing that cursed song, asking his son to release him.

The song was still important—important enough that the Widow would kill anyone who had it. But she hadn't killed Relic...

"I followed him here," Gate said, tapping his boot on the concrete floor again. "His drums were in this room, with a junky PA system set up next to them. There was a copy of that song with a note next to it...telling me to..."

Relic knew where it was going, but he let Gate finish the tale.

The janitor looked up to Relic, his tired eyes rimmed in red. "He begged me to destroy it all, kid." His voice almost broke. "Part of me knew that doing it might make it so he could never come back...but he was my best friend. Damn me if I didn't burn it all."

Relic was left there to comfort a sobbing middle-aged janitor as the final school bell rang.

Chapter 13

Despite the revelation that his dad was somehow stuck in his nightmares, Relic found himself on autopilot Friday night. He and Bree hadn't really discussed Natalie's murder or even acknowledged the fact that they were going to homecoming. Instead, they spent most of the afternoon in Relic's basement watching *Mr. Bean* and planning out next morning's practice.

Thankfully, Relic didn't dream that night. Whether it was because Bree slept over or his mind was literally too exhausted to handle whatever subliminal messages his dad wanted to send him, he didn't care. He woke up on Saturday refreshed and ready for Altar Stone practice.

Nick arrived early, dropped off by his dad who was heading to a worksite. Doug Weber was a construction worker or handyman, Relic didn't know for sure because Nick didn't talk much about it. But from the look of the truck that Nick grabbed his bass guitar case out of, money was tight, and Doug made do with whatever tools he could scrounge together.

Relic and Bree led Nick down to the basement, discussing which covers they would work on today. The three of them had agreed to learn Metallica's "Master of Puppets" and Offspring's "Self Esteem," which seemed like a decent middle ground for their collective musical tastes. Even though Nick was in a punk band—or had been, Relic wasn't sure of the state of Bag of Sax now that Nick was in Altar Stone—his tastes were a bit more varied than Relic's, but nowhere near as eclectic as Bree's.

Bree and Nick plugged into the old Unknown Oath amps that Relic had dug out of the garage. They weren't the best pieces of gear, but at least they still worked, and it saved them from having to lug more equipment to each practice. After they were all tuned up and Relic was stretched out, they kicked into their covers. Altar Stone's first real practice was euphoric. Relic was in such high spirits that he didn't even feel that strange jealousy when he saw Nick and Bree jokingly crossing their instrument necks as if they were showing off to a crowd—he simply smiled with them and spun his sticks between cymbal chokes.

It's happening, he thought, *I'm in a band!*

During the breakdown of "Master of Puppets," Relic inevitably began thinking about his father. He wondered if this is what really pulled Steven away from his family—the possibility of doing this for the rest of his life—touring Europe, playing in front of huge crowds, recording legendary heavy metal tracks in luxurious studios. Even if a supernatural murderer factored in, part of him really wondered if he could blame his dad for wanting to chase that dream at the cost of not being able to be there for his son.

Something about that thought angered him, and as he kicked into the tom rhythm—which was supposed to be following Nick's bassline—Relic began playing something else.

"Alternus."

With his eyes closed, Relic slid into the ritualistic rhythm from his nightmares, imagining he was his father. It wasn't adulation that made him become the Steven Meyers from his dreams; it was more a sense of revulsion. As if Relic wanted to prove that he could be better than the man who abandoned him, leaving his wife and son to deal with some murderous ghost and her pack of mutant dogs.

He pounded his toms violently, clearly aware that the accompaniment from Bree and Nick had fallen away.

"Relic!"

Ignoring their shouts, he kept playing, increasing the tempo, the skin on his fingers tearing as his blisters broke open again. Another clattering rhythm joined Relic's thundering toms, like blades on glass, tapping faster and faster to keep up with Relic beats. His eyes tightly closed, he pictured the mists gathering behind him just like they had in his first dream about Delilah. But this time she was twisted, pale hands ending in crooked, sharp fingers that reached out to embrace the drummer who was part Relic and part his father.

"Relic!"

The tapping on the window turned into a hideous screech, like nails on a chalkboard, and finally Relic opened his eyes to see Nick and Bree staring at the basement window. A giant claw was scratching at the glass, trying to get to the haunting rhythms that pounded within. In a trance, Relic still played the tom pattern, even though his face stared at the creature's limb in horror.

Relic did one final tom roll and hit the crash to end the section of "Alternus," and at that exact moment, the claw reached back and smashed the window.

Dropping his sticks and falling off his drum throne, Relic rolled away from the shards of glass that fell inward. A familiar low growl echoed in the basement.

"What the hell is that?" Nick yelled, putting himself between the window and Bree.

Relic scrambled around his drums to get a better view, but all he saw was a broken window framing a peaceful, sunny Saturday morning.

The teens stared for a long moment in disbelief, until Bree finally yanked her guitar off and scrambled for the stairs.

"Wait!" Relic called, chasing after as Nick took off his bass. "Don't go outside!"

"What kind of dog was that?" Nick asked from behind them.

When Relic got upstairs, Bree was looking out the living room window as Dina came out of the kitchen removing her headphones.

"You guys done already?"

"I don't see it," Bree said, her voice understandably panicked.

"See what?" Dina asked, joining Bree at the window.

"Some huge dog just busted the window down there, Mrs. Meyers," Nick said, slightly calmer. He leaned over Bree to scan the front yard.

Dina's head jerked to Relic as she moved away from the window. He gave her a look that he hoped said, "The beast was back." In that moment, he thought of the copy of "Alternus" he stole from Natalie's apartment which was hidden in his bedroom. He wondered if that's what had drawn it here. But then he remembered that the last time this thing visited his home, his mom had just gotten rid of the tape.

"I've, uh, heard of some strays being seen around here," Dina lied. "You better stay out of the basement. I'll call someone to fix the window." She looked pointedly at Relic. "No more practice today."

"Yeah," Relic said, looking out the window but not seeing anything.

As Dina returned to the kitchen, Bree turned to Relic, frowning. "What was that you were playing?"

"Yeah," Nick said, still looking around out the window. "It was badass." He glanced over his shoulder at Relic. "You write that?"

Relic looked at Nick, then back at Bree. As much as he didn't want to lie to her, he nodded. "Yeah. Just something that came to me."

"Really?" Bree asked, skeptical.

Afraid that she would see the truth on his face, Relic looked down and scratched the back of his head. "I just don't really like what Lars played on that Puppets breakdown. It's kind of boring."

"Yeah, well, Lars is boring," Nick said, looking back outside.

Relic found that entirely uncalled for, but he was glad for the diversion. "Looks like practice is shot for the day," he said. "Damn dog."

Bree went to the stairs. "I'm just going down to get my guitar so I can practice at home. Be right back."

As Dina was talking to the window company on the kitchen phone, Nick turned around and sat on the sofa's armrest facing Relic. In a low voice he said, "You know, I only asked her to go to the dance as a friend."

Relic frowned, waiting for him to say something else, but Nick just kept a level gaze. "Okay."

"Well, I didn't want you to think that I was just joining the band to get with the girl, you know?"

It was then that Relic reminded himself that Nick had gone to a different middle school. He didn't know Bree was a lesbian, just like he didn't know Relic's dad wasn't a mass murderer. But he didn't feel like it was his place to speak for Bree's sexuality, so he just nodded. "That's good. Though I guess there are worse reasons to join a band."

Relic laughed with Nick as Bree came up with her guitar.

"I'm going to head home," Bree said, nodding toward the front door.

"No you're not," Dina said, coming out of the kitchen waving a finger. "I'm going to drive you home. You, too, Nick. I don't want you two walking around outside if there's some wild dogs on the loose." She snapped her fingers at Relic, "And you and I need to go shopping. I'm sick of seeing you in that one pair of shorts. Besides, Calvin wants to meet up for lunch."

Relic groaned, not because he hated shopping (he did) but because he was hoping to be alone so he could watch that damn video of his dad's show before meeting with Larry tomorrow.

"I don't want to hear it," Dina said. "Move it. Don't make your bandmates wait."

After dropping Bree and Nick off, Relic and his mom went to meet Calvin for lunch at the Roanoke Mall.

"Heard you started a band," Calvin said after the waitress dropped off their drinks. The Applebee's was attached to the mall, with the dining area windows facing the parking lot. Relic found his gaze wandering outside, looking for giant dogs. "What's your guys' name?"

"Altar Stone," Relic replied, eyes still searching the rows of parked cars.

"Rad," Calvin said, dejection in his voice.

Even though Relic knew quite well he was being dismissive, he didn't have it in him today to try to bond with his mom's new boyfriend.

"Why don't you tell Cal about your big date coming up?" Dina suggested, taking a sip of her iced tea.

Relic finally turned to face his dining companions, scowling at his mom.

"Date?" Cal took a slug of his soda.

"It's just the homecoming dance," Relic said. "I'm going with the band."

"And the new girl in town," Dina added with a wiggle of her eyebrows.

"Jesus, Mom, where do you hear this stuff?"

Dina scoffed. "Where else? I'd barely know anything about what goes on in your life if it weren't for Red."

It unsettled him that Bree had spoken to his mom about the dance. He would have been very curious to hear what she would have said about going with Nick—his mom was already convinced that Bree was straight; this would only ensure that things would get weirder.

Fortunately, the conversation quickly shifted to how Constrained Media was sponsoring homecoming this year, and Relic was able to finish lunch and properly prepare himself for clothes shopping.

Leaving the restaurant, they joined the rest of the Laramie consumers flooding the mall. As much as Relic hated shopping, he did enjoy being inside malls. It reminded him of being stoked to visit the toy store and the arcade as a kid—bright lights and constant energy. Walking the mall as a teen still gave him a similar feeling, but it was mixed with the social dread of seeing someone you only halfway knew and being unsure if you should greet them or not.

"Where to first?" Calvin asked.

"Oh," Dina said with a laugh, "that place over there seems appropriate." She pointed over the crowd toward a sign in the distance.

Crane & Co. Athletic Supply.

"We can replace those gym shorts," Dina said. "Maybe meet your girlfriend."

Teasing aside, Relic was actually eager to see the place. He doubted Delilah or her dad would be there, but he was curious, nonetheless. "Sure."

New stores had a very notable smell to them, and Crane & Co. was no exception. Everything in the place looked unspoiled and pristine. Relic had flashbacks to little league as they passed by kid-sized mannequins wearing catcher gear and batting helmets.

"We should grab some tennis racquets while we're here," Calvin said.

"When am I ever going to have time to play?" Dina asked miserably. "I feel like Rook has me on doubles almost every day."

"I told you to cut back," Calvin said. "You said you could afford it now. Need a mental break from that place."

"I know," Dina sighed. "Relic, why don't you go pick out some clothes. We'll be wherever the hell the preppy sports section is." Calvin laughed as they walked away holding hands. Relic watched, feeling a strange mix of happiness for his mom and bitterness for...well, himself, he guessed. He couldn't really make himself feel anything for his dad right now.

Feeling morose, Relic wandered toward the gym shorts. As he passed by the shoe department, he heard a familiar voice.

"You're going to need something better than the other guys have, Tyler. You're only as good as your gear."

Relic peered between two racks of shirts to see Barry Richardson kneeling down next to his son, Tyler, who sat on the bench. Tyler had one foot in a cleat and the other in his own shoe.

"They're just shoes, Dad. I'll be fine with what I have." Relic couldn't remember ever hearing Tyler Richardson sound so pathetic.

Barry leaned in toward his son. "You sound like a whiny little faggot, son. Is that how you want to sound?" His voice was low, but Relic didn't miss a word. The anger in that voice was shocking, the crude language appalling, even for an offensive teen like Relic. He always knew Barry was a "tough love" type of guy, but this was absurd.

"Would you rather I buy you a pair of Barbie sneakers to play in? Or do you want to sack up and find a pair of shoes here in the *men's* department?"

Tyler didn't answer. He reached down and tied the cleats, yanking the laces so hard that the veins in his forearms popped.

"Is that you, Barry?"

Tyler's dad looked up. "Marshall! Didn't think I'd catch you here!" Barry made a show of patting his son on the back like an old chum as he got up and went toward Delilah's father, who Relic didn't expect to look so young.

Marshall Crane wore a V-neck shirt with a tan sport coat over it. He had salt-and-pepper hair combed perfectly to one side and a matching mustache. He stood just as tall as Barry Richardson, whose hand he now shook vigorously. They spoke to each other in low voices so Relic couldn't make out what was said, but they were acting like old friends.

Relic moved away, afraid that Tyler might see him eavesdropping. As miserable as Tyler had made Relic's middle school years, somehow it made sense to Relic, and he was almost empathetic. Barry's homophobic remarks might just be part of his idiotic method of trying to make his son more like him—that antiquated version of macho—but maybe it also stemmed from something he had observed in his son.

As Relic browsed the available gym shorts, he couldn't help but think back on those times he and Tyler used to do dumb stuff together as kids, like flash their penises at each other—juvenile shenanigans that little boys engaged in without an ounce of concern about sexuality. Was there a chance that Barry saw any of that behavior and actually thought his son was gay? It seemed a ridiculous concept to Relic, but why else would Barry treat his son—a star athlete and one of the most popular guys in his grade—so cruelly?

Ultimately, it didn't matter. The only thing Barry Richardson strengthened with his little pep talk was the disdain Relic already had for him. He always assumed Barry was the type of guy who used shame and hateful language to fight his own insecurities and failings. Whatever Tyler had ever done or said to Relic, it was truly Barry's own sentiments and teachings flowing through his son.

Relic grabbed a couple pairs of shorts and went to catch up with his mom.

That night, Bree had to visit her grandparents in the country and Calvin had taken Dina to a movie, giving Relic the perfect opportunity for a private viewing of Larry's video. Normally he may have dreaded being alone in a dark house while there was a murderer on the loose and wild dog-things smashing his windows, but he had put this off for far too long, and the anxiousness he felt outweighed any notion of fear.

Opening the package from Larry, Relic found a simple VHS tape in a clear case. It had a label on it that read: "Unknown Oath – Halloween Bash – 1982 – Laramie, IN."

Knowing the basement TV had better display than the little one in his bedroom, Relic grabbed a Diet Coke and a bag of cheddar sour cream potato chips and hurried downstairs. He was grateful the window people had replaced the broken glass so quickly as rain was now hammering against it. Lightning flashed before a roar of thunder made the overhead light flicker.

Relic ignored it and popped the tape into the VCR, grabbing the remote. He got comfortable on the old recliner that sat closer to the TV than the couch and pressed play. After a small section of static and wavy lines on the screen, the picture cleared up to show a grainy view of a small stage. A few teenagers were setting up amps and drums, including Steven Meyers.

Unable to breathe, Relic watched as his dad—looking barely any older than himself—fiddled with his cymbal stands on the stage. He felt like a time traveling ghost, sneaking glimpses of things he wasn't meant to see. There was a distinct thrill about it, and Relic shoved chips in his mouth as he watched the young members of Unknown Oath prepare for their show.

After what felt like nearly thirty minutes of setup footage, the show began with a roar from the small crowd that came through the TV like incomprehensible feedback. From more recent concert footage Relic had seen of the band, it was clear he was watching Unknown Oath before they had truly found their sound. Their set consisted of a few covers and some originals that would later become much different songs. But the most notable part of the show was when they played "Alternus."

"This one is about an accursed place," Ricky shouted into the mic, his young voice nearly hoarse from not using it properly, "a place where music dies and murder thrives!"

Jeff held up his guitar as he let a power chord ring out, Steven pounding that familiar rhythm on the drums. Gate's bassline seemed to shake the camera, the picture wobbling slightly.

"Let me see your hands up!" Ricky was clapping along to Steven's steady bass drum. The crowd clapped along.

The picture started getting fuzzy. Relic tried to adjust the tracking on the remote, but it didn't seem to affect it all. The tape's audio was getting all distorted so he couldn't even hear the song, and the static kept screwing up the picture.

"Dammit," Relic said, moving to get up from the chair. But as he paused the tape, he nearly choked on his chips when he saw what was frozen on the screen.

A pale white claw was formed out of the wavy static lines, and the words "release me" appeared as blocky white letters where normally PLAY or STOP might appear in the top right of the screen.

Relic blinked and it was gone, replaced by normal static.

He pressed play again to see what would happen, but the static just got worse. He fast-forwarded it a bit until the picture cleared up. When it did, it was a different show with a bigger stage, and a different band was playing. Behind the drummer was a big banner that said "Unkind Ways" and the band was in the middle of a synth-heavy pop song.

Relic made a disgusted face, not enjoying the music at all.

Once the song was over, the singer, who was playing keyboard, spoke over a spattering of applause. "Thank you for sticking around, meatheads." This drew a wave of boos which seemed to delight the singer, who was a pale and scrawny guy who dressed like a vampire from *Buffy*. "I'm Guy Valentine and we are Unkind Ways." More boos.

"Maybe you'll enjoy this one," Guy said, motioning to the drummer who began playing a simplified version of the same rhythm that had haunted Relic since he found his dad's demo. Guy made a show of headbanging—clearly mocking the music—drawing more ire from the crowd. Just as he straightened himself and moved toward the mic, someone leapt on stage and shoved Guy.

The ambusher grabbed the keyboard and threw it off the stand, eliciting a roar from the crowd. The long-haired assailant was none other than Relic's father.

"What the fuck!?" Guy shouted, struggling to his feet.

Steven stood over him and shoved a finger in his face, the drums still going sloppily behind him. "Don't mess with us, Valentine!" Steven turned to the drummer. "And you better fucking can it, Ernie! I'm serious."

"My keys, man!"

Steven turned to face Relic through the TV. "And turn that shit off!"

Static.

Relic watched the grainy display, wondering what the hell he just watched. Why did Larry want him to see that?

Pressing the power button on the remote, Relic shoved another handful of chips in his mouth, feeling slightly let down. Guess he'd have plenty of material to discuss during the interview with Constrained Media tomorrow.

Chapter 14

"You sure you want to do this, Relic?"

Staring at the Crosstown hotel entrance from his mom's Mazda, Relic honestly wasn't sure. But he knew he had to. Last night, he had dreamed about Natalie's murder again, and he knew if he didn't try to stop whatever was happening, it would just keep haunting him for the rest of his life.

He had to get that tape from Larry.

"Yeah," he said as he reached for the car door's handle. "I feel like I have to at least tell them my side of things," he lied. It sounded like something that a normal kid in his situation would want to do, if his absent father was a central part of a big documentary.

Dina rubbed his back. "Alright, I'll be around the corner at the bookstore. Just feel free to leave if you get uncomfortable or anything."

Relic got out of the car and approached the elegant hotel. He had never been in the place, but he had always noticed it when riding downtown. He pushed through the massive rotating door and saw Delilah sitting on a velvet-cushioned chair in the lobby.

"Hey, Relic," she said, smiling at him.

Before he could reply, another voice came from behind him. "There he is!"

Relic turned around to see Larry approach from the hotel bar with three other people in tow. A young woman in slacks and a silky blouse carried two cups of coffee with a leather planner tucked under her arm while two younger men followed behind her, each lugging black bags over their shoulders.

"Glad you could make it, young man," Larry said as he extended a meaty hand for Relic to shake. After the greeting, Larry motioned toward the hallway beyond the bank of elevators. "We have one of the conference rooms mostly set up—Ms. Crane, why don't you join us, and we'll get started."

Delilah and Relic followed the crew around a few turns in the hallway, listening to the young woman read off Larry's agenda for the day. "Today's shoot needs to wrap before 2 P.M. if we're going to make our window at the Wane Street place," she said as she handed him his coffee. "They are prepping for a wedding later this week, so we can't miss it unless we want to hire an editing team to dirty up the shots in post."

"We have plenty of time," Larry assured with a wave of his big hand.

They pushed open the double doors to the conference room and Relic felt a thrill seeing all the lights and mics that filled the room. One corner of the room was blasted by several lights, decorated to look like some arcane study, with a bookshelf that certainly came from somewhere else and two candelabras flanking the set.

"Ladies first," Larry said, giving Delilah a creepy smile. "Why don't you grab a seat on the left there, Miss Crane. I'll be on the right. Molly!" A young woman who couldn't have been older than eighteen or nineteen scrambled out from behind a black curtain carrying a makeup case. "Give Miss Crane a quick pass and then cover up as much of my ugly mug as you can."

"Wait, are you doing the interview?" One of the guys carrying a black bag asked, a handsome man with a chiseled jaw and just enough of a five o'clock shadow. Relic was sure he had seen the man in something before. "Why am I here, then?"

"To take some notes," Larry snapped. "That last interview, you let the chief walk all over you. You can record your scratch tracks for the voiceover transitions, just keep it down."

The man gave Larry a sour look as he dropped his bag and took his coffee over to one of the tables along the edge of the room. Larry may be treating Relic and Delilah kindly, but he was clearly an asshole. That told Relic that they had something Larry wanted, which was good, because Relic *needed* something that Larry had and could use some leverage.

After Molly adequately prepared both her subjects, the other man in the company got behind the camera as several more crew members filed into the room to operate the lights and audio equipment. Relic sat back and watched it, fascinated to see how this all worked behind the scenes.

"Alright," Larry said, turned slightly toward Delilah on the set, "just be natural and we'll keep this short and sweet."

"Sure," Delilah said, unbothered. Relic thought he caught her shooting him the occasional glance, but he told himself that was just wishful thinking.

Soon, the cameras were rolling, and the interview had begun. "What did you know about Laramie, Indiana, before moving here?"

Seeming completely at ease in front of the cameras, Delilah took in a deep breath before answering. "I guess just the normal stuff—some weird murders, monster sightings." She motioned with her hand as if she had just remembered something. "Oh, and I knew that this was where the Rothen Corporation was founded."

"Well," Larry said with a nod, "not founded, but its American presence was established here, certainly." He weaved his sausage-like fingers together and laid them on his lap. "But tell me more about the monster sightings you had heard of. Did you chalk all that up to tabloid fodder?"

Delilah's eyes flashed to Relic's—this time he knew he wasn't imagining it—if only briefly. Her calm demeanor seemed to crack a little bit, her teeth chewing on her lower lip as she considered the question. "I guess not," she finally said. "I mean, why would there be so many stories like that coming out of one city in Indiana?"

"Very astute," Larry said, his tone a little condescending. "So you believed there were *actual* monsters lurking in Laramie, and yet here you are, as brave a young woman as I've ever seen."

The corner of Delilah's mouth rose in a smirk, releasing a small laugh. "I guess. My dad wanted to move here for work; I didn't have much of a choice. If that's brave, consider me Buffy Summers."

Relic couldn't help but smile at that.

Larry smiled, too, but there was something sinister and joyless about his leer. "You mean your adopted father, Marshall Crane. Right?"

Delilah's smile faded and her relaxed posture tightened, her eyes were now like daggers pointing at Larry.

"Would you be open to discussing your biological father?" Larry asked, his tone unchanged despite the clear discomfort his interviewee displayed.

"No," Delilah said flatly.

Larry cast a quick glance at the cameraman, a sleazy smile still waxed across his face. "Are you sure?" he asked the camera. "I think the perspective would be useful as we discuss the events to which he was so closely tied."

Delilah crossed her arms, leaning back in the chair and crossing her legs defiantly. That strong pose with those black fishnet stockings she wore made Relic fall in love all over again. He was going crazy for this girl, and he did not like how Larry was pressing her.

At the same time, Relic couldn't help but be insanely curious who her father was now. But it wasn't his or Larry's business, he supposed.

Larry tried to re-engage Delilah on some more tame topics, such as the Widow of Wane Street, the West Laramie Werewolves, or even the 1988 zombie riots, but even Relic could tell that there would be no more useful content coming from Delilah Crane. Finally, after another fifteen minutes of wasted footage, the interview ended, and Relic was invited to the set.

As Relic passed by Delilah, he wanted to say something that might be consoling, but the best he could manage was, "Good job." *Idiot idiot idiot!*

Regardless, Delilah offered him a weak smile as she moved toward the door.

"Oh, Miss Crane!" Larry called from his chair, refusing to get up. "Do stick around if you can. I think you might find Relic's segment interesting."

Relic saw Larry give a discreet nod to one of the cameramen, and in turn the guy rotated his camera slightly so he had Delilah—who had taken Relic's previous seat off set—in view.

What the— Relic's thoughts were interrupted by the makeup girl, Molly, who was brushing stuff all over his nose and cheeks.

"Welcome to show business," Larry chuckled. The same preparations made for Delilah's interview were repeated for Relic's segment.

Once the cameras were rolling, Larry wasted no time. "When people think of Laramie, Indiana, they probably think of three things: the supernatural, the Rothen Corporation, and the heavy metal band, Unknown Oath. One of those things has two gold records under its belt but has completely fallen off the radar in recent years." He made a motion toward Relic, who was already regretting his agreement to sit in front of a camera with Larry. "Relic Meyers, son of Unknown Oath's drummer, Steven Meyers, tell me: when was the last time you corresponded with your father?"

Relic nervously glanced from the camera to Delilah, who was glaring at Larry. Shifting his eyes to his knees, Relic said, "I got a letter from him a few years ago, around Christmas. He said he was coming home."

"Did he?"

Relic shook his head. "No, that was the last we heard from him." Annoyingly, he felt his voice give out there, as if he were about to cry. He didn't feel sad, but the discomfort of the camera on him and seeing Delilah so upset was screwing with his emotions.

"Is it true that your father supported you and your mother over the years? Financially, that is."

Relic looked up to Larry, his heart racing. "I—I don't think I'm supposed to talk about that…"

Larry waved a chunky hand. "Don't worry about it." He turned to the camera and made a throat-cutting motion. "We'll edit that out. Relic, are you quite certain your father never returned home in 1995?"

The question threw Relic completely off guard. Before he answered, he remembered Gate's story about his dad saying he was going back to Laramie. But deep down, Relic refused to believe that his dad would come back and not at least visit his son.

"Relic?" Larry was leaning forward now.

"No," Relic said decisively. "I told you, the letter he sent was the last I heard from him. I wrote him like a hundred letters, and he never wrote back." Relic felt a tear in the corner of his eye now and he was growing angry—he refused to let himself cry over this.

"Well," Larry said, twisting his head as if he was about to say what a shame that was, "we have proof that Steven Meyers indeed flew back from Copenhagen on December 31st, 1994. Can you think of any reason that he wouldn't contact his wife and son?"

Clenching his fists, Relic willed himself with everything he had not to cry or scream or punch this fat jerk in the face. He took a deep breath and replied, "No."

"Perhaps it was because he was being sought after by the police here in Laramie in connection to the murder of Guy Valentine in April of 1995?"

From the corner of his eye, Relic saw Delilah stand up then, but his focus was on Larry's words. *Guy Valentine,* he thought, wondering where he had heard that name. It wasn't the first time his father was tied to some murder, but this one didn't ring any bells. Except that name...

Then, it came back suddenly. The video from last night.

"I'm Guy Valentine and we are Unkind Ways."

The singer that Relic's father had attacked on stage. When Relic looked up to Larry, he saw a mocking smile.

"You watched the tape, didn't you?"

Relic stood up. "My dad isn't a murderer!"

Leaning back in his chair casually, Larry slowly crossed his legs. "You have seen him recently, haven't you, Relic?"

The arrogant, judgmental look on the man's face revolted Relic, and he didn't know how to handle it. "Give me the tape," Relic demanded, surprising himself with how he hadn't already succumbed to tears at this point. "It's dangerous."

"Dangerous? How?" Larry asked, his glance going from Relic to the camera. "Is your father still looking for any remaining copies? Is that why he killed Guy?"

"Relic," Delilah said, now standing near the set, "let's go. He just wants to profit off your family." She glared at him. "And mine."

Larry was still smiling, enjoying this chaos he was creating. "You're awfully protective of a Meyers."

Relic didn't want to listen to any more. "Just give me the tape, please. My mom sold it to the place you got it from, and I need it." He tried a Hail Mary. "It's all I have left of my dad."

"I'll make you a copy," Larry said with a wink.

"Don't!" Relic said, once again surprising himself with his assertiveness. But he felt Delilah's touch on his arm, pulling him away from the set.

Larry's eyes shot to Delilah. "You are a fascinating one, young lady. With everything this boy's father has done to your—"

Delilah closed the gap between herself and Larry so fast that Relic gasped. She leaned over his chair so that her face was so near his that they could have been kissing—which both grossed Relic out and made him envious of the fat man. Her hands were on his chair's armrests, which squished against his lavish sport coat.

"Not. One. More. Word." Delilah's voice was soft and deadly, and the room fell silent as she spoke. "You know who my father is. So wrap this up and do not bother me or Relic again. Understand?"

There was a drawn-out silence before Larry finally said, "I guess that's a wrap today, everyone."

Delilah returned to Relic's side, crossing her arms and giving him a consoling look.

"Thank you for your time today, kids," Larry said, snapping his fingers for one of his assistants to bring him his coffee. "Now, fuck off."

As they left that horrid room, Relic tried to calm his heart, which thundered like a machine gun. But when Relic felt Delilah's hand grasp his, he thought his chest might just explode.

"This way," Delilah said, flashing him a quick smile before she pulled him toward the elevators. As much as Relic wanted to ask what was going on, he would literally follow this girl into Hell, so he kept his mouth shut and kept pace with her. After she pressed the up button near the elevator doors, they waited, still holding hands.

Relic felt like he was in some kind of spy thriller movie.

The elevator dinged, and when they were on, Delilah pulled out her other hand that was tucked under her arm. In it was a small envelope with the number 424 on it. She used a black-nail-tipped finger to press the 4 button and the doors closed.

As much as Relic didn't want to spoil this magical moment, his curiosity was getting the best of him. "So, what are we doing?"

His mind raced with possibilities: *We're going to go have sex!* felt both terrifying and improbable, but that's what happened in spy movies, right?

Delilah gripped his hand tighter when she held up that numbered envelope. "You said you needed that tape, right?"

It took Relic a moment to realize what she held, but he couldn't contain his laugh when it dawned on him. "You swiped his room key?!"

She tucked it back into her hand and grinned. "You can learn a few tricks growing up in the system."

The elevator dinged again, and they were on the fourth floor. Unfortunately, Delilah let go of Relic's hand as she put both hands on the elevator's doors so she could look in either direction down the hallway.

"Clear," she said, moving swiftly. Relic followed. Room 424 was around the corner, and a quick swipe of the key card gave them entry. Larry's room was already cleaned, fortunately, so there was no chance of room service catching their larceny.

Relic remembered something Larry said. "Is there a safe?"

Delilah went straight for the closet, which had a folding door. Inside, they saw their prize: a small metallic safe with a digital keypad. *Damn*, Relic thought, doubting Delilah knew how to crack that. He was also unfortunately not the star of this spy thriller, with pockets full of gadgets.

However, Delilah flipped over the envelope the room key had been in and they both shared a laugh. The numbers 6969 were crudely jotted down on it.

"I pity the woman who has to do that for a movie part," Delilah said, punching in the code.

Relic felt the first relief of the day when he saw the tape sitting alone in that safe. He snatched it quickly, and together they hurried out of the room, down the hall, and back into the elevator which was still on the fourth floor. On the ride down, Delilah was leaning back on the decorative banister in the elevator, breathing heavy like she had just ran a marathon.

She smiled at Relic. "That was fun."

Relic just stared at her, completely smitten. "I can't believe you did that, Delilah." He looked down at the tape, tapping it. The relief—everything they just experienced together—was doing a number on him, and he felt like he was about to cry again. "Thank you."

"You're welcome," Delilah said, a shyness in her voice.

He looked up at her. "No, really…" Stepping toward her, not really sure why, he showed her the tape. "I don't think you know how huge this is. I just…"

She held his gaze, slightly biting her lip.

After the last few hours, kissing her was the easiest thing he could possibly do at that moment.

It was his first real kiss—that time he and Bree pretended to kiss didn't really count, he always told himself—and he couldn't think of a more perfect first kiss. Relic felt Delilah's hand on the back of his neck, and he put his free hand on her waist, feeling the studs on her black leather belt. It was brief, but would live in Relic's mind for the rest of his life.

They broke away from each other when the elevator dinged, and both laughed at their reaction. They quickly and awkwardly exited the hotel.

"That was…intense," Relic said as they walked outside, he felt too shy to even look at her now that they were back in the real world.

"Yeah," Delilah said. "I should probably get home and let my dad know how that went."

Relic tensed and looked at her. The fear must have been clearly apparent in his eyes.

"The interview," Delilah said with a laugh. "I just meant the interview. My dad knows Larry, and I want to make sure he knows how much of a dick he really is."

Laughing, Relic nodded. "Yeah, I should go meet my mom at the bookstore. I'll see you at school tomorrow?"

"You better," Delilah said with a wicked smile.

Relic floated toward the bookstore in a complete and wonderful daze.

Chapter 15

"Where'd you find this?" Gate asked the next day, inspecting the tape Relic had stolen from Larry's hotel room. "I thought we got them all."

Relic wasn't quite sure yet if he wanted to disclose that there was a copy of this tape in his bedroom—he had already convinced himself it was safe where it was. "I found it in our storage unit, where Ted Packer was killed."

Gate looked from the tape to Relic, and it was clear he was making the same connections that Relic had already made. "It's happening again," Gate said, getting out of the chair in the middle of the maintenance room—the chair that marked Steven Meyers' last known whereabouts. "We need to destroy this thing."

"Wait," Relic said, not even sure where he should begin. "There's some stuff I haven't told you."

Just then, the morning bell rang.

Relic looked up at the grimy clock over the exit. "Shit." He moved toward Gate, pointing to the tape. "Look, just don't do anything with it yet. Hide it or something, but there might be something we can use it for."

At this point, Relic was just making stuff up—he was so far out of his element that he felt like he was speaking someone else's thoughts. But he couldn't shake the feeling in his gut that he needed to help his dad, and he wouldn't be able to without that song.

"Kid, you don't want to mess with this," he held up the tape, "whatever body count you think this song has…you don't even know the half of it."

Relic grabbed his backpack, honestly not overly concerned if Gate smashed the tape—he did have that copy—but he begged again. "Please, just wait until after school. I'll stay behind and we can talk about it."

He waited until Gate tucked the cassette into the pocket of his green coveralls. "Go on, kid. Get better grades than your dad."

About eight minutes after leaving the basement maintenance room, Relic was standing in front of Ms. Duncan's class trying to remember how to speak English. You'd think that after surviving werewolf attacks, discovering his dad might be stuck in a different dimension, and kissing the girl of his dreams, speaking in front of a small group of peers would be cake for Relic. But as his throat dried up and his hands kept shaking, he was reminded this was still high school, and he still felt at the mercy of his peers.

"The West Laramie Werewolves were an urban legend that stemmed from a series of dog attacks," Relic said, his eyes surveying the class nervously. He could see Ms. Duncan with her legal pad sitting with her legs crossed to the side of the room. She was jotting things down that Relic convinced himself were all the things he was doing wrong. "There were two main instances that sort of led to these stories.

"Back in, like, the 1800s, there were a lot of Great Danes brought over to the United States." Relic did his best to summarize what Bree's dad had told him about the werewolf stories. "Apparently, they were the most popular dogs amongst the upper class, and, uh, the Widow of Wane Street had like five of them."

Relic stared at the class as his mind wandered back to the restroom, when he was stuck in a stall and one of those massive creatures growled. He heard it now, overpowering the thoughts in his head.

"Relic?"

"Huh?" He blinked the memory away, looking at Ms. Duncan. There were a few snickers in the class, and he forced a smile as if he were part of the joke and not the butt of it.

"What is the story you wanted to tell the class?"

"Oh, right." Relic adjusted his posture and started again. "In, uh, 1983, my dad's band—"

"Who's your dad's band?" Tyler Richardson called out from the second row, his voice dripping with mockery.

"Quiet," Ms. Duncan warned.

Relic tried not to look at him. "My dad's band, Unknown Oath—"

"Whoa! Your dad is *the* Steven Meyers?" Tyler mocked again, drawing more than a few chuckles, each one sending needles into Relic's eyes. Fighting the tendency to cry when embarrassed or angry, Relic took steady breaths to restrain the tears.

"One more outburst, Tyler," Ms. Duncan said, "and you will lose a letter grade on your presentation. Do you understand?"

Relic glanced at Tyler and saw a gloating smile, completely relishing in his one-time friend's misery. *What happened to you, man?* At that moment, Relic couldn't feel a shred of pity for the young man who he saw verbally abused by his father just days ago.

"I apologize, Relic," Ms. Duncan said in a calmer tone, "please continue."

Relic took a deep breath and kept his eyes down as he calmed himself, just wanting to finish this presentation without further incident. Fortunately, he knew this story all too well. "Unknown Oath was performing a show at the university, and there had been several 'werewolf sightings' that spring." Relic used finger quotes to show what he thought of these sightings. "At the show in April, there was an incident when a Great Dane attacked the venue where Unknown Oath was playing and two people were killed—one was mauled by the dog and the other was, I guess, trampled by the people trying to get away."

Hoping he was done, Relic let an awkward silence hang between him and the class. Finally, Ms. Duncan asked, "And what significant historical event happened around the time of this attack?"

"Oh yeah," Relic said, shaking his head in a show of forgetfulness. "I guess there were a few laws passed about animal testing? Because there used to be an animal lab outside of town where Rothen, I guess, tested their drugs on animals. Some people said the 'werewolves' were dogs that had been illegally experimented on in those labs and they escaped."

Another silence.

"And do you know what any of those laws were specifically?" Ms. Duncan asked with raised eyebrows.

Relic lowered his eyes. "No."

"Alright," she replied as she jotted something down on her legal pad—*a big fat F*, Relic was sure. "Thank you, Relic, that was a very interesting story. Do we have any volunteers, or am I going to have to keep picking you all randomly?"

"I'll go," Bree said eagerly with a raised hand. Relic glanced at her on his way to his seat, and the consoling look on her face eased any lingering tension from the display. He could still feel Tyler's eyes on him, but he tried to ignore them as he sat down and focused on Bree.

"I want to go back to something Relic said during his story," Bree said, sounding as natural as if she were just talking to Relic in his basement. He was so insanely jealous of her confidence. "Back in 1843, here in Laramie, Cecily Moreau—who I'm sure most of you all know as the Widow of Wane Street—was accused of killing her family and feeding their remains to her starving dogs, giving them the taste of human flesh and giving birth to the rumors of the werewolves Relic spoke of." She took a deep breath, "But one thing we don't hear much about is her husband, Gustave.

"Gustave was a well-regarded French composer who brought his family over to America from Italy. The Moreau family came to Laramie because of the Chambers Music Hall that used to be right here where the school was eventually built—it burned down in like the 50s or 60s, I think—and Gustave was close to the Rothen family who built the hall and the school. Anyway, Gustave was, like, super paranoid about this thing called the Curse of the Ninth, because he was working on his ninth symphony and apparently there were lots of famous composers who mysteriously died after they performed their ninth symphonies."

Relic was mesmerized by Bree rattling off these facts. He always knew she was much smarter than him and always got better grades, but she must have done a ton of research. Now he felt even more embarrassed by his presentation.

"So this is your story?" Ms. Duncan asked. "About Gustave's obsession with the Curse of the Ninth?"

"Yeah," Bree said. "Apparently when Cecily murdered him, lots of people were saying that he cursed her somehow—like as a way to avoid him dying due to the Curse of the Ninth—because historically around this time, there was a big Spiritualism movement in America—which is my historical event, even though it wasn't just a single event but instead a sort of cultural shift—"

"Excellent," Ms. Duncan said, clearly trying to prevent Bree from taking up more time. "Very insightful, Bree. I love how you touched on one of the biggest movements in the 19th century. Maybe you can all see why there are so many stories like that in Laramie, due to what was happening in the country as a whole. Thank you very much, Bree. Who's next?"

As Bree made her way back to her seat, Miranda Cartwright stood up on the other side of the classroom. "I'll go," she said, holding up a black VHS tape. "I have a visual aid—you said we could get extra credit, right?"

"Yes," Ms. Duncan said, motioning to the front of the classroom. "The VCR there is all ready to go; just use the remote."

Miranda flipped her hair over her shoulder and strutted toward the media cart that had a strapped-down television on top and a VCR on the lower shelf. "My story is from 1986," Miranda said in an exaggerated presenting voice, her back to the class as she put the tape in. "There was a super ugly guy named Errol Vaughn who lived in this gross shack down by the Wabash River, and he kidnapped people and drowned them. It was like all over the news." She pressed play on the VCR. "And my historical event is, like, super important. It was the year Madonna released this song."

As the TV's picture adjusted, Relic nearly threw up. "No," he breathed.

"Press play!" Bree's youthful voice shouted from the fuzzy recording of her living room. She was wearing her mom's leather jacket that was way too big, and little fifth-grade Relic wore a feather boa around his neck that was probably from the family's Halloween costume box. "The green button!"

"What the hell?" Bree said from the back of the room as several students started chuckling.

The song kicked on and all the horrors that Relic had experienced these last couple weeks seemed so insignificant in this moment of pure torment. This was his personal hell.

As the infectious synth melody of "Open Your Heart" mingled with the rising laughter in class, Ms. Duncan stood up. "Alright, Miranda, that's not appropriate."

"Woo, Relic, shake that ass!" Tyler shouted as he clapped in mock applause, turning the entire classroom into a comedy club that just got hit with the punchline.

Relic couldn't take his eyes off the screen, watching in horror as a treasured memory—of him and his best friend experiencing a rare moment of unbridled joy—become tarnished forever. Because of two preppy scumbags. He clenched his fists, his sadness and shame becoming a fiery rage.

"Now, that's enough!" Ms. Duncan said, raising her voice and swiftly closing the gap between her and the TV. She turned it off and rounded on Tyler. "As promised, that's one letter grade off your presentation, Mr. Richardson. And you, Miss Cartwright, can see me after class."

The bell rang as the laughter died.

"The rest of you, be prepared to share your stories next class," the teacher said, her voice much less pleasant than usual. "And any more nonsense will result in a zero. No exceptions."

Normally, Relic would be the first one out the door when the bell rang, but he took his time collecting his things. Despite the blood pounding in his ears, he heard Bree on his left.

"What the fuck was that, Miranda!?" she hissed.

"I thought you guys would like it," Miranda said in a tone of feigned innocence. "Maybe you should do that routine at the talent show."

"Take a seat, Miss Cartwright," Ms. Duncan said, approaching Bree. "Is this yours?" She held out the VHS tape.

Furious, Relic stepped over and snatched it out of the teacher's hand as he stormed out of the classroom.

"Relic," Bree called, but he ignored it, stalking the hall toward his locker where he expected to find Tyler. "Wait!" He heard her footsteps quickening behind him.

He turned, even more furious. "Why would you give her this?!" He held up the tape, scowling at her over it.

Bree's expression looked like he had just hit her. "I didn't give it to her. We used to record videos at her house with my dad's camera. I must have accidently left some tapes over there. I didn't think—"

"You didn't think that your ex-girlfriend was a massive bitch?!"

The hurt expression on Bree's face turned to anger. "She's not my ex-girlfriend, you asshole." She turned and stormed off.

Still overcome with shame and fury, Relic could only watch her go. He didn't want to hurt her, and he had no clue what the whole story between Miranda and Bree actually was, but he still had a score to settle. He turned back toward his locker and saw Tyler alone, his back to Relic as he exchanged books in his locker.

Too angry to consider his options, Relic followed his idiotic, male primal instincts and shoved the star quarterback of the football team into the locker. He heard several "ooohs" as students gathered around the edges of his vision, but he was only focused on the jerk who slowly turned around to flash him a cocky smile.

"You looking for a new dance partner, Meyers?" Tyler asked, pushing his perfect hair out of his eyes. That got a few laughs from the onlookers.

Relic held up the tape. "Guessing you put her up to it, right?"

Tyler scoffed. "Put her up to what? I didn't give her that tape. Ask your friend, Ellen DeGeneres."

Something dark and hateful bubbled up from Relic's memory. "How about I ask your shoe salesman? Did you find any Barbie shoes that fit?"

Tyler's arrogant expression melted to confusion, then anger. "You spying on me now, fat ass?" He stepped forward and shoved Relic. It wasn't hard, it was more of a challenge, as if he wanted to provoke Relic. "Taking after your dad? Sneaking up on people before you kill 'em?"

Overcome with adrenaline and aggression, Relic dropped the tape and grabbed Tyler's shirt with both fists, pushing him against the lockers.

"Come on, Meyers," Tyler taunted through his teeth, "hit me. Everyone's watching."

Relic couldn't help but shift his eyes in either direction, seeing the crowd waiting for something to tell their friends about. He wanted nothing more than to cave Tyler's teeth in—even though he had never hit anyone before—but something restrained him.

"Come on!" Tyler growled. "You know you want to, Meyers."

"Break it up!" A voice bellowed from down the hall.

Something about it triggered Relic, and he tightened his grip on Tyler's shirt, remembering all the times this bully made his life miserable in middle school—made all the worse by the pleasant memories he had playing baseball with Tyler in simpler times.

"Come on, fat boy," Tyler taunted in a whisper, his breath hot in Relic's face. "What are you waiting for?"

It took everything within Relic to let go of Tyler's shirt as a teacher shouted for the gathered kids to break up. But when Tyler said, "I guess he lets his dyke friend fight his battles," Relic lost it and threw his right fist into Tyler's face with all his might.

Chaos broke out among the gathered crowd, shouting for blood. But the teacher—who Relic couldn't even see—shouted it all down. "Move along! You two, break it up now!"

Relic could barely comprehend what was going on around him, consumed by the pain in his right hand. He had never punched anyone before, and he worried that he may not be able to hold a drumstick with his injured hand.

"Both of you, to the principal's office," the unnamed teacher commanded, ushering kids away from the scene. "Now."

After a short visit to Principal Sinclair's office, Relic was given one front-row ticket to detention that afternoon. First though, he had to sit with the school's secretary while she called his mom to leave a message about him needing a ride home, since he had to miss the bus to stay back to serve his time. When the secretary was unable to reach Dina, Relic lied and said he had a ride, knowing he had to meet up with Gate whenever he could get out of detention. But the stubborn secretary left a message for his mom anyway.

Tyler seemed extremely pleased during the whole procedure, as if Relic had played his part perfectly. Why the star quarterback of the Chambers High football team would want to be sitting in detention after school was beyond Relic, but he was thoroughly annoyed to think that he had somehow given his nemesis exactly what he wanted.

The rest of the day's classes were a blur of frustration and dread. By the time Relic had to report to his disciplinary obligations, he felt completely defeated, resignation replacing any anger he once harbored over the morning's events. As he dragged his feet into the basement classroom and laid his eyes on Tyler, Relic saw a guy who was totally pleased with himself.

The heavyset teacher, Mr. Proctor, looked up from an open newspaper on his desk with bleary red eyes, motioning to the seats.

"Get comfortable," the man said from below his bushy mustache. "My only rule here is that you stay quiet until that clock hits 4:45. Understood?"

Relic nodded and made his way to a seat as far away from Tyler as possible. They were the only two students, but there were only two rows of desks in the room, so he couldn't be as far from Tyler as he would have liked.

The first five minutes of detention were an infinity; Relic tapped his foot quietly as if he were playing an AC/DC song at triple the BPM, watching the hands of the clock slowly tick away. It wasn't until Mr. Proctor excused himself to go to the restroom that Relic finally looked over at his tormentor. Spinning a mechanical pencil through his fingers, Tyler looked perfectly pleased with himself, despite the red mark on his left cheek where Relic had smacked him.

As Relic stared at him, he thought about all the real problems he was dealing with—the "Alternus" murders, the werewolves, his father—and felt so ridiculous that he had allowed Tyler Richardson to make him feel any sense of fear or shame. However, he couldn't shake his curiosity…

"I don't get it, man," Relic finally said. "I mean, I can guess why you're always going after me…I quit playing sports, and the way your dad treats you, I bet you think you're doing me a favor by trying to shame me for being a quitter—the kind of stuff your dad does to you. But why make Miranda do your dirty work? What did I ever do to her?"

Tyler waited until Relic was done talking before he turned in his direction, still wearing that arrogant smile. "You think you're worth that much effort? I told you I didn't tell Miranda to do anything. What makes you think it had anything to do with you?"

Relic could only glare as he considered those words. *Bree?* He hadn't considered Bree getting embarrassed over that, remembering how she and Natalie had been laughing about the memory at The CD Palace. Relic never knew Bree to let any sort of teasing get to her—and he knew how much she had to endure due to her orientation.

"What's her problem with Bree?"

Tyler shrugged. "I don't care, ask Miranda. She probably doesn't want Bree stalking her anymore."

"Stalking?" Relic was genuinely perplexed. "What are you talking about?"

"Apparently Bree was pretty gay for her, used to stalk her and stuff."

"What?! Dude, Bree never stalked Miranda. She just—" Relic cut himself off then, realizing he only had his own assumptions to go off of. And with how Bree reacted to his comment earlier, now he wasn't sure what the deal was between her and Miranda. He did know that it wasn't his or Tyler's business. "Whatever," Relic said, kicking his feet up onto the book rack on the desk in front of him, "just seemed like something you would do, since you're so obsessed with me apparently."

Tyler laughed. "Figures you'd think that, Mr. My Dad Plays Drums For a Has-Been Metal Band," he pantomimed with his hands, "thinking everything's about you."

Despite the mockery, Relic felt a particular weight to those words. In a sense, none of this was about him—this was all about Barry Richardson treating his son like shit. Knowing that he'd be unable to change anything about Tyler, Relic resisted the urge to get into some stupid argument, and instead spoke how he really felt.

"I'm sorry your dad called you that."

The palpable tension lifted then as Mr. Proctor came back into the room, and Tyler stopped twirling the pencil through his fingers. "I'm sorry your dad killed a bunch of people."

"Ah ah ah, no talking," the teacher said as he plopped down behind his desk. "We're almost home free."

"Excuse me, teach," a familiar voice said from the doorway. Gate leaned in, peering at Relic and then back to Mr. Proctor. "You think I could borrow one of your inmates? Got some gum to scrape off some seats and figured it might be a good use of their time."

"That sounds like a marvelous idea, Gerald," Mr. Proctor said, adjusting his newspaper. "Any volunteers?"

Relic got quickly to his feet and slipped on his backpack, eager to escape. As he looked over at Tyler, who was leaning his head back to see the clock tick slowly toward 4:26, Relic's sympathy was still getting the best of him. He gave Gate a knowing stare. "Do you think you'll need both of us?"

Gate's eyes went to Tyler and then back to Relic before saying. "I suppose."

"Wonderful!" Mr. Proctor said, getting up again. "Keep an eye on 'em until 4:45, Gerald. I've got some traffic to beat."

Once the teacher was gone, Tyler stood up and walked slowly toward Relic and Gate. "Scraping gum for ten minutes is a pretty lame revenge, man."

"You can get lost, kid," Gate said to Tyler as he turned away, motioning for Relic to follow him. "We don't need you."

Relic looked at Tyler, who seemed very confused. "Figured you were just trying to get out of football practice. That's why you wanted me to hit you, right? It kind of just occurred to me today—all the times you've messed with me...you've never tried to beat me up or anything. Got me wondering what kind of bully does that, you know?" Relic took a few steps toward the door. "I kind of get it. If my dad was around and treated me the way your dad did..."

As Relic was about to leave the room, Tyler said, "I hate sports." He waited until Relic turned around to continue. "I guess I was pissed at you for being able to quit with no one hassling you—made me jealous. I told my dad last year I wanted to join choir and he called me a fag." He looked at the ground. "He made me try out for football instead, after sending me to conditioning all summer and paying this former pro to train me."

"That sucks," Relic said. "I didn't know you sang."

Tyler looked back up, anger in his eyes. "Yeah, well I don't. You tell anyone and I will see what other tapes Miranda has of you guys."

There's the Tyler I know, Relic thought miserably as he watched the troubled teen take his leave.

Chapter 16

"Alright, junior, give me one good reason not to smash this thing."

Relic looked at Gate, taking a breath to buy himself some time. "I haven't told you some things, and I feel like if this is the last copy of this tape," Relic tried not to cringe at that, remembering the copy in his room, "we should talk about them."

Gate crossed his arms and leaned against the concrete wall in the maintenance room. "I'm listening."

Relic explained his dreams, the werewolf attack at home, the situation with Larry...everything that had happened in the last couple weeks that may have some relevance. Well, except for him taking the copy of the tape from Natalie's place.

"So you're saying this tape is leaving a trail of bodies, and you brought it to your high school?" Gate shook his head in disbelief.

"Whatever is killing these people is doing it in the dark," Relic said, his voice rising, "without witnesses. Don't you think the school is the safest place for it? Besides, that scumbag Larry is still alive—not to mention, it could have killed me when I played the song, but it didn't. It's almost like it wanted me to."

"Exactly," Gate said, holding up the tape, "it's the Widow, kid. Not a doubt in my mind. And this goddamn song is what freed her from whatever curse your dad found out about. I mean, you're kind of right, she never killed any of us, even though the bitch had plenty of chances." He shook his head, "All that aside, of course she wants you to play it, that's probably why she's back now!"

"That's just it," Relic said. "She's still here and my dad's not. But whatever he did made it so she couldn't kill just anyone—like, he crippled her or something.

He knew something we didn't—how to weaken her—and we need to find out what."

Gate nodded. "Trust me, man, I tried. Your dad didn't leave me a single goddamn breadcrumb. We were best friends—I would have found it by now."

Relic looked at the tape in Gate's hand. "What if he did?"

As Gate's eyes fell onto the tape, the words "release me" flashed in Relic's memory again. His heart racing, he walked toward the chair that sat in the middle of the room, marking Steven Meyers' final jam session.

"What if my dad's trapped somewhere? What if whatever he did to try to trap the Widow, trapped him there with her as well?"

Gate paced over to where Relic stood, his eyes distant, considering the idea. "He used to talk about this cult he read about in that book Jeff found in his grandparents' attic. That's where he got the name; he said they were called the Cult of Alternus."

Relic could have sworn he just heard a whisper then: "release me..."

"What book?"

Shaking his head with a look of dismay, Gate replied, "Don't get excited, kid, it's gone. Steven brought me to it after the battle of the bands, when we first played the song live—insane show, man—all we found was a pile of dust where he had left it. It's like the song destroyed it or something. Stick said he used the book to write the lyrics to 'Alternus,' but he could never find another copy of it."

Relic was no expert of the occult, but it certainly sounded like the effects of some elaborate ritual. As awesome as the concept of a heavy metal band completing a ritual with their music would have normally sounded to Relic, right now it made him ill. *Did Dad know what he was doing?* Relic wondered, hoping the answer was a resounding "no." Thinking of all the times he had been teased for having a psychopathic murderer for a dad, he hoped all those kids hadn't been right. Because if Steven Meyers had any idea what he had been doing, maybe he belonged wherever he was...

"Did he ever tell you what that name meant?" Relic wasn't quite sure why he suddenly wondered that.

Gate nodded. "Like, some other dimension or some crazy shit. He said something about the cult believing there was a place where these, like, ghosts or something came from. I remember him saying something like these spirits couldn't create—or even conceive—stuff in the same way humans could, so they fed off our imaginations, our art." He held up the tape. "Our music."

Relic thought back to his dreams of his dad, playing drums in some strange other world like a ghost battery, feeding millions of murderous spirits. What if that was Alternus? Was he able to go there in his dreams? Or was he just imagining what the place looked like? He wanted to laugh suddenly, feeling insane for trying to logic stuff like this out.

"Anyway," Gate said, "this cult had a bunch of high society members, Stick said. I forget who, but I think he mentioned the Widow's husband and one of those Rothen ladies..."

"Gustave Moreau?"

Gate looked at him. "Yeah, that dude."

Relic remembered Bree's presentation about the Widow and the Curse of the Ninth, and all the rumors about how Gustave had somehow doomed his wife to avoid the curse himself—whatever that meant. Felt like something was there...

"Relic Meyers, please report to the office," a muted mechanical voice called from the hallway intercom, "Relic Meyers, please report to the office."

"Shit," Relic said, grabbing his backpack. "My mom's probably here." He looked at the tape in Gate's hand and added, "I don't know if it's safe here, but I feel like it is. I also feel like it might be the only way we could find my dad."

Gate tucked it into the pocket of his coveralls. "I'll just make sure no one else finds it. Stay out of detention from now on, kid."

"That little asshole," Dina said as they got into Calvin's ridiculously clean Jeep. "I thought maybe he'd have grown up by now. Still, Relic, don't get yourself in trouble over him—he's so not worth it."

"I know," Relic grumbled, not wanting to talk about Tyler in front of Calvin. "Hey, Calvin. Thanks for the ride."

"No problem, bud," he said as he pulled away. "You guys want to grab some dinner?"

Really, Relic just wanted to go to bed. "Drive thru is fine."

"Actually," his mom said, laying a hand on Calvin's arm as he steered them away from school, "let's go somewhere nice." She looked back at her son. "Your choice, kiddo."

"What's the occasion?" Relic asked.

His mom ignored the question. "Anywhere you want. Seriously."

"Rook's?"

"No, you little shit!" Dina shouted, laughing. "I'm not going back to work on my night off!"

Relic suggested his favorite Italian place, Esposito's, where they rarely got to go. But he got a sort of sick pleasure picking the most expensive place he could think of, knowing that Calvin would most certainly offer to pay.

As they ate breadsticks and Relic told them about the cause of his detention, Calvin and his mom were surprisingly supportive of his predicament.

"I don't know what I would do in that situation," Calvin said, taking a sip of his cocktail. "I'd say if you just punched the guy one time over that—I don't know, to me that seems like a pretty level-headed reaction."

Relic grinned. "Yeah, but it wasn't him that did it. So I was kind of out of line."

"Wait," Dina said, breaking off a piece of breadstick, "so who played the tape? Miranda?"

Relic nodded. "I guess Miranda has some problem with Bree now."

"I'll tell you what her problem is," Dina said angrily, "Miranda probably got called gay for hanging out with Bree and did what all shallow teen girls do and decided she had to throw Bree into the line of fire to stay out of the crosshairs herself."

"I thought they were like...together last year," Relic said, swirling his straw in his Diet Coke. "But Bree seemed pretty pissed when I said she was her ex-girlfriend."

"Relic," Dina said, more calmly, "I told you, Bree is not a lesbian. I mean, she can be whatever she wants, and she has her whole life to figure that out, but she isn't. I admit, I also thought she might have been before, but after talking to her recently...I'm pretty certain she's not."

Frowning, Relic had trouble accepting that. "Why hasn't she ever said anything, then? Everyone says she is. I've even sort of said so in front of her." Or had he? He couldn't really recall a specific direct discussion about it, but he certainly had to have implied it at one point.

"Why should she?" Dina asked, taking a sip of her wine. "You think she's going to open up to a bunch of kids who tease her about her orientation? And you," Dina added, pointing to Relic with her half of a breadstick, "she probably thinks you should know by now."

"Know what?"

"Are we ready to order?" the waitress asked, bringing Relic a fresh Diet Coke even though his was still half full.

"Definitely," Dina said, and they each put in their order. Afterward, she crossed her hands and looked at Relic, "Calvin and I have something we'd like to talk to you about."

Oh shit, Relic thought. Never the words you wanted to hear when being treated to your favorite dinner. It's either bad news or a lecture or both.

"As you know," Dina continued, "Cal and I have been seeing a lot of each other lately. I hope you'll agree with me that he's a very nice man who's always there for us."

"You're getting married?" Relic asked, looking directly at Calvin.

"No!" Calvin gasped with a laugh, "No, no, no."

"Four?" Dina said with a laugh, glaring at him. "That required four noes? Really, Cal?"

"I just mean, we wouldn't drop that on you, like, out of nowhere, Relic—besides, your mom is still technically married."

Dina looked back at her son. "Yeah, those sorts of things take time, Relic. No, we just wanted to let you know that we've begun dating. Because I think you should know, and Calvin suggested that we tell you."

"Ok," Relic said, not really sure how to feel. As usual, he couldn't logically fault his mom for moving on after being abandoned by his dad, but he couldn't help the bitterness he felt over it.

"Ok," Dina repeated, grasping Cal's hand as she smiled at both of them.

As bitter as he was, Relic couldn't help but smile as well as he bit into another breadstick.

That night, Relic got a surprising phone call.

"I heard you got in a fight," Delilah said. "You alright?"

Relic tried to adopt the coolest boxer voice he could muster. "You should see the other guy."

"Huh?"

"Never mind," Relic mumbled, messing up a perfect joke. "It was just a stupid thing with Tyler. We worked it out during detention."

"Oh, good," she replied.

An awkward silence followed.

"So, my mom just told me that she's dating someone," Relic said, struggling to think of something to say.

"Has she not dated since your dad?"

"No," Relic said, having nothing else to really offer on the topic.

"Oh, that must be weird."

"Yeah." Another awkward silence followed. He almost jumped into the story about when he thought his mom was dating a couple years ago, but there were a lot of details to that story that only Bree would have appreciated.

"Well, I just wanted to see if you were okay," Delilah said.

"Yeah, thanks, I'm alright. See you in art tomorrow?"

"See ya." She hung up.

Relic hung up the phone, but kept his hand on the headset, tapping it with a finger. He picked it back up and called Bree.

"Hello?"

"Hi, Mr. Thompkins, it's Relic."

"Oh, hey! I figured you'd be at Nick's."

"Huh?"

"Bree went over there to practice after school."

"Oh, right," Relic said, pretending to know exactly what he was talking about. He pictured his bassist and guitarist making out on Nick's couch and wanted to die inside. "I'll just catch her at school tomorrow."

Now filled with violent energy, Relic went to the basement to pick up his sticks and hit things very hard and very fast.

Hours later, Relic fell asleep watching his guilty pleasure movie, *Baby Boom*—one of the free used VHS tapes that he had gotten during the infamous "buy four, get two free" sale at The CD Palace. The last thing Relic remembered was seeing Diane Keaton's character, J.C., move to the country with her inherited kid before he was once again standing before his father silently playing drums in what he now accepted to be Alternus.

"This place sucks!" Relic yelled at his dad, his voice once again not making a sound. "How do I get you out of here?!"

Headbanging, Steven Meyers kept playing the same pattern now imprinted on Relic's heart. Even though he hadn't really sat and fully learned the rhythm, Relic was certain he could play "Alternus" to perfection at this point.

As his dad played, Relic continued to hear nothing. The atmosphere around him was swirling fog that obscured deformed shapes in the distance. Relic felt the presence of spectral watchers, reaching for him from beyond the shrouds, but something kept them at bay. As his eyes were drawn back to his dad, Relic realized that it was the drumming that protected him.

He wasn't empowering them; he was keeping them at bay.

The world shifted then, as if that realization pulled him from his safety, thrusting him—whirling and flailing—back into the cold bleakness of reality. It was there that he saw Larry Belinsky take shape, his large form solidifying from a cloud of impotent rage.

"You get that kid and his little slut back here!" Larry shouted into his phone, pacing back and forth in his hotel room. Relic looked around, seeing his surroundings through a strange black and white haze. He tried to look at his hands to see if he was also monochrome, but he had no physical form—it was like he was just a set of eyes, only here to observe in terrified suspense.

There was a knock on Larry's door.

"I don't care if you have to drag their parents with them," Larry snarled into his phone, walking toward the door. "You can even tell Marshall Crane that I said the little twerp he picked up for a publicity stunt is a goddamn thief!"

He yanked open the door. "What?!"

Relic could see that no one was at the door to Larry's room. The producer peered out into the hall, looking both ways. "What the hell..." After a moment, he slammed the door and went back to yelling into his phone.

"Stick's kid lives over in Greenbriar, start there. I need—"

Another knock, this time followed by a familiar scratching as if someone was dragging a blade down the length of the door.

"Goddammit," Larry said under his breath as he stomped back toward the door. "I'll call you back." He tossed his cellular phone onto his bed on the way back to the door. He again pulled the door open to an empty hallway. But Larry must have seen what just caught Relic's eye, because the man paused and bent down to examine the lower part of the door.

The words were scrawled vertically, but they were unmistakable to Relic.

"Release me?" Larry asked himself. "Is this some kind of game, Relic?"

Miles away, Relic's heart thundered in his slumbering chest. Did Larry somehow know he was here?

Larry held the door open as he peered carefully down either side of the hall. "Delilah?"

There was no answer. Larry stood in the hall, holding his door open as if afraid to go back into his room. His eyes were fixed on the words as a strange smile spread across his lips. "Same words your dad wrote at all the murder scenes, kid. This some kind of threat?"

Again, Relic felt like Larry was talking to him, but he wasn't actually there—*or here? Whatever*—to reply, as much as he wanted to tell the giant idiot that his dad wasn't the murderer. Like it would do any good.

"Tell you what, kid," Larry said, still staring at the words. "Go ahead and keep the tape. I won't report it to the cops. I'll chalk it up to a loss. Just call your dad off. We'll finish up our little production, and you'll never hear from us again."

There was a sound of a door opening down the hall. "Hey, buddy, keep it down. People are trying to sleep in here."

"Blow me, pal," Larry grunted, still staring at his own door.

Relic heard the unseen complainer grumbling, followed by a door slamming shut. For a long moment, Larry just stared at the words etched onto his door, waiting for something to happen.

Finally, Larry spoke again. "We got a deal or what, kid?"

I can't talk to you, Relic thought, *I'm not even here, you psycho.* Relic knew how absurd the notion was, but he had become all too used to being the Widow's phantom cameraman, and he could feel her presence here, as if he *were* her. But Larry certainly didn't see him.

Suddenly, Larry's cellular phone rang from his bed, startling the big man back into his room. He picked up the phone, backing up toward the closet as if he saw something terrible on the bed. He pressed a button to receive the call as the phone rang again, pulling it up to his quivering cheek.

"Yeah?"

Relic heard the haunting voice that came through the device as if it were up to his own ear.

"Release me," it said, the same whispering voice that had followed Relic from his dreams.

"I can't," Larry said, his chin shaking as his eyes darted from one dark corner of the hotel room to the other. "I don't know how. Just tell me how."

There was no answer.

"Please," Larry said, "I don't have the tape anymore, look." With the phone still held to his ear, he opened the closet to reveal the safe where Relic and Delilah had found the demo. "It's gone!" His voice was a frantic hiss as he motioned toward the open safe sitting atop a small wooden alcove where his shoes were tucked away.

"Release me," the voice said again, a skipping record that repeated the same words at the same terrifying frequency.

Larry spun around, his eyes wild. "I can't, you bitch! Leave me alone!"

There was a click on the phone as if the other line disconnected, and Larry suddenly clutched his chest. He dropped the phone as he stumbled back onto his large ass, both hands clutching his shoulder as if he were having a heart attack. Relic saw blood begin staining Larry's sweaty shirt, and the man's eyes went wider than before. He looked down at the blood and ripped his shirt open to reveal a pair of hairy, sagging breasts. The words "release me" were being carved onto his chest—right over his heart—by an invisible blade.

Larry choked as if he couldn't speak through the pain, falling to his back. As his body thudded to the floor, it seemed to shake the entire room, and the open safe fell off its shelf and smashed Larry's head with a sickening sound—like a watermelon full of rocks being run over by a car.

The hotel room began to fade as Larry's body went still, the thundering drums of "Alternus" taking Relic back to reality.

When he woke up, Relic was wearing headphones listening to the tape he had taken from Natalie's. He must have somehow found the tape and put it into his portable cassette player in his sleep.

Strangely calm after a sickening nightmare, Relic stayed in his bed, staring at the ceiling. He rewound the tape and played it from the beginning. And then again. And again.

By the time the sun began to rise, he felt like he knew every part of that wretched song.

And he was ready to play it.

Chapter 17

The next morning, Relic left early to go to Bree's. Normally, she would come to his house since it was on the way to the bus stop, but despite everything else that happened yesterday, he really wanted to apologize to her.

"What are you doing?" Bree asked him, walking across her front yard.

"What are *you* doing?" He grinned, adjusting his backpack.

Bree looked down as she approached, appearing uncharacteristically shy. "I was going to come over early so I could apologize."

Relic was genuinely taken aback. "Apologize for what?"

"I'm sorry I snapped at you yesterday after history. I should have told you about what happened with Miranda." Bree kept walking past Relic, so he fell in with her as they took a slow pace toward the bus stop. "I know you think me and her were like...together, but that's not what it was like. People kept talking about me and her being lesbians, like, all through eighth grade. So I tried to talk to her about it before I left for the summer, but she got all weird, like I had pretended to be her friend or something."

Relic wasn't quite sure what to make of any of this. "So, do you mean, like, you were into her, but she wasn't into you?"

Bree stopped and turned to him. "Relic, I'm not a lesbian."

Relic just stared at her, not sure what to say. Apparently, his mom was right. But how had he convinced himself with such certainty that Bree was gay?

"I know everyone thinks I am, and I know you did—hell, even my parents did until this summer," Bree said, shaking her head and looking away, "which is fine, I never argued the point, because, honestly, it was just easier for me. I was always so annoyed that it mattered if I liked a girl or not—I mean, so what if I do? Does that mean I can't like a guy too?"

Even though his own mind was now racing, Relic couldn't stop coming back to the memory in sixth grade, when they were camping out in Bree's back yard using her family's tent. Back then, they used to wrestle sometimes, and Relic always welcomed the opportunity to touch her—being a curious boy, there was a lot about the female anatomy he naturally wanted to explore. That night, Bree had been reaching up under his shirt occasionally, so Relic assumed it was an invitation to do the same, but Bree smacked his hands away when he tried and got super weird. That was their last night of wrestling and the first night Relic realized they were meant to just be friends—which at the time was fine by him, because they were awesome as friends.

He realized now, too, that it was also the night he first thought she was a lesbian. It may seem judgmental or stereotyping, but from the way Bree spoke, dressed, and behaved, it was easy to see why people would make assumptions about her, as much as Relic wished that wasn't how it would be.

"I'm sorry I listened to everyone else instead of asking you about it, Bree." Relic felt uncomfortable saying this out loud, but he knew he needed to. He needed to keep his friend. If he could be direct with Tyler fucking Richardson, he could be up front with Bree. "I think that night in the tent—I'm not sure if you remember—but back then, I think I got the wrong idea about us, and when you kind of hit me for trying to grab your...well, your—"

Bree laughed. Like, a bent over full-bodied laugh that made Relic recoil. When she caught her breath, she looked back at him. "Dude, I stuffed my bra back then. I thought you would find out."

After a moment of silent disbelief, Relic's mouth fell open, and he began to slowly chuckle.

Bree grabbed her chest. "I didn't have these, man, and Miranda did—lots of girls back then started to get them—and I went through this phase where I thought I had to fit in or something. I just didn't want you to know."

Relic laughed with her, but he couldn't help being slightly hurt that she would have hid that from him. Then again, it was probably nothing to her—to her she was just trying to avoid an uncomfortable explanation—while to Relic it held much more significance.

They continued their slow walk to the bus stop, recovering from their laughter.

"Oh, man," Relic said, as the levity died. "So you didn't think I was a creep back then?"

"No way," Bree said, "I think I was grabbing you more than you were grabbing me. We were kids, dude. Trying to figure stuff out."

Yeah, Relic thought ironically, *trying to figure a lot of stuff out...still.*

"Well, that's a relief," he said, "that's one of those memories that sticks with me. I think that's when I convinced myself that you were into chicks and probably why I stopped thinking we might eventually start dating."

"Oh," Bree said teasingly, "so if I don't want to get with *the* Relic Meyers, I must be gay?"

"No," Relic began, blushing.

"I'm joking, dude," Bree replied, putting a hand on his shoulder which felt so much different now to Relic. "No, I know what you mean. I think the reason I never said anything before is that—well, everything would change, man." She motioned back toward their houses. "I love hanging out, and our parents let us sleep over and stuff—I'm sure because *they* all think I'm gay, even though I sort of implied to your mom that I'm not."

"Yeah, thanks for that, by the way," Relic said in his own teasing voice.

Bree laughed. "Anyway, I just wanted to say, sorry for hiding that from you. I'm pretty sure Miranda did that yesterday because she still wants to distance herself from any possibility that she might be gay with me."

"I'm sorry I called her your ex," Relic said. "You could score a much better babe than that."

Bree shoved him playfully.

Despite all the emotions that her honesty awoke within him at the moment, Relic mostly felt guilt. Bree just opened up to him about something deep and personal, and he was keeping so many secrets from her—the dreams, the tape, the murders, Gate, his father, the Widow, his kiss with Delilah.

Delilah, he thought, remembering that uncomfortable call last night. Not even a day ago, he thought he had found the girl of his dreams, but with what Bree just told him...

"Just promise me something," Bree said as they rounded the last corner toward the bus stop. "Don't tell anyone. Just let them think or say whatever they want. I don't care if people think I'm gay—like that's such a bad thing, right?" She kicked a rock. "I'd kind of rather them make jokes about that than tease us like they did back in fifth grade."

Relic nodded but wondered what she meant by that. Would she be offended if people thought they were dating? Or was she just trying to protect him from being teased? As if he wasn't used to it in some form or another by now.

"Alright," he said. "I'll keep it between us. But what about homecoming?"

She looked at him. "What do you mean?"

"Well, you're going with Nick, right? Won't people kind of assume you guys are, like...together?"

Bree looked off in the distance, as if that thought had never occurred to her. She shrugged and shook her head, "I don't know, man. Guess it's a useless thing to worry about."

"What if we just didn't go," Relic suggested in a half-joking tone.

Chuckling, Bree shook her head. "We should go—seemed like Nick really wanted to."

Awfully concerned with what Nick wants, Relic thought bitterly, silently scolding himself for being jealous when he had smooched the new girl in town after committing what was probably a felony.

As they neared the bus stop, Relic saw Delilah, along with Paul Stevens, Miranda Cartwright, Tyler Richardson, and all the rest.

"That wasn't your dad, right, Relic?" Even when he was shouting, Paul still managed to sound like a snoring hog when he spoke.

Relic didn't answer, just gave him a confused look.

"That movie guy," Paul said, pointing in some random direction as if that were any clue as to what he was talking about. "Killed at his hotel. Said it was the same M.O. on the news, which I think means..." another snort, "motive."

The revelations from Bree made him completely forget about the nightmare last night. It was as if this kind of stuff had become normal for Relic—normal enough for teenage hormones to seem more important than supernatural killings. He turned to her now, and his face must have not been as shocked or confused as she expected, because she gave him an expectant look—as if she was waiting for some sort of explanation.

He shot Delilah a look as he approached, but she was waiting for more details from Paul.

"You mean Larry Belinsky?" Relic asked, trying to sound as clueless as possible. "He's dead?"

"Man, your dad's been busy," Tyler said, but Relic could hear the weightlessness in his tone—dude was taking swings entirely for show.

"Shut up, Tyler!" Bree snapped. "What happened?" she asked Paul.

Relic joined Delilah and she subtly took his hand as Paul crudely relayed what he had heard on the news. Not sure how, but Relic could sense Bree on the edges of his vision notice the hand holding.

Paul's speech was slow and slobbery. It sounded, for the most part, exactly as Relic had dreamed it. Struggling to understand what kind of connection he had with the Widow—so close that she would invite him along on her killings—Relic's mind wandered as Paul told his tale. He was so lost in thought that he didn't see the police cruiser pull up.

"Relic?"

He let go of Delilah's hand as if he had just gotten caught doing something terrible. He turned to see Officers Hayes and Barnes.

"We have to stop meeting like this," Hayes said without an ounce of humor on her face.

The roar of the bus came around the corner.

"You looking for his dad?" Paul asked.

"Go catch your bus," Barnes said, motioning for Relic to follow him. "We'll get you to school on time, bud. Oh, and you too, Miss Crane."

There were plenty of whispers and giggles from the other students as they lined up for the bus.

"Can I stay," Bree asked, her eyes fixed on Relic.

"No, you go on," Hayes said, motioning to the bus. "We have sirens, so we'll probably get your friends to school before you guys get there."

"Come on," Barnes said, much less chipper than the previous times Relic had encountered him. "We can talk in the cruiser. Hopefully, it'll be the only time you two ride in the back of one of these, right?"

Relic and Delilah didn't hold hands in the back of the cruiser, the former felt like a criminal and the latter looked like she was trying not to give anything away from her expression. She looked...blank.

A loud, staticky voice squawked through the radio before Hayes turned down the volume so she could grill the kids without having to yell. "I heard you two were at the Crosstown on Sunday, filming some interview material for a Larry Belinsky of Constrained Media."

"Yes," Delilah said, her voice sounding almost robotic.

"Guessing your parents knew you were there?" Barnes asked.

"Yeah," Relic replied quickly. "They had to sign forms. My mom was at the bookstore around the corner."

Barnes nodded, satisfied. "You guys probably heard that Larry was killed last night in his hotel room."

"Are we suspects?" Delilah asked again, once more sounding completely mechanical. Something about her current demeanor really unsettled Relic, and he almost wanted to scoot away from her.

But she still looked super hot, and he had trouble not thinking about their kiss every time he looked at her, despite their bizarre circumstances.

Both officers laughed at that. "We aren't interrogating you," Hayes said. "We're actually worried about the two of you."

"Relic," Barnes said, his voice soft and kind now, "whoever is doing this clearly has some sort of interest in you or your family. You have been somehow associated with each murder scene or victim. We want to keep you safe, but we need something to go on here if we're going to catch this monster."

"Have you seen anyone suspicious lately?" Hayes asked, turning around in the passenger seat and removing her sunglasses. "Maybe someone in Belinsky's company? That's a lot of outsiders in town, and trouble seemed to only start when they showed up."

Relic thought about Larry's crew, but honestly Larry himself was the only one of them that truly concerned Relic. The guy just seemed like a total creep. He shook his head, looking back up at Hayes. "No, it's honestly been a pretty normal couple of weeks." It was hard for him to keep a straight face while telling that kind of lie.

"Should I have my dad get my lawyer?" Delilah asked, crossing her arms.

Relic wanted to tell her to chill out, but her behavior honestly kind of frightened him at this point.

Hayes gave her the fakest smile Relic had ever seen. "No need, ma'am. We would just like both of you to come to us if you see anything out of the ordinary. Any information you might have regarding someone wanting to hurt Mr. Belinsky, please let us know."

The rest of the ride to school consisted of Officer Barnes trying to make small talk with Relic, but the tension in the car made it difficult to carry on much of a conversation. They mostly rode in silence, with Officer Hayes occasionally responding to the radio. The teens were dropped off in front of Chambers High, and Relic was relieved when Delilah excused herself to use the restroom—giving him a light peck on his cheek—while he proceeded to his locker.

Unfortunately, Tyler was waiting for him. He was standing in front of his open locker, staring blindly at its interior. But when Relic approached, Tyler leaned against the open locker door and spoke quietly to Relic.

"What's up with you and the janitor?"

Relic spun his combination lock, instinctively following Tyler's lead by not turning toward him. Out of the corner of his mouth he asked, "What do you mean?"

"Your dad's old bass player," Tyler said so only Relic could hear, "why are you guys sneaking around?"

Frozen, he shifted his eyes toward Tyler, who was giving Relic a knowing look. It unsettled Relic seeing his former bully not wearing that arrogant smile. "How did you know?"

Tyler scoffed. "Takes more than a haircut and a mustache. Dude's face is all over the albums."

The second revelation shocked him more than the first. "You listen to Unknown Oath?" To Relic's recollection, the only music that Tyler listened to was *Jock Jams*, those compilations of songs played during interludes at sporting events.

Looking back into his locker, Tyler shrugged. "*Lead Her Astray* mostly—Ricky's vocals are pretty sick on that one. Not a huge fan of the later stuff." He peered back over to Relic, his expression almost sincere for a change. "Is your dad really in town? I won't tell anyone if he is."

Relic shook his head, not sure how to respond. He had to give Tyler something, otherwise his curiosity might cause more problems for him. "I don't know where he is, but Ga—I mean, Gerald has an idea how we might be able to find him."

Tyler looked back to his locker and slammed the door, as if bored of the topic—*Whew*, thought Relic. As Tyler turned to leave, Relic tapped his elbow with a knuckle.

"Don't tell anyone about Gerald," Relic said when Tyler locked eyes with him. "I don't think he wants anyone here to know who he is."

Tyler looked over his shoulder before he leaned in close to Relic, his normal cocky smile returning. "Seems like we both got things to keep to ourselves." He shoved Relic into the locker; not quite that hard, but enough to make Relic's teeth rattle.

Relic hung his head, wondering how much more complicated his freshman year could get.

The bell rang, and on the tail end of it, the words "release me" echoed in his mind.

"Oh, fuck off," Relic mumbled as he slammed his locker door and went to class.

On the bus ride home from school, Bree and Relic got caught up talking about Altar Stone and their need for a singer.

"I mean, you can sing, right?" Relic remembered Bree remaining a member of middle school choir up until seventh grade. She had several solos at her performances.

She shrugged. "I'd rather just play guitar. If worse comes to worst, yeah, I could sing. But it wouldn't hurt to find someone who can just focus on that."

A sick part of Relic wanted to suggest Tyler as a contender, even though he hadn't actually heard him sing and Relic would be risking serious bodily harm if he divulged Tyler's secrets to anyone.

They continued talking about Altar Stone and which covers they wanted to prepare for the battle of the bands until they reached their stop. Their normal walk home was disrupted by Delilah who walked on the side of Relic opposite Bree.

"Sorry about this morning," Delilah said. "Cops kind of freak me out."

Bree—who must have forgotten about that entire situation with the police—asked for the details then. Relic left out the part about him and Delilah stealing Larry's tape and kissing in the elevator. When Delilah wrapped her fingers through his now, he felt so many levels of discomfort: he was still weirded out about Delilah's behavior around the cops, he was still hiding so much from his best friend, and after Bree's confession this morning—Relic didn't even know how to act around these two together.

Regardless, Relic squeezed her hand and said, "Seems like they're just grasping at straws. Like they don't have any idea who this is."

"I think the news is right," Bree said, keeping her eyes on the sidewalk. "It's gotta be some sort of copycat."

"Copycat?" Delilah asked.

Relic and Bree shared a look, remembering how new Delilah was to Laramie. Relic told her about the murders in Laramie that led up to the Dire Decade. "My dad's band were suspects for a while," Relic told her, "because there were so many killings near their shows. That's why people always give me shit about my dad being back."

He slightly loosened his grip on Delilah's hand, certain that she would want to let go of his after hearing about his dad. But she tightened her grip and ran her thumb gently over the back of his hand. Relic's body reacted predictably, and he nearly tripped over a crack in the sidewalk.

"I heard about some of that," Delilah said. "I just didn't know these murders were so similar."

"Well," Bree said, "mostly just Ted." She wiped her nose and sniffed. "I still don't get why they killed Natalie."

"Maybe it's something to do with The CD Palace?" Delilah suggested.

Relic tensed, hoping not to open this discussion. "Maybe," he said, quickly diverting things. "Oh hey, Bree, we still on for *Buffy* tonight?"

"Better be," she said with a smile.

"You guys like that show?" Delilah asked. When they both nodded, she gave them a sort of pitying look. "I don't really like its take on that stuff. Kind of makes a joke out of it all."

That's kind of the point, Relic thought, slightly annoyed. It was a fun show, not meant to be taken that seriously. The hand that Delilah gripped seemed to start sweating a lot.

"You want to come?" Bree asked, tightening Relic's intestines.

Delilah shook her head, "No, that's alright. I have to practice tonight with Sebastian. Relic, could we talk before I head home? Maybe at your house?"

"Sure," he said, curious what she wanted to talk about without Bree. "I'll see you in a bit, Bree."

"See ya," she said, her voice a bit deflated as she walked toward her house alone.

Relic led Delilah into his house, giving her a brief tour of the upstairs. She insisted on seeing his room.

"Sorry it's such a mess," Relic said, kicking some of his dirty clothes under his bed. "I spend most of my time in the basement where my drums are."

She motioned toward the Unknown Oath posters on his wall as she took a seat on his bed. "You still listen to your dad's music?"

"Alternus" played in Relic's head. "Yeah," he said. "I kind of grew up on thrash stuff, but lately I've been getting more into European power metal, like HammerFall." His eyes strayed from Delilah to the cassette player on his headboard shelf that had the copy of "Alternus" in it. *Shit*, he thought, gradually moving toward it. *Have to hide it...*

As he inched closer to the bed, Delilah shifted to face him. "Relic, we need to talk about Sunday."

He stopped moving. "We do?"

She stood up, taking his hands in hers as she looked up into his eyes. Her dark pupils were wide, and the black eyeliner framing them made it seem like he was staring at some sinister being seeking to devour him.

Honestly, he'd be alright with that.

"You need to know that I didn't kill Larry."

Relic almost laughed. The notion hadn't even remotely crossed his mind. Though, now that she said it out loud, it was the first time he considered the position they were both truly in. They both snuck into what would soon be a murder scene—Relic's third one in under three weeks—and stole something from the victim. Also, Delilah still had the room's key card.

"I know," Relic said, despite the doubts now flooding his mind.

She held his gaze. "It's just, I know how it kind of looks. I got mad at him when he was asking about my real dad," her eyes drifted then, scowling, "which is totally none of his business." She dug her nails into Relic's fingers, but he just gritted his teeth behind tight lips. Releasing the tension in her fingers, she locked eyes with him again and cocked the corner of her mouth in a grin. "Sorry. He shouldn't have done that, just like he shouldn't have tried to trick you. But I didn't kill him. I didn't even keep that room key—I threw it in a bush when I was walking home."

"I believe you," Relic said, feeling more than uncomfortable. While he thought maybe he was still in love with this girl, he was also growing more and more unsettled by her. Maybe that's what love was like?

She hugged him then, and Relic internally swore that she could unsettle him as much as she liked—he couldn't let himself mess this up just because he got occasionally rattled by her.

"You didn't do it, right?" Delilah asked, her head still resting on Relic's shoulder.

The question sent Relic straight back to his nightmare, hearing that sickening crunch of Larry's skull being smashed. He could smell the blood.

"No!" Relic said, a little too sternly. Delilah was jolted back from him, her eyes wider than before as she looked up into his. "Sorry, I didn't mean to scare you. I just—no, I haven't been back there. I didn't want Larry dead. I mean, he was a dick, but it's not like people haven't harassed me about my dad before. I wouldn't let it bother me enough to do something like that."

"No, I'm sorry," Delilah said, her eyes returning to normal. "I didn't mean to accuse you or anything. I mean, to be completely honest, I wouldn't have been shocked if you did kill him. He was scummy."

Relic laughed, not sure why—that wasn't really a funny prospect, murdering someone.

"I just want us to be honest with each other," Delilah said, stepping closer. "I really like you, Relic."

"Yeah," Relic said, his throat tightening up. "I like you too, Delilah."

Delilah leaned in closer, bringing her mouth up to his as she slid a hand up to the back of his neck. Relic felt her tongue in his mouth this time as she pushed her body against his, her hand firmly on his lower back.

Just like most American boys in their prime, Relic had seen tons of steamy scenes in movies, so he thought he would always know what to do in this type of situation. But his normally dexterous hands felt like he had just had them surgically attached to his wrists and he was just now learning how to use them properly.

He reached for her shoulders, then moved his bumbling hands down to her sides, then let one stray to her butt right before he felt like a creep and moved it back to her waist. All the while, her tongue explored his mouth and he felt like they were both trying to eat each other.

Despite how bizarre it all was for Relic, it was also amazing. It wasn't long before his mind was flashing back to that dream he had the first day he met Delilah, almost as if it were some kind of portent. He felt like he was about to explode again, but the phone rang before he could, startling them both.

"Sorry," Relic said, adjusting his posture as his body calmed down. "That might be my mom at work—sometimes her car craps out."

Delilah smiled, licking her lips. "Better get it then," she said teasingly. "I'll be here."

Relic scrambled out of the room as the phone rang for a third time, racing to the kitchen before the machine kicked on.

"Hello?"

"That you, kid?"

Relic looked behind him, making sure Delilah hadn't followed him. He lowered his voice and moved further away from his room, "Gate?"

"I didn't see you at school today, but we need to talk."

Nodding, even though the man couldn't see him, Relic agreed. "I can come to the basement in the morning."

"No, I mean now. You got somewhere you can listen?"

Of all the goddamn times, Gate, Relic thought, still watching to make sure Delilah wasn't leaving his room. "Make it quick if you can."

"Cops were here again. Asking me about that producer that got killed—same message left behind as the other two. They want me to come downtown to make a statement. I don't know what else to do with this tape, kid. If you don't have any bright ideas, I say we burn it like we planned. Maybe that'll keep the bitch quiet—for a while, at least."

"Like you said, Gate, she never came after you. I think I may have an idea; I'll tell you tomorrow, okay?"

There was a pause. "I don't like waiting, man. Cops could decide to search my place or the school after talking to me, if they don't like what I have to say."

"Look, I can't exactly tell you now—"

"Relic?"

As his heart tried to burst from his chest, Relic turned around to see Delilah. "One sec," he said into the phone before covering it and moving toward Delilah. "Sorry, it's just...uh, it's just my bassist—you know, Nick?"

Delilah smiled holding up a hand so he wouldn't have to explain. "It's fine. I just better head back home. I have practice tonight."

"Oh sure," he said, trying to hide his disappointment that things wouldn't progress further this afternoon. "See you at school tomorrow."

She nodded and kissed him one more time before making her exit.

Relic stood frozen, hanging onto the feel of her lips even after the front door shut.

A tiny voice called, "Kid?"

Relic put the phone back up to his ear. Realizing he couldn't lie anymore—he had to prove his theory to Gate—he quickly explained what actually happened at Natalie's apartment and then the hotel, once again leaving out the part about him smooching in an elevator like a badass spy.

"Jesus, kid. You can't keep this shit from me."

"I know, I know," Relic assured him. "But it's fine, like I said before, the killings skipped me—the Widow went right from Ted to Natalie, even though I had the tape. She either can't or doesn't want to hurt us."

"Yeah, what about her dogs?"

Relic had almost forgotten about both of those attacks. But now that he thought about it, neither time was he really close to injury. It was almost like those attacks were meant to scare him. But why?

"Kid," Gate said after another moment of silence, "just do me a favor. Bring the tape tomorrow. At least keep them together."

Something about that sounded totally wrong to Relic, but he agreed nonetheless. He was far from an expert on this whole thing, all he could do was go with his gut. "I'll bring it tomorrow," he said, "but you bring me anything you can on how this all started back in the day."

"Your pops destroyed it all," Gate said.

"Then remember whatever you can," Relic demanded. "I have an idea, but I need to know as much as possible about how this all started."

"I was drunk a lot back then," Gate said, and Relic could hear the gap-toothed grin on his face, "so I'll just get good and drunk tonight and see what happens."

Relic laughed, glad for the levity. "Sounds like a plan. See you in the morning."

Chapter 18

R elic headed over to Bree's house after a short drumming session to work off the lingering tension Delilah had left him with. He rang the doorbell when he got to the Thompkins' house. Bree took a while to answer the door, but when she did, Relic howled in laughter—something he hadn't done for what felt like way too long.

Standing in the open doorway, Bree wore an oversized Molly Hatchet shirt that had to have belonged to her dad. Her chest was sticking out as if she had two watermelons tucked up under the shirt.

"What's up, dude?" Bree said in a very deep voice. "I got the tent set up out back—thought maybe we could camp out. Maybe wrestle a bit?"

Bent over in a dry wheeze of a laugh, Relic couldn't breathe. He was so grateful for Buffy Tuesday at the moment—so grateful for Bree. "I'm gonna piss my pants, dude, stop." He staggered into the house.

Bree gave him a playful shove as she shut the front door. "Sorry, couldn't resist. Took me like twenty minutes to roll up all these towels though."

Finding a seat on the living room couch, Relic grabbed the TV remote and tried to catch his breath. But he froze awkwardly in place as Bree pulled her shirt off. Her two fake breasts made up of wads of bath towels fell to the floor as she tossed her huge shirt onto the nearby loveseat. Wearing nothing but her shorts and what Relic guessed was a sports bra, Bree plopped down on the couch next to him, comfortable as ever.

Don't look, man, don't look, don't look. No matter how much his mind tried to take control, his body resisted, and he turned to face Bree, his eyes straying to her boobs. *Idiot!* He finally managed to jerk his eyes upwards.

"Where are your parents?" he asked, hoping his voice didn't sound as rattled as he was.

Bree pulled her legs up and crossed them on the couch, hugging a pillow as she reached for the cordless phone. "Date night. Mom's actually not traveling this week. They left us pizza money. You in?"

Relic clicked on the TV, trying to keep his gaze away from all the revealed flesh in the room. "Abso-freaking-lutely."

As Bree called in their order (their standard large sausage pizza and bread-sticks with extra cheese dip), Relic flipped channels while waiting for *Buffy* to start. They had another ten minutes until the rerun began. As he was flipping, he stopped on VH1, which was airing a news segment. He saw the familiar face of Ricky Warren from Unknown Oath with the words "WANTED" printed under his headshot.

"...the police have not yet released any additional details, but former singer of Unknown Oath, Ricky Warren, is wanted for questioning in connection to the murder of lead singer of Gator Sponge, Holden Fey. Found strangled on the Gator Sponge tour bus in Boston two nights ago, Fey was said to have objected to his upcoming replacement. Warren and Fey publicly feuded for weeks leading up to Fey's last show with the band, but witnesses say..."

"Holy shit," Bree said, hanging up the phone.

Relic switched the channel.

"Hey, wait!"

"I don't want to know," Relic said, already imagining Paul Stevens at the bus stop asking if his dad's singer was the one killing people. He had come over here to forget all this crap for an hour or two. "I'm sure we'll hear all about it tomorrow."

Bree was silent as Relic kept flipping channels, finally stopping when he sensed her discomfort. He set down the remote as a toy commercial filled the silence and turned to face Bree. Suddenly, he didn't seem to have a problem keeping his eyes above her neckline. The expression on her face made him want to tell her everything that had been happening.

"What's wrong, dude?"

Relic swallowed, wondering where to start. "My dad came back here a few years ago."

Bree scooched toward him. "What?! How do you know?"

Careful, man, he told himself, knowing that it wasn't just his ass on the line right now. Gate didn't want his real identity getting out there. Relic knew he could trust Bree, but still he kept it vague out of respect for his dad's friend. "Someone who works at school told me; they went to school with my parents." Bree wasn't as focused on those details, fortunately, so he continued. "Apparently, my dad was trying to fix something from before he left."

"Fix something?" Bree raised a skeptical eyebrow. "But he didn't come see you, right? What else did he need to fix besides the family he bailed on?"

Relic laid out all the details he had gathered thus far, asking for her to keep an open mind when he referred back to the Widow and the werewolves. He was glad she didn't laugh at him, but he could still sense skepticism in the way she regarded him. It was as if she was trying to decide if he was crazy or not—which was fair, Relic assessed. He was still trying to figure that out as well.

"I think my dad," Relic shook his head, struggling to even speak his thoughts aloud to her. But when he remembered how Bree had opened up to him, he knew he owed it to her. Looking up, he finally said, "I think he trapped himself somewhere, and he's asking me to release him."

The *Buffy the Vampire Slayer* theme song kicked on, but Bree and Relic were too focused on each other. "You don't think the Widow is asking you to release her?"

Relic nodded. "Yeah, but if she's out here killing again, she's already...like, released, right? At least partly. Whatever my dad did kept her quiet for, what, ten years? Maybe he can help us do it again?" Relic motioned to the window. "But we won't know unless we bring him back."

Bree's eyes were distant as she turned from Relic to the TV. "Man," she said, taking a deep breath, "this is like fodder for an episode of this show. Can't believe we're even talking about this—just yesterday, I was presenting the Widow as an urban legend in history class."

Just then, Relic heard a howl in the distance through the nearby window. He grabbed the remote and muted the TV. "Did you hear that?"

Looking back at him, Bree narrowed her eyes. "Huh?"

They could hear the muted sound of crickets outside.

"Remember that dog attack during practice?" Relic whispered.

Bree's eyes went wide, her face leaning so close to his that their noses almost touched. "That was the same thing that attacked you on the shitter?"

"The West Laramie Werewolves," Relic whispered. "He told me not to tell you about them—he said the more people who knew about them, the worse it would be."

"Who?" Bree whispered.

This time they both heard the howl, and from the look that Bree gave him, she probably felt the same icy chill racing down Relic's spine.

Bree put herself between Relic and the window, peeking over the back of the couch as she tried to see outside. "What do we do?"

"Probably get away from the windows," Relic suggested, putting his arm around Bree's waist. Despite the horrific situation, he couldn't help feeling like an action hero as she hugged his arm in response. "Let's get upstairs and call the cops," Relic suggested, not sure what else they could do. Relic tried to pull Bree toward the stairs, but a slam at the front door threw them both back onto the couch.

"Shit!" Bree swore, sucking in a gasp of air.

The slam came again, and the door shook in its frame. Relic was frozen in fear, but he felt Bree disentangle herself from him and dart in the opposite direction.

"Wait!" He called, keeping his eyes locked on the door as it slammed again. Whatever it was, it was going to break down the door within seconds. Still, Relic couldn't force his limbs to move. He was pulled back into the basement restroom in Chambers High, when that creature's low growl had rendered him completely paralyzed.

He snapped back to reality when the next slam came, flinging open the Thompkins' door. The front half of a snarling beast came down forcefully onto the hardwood floor of the entryway. Each of its paws looked like the size of Relic's old catcher's mitt. "Werewolf" was the first thing Relic thought of when he saw the creature, but there was nothing cool or "Hollywood horror" about this thing—it was a nightmarish monstrosity with murder in its eyes. Those eyes were locked on Relic, and the thing snapped its jaws as it entered the house.

"Bree, run!" Relic screamed, scrambling off the couch. Behind him, he heard the thing turn the coffee table into kindling, just barely leaping over Relic as he ducked and raced into the kitchen. "Bree!"

Relic froze, not seeing any sign of her. There was no back exit in the kitchen, so he made to turn toward the garage, but he was too slow.

"Ah!" Relic felt ten daggers rake his back with what felt like two hundred pounds behind them, shoving him to the kitchen floor. "No!" He screamed in a high girlish voice, thinking he was about to die. Visions flashed in his head—not of important moments in his life, like the stories say—of Bree scrambling outside to safety. He hoped she could get away. If he was about to die tonight, he'd want it to have at least not been in vain.

Managing to roll over, Relic tried to push the thing away. The werewolf drooled all over his face as it snarled, snapping its teeth as it tried to eat him. From somewhere, Relic found the strength to keep the thing just far enough away, grabbing fistfuls of its ragged fur and pushing with all his might. Desperation and futility can do strange things, and for Relic, it currently inspired him to begin singing.

"The curse has come!" His voice was super off key, as he couldn't sing to save his life, but he felt the lyrics to "Alternus" deep in his chest as he shouted, "From far beyond!"

The wolf recoiled from him, its salivating maw snapping shut. Its menacing eyes still bore into him, and its weight didn't slacken, but it seemed to be suddenly entranced by the words.

Relic began mouthing the rhythm, "Boom boom, cha-boom, ba-boom-cha. Boom boom, cha-boom, ba-boom-cha."

The beast growled in response, as if waiting for Relic to stop so he could begin feasting. Relic closed his eyes and kept singing, hoping to continue distracting the beast from his dinner.

"Release me from this place!" Relic shrieked, his voice cracking as he tried to hit Rick's wailing notes. "I am trapped within by mistake!" Suddenly visions of his father flashed through his mind, still drumming in his lonely abyss. The lyrics to "Alternus" suddenly took on a whole new meaning, as if his dad were singing directly to him.

With the creature on top of him, Relic was running out of air, and soon he could hardly breathe, let alone sing. The beast took the opportunity, pulling its head back and unhinging its jaw wide enough to swallow Relic's entire face.

Relic closed his eyes again, summoning all his remaining strength, but it wasn't enough. He felt the beast overpowering him. Just as he was sure he would feel its jagged teeth dig into his flesh, he instead felt the creature spasm, letting out a pathetic whimper before it thrashed to the side. Relic pushed the thing away again, this time managing to slide out from under it.

He watched in shock and wonder as Bree—in her skimpy shorts and revealing top—yanked a long kitchen knife from the beast's side, spraying blood all over the tile. Like some savage Amazon warrior woman from one of their fantasy games, she buried the knife again into the werewolf, her face a mask of primal fury. The thing shuddered, kicking its legs in a futile attempt to escape its demise. But Bree screamed as she tore the knife free and stabbed it again, making it go still.

"Holy fuck," was all Relic could say between ragged breaths.

Bree let go of the knife's handle, leaving it buried in the coarse, blood-matted fur. She took a careful step away from the thing, watching for any life left in it. Satisfied, she turned and extended a bloody hand down to Relic.

"Are you alright?"

No, Relic thought, his gaze shifting between a dead werewolf on the Thompkins' kitchen floor and the bloodied, half-naked form of his best friend who was now a literal monster slayer. *I don't know what alright is anymore.* He took her hand, shakily pulling himself toward her.

"Whoa," a voice said from the living room.

Relic scrambled to his feet to put himself in front of Bree, both of them breathing a simultaneous sigh of relief when they saw a pimple-faced pizza boy holding their dinner. His wide, terrified eyes were fixed on Bree's blood-splattered torso and the dead monster in the kitchen.

Bree pointed to the living room with a bloodied hand, and in a much-too-calm voice said, "Money's on the end table by the couch." She hugged Relic from behind, resting her head on his back as she added, "Keep the change."

They waited on the porch for the cops to come, neither of them really hungry for pizza at the moment—or ready to watch Sarah Michelle Gellar beat up fake monsters. The friends just sat in the momentary silence of the evening until the sirens and flashing lights showed up. Relic had his arm around Bree, who now wore a towel over her shoulders. They both stood up to meet Officers Hayes and Barnes as they got out of the police cruiser.

"Oh my god," Hayes said, seeing all the blood on Bree under her towel. "Barnes, check on that ambulance, tell them to punch it!"

"I'm fine," Bree stammered. "It's not my blood..."

Hayes looked to Relic as if it were his. "What happened? Dispatch said there was an animal attack?"

"Yeah," Relic said, pointing to the house, "some kind of...dog, or something. Bree stabbed it with a knife. It's dead in the kitchen."

Hayes drew her gun and held it at her side with both hands. "Barnes, stay with them."

Officer Barnes had his gun drawn as well, putting himself between the teens and the house. "Move toward the curb," he commanded, keeping his eyes on the house. The three of them watched through the window as Hayes surveyed the living room with her gun swinging left and right. She stopped when her back was to the window, looking into the kitchen.

The radio on Barnes' shoulder crackled. "Barnes, get in here." The ambulance sirens wailed in the distance, getting closer.

"Stay here," Barnes said, moving quickly to the house. Relic and Bree watched as the cops stared into the kitchen, clearly shocked at what they saw. Paramedics came to check on them, but after a quick examination—Relic's back was surprisingly only slightly bruised—they went to the front door and asked the officers if it was safe to enter.

When they saw Hayes motion for the paramedics to go into the kitchen, Bree brushed Relic's shoulder with her hand and asked, "What are they going to do with a dead dog?"

"That's not a dog," was all Relic said. But they both got quiet as the officers came back outside, Barnes staying back to use his radio while Hayes approached them.

Hayes hooked a thumb over her shoulder back to the house. "Did he come in like that?"

"Who?" Relic asked, confused.

"The intruder," Hayes said. "Did he not have any clothes on?"

"It's a dog," Bree said, almost angrily, "of course it wasn't wearing clothes."

Hayes was taken aback by that. "He had a dog with him?"

Frustrated and still reeling from the adrenaline, Relic pushed away from the car and moved toward the window. "Hey," Hayes called out, causing Barnes to turn around.

"Stay back, Relic," he said. "This is a crime scene!"

But before either of them could stop him, Relic neared the window so he could see inside. In the kitchen he saw the paramedics tending to a naked man with long shaggy hair and a beard, who also had a knife stabbed into his bloodied back.

"What—no," Relic blinked several times, making sure he wasn't seeing things. As one of the paramedics shifted the man to his side, Relic could see the words seared into his flesh as if by an iron brand.

Release me.

"Come on, kid," Barnes said, turning Relic away from the window and leading him back toward Hayes and Bree.

"What do you mean a man?" Bree asked. "It was like a giant hairy dog, trying to eat Relic."

"He does look hairy," Hayes said. "Look, this has happened a lot before. People get attacked, their blood gets pumping, and they see things—people become monsters, their features become exaggerated. It's part of the human defense mechanism. Your mind is trying to convince you that whatever attacking you is scarier than it probably is, forcing you to fight back. We get it all the time."

Bree scoffed, looking at Relic. "No way, we know what we saw!"

Relic swallowed, remembering what Gate had told him in the basement at school. The night he finally tells Bree about the werewolves, they get attacked by one—it couldn't be a coincidence. It's almost like the thing was waiting for Relic to tell someone, infecting them with fear so it could finally attack.

None of that made sense to Relic yet, but what did make sense is that there was a dead man in Bree's house and if they kept talking about monsters, it might raise even more questions than they had answers for.

"I don't know," Relic said, giving Bree a knowing look, hoping she would follow his lead. "It happened so fast. Whatever it or he was, it tried to kill us—busted down the door and attacked me. If Bree hadn't grabbed that knife...I'd be dead."

Bree's anger melted from her face, replaced with doubt. But she didn't object, for which Relic was grateful.

"You see those burns on his body?" Barnes asked Hayes, turning his back to the kids and speaking under his breath. "Might have found our guy."

The murders, Relic thought. *They're going to try to pin the murders on this guy.* It was a slightly relieving thought, because it would shift any attention away from them, including Gate Murphy.

"Look," Hayes said to Bree, "this clearly looks like a self-defense situation. Once your parents get home, we'll get your statements. Can you guys sit tight while my partner and I go have a look around?"

Relic and Bree nodded, waiting near the squad car until Bree's parents pulled up. They were understandably panicked, but the police assured them that the house was safe.

"We suggest you find somewhere else to stay for the night," Hayes said. "We can probably have things cleaned up by early morning, but there's no reason to wait around for us. We'll have a patrol car outside to keep an eye on things."

"Thank you," Russ Thompkins said, holding out a hand to shake Officer Hayes' while using his other hand to hug his daughter. He turned to Relic. "Is your mom home?"

"She should be soon," Relic said, and the Thompkins informed the police that they would take him home after all the questions had been answered.

The Thompkins dropped Relic back at his house, and Bree walked him to the door.

"We'll talk tomorrow," Relic said. "Try not to tell your parents too much about the whole werewolf thing..."

Nodding, Bree looked down at her thumbs, picking at the blood still dried up along her cuticles.

Relic put a hand over hers. "I'm sorry, Bree."

She looked up at him. "For what? You didn't do anything."

He didn't know how to explain that telling her about the thing might have brought it to her—the whole concept seemed more and more crazy the closer any words came to leaving his lips. "I'm just sorry you had to do that. Even though..." he moved his hand up to her cheek, "I mean, it was super badass."

She laughed, smashing his hand between her cheek and shoulder. Putting her arms around him, she hugged him fiercely. "I thought we might die," she whispered.

"Me too," he whispered back, wanting to say more, so much more. But when she patted him on the back, he loosened his arms. She motioned to the approaching headlights speeding around the corner.

"She must have heard," Bree said. They watched as Dina pulled to a skidding stop in the driveway and rushed over to embrace Relic and Bree. They had to calm her down a bit before Bree could get back in the car with her parents, and then Relic had to spend even more time explaining exactly what had happened to his mom once they got inside the house.

"You did the right thing," she said, putting a hand gently on his cheek like Relic had done to Bree. "Trust me, with how things are around here, the more you say the worse things seem to get." She put both her hands on his shoulders. "But promise me, Relic. Be honest with me—I know how bad things can get, after everything that happened with your dad...just please, don't keep anything from me. You can tell me anything."

I can't, Relic thought miserably. *Not this.* But he nodded anyway and let her hug him for another ten minutes before finally convincing her he could really go for some sleep. When he finally got to his room, he collapsed immediately and fell into a wonderful, dreamless sleep.

The next morning, he woke up right on time, got ready for school, and went to get the "Alternus" tape to take to Gate—they had to figure this out...as in, today.

However, the tape—once again—was gone.

CHAPTER 19

R elic was in a panic all morning. He tore his entire room apart looking for the tape, even though he knew exactly where he left it. A thousand possible scenarios spiraled through his mind, each one more improbable than the last.

Did his mom take it again? No way. After last time, she would have confronted him about it; she likely would have been way too pissed to let that slide. Besides, he couldn't even ask her about it because then he'd have to figure out how to explain how he got the thing out of Natalie's apartment.

Did the Widow somehow break into his room and take it? If she wanted the tape, she could have gotten it a long time ago. All signs pointed at her wanting Relic to have the tape, so that didn't make any sense either.

Any possibilities that hinged on a break-in seemed unlikely, as there were no signs of entry or rummaging around looking for the tape. Unless James Bond was after this thing, it just didn't seem probable that someone snuck in and stole it.

The only other person who had been in his room—that he knew about—was Delilah, and she didn't even know about the tape.

Did she?

"Relic, aren't you going to miss the bus?" His mom sounded winded, and when he opened the door, he heard that she was doing aerobics in the living room. Her workout videos had the most annoying music.

As he rushed to the kitchen to grab some breakfast, he considered telling his mom about the tape to see her reaction, but he had no time to talk and even less hope that it would shed any light on the situation. Before leaving, Dina reminded Relic—through heaving breaths—that they had to go to the police station right after school to give their statements, "I'll pick you up, alright?"

Like I need more things to worry about, Relic thought as he said goodbye.

Not having Bree to talk to as he walked to the bus stop, Relic grew more anxious and frustrated. He imagined the Widow out there, stalking whoever had the tape—it was only a matter of time before there was another murder. An unbidden thought came to him that another killing would actually be helpful, putting him back on the trail; disgusted with the notion, he pushed the idea away and quickened his pace to the bus stop.

"Yo, Meyers," Paul Stevens called out as Relic crossed the street. "Is it true you saw the murderer last night? It wasn't your dad, right?"

Relic sighed, claiming a spot to stand on the sidewalk between Paul and the pop-squad consisting of Tyler, Miranda, Valerie, and Tammy. There was no sign of Delilah.

"I'm not supposed to talk about it," Relic told Paul. Hayes and Barnes had instructed him and Bree not to discuss anything about the event last night until they gave their official statements after school.

"Where's Bree?" Miranda asked in an accusatory tone, as if she were catching Bree skipping school. But Relic supposed it was because the girl truly cared about her former friend.

"She stayed at a hotel with her parents," Relic replied. "The house is still a crime scene."

"You alright?" Tyler asked, taking Relic aback. His tone was not at all accusatory or mocking, and Relic couldn't remember the last time he even heard Tyler speak so normally.

Relic just nodded. "I got shoved. The cl—" He stopped himself, almost saying the claws didn't break his skin. "The guy just tackled me, and then…" He couldn't really tell the rest, given the police's instructions. "I'm sure you'll hear about it all pretty soon."

"But it wasn't your dad?" Paul asked earnestly between snoring breaths.

"Fuck off, Paul."

As the bus roared around the corner, Relic still saw no sign of Delilah.

Gate sat and listened calmly as Relic explained everything that had happened last night, defying the cops' request. When he mentioned seeing the beast turned back into a man, Gate tightened his lips and nodded slightly, as if expecting it.

"There were four of them," Gate said, once Relic was done explaining everything—everything except the stolen tape.

"Four of what?"

"The werewolves," Gate said, getting up from his chair and going to his locker to rummage around. "That means there's one left. I got Gimpy Reece before school started—sonofabitch tried to jump me outside of a bar. Donnie was the one that I bagged in the basement before he got to you. I was hoping the rest of the band might have skipped town when the Widow showed up, but since your friend put Vern down—had to have been Vern, Jason was never that stupid—"

"Whoa, whoa, whoa," Relic said, motioning Gate to stop. "What band?"

Gate turned around, forgetting what he was looking for in his locker. "Lunaral Dirge. You never heard of them?"

Relic shook his head, but with the topic being werewolves, he thought a band name playing on the words "lunar" and "funeral dirge" was way too on the nose.

Running a hand through his thinning hair, Gate sighed. "I'm sure you missed out on a ton of stories with your dad on the road. Well, Lunaral Dirge was this local band that had beef with Oath. We played a lot of shows together, but we always butted heads about something—those guys thought they were Led Zepplin or something.

"Anyway, at the battle of the bands, when the shit went down, I guess they were doing dope down here," Gate motioned to the middle of the room where his chair was, shaking his head. "Why this place is significant is beyond me—some sort of hotspot. Well, whatever happened here, it turned them into those things."

Relic pretty much had to accept at this point that these were *actually* werewolves they were talking about, not just some giant dog urban legends.

Gate was staring at the chair, narrowing his eyes and cocking his head as if trying to remember something. "Your dad used to talk about Alternus being this place we can only see in nightmares... It's like insubstantial horror: can't really hurt us, but can scare the shit out of us. And these things...he called them Alternians," Gate said with a shrug, "could turn people into...essentially, monsters." Gate motioned to Relic, "Like werewolves."

As Relic's vision fixed on something—rationale or reason—that wasn't there in the room, he puzzled it out aloud. "So these jerks are down here getting loaded while you're up in the auditorium playing 'Alternus,' something happens down here, releasing the Widow and turning these guys into werewolves?"

Gate smoothed out his mustache as he listened, nodding along. "That's about the size of it."

"So you guys just...played the song, right? Nothing else different?"

"Well," Gate said, motioning with his hand. "That was the first time we had ever played it live. I mean, we had rehearsed it at Packrat, but that was the first time in front of a crowd."

Was that the important part? Relic wondered. *The crowd? A big gathering like...a ceremony or something?*

"What if we do it again?" Relic asked.

Gate looked at him, his brows creasing. But he didn't shake his head.

"Hear me out," Relic said. "If Unknown Oath nailed this song in front of a stoked crowd and somehow opened up some weird portal under the school, don't you think that's what my dad was trying to recreate by coming back here?"

Like a statue, Gate listened, waiting for more.

Relic's mind felt like a runaway train right now, making all kinds of conclusions that he couldn't possibly know, but something felt so *right* about this idea. "Maybe he thought all the tapes were gone, and there was nothing keeping the Widow here. But because there was another tape left, whatever he did only partially contained her because the part of her on that tape remained. But he didn't leave anything behind here for us to go off of, right? So now our only choice is to finish what he started." He pointed up. "My band plays—"

The bell rang then.

Gate shook his head as if already rejecting whatever plan Relic was going to lay out. "Better get to class, kid," he held out his hand. "Leave the tape here, I'll keep 'em together."

Relic showed his teeth in a sign of embarrassed admission. "Well, actually..."

After managing to get through a school day without any major incident, Relic was pleasantly surprised to find Bree at the school entrance, also waiting for her parents to pick her up and take her to the police station. They discussed how they were bombarded with questions from other students—and even teachers—regarding the attack last night, and Relic nearly let his conversation with Gate slip to Bree several times. Fortunately, he caught himself and diverted the talk.

Though, if he was going to enact his big plan, he would have to tell her something soon. And Nick. And they still needed a freaking singer...

Russ pulled up with Dina in the passenger seat, and Relic was grateful to get to ride with Bree. The afternoon traffic was bad enough on the ride downtown that Relic was ravenous for dinner by the time they all sat down in an office at the police station.

"Thanks for making time," Barnes said, offering Russ and Dina coffee—they both declined.

"Let us know how we can help," Russ said, taking a seat on Bree's side opposite Relic.

"Did you find out who that maniac was?" Dina asked, taking the chair next to her son.

"We can't disclose that yet," Hayes began, preparing her notebook across the table.

"Relax, Mindy, it's going to get out anyway," Barnes said, giving Dina a knowing look. "It was Vernon West."

"Vernon?!" Dina gasped.

Russ leaned over the table. "You mean from that band, back in school?"

Barnes nodded. "There have been a few complaints about his behavior, especially over at that bar they still played at up until a couple years ago. What was it called?" He turned to Hayes.

"O'Reilly's," Hayes said, checking her notes. "They called themselves Funeral Dirge."

"It's actually Lunaral Dirge," Relic corrected, immediately regretting it as all eyes shifted to him.

"Did you know the perp?" Hayes asked, raising an eyebrow.

"No," Dina answered for him, giving him a sharp look before turning to Officer Hayes. "We just have lots of posters and fliers around the house from old shows around town."

Nice save, Mom, Relic thought as he sighed inwardly in relief.

"Did he say anything to either of you?" Barnes asked. "Before the attack?"

"No," Relic said, once again explaining what happened, leaving in enough vagueness that their animal claims still made sense. Dina covered her mouth at several points during the story, gasping or whimpering accordingly. Relic could see Bree's dad's hands tighten into fists—he had never seen Russ angry before.

"Honestly, he should have been locked up," Russ said to the cops, almost accusingly. "He was doped up all through high school, and probably bringing all sorts of drugs into town—him and his vagrant crew."

"Well, he was locked up quite a bit between '91 and '93, and then again last year," Hayes said, checking her notes. "All assault charges, or disorderly conduct, but nothing to keep him away. He was out on parole up until...well," she closed her notebook and looked to her partner.

Keith Barnes leaned over the table, resting both his elbows on it. "Look, folks, this seems like a cut-and-dry self-defense scenario. With Vern's past, and the state in which he was found—pumped up to the gills with street drugs—I don't think we need to drag this out any longer. We'll type up our report with the details you've given us, and we can hopefully put this to bed by the end of the day."

"Is he the murderer?" Bree asked, her eyes shifting from the cops to Relic, as if he had the answers. "Did he kill Ted, and Natalie, and that producer?"

Hayes leaned in to prevent Barnes from answering too quickly. "We can't discuss an open investigation. But there are clear indications that he would be a suspect."

"Especially with those words burned all over him," Barnes said, raising his eyebrows at Dina.

"Barnes," Hayes said sternly, "I believe we're done here, yeah?"

"You said he was hopped up on drugs, right?" Dina asked. "Do you think that's how he was able to break down the door? I've heard people on PCP can punch through a car window without really feeling it."

As the officers got up, Barnes nodded. "Well, he was loaded up on crank and also, oddly enough, something called Nexaphane, which apparently isn't even on the market."

"Nexaphane?" Bree asked, looking to her dad. Relic remembered Russ talking about that the other night, some sort of anti-hallucinogen or antipsychotic that Rothen was developing.

Russ looked from Bree to the cops. "Well, my wife works at Rothen, and we have heard that name before at the house."

Officers Hayes and Barnes shared a brief look between each other and simultaneously turned to Russ.

Hayes opened up her notebook and jotted something down. "Do you think we might be able to speak to your wife, sir?"

"You'd probably have to go through her superior, but I'd be happy to give her your number."

They exchanged information before leaving.

When Relic got home, there was a message on the answering machine from Delilah. She sounded worried, saying she heard what happened last night and wanted to make sure he was alright. Even though he felt ready to turn his brain off for the day, Relic picked up the phone to call her back.

"I saw the news," she said, answering the phone after only a single ring. "Are you and Bree alright?"

Relic assured her he was fine, even though he felt far from it. Despite Vern's claws not breaking his skin, they had left painful bruises on his back. Not wanting to get into too much detail, he diverted the conversation. "What about you? Were you home sick today?"

"Yeah," Delilah said, her voice getting quieter. "Just...girl stuff."

"Ah," Relic said, not wanting to open that door any further. There was a brief pause, and Relic almost dared to ask her about the tape. He couldn't imagine her taking it, or her even knowing what it was or where to find it, but he had no more theories to pursue.

As if reading his thoughts, Delilah said, "Um, Relic...about yesterday."

Admit it! You took it, didn't you?! "Yeah?"

"Would it be alright, if we," she paused. "Would you mind if we took things slow?"

Remembering the rush he had gotten last time he was with her, the request was like a punch to his kidney. At the same time, he was kind of relieved—it was one less thing for him to stress about. Even though it was probably the part of his life that was the least stressful at the moment.

"Yeah," he said. "Sure. Sorry if I did anything—"

"Oh, no," she interjected, "that was all me. I just...I'd like to wait until homecoming."

Wait...what?! He felt like he was getting mixed signals now. The homecoming dance was a couple weeks away, and he had no idea what she was waiting for. Were they going to have sex?! His heart began thundering in his chest and his throat went dry. "Oh yeah?" He couldn't think of anything else to say.

"Yeah, I just...I really like you, Relic. And I'd like things to be sort of special, and memorable, ya know?"

No, I don't know! His mind was racing, and he was not prepared for this sort of relationship after the last forty-eight hours he'd had. "Yeah, I get it," he finally said, even though he really didn't.

"Good," she said in a way that Relic could tell she was smiling. "I just didn't want you to think I was being weird with you after yesterday. Like, I'm not a prude or anything, but I also don't want you to think I'm a slut."

"I'd never think that," Relic said with a laugh. "It's totally fine. I'm glad we talked about it."

"Alright, well, I'll let you go, Relic. I'm sure you've had a day."

He offered a weak laugh. "Yeah, it's been crazy."

"Well, get some sleep. Oh, and Relic…"

"Yeah?"

"Release me."

He froze, his racing heart stopping dead in its tracks. "What?"

There was no answer, just silence.

"Delilah?"

The dial tone kicked on and Relic stood there listening to it for almost a solid minute. When he finally hung up, he debated calling again, just to be sure. But what good would that do? Besides, what would he say? "Hello, Delilah, was just calling back to see if you were actually the Widow?"

After a moment of reflecting, Relic instead turned to go downstairs to drum, grabbing his HammerFall album on the way. With how much he had been hearing voices in his head, there was really no reason to assume Delilah had actually said anything. He needed to clear his mind and then get some sleep.

He was so determined to get his mind off everything, he even pretended not to hear the howl outside as he passed by the front screen door.

But he did shut the door and lock it, just in case.

CHAPTER 20

T he next week seemed to pass without any of Laramie's usual brand of bullshit.

School had seemed more tolerable to Relic since he and Tyler had developed a sort of standoff, and Delilah had decided that they should take their relationship slow—which Relic took to mean holding hands and the occasional peck on the lips was about the extent of their physical contact. She hadn't invited herself over to his house after school since that first time, and she never even really talked about her own home.

A normal freshman might find that an odd quality in their girlfriend, but Relic had been way too preoccupied convincing Gate to help them with his plan.

"Look," Relic said in the basement maintenance room on the following Friday afternoon, "it's been a week and no one's died. And that other wolf-dude hasn't shown up, so I think we've bought ourselves some time."

"It doesn't bother you that there's another copy of that tape out there?" Gate asked.

"Who says there is? What if whoever or whatever stole it has already broken it or taped over it or something? Besides, with how close together the other murders were, you'd think something would have happened by now, right?"

Gate shook his head, looking at the ground in futility. "You're asking the wrong guy, man. When it comes to this shit, your dad was the thinker. I was just his sounding board."

"Well let me think for now, then," Relic insisted, feeling a strange sense of assertiveness in the wake of Gate's doubt. "You can be my sounding board until we figure out how to get Dad back here."

Staring at the ground for a long moment, Gate finally looked up and nodded. "I owe your dad everything, kid. The least I can do is trust his son's instincts. What do you need from me?"

Relic knew that Altar Stone would need Gate's guidance if they were going to have "Alternus" down by the battle of the bands, but it might be tricky to have Gate over to his basement when his mom would be able to identify him. He was also hesitant to play the song at home, given that the last time he played the drum part, a werewolf busted his basement window.

Looking around the maintenance room, Relic had a sudden idea. "Could the band set up down here? Like, after school?"

Gate chuckled, looking around the room. "Funny you ask that. I remember skipping class with your dad and hanging out down here when it used to be a boiler room. No one ever really came down here. We used to talk about how it would be a perfect practice space."

"So, yeah?"

Nodding, Gate replied, "Yeah, I think so."

"Good, because we're going to need your help if we want to really nail down the song."

"And you're sure about this?" Gate's expression was more doubtful than the tone of his voice, as if he just wanted additional reassurance. "I mean, you said last time you played that song, one of Jason's crew came to your house."

Relic considered that, but then replied with, "Yeah, but wouldn't you want to lure him here? If he's the last one, and he needs to be put down before he hurts anyone else, shouldn't we try to draw him here and trap him or something?"

Gate looked genuinely impressed with the suggestion. "Not a bad idea, actually. And practicing at night will be less risky—I can put in some overtime requests to do some of the repairs that are backlogged, which should give us the cover we need."

After settling their weekend plans to turn the maintenance room into Altar Stone's new rehearsal space, Relic next had to figure out a subtle way to transport their gear to school without drawing any parental suspicion. But he already had an idea for that. The bigger issue still was finding a singer...

Relic called a band meeting after school, telling Nick and Bree to meet up for practice that night. He would have preferred to have divulged more of his plans to Bree, but because he had to get Nick on board quickly, he chose to include them both so that they were all on the same page. He had no desire to try to remember who knew what with all these lies floating around.

"I had this idea," Relic said, twirling his sticks in his basement as Bree and Nick tuned their instruments. Relic sat in front of his drums, legs crossed. "I'm sure everyone's going to be covering songs at the battle of the bands in April."

"Yeah," Nick said, "Bag of Sax is doing a Green Day song I think."

"I thought you said you quit?!" Bree asked, affronted. "Will they let you play in two bands?"

"No, I did," Nick said, "but their new bassist is in my study hall. Some girl named Shannon—looks kind of like the singer from No Doubt."

"Guys, listen," Relic said. "There's going to be a lot of covers, especially mainstream songs. Delilah said something about Autumnal Fall covering some Depeche Mode shit."

Bree stuck her tongue out, making a barf face.

"I think we could stand out playing something no one's really heard," Relic said, choosing his words carefully.

"An original?" Bree asked excitedly. "I have some riffs."

"We don't even have a singer yet," Nick complained, resting both hands on his bass. For some reason, Relic caught himself wondering if those hands had been on Bree during their little "practice" at Nick's house the other night. But he forced the thought away and stood up.

"I mean, we could try to write some stuff, but I think it's better if we have something we can start practicing right away."

Bree rolled the volume knob on her guitar and started playing the opening riff to HammerFall's "Child of the Damned," which she knew was Relic's favorite. He couldn't help smiling.

"What's that?" Nick asked.

Muting her guitar, Bree let it drop to her side as she turned to give Nick a look of stunned disbelief. "Are you serious, man?!"

Even though he didn't know why that set her off, Relic held up his hands to diffuse whatever it might escalate into. "Killer suggestion, but I had something else in mind. Something that probably no one in the crowd has heard—even though I'm sure most of them haven't heard HammerFall either."

"Hit us with it," Nick said, motioning to bring it on.

Relic explained how Unknown Oath had won their battle of the bands in 1976 playing a song that, essentially, had since been lost to time. He obviously excluded details about the truths around the song, relying more on the urban legends surrounding it.

Bree stepped closer to him. "Are you talking about the 'Alternus' tape? From storage?"

Given everything that had happened, Relic had almost completely forgotten that Bree was the one who had originally found the "Alternus" demo in his dad's box of junk. Hoping his shock wasn't too noticeable, he nodded his head to confirm.

"Oh, shit, seriously?" Nick cracked his knuckles. "Yeah, dude, we have to play that. Break it out. I've always wondered what that song sounded like."

"I actually don't have it," Relic admitted. "It's at school." He turned to look at his drums and then back to his band. "How do you guys feel about practicing there?"

Bree and Nick shared a confused look.

"I thought we were going to see *Event Horizon*," Calvin said the next day as he watched Bree and Relic disassemble the drum set in the Meyers' basement. "We'll miss the showtime."

"We can catch the next one," Relic said, folding up a cymbal stand as Bree tucked the last crash into the cymbal bag. "I really want to surprise Mom."

Since none of Altar Stone's members could drive yet, Relic had to get creative in regards to transporting their gear without drawing too many questions. Calvin—who was eager enough to bond with Relic that he would probably go as far as helping him hide a body—was the perfect patsy. Relic knew that Calvin's Jeep was the most logical choice to get all their stuff in one trip, but he just needed a good reason for Calvin to keep quiet about it.

Surprising his mom was the best option. Dina had long groaned about the junk piling up in the garage because the basement was the only place Relic could play drums. A brilliant idea came to him when Calvin offered to take him and Bree to the movies on Saturday morning while his mom worked. He explained to Calvin that he was going to surprise his mom for her birthday—which conveniently was the day before the homecoming game—by cleaning out the garage, but he had to move the drums to Nick's house...unfortunately, Nick's house was getting renovated—it wasn't—and they had to stash their gear at school in the band room until it was ready.

As proud as Relic was of his plan, he did feel a little guilty pulling the wool over Calvin's eyes. He promised himself that he would indeed clean the garage out on Sunday, which would lend some authenticity to his genius scheme.

Calvin grabbed a bass drum. "You ever think of getting a smaller set?"

"Heresy!" Bree shouted.

"We will not tolerate such blasphemy!" Relic added in a similar tone.

"You guys are dweebs," Nick said, coming back down the stairs, stepping out of the way as Calvin struggled to get the bass drum up the stairs. Once he was gone, Nick moved closer to his bandmates. "So, why can't he know about this, anyway? What's with the secrecy."

Relic was prepared for this. "My mom is kind of weird about that song. In fact, she's pretty weird about me playing drums at all, which is why I'm doing this for her birthday—getting it out of her sight, at least for a while. But I don't want to play that song here. There's just a lot of baggage with my dad and all."

Satisfied, Nick nodded, moving to grab a couple cymbal stands and following Bree who lugged his cymbals up the stairs.

I guess that's that, Relic thought, having expected a little more resistance. He grabbed the last two drums and followed them upstairs.

Knowing that Calvin had gone to school with Gate, Relic had to do some clever maneuvering when they got to the school. If Calvin mentioned anything to Mom about Gate working as the school janitor, well…that just might complicate things more than they needed. Fortunately, Relic was able to get out of the Jeep so he could direct the vehicle as Calvin backed it up toward the loading dock. Gate was waiting where they had planned, but Relic motioned for him to leave the door open and stay out of sight.

It was all downhill from there; they unloaded the drums and amps without incident with plenty of time to catch the next showing of their movie, with Nick tagging along despite not having really been invited.

As if things hadn't gone smoothly enough, Calvin treated the band to lunch at Fazoli's next to the Eastside 10 theater where *Event Horizon* was still playing. The movie itself was awesome, and Relic was overall having a badass day. But after they dropped Nick off, Bree also began getting out of Calvin's backseat.

"I'll have my dad pick me up here later," she said as Nick got their guitars out of the back. "Nick and I are going to practice a bit."

"Oh," Relic said. He'd hoped that they'd get to hang out that night. "Okay. Catch you guys later, I guess."

"Have fun!" Calvin said.

Bree slammed the door and waved. As Calvin put the Jeep into gear, Relic watched as his bassist and guitarist playfully shoved each other with their elbows, flirting their way up to Nick's front porch. The rest of his day's victories seemed completely spoiled now, knowing he wouldn't get to watch *Mr. Bean* and eat junk food with Bree like they usually did on Saturday nights.

"What about you, pal?" Calvin said, turning on the radio and adjusting the volume to barely a whisper. "Want me to drop you at your girlfriend's place? Or maybe pick her up?"

Relic shook his head. "No, I think she's got band practice, too." Honestly, he didn't really know, he just wasn't in the mood to be around anyone now. "Let's just head home and make sure my mom doesn't creep into the basement for some reason."

Calvin laughed. "Sounds like a plan."

After a pretty low-key evening, Relic went to bed early, looking forward to being unconscious so he couldn't think about Bree and Nick doing whatever they did when they were alone. Having spent more than half his life with Bree, he was still not used to this strange jealousy that kept plaguing him, especially when he had a girlfriend.

Thinking of Delilah made him feel even more morose. "Taking things slow" made him feel less and less enchanted by her. He was attracted to her, sure, but they didn't have as much to talk about as he'd hoped, and whenever he hung out with her near her goth friends, he felt so out of place. Even though he wasn't looking to get married or anything, he still didn't really like the idea of being with someone that didn't share more of his interests.

As he lay in bed thinking about all those things, he fell into an anxious sleep of bizarre dreams, none of which he would later recall with any particular detail. However, the rhythms that had come to ruin his more tame nightmares brought him back to the foggy place where his father slaved away behind a wicked-looking drum set. This time, there was no deafening silence…Relic heard every beat clearly, as well as every pleading word his father spoke to him.

"Release me…release me, son…please…my son…"

Chapter 21

Every evening the following week—with the exception of Tuesday for Nick's football practice (not to mention *Buffy*) and Friday night for the homecoming game—Altar Stone practiced "Alternus" in the Chambers High maintenance room with Gate advising them.

Monday night took a while to get started, as Bree couldn't believe that Unknown Oath's bassist was their janitor.

"Dude, you were sick on *Lead Her Astray*!" Nick was fanboying over meeting one of his favorite bassists as Bree confronted Relic.

"How long have you known?"

Relic had to tell her the truth of their meeting, about how Gate was the one who'd saved him from the bathroom werewolf. "Let's talk about it later," Relic whispered when he was done, glancing toward Nick, who was asking Gate how he played with his bass so high up.

"We better," Bree warned.

He was both surprised and extremely grateful that Bree agreed to keep it quiet for now. She had every right to blow up on Relic for hiding something so huge from her.

As if reading Relic's mind, Gate then asked the other members of Altar Stone to keep his identity to themselves. "I owe a lot of money around town, and the last thing I need is collectors knowing where to find me." He gave them both stern looks, avoiding Relic's gaze. "I could lose my job."

Relic guessed that was a lie, but it seemed like a fine idea for a cover story, so he didn't press Gate for more information.

Once the secret was out, they could focus on the music. Gate started with the rhythm section, breaking out the cassette tape and popping it into the extremely old tape deck that sat on a grimy shelf above the sink. The intro was the most involved part of the song, with the tom pattern that Relic had nearly perfected from all the times it accompanied his nightmares.

Those first few practices were not much fun, as there were a lot of complex parts to iron out. But Relic could tell that they had the talent to pull it off. It was just a matter of getting all the sections together so they could start playing the song in its entirety as soon as possible.

"Who's going to sing?" Gate asked when they were wrapping up on Thursday night.

Relic turned to Bree, who was winding her guitar cable over her arm. She made a painful face. "I will if I have to, but it's probably going to sound weird. Ricky has way more range than me."

"Maybe we could find someone in choir," Nick suggested, snapping his case shut and standing up. "I used to go out with Tammy in seventh grade, and she said there were a few guys with her in choir who were into metal and rock."

That sounded promising to Relic. "See if she still knows them."

Nick laughed, casting Bree a quick glance. "Dude, Tammy won't talk to me anymore. Not the best breakup."

"We can ask around," Bree assured them, heading toward the exit. "You got a ride, Nick?"

"I'll walk," he said, "I just live over past Teal Road."

"I'm heading that way," Gate said. "I'll give you a lift."

"Awesome!" Nick replied, clearly eager to spend some more time with one of his idols.

Once Relic and Bree were alone on the stairs leading up to the school's entrance, Bree smacked his shoulder. "You couldn't tell me your dad's bassist is our goddamn janitor?! Or that he killed a freaking werewolf a week before one crashed Buffy Tuesday?!"

Relic had no good response, other than, "I didn't know how to talk about it, Bree. I mean, you gotta admit, this is all so fucking crazy!"

"Yeah, but we tell each other everything, man!"

Do we? Relic wondered, remembering what it felt like watching her walk to Nick's house. "I'm really sorry, Bree. I thought all of this was just, like, me imagining things. And Gate—I don't know, I thought maybe he might be my only shot at finding my dad, and I didn't want to mess that up. He told me I couldn't tell anyone, just like he told you guys."

Bree set the end of her guitar case down on the ground, leaning it against the brick wall near the main school entrance—no sight of her dad's car yet—as she turned to Relic. "I get it...I just...ugh!" She hit her guitar case, clearly frustrated. "Is there anything else I don't know?" Her dazzling green eyes were tractor beams, not letting his own eyes stray from her gaze. "Tell me now if there is, or I'm going to kick your nuts up into your throat."

"Jesus," Relic said through a ragged laugh, trying to keep his composure with her piercing eyes on his. He nodded. "There is something." He finally broke from her gaze, watching the traffic through the door's narrow window. "My dad...I've been...dreaming about him."

"That seems pretty normal," Bree said.

Relic looked back at her. "No, I mean...these are, vivid dreams. Like I'm watching him where he is now, and hearing him. He keeps saying..." He swallowed, feeling a lump in his throat. "He keeps saying 'release me,' and I wasn't sure it was him before because the voice is all distorted, but now whenever I hear those words, he calls me son."

Bree's eyes grew wide, and there wasn't an ounce of disbelief in them. "The murders...that—that wolf-guy..."

Relic nodded.

"What's it all have to do with your dad?"

He had to explain his theory about Unknown Oath summoning the Widow by playing the song at the battle of the bands, including the new details he learned about Lunaral Dirge and Guy Valentine's band, Unkind Ways. "It's all connected. Something happened that night, some kind of door was opened, releasing the Widow. Then my dad came back to fix it and got trapped or something...I don't know."

Bree's eyes were distant, as if she were working out some complicated math problem.

"I know this all sounds so insane," Relic said, turning to pace in front of the stairs. He rubbed the raised skin on his index fingers with his thumbs; the blisters had now become calluses after so many band practices. He turned back to Bree. "But this town is insane, so I have to believe it, you know?"

"It kind of makes sense," Bree said, her eyes still focused on something that wasn't there. She motioned with her hands, a sequence of events. "If your dad came back here and stopped the Widow somehow, then us finding the tape triggered something...like, woke her up?" She finally looked back to him. "Which is why we have to play the song at the battle of the bands, right? You want to free your dad?"

Jesus, she got that quick, he thought with a good measure of annoyance. *I really should have looped her in sooner, dammit.* But he just nodded.

There was a car horn outside signaling that Russ Thompkins had pulled up.

Bree grabbed her case. "Why are we going to a stupid homecoming game tomorrow?! We should be practicing!" She shoved the door open, and Relic could only follow her, shaking his head in both disbelief and utter relief.

Bree and Relic were dropped off at the homecoming game the following night by Dina and Calvin, who said they would be nearby getting dinner if they needed anything. The game hadn't started yet, but Relic could hear hoots and cheers from the excited crowd already filling the stands. A couple times, he thought he heard a wolf howling, but after glancing at Bree—who clearly hadn't heard anything strange—he convinced himself he was hearing things yet again.

Delilah met them at the concession stand near the bleachers. She waved shyly to Bree as they approached and then took Relic's hand as she joined them. It was an innocent thing, but for some reason it felt weird to Relic, holding Delilah's hand in front of Bree.

"You go to a lot of games?" Bree asked, having to shout over the crowd.

"Yeah," she said, "my dad always sponsors local teams, and I grew up around sports. I know people probably can't tell from looking at me, but I love football."

Relic groaned inwardly. While he loved sports as much as the next kid in grade school, especially baseball, he later grew to despise the culture around organized sports, particularly when it came to youth sports. But he kept his mouth shut.

"I don't know the first thing about football," Bree admitted, "but I'm excited to see how Nick does."

And Relic's mood darkened a little more. He wished he didn't have such resentment toward Nick due to the current situation; his bassist was a super nice guy, and Relic didn't think he would have such a beautiful girl latched onto his arm if it weren't for him. But it felt like Nick was ever so slowly stealing Bree away from him.

"Release me, son?"

Relic snapped his head toward Bree. "What?!" .

Bree recoiled, her face scrunched up in confusion. "I said Reece's anyone? I was going to grab some snacks, you freak."

"Oh, yeah," he said, trying to laugh it off, "for sure."

"I don't like peanut butter," Delilah said—*Ugh, strike two,* Relic thought, *well, strike three if we're counting taste in music*—waving away the offer. "But if they have any Twizzlers, I wouldn't say no."

"Two peanut butter nectar of the gods and one chewy red stick," Bree said, shooting finger guns at them, "coming right up." She got into the concession line while Relic and Delilah found some seats. Fortunately, most of the other big groups of students were clogging up the higher bleachers, so there were plenty of open seats toward the front, where Relic knew they could make a quick escape once this whole ordeal was done.

"Excited for the dance tomorrow?" Delilah asked, hooking her arm through Relic's as he sat down next to her. They saved a seat for Bree near the stairs.

Honestly, he wasn't. Besides not liking dancing nor the music associated with it, Relic was dreading what Delilah may or may not have in mind for them afterwards. The side of him that enjoyed watching sleazy teenage comedies centered around cringy dudes trying to get laid had already envisioned plenty of outcomes, but he was torn between whether or not he even wanted to engage in that stuff with Delilah.

He turned to her, and all that doubt melted away like the wax of a candle retreating from a flame. "Yeah," he smiled. "I really am."

The crowd suddenly started cheering as the marching band took to the field, playing the school's anthem. Bree arrived shortly after, and they had snacks while they watched the performance. There were only a handful of times that Relic's freshman year felt at all normal, but this was one of them. He didn't hear any howls or whispers of release as he watched the homecoming festivities with his best friend and his sort-of-maybe girlfriend.

"Ladies and gentleman, please welcome our visiting team, the Benton Central Bison!"

There was an overwhelming wave of boos that accompanied a spattering of applause as the rival team took to the field. It amused Relic that the other high school's colors were so similar to Chambers High—green and gold—with the main difference being Chambers High had a much more vibrant shade of emerald green compared to Benton Central's more drab forest green.

"And please give a warm welcome to their sophomore linebacker, Adam Lavenza!"

This time, the crowd unanimously exploded in applause, with Delilah taking her hand out of Relic's arm to join in. Relic and Bree exchanged confused looks as most of the bleachers got to their feet to cheer this person onto the field.

"Who?" Bree asked, looking at the Bison as they gathered on the opposite side of the field.

"Adam Lavenza," Delilah shouted over the noise, as if that were enough to explain it. "You guys didn't hear about his accident?"

As Delilah detailed the story, Relic picked out the monstrous teen in question. Adam Lavenza looked like a gorilla, with thick arms that looked too big for his slightly hunched body. While his teammates were goofing around and rallying their few fans in the bleachers, Adam stood like a troll patiently guarding a bridge. Relic got a terrible feeling in the pit of his stomach, reminding him how he had felt in his dreams of the Widow.

According to Delilah's summary of the event, Adam Lavenza had been in a horrible car crash last week, and he was taken to a hospital where he was—mistakenly—pronounced dead. But Adam's father, Dr. Frank Lavenza, was a renowned surgeon, and he had reportedly saved the boy's life when everyone was sure he would die. Delilah said it had been all over the news, and no one expected him to be able to play today.

Relic couldn't take his eyes off the good doctor's kid. His arms appeared to have fresh scars all over, and his skin looked sort of pallid. And the way he just stood there, looming...he looked menacing and inhuman.

"I'd hate to go up against him," Bree said.

"Yeah," Relic agreed. "Nick better steer clear." He didn't voice his other concern as the announcer introduced the home team, knowing the quarterback was really the one who should be watching out for a monstrous linebacker. Tyler Richardson was leading his teammates out onto the field, pumping his green helmet in the air. For someone who apparently didn't want to be on the football team, he really seemed to enjoy the perks.

The crowd went wild, and Relic found himself clapping along, caught up in the energy. Deep down, he was stoked for Tyler, even if he didn't want to admit it out loud. They had a lot of good memories together, and Relic hoped they might someday reconcile. But for now, he was just hoping Tyler didn't get mauled by whatever the hell old Doctor Frank had stitched together.

Once the game started, Relic was quickly reminded why he'd lost his taste for sports. While he would admit it was more enjoyable to watch the game live, he would much prefer to be at a movie or concert. He tried to share Delilah's enthusiasm for the home team's performance—which seemed to be good—or Bree's boisterous support for their bassist who had already caught two passes, one of which was nearly a touchdown, but he just found himself eager for the game to be over.

The chaos began right at the start of the second half.

After the cheerleaders did their halftime performance of Backstreet Boys' "Everybody," the marching band came out to do some pop medley and Relic excused himself to go pee. On his way back from the restroom, he heard his father again.

"Release me, son...hurry."

The sounds of the game fell away and the rhythms of "Alternus" made him nearly stumble, bumping into a stranger.

"Watch it, fatty!"

Some skater in huge pants shoved him, but Relic barely even noticed. He closed his eyes and rubbed his head, waiting for the thundering drums to cease. When they finally did, he heard a wolf's howl echoing on the edges of the announcer's voice.

"Welcome back to the second half, folks! Our Ravens have got the Bison chasing them 14 to 3! But the Bison are bringing in their star player—recently recovered from his injury—number sixty-six, Adam Lavenza!"

The crowd went ballistic, and Relic spun around, looking for any sign of werewolves. All he saw were rabid sports fans, and he shook his head, hoping the dread he felt was just paranoia. He got back to his seat just when Nick caught the kick-off, sending Bree into a frenzy.

"Oh, he's got it! Go, Nick! Go!" She squirmed in her seat as she clapped, and Relic joined in, albeit a little reluctantly.

Nick was more lithe and long-limbed than many of the opposing players, and he dodged several tackles as he neared midfield. However, Relic saw what waited for him. Adam Lavenza no longer looked like a lumbering ogre; he was a human freight train barreling down on Nick faster than someone of the linebacker's size had any right to move.

"Oh, shit," Bree breathed, barely audible to Relic through the roar of the crowd.

Relic saw the hit before it happened, and he knew it would be bad. However, nothing prepared him for the sound of the helmets crashing together and the scream Lavenza knocked out of Nick as Altar Stone's bassist was heaved up into the air and then thrown back nearly ten yards, landing awkwardly so that one leg was pinned under his body.

"No..." Bree's voice was weak, but Relic could still hear it as the rest of the bleachers gasped. The ref threw a flag as the Ravens' coaches rushed out to check on Nick. The announcer came on to attempt to keep the crowd calm, but several students and some adults were shouting threats at the Bison's linebacker who walked away from the incident unharmed, resuming his hunched over troll posture near the rest of his team.

After a few tense moments, Nick was up on his feet, limping on one leg as the coaches helped him to the bench. He had his helmet off and waved to the crowd, giving Bree and Relic a thumbs up and a smile, although it was clear he was in pain.

"Man," Relic said in relief, just now noticing Delilah's iron grip on his arm. "Glad he's alright."

"Something's wrong with him," Delilah said softly, and Relic saw that her eyes were fixed on the Benton Central ogre that stood like a statue near his team's huddle.

Relic heard the howl again, and he noticed Delilah's eyes shift away from the field. He followed her gaze, out to the dark trees beyond the lights of the game. There was nothing to see, but he felt her grip grow even tighter on his arm.

"I'm going to go check on Nick," Bree said, her own gaze down near the sideline where Nick took a seat on the bench so one of the assistant coaches could check his leg. Relic almost got up to go with her, but he heard the howl again. He turned to Delilah, wondering if she heard it. Her eyes went from the trees back to Relic, a guilty look on her face.

She raised her eyebrows. "What is it?"

She heard it, he thought, *I know she did.* Why she was hiding it, he couldn't begin to guess. But the ref's whistle blew, and the game resumed.

As the teams lined up, Relic saw Bree down near the sidelines talking to Nick, who seemed to be alright. The coach was wrapping his foot, meaning he had probably sprained his ankle. Relic would have been relieved if he weren't watching Tyler look like a child as he took position staring down the goliath that loomed over the Bison's defensive line.

Time slowed to a crawl as Tyler counted down the snap, and Relic heard the howl again, drawing his eyes to the darkness beyond the blinding lights. A shadow dashed between the white globes, too fast to be anything natural.

"Release!" Tyler yelled from the field, his hands tucked between his large teammate's ass cheeks. "Me!" His words were drawn out echoes in the slow passage of time, and Relic couldn't turn away from the thing that came toward the field, taking shape as it now leapt the fence.

It was the last werewolf, charging on all fours as Tyler screamed, "Son!"

The present snapped back before Relic could react, Adam Lavenza plowing through the Ravens' front line as if they were toddlers. Tyler scrambled back in a panic, having no one to pass to; Nick's replacement was a sluggish wide receiver who hadn't yet gotten clear of his opponent. Relic was frozen in place as Tyler backpedaled right into the werewolf's path.

"Look out! Dog!" some people shouted, but still Relic couldn't move. He felt Delilah let go of him, but he couldn't look away from the tragedy unfolding on the field.

The werewolf opened its jaw and snapped at Tyler, but the quarterback must have heard its growl at the last minute, pulling his arm—and the ball—away just in time. Unfortunately, Adam Lavenza was upon him on the other side.

The linebacker's massive arm came swinging around his body and caught the werewolf's jaw, sending it flailing through the air back toward the fence it had leapt over. Adam seemed unbothered by the creature, his seismic punch next connecting with Tyler's arm, which was now in an awkward position having just avoided being chewed on. There was a sickening crunch as Tyler's throwing arm was pulverized by Lavenza, and the star quarterback went sprawling in a direction opposite the werewolf.

That's when the place went crazy.

Relic turned to see that Delilah was gone, with no sign of her amidst the sudden stampede of rushing bodies. On the field, the Ravens were trying to wrestle Lavenza to the ground, but the enormous dude was shoving them all aside like a rhinoceros fighting a flock of birds. Dozens of adults scrambled to check on Tyler who writhed on the ground, but Relic's eyes scanned the madness to find the werewolf.

He finally spotted the creature getting back onto its feet, the savagery knocked out of it by Dr. Frank's monster of a kid. Relic moved toward it, not sure what the hell he was going to do against a goddamn werewolf, but he knew he couldn't just let it get away. Weaving through the crowd, he kept his eyes on it, following as it slipped between the lights. Its shape started to shift, looking less hunched over and more upright as it crept along in the darkness.

It was heading for the school.

The song, Relic thought. *The song drew it here!* He broke off into a full sprint toward the loading dock, hoping the side entrance was unlocked. He was sort of grateful for the diversion on the field, but he couldn't help feeling guilty abandoning Bree and Delilah in that madness. But technically, Delilah bailed on him first.

Relic reached the side of the building, yanked the door open, and ran for the stairs to the basement. He could hear clawed feet on the tiled floor below. There were muffled voices, but he couldn't make out what was said. Forgoing any chance of stealth, he ran as fast as he could, taking several steps at a time.

"Hey!" It was Gate's voice, echoing from around the corner. "Get back here!"

Relic ran toward it, and when he turned the corner, he saw a sprawled naked man on the floor, the hilt of a strange knife protruding from his back. Gate stood over the man, a wet mop in his hand and a puddle of chemicals near his feet.

"What happened?" Relic asked.

Gate nodded to the strange blade in the man's back. "Belong to one of your friends?"

CHAPTER 22

Relic let Gate take care of the body as he went back to check on Delilah and Bree. He found both girls near the entrance to the football field, gathered with many other spectators watching Tyler, on a stretcher, get rolled toward the back of an ambulance. As Relic approached, Tyler—who was sitting propped up his arm in a sling—gave him a level stare. Something about the fear Relic saw in Tyler's eyes seemed to bring them both back to grade school.

"You alright, man?" Relic asked, stopping near the back doors of the ambulance.

"Please stay back, son," one of the paramedics warned as he and his partner lowered Tyler's stretcher so they could load him into the vehicle.

"Yeah." The quarterback's eyes locked on Relic. "Did you get it?"

Not knowing why Tyler would think he was some kind of a werewolf hunter, Relic nodded. "Yeah, he's down."

"Good," Tyler said, giving Relic a nod. "Thanks."

Before Relic could reply, Tyler was lifted into the ambulance.

"Where were you?!"

Relic spun around to see Delilah waving him over to her and Bree on the curb. He dodged the paramedics and joined the girls.

"I went looking for you," Relic lied, pointing over his shoulder. "I thought I saw you run toward the school." At least it didn't sound completely crazy.

"Did you see that Neanderthal try to kill everyone out there?" Bree asked him, pointing her thumb over her shoulder toward the field. "They had to sedate him or something. Saw some of those armed Rothen guys escort him into a truck." She shook her head. "There's no way they can let that dude play again."

"Where's Nick?" Relic asked, looking over their heads as everyone was filing out into the parking lot.

Delilah pointed to the ambulance that now pulled away. "The coaches drove him and a couple other players to the hospital, just to get them checked out."

Neither of them mentioned a giant dog, nor did Relic hear anyone else talking about it around them. All the talk was about Adam Lavenza, which was a bizarre situation itself, but Relic was relieved that no one would be looking for a werewolf carcass.

"There's your mom," Bree said, motioning to Calvin's Jeep navigating the rush of traffic trying to get out of the parking lot. Dina's arm was waving to them out of the passenger side window. "Let's go see if she can take us to the hospital and keep Nick company."

Relic set aside his jealousy and agreed, since he was also genuinely concerned for both Nick and Tyler. He turned to Delilah. "You coming?"

"No, you guys go ahead," she said, putting her hand on Relic's shoulder and stepping over to kiss his cheek. "I left something on the bleachers, so I'll just wait for my dad to get here."

Even though he was curious what she had forgotten, Relic didn't argue. He joined Bree as they made their way toward Calvin's Jeep, but when he looked over his shoulder to wave to Delilah, she had already vanished.

As Bree told Calvin and Dina the tale of the homecoming game on the way to the hospital, Relic—after assuring his mom several times that they were alright—pondered over the events of the evening. Mostly, he was curious about that strange knife and who had used it to kill the last of the Lunaral Dirge pack. Before leaving Gate to deal with Jason's body, Relic had watched the janitor pull the knife out to inspect it.

"This come from some kind of museum?" the janitor had mused aloud, turning the bloody weapon over in his hand. It was similar in shape to a combat knife, but the handle was carved from some sort of marbled material, with red and violet veins running through a gray surface. The blade itself was made from a green material, not quite jade and not quite emerald, but somewhere in between. It was hard to tell with the blood covering it.

"Not from any museum around here," Relic guessed. Leaning toward the knife, he could see strange, jagged characters along the serrated side of the blade. "I've never seen any language like that."

"I have," Gate said, lowering the knife before telling Relic to get back to his friends. "We'll talk about this later."

Back in the car, Relic was startled when Bree laid a hand on his bare knee. He turned to her, seeing that she was waiting for some sort of response.

"Huh?"

"What'd Tyler say to you," Bree repeated, "before he got in the ambulance?"

Relic looked ahead, seeing his mom and Calvin discussing the stopped traffic, then turned to give Bree a knowing look. "Something about a dog."

He could tell she understood.

Dina insisted that they stopped for a quick dinner before going to the hospital. "Give the doctors some time to work," she said. "We don't want to get in their way."

Despite the crazy events of the evening, Relic definitely wouldn't say no to a burger.

St. Regis' Hospital seemed fairly active. Relic wasn't sure if that was normal or not, but he would guess this wasn't exactly a typical Friday night. Calvin, Dina, Bree, and Relic came in through the emergency room entrance. The waiting room consisted of three middle-aged men holding bloody bandages to wounded limbs, a sobbing child who didn't look injured but whose mother cradled her as if she might break, and a few other people who looked like they might be drunk or high.

Relic heard Calvin whisper to Dina, "What's going on tonight?"

"Full moon?" Dina asked, shooting a glance to Relic as if she hadn't meant to say that.

"You here for the football guys?" a voice called.

Relic and his companions walked over to the front desk where a nurse was typing at a computer.

"We're here to see Nick Weber," Bree said.

The nurse pointed to the door without looking away from her monitor. "Through the door and on your right."

They followed her instruction and found two assistant coaches standing in another waiting room with Nick and two other players, still in their football gear.

"Don't worry," Nick said from a chair, showing Bree and Relic his hands and wiggling his fingers. "I can still play bass." Bree hugged him while Relic clasped one of his hands like Dillon clasped Dutch's in *Predator*.

"Where's Tyler?" Relic asked, looking around. The other two players—Joe Reynolds and Mike Ferguson—had ice packs on their arms, each one covered in bruises.

Joe nodded toward an open door across the hall. Relic could see two adults talking animatedly through the doorway. "That hillbilly jackoff destroyed our chances at state," Joe mumbled.

Relic snuck away as Bree consoled Nick, avoiding Dina as she chatted with the coaches about what had happened at the game. Leaving the waiting room, Relic quietly approached the door to eavesdrop.

"...look, Barry, I can't force the kid to see him."

Relic saw Barry Richardson point a finger at the doctor. "Just write the referral, I'll make sure he understands."

"Dad, I understand, but I don't want to see him," Tyler insisted from further in the room. "You saw his son. Whatever he did to him, I don't want that."

"You're never going to throw again, Ty! We need to jump on this, or everything you've worked for is going down the toilet."

There was the sound of a pen on a metallic clipboard. "We'll get an MRI, but I've seen a lot of torn rotator cuffs—this one is likely the worst I've encountered. Your dad's right, Tyler. You may be able to throw someday, but you'll never get back to where you were."

There was a sudden crashing sound, and Relic could see a metal trash bin roll across the floor.

"Alright," the doctor said, "let's take a walk, Barry, maybe grab some coffee. Tyler, just relax here. I'll have a technician come get you in a few."

Relic turned away and leaned against the wall when he heard them leaving the exam room.

"Think about your future, kid," Barry said to his son as he left, his voice thick with restrained fury. "You don't want to wind up a deadbeat like your brother." He continued to vent to the doctor as the two of them walked past Relic without noticing him.

After they'd turned the corner, Relic slipped into Tyler's exam room.

"What are you doing here?" There was none of the usual venomous mockery in Tyler's voice.

Relic looked at him, sitting in a chair next to the exam table in a green Chambers High t-shirt probably borrowed from the P.E. lost and found. His football pants were smeared with blood, dirt, and grass stains. He still wore the sling, keeping his right arm pinned across his body.

"You alright?"

Tyler laughed. "Nope."

"I...I heard your dad—about you not being able to play again." Relic shifted uncomfortably, not sure what to say. "Sorry, man."

"Sorry for what?" Tyler said, once again without sarcasm. "Besides almost dying, I couldn't have asked for a better Friday night." His eyes got distant as he looked at the wall. "I just hope my dad doesn't try to get me to take up soccer or something."

Relic knew Tyler's dad had pushed him hard in sports, but he hadn't known the extent of the pressure involved. "Sports that bad now, huh?"

Tyler looked back at Relic, some of the attitude returning to his expression. "Sports are fine, unless you treat them like life and death." He glared at the door as if his father were there. "He calls my brother a deadbeat—Shawn was almost valedictorian! He's studying molecular engineering. But since he doesn't throw a baseball around, I guess he's good for nothing."

"So what now?" Relic asked. "Since you're done with sports. Still thinking about," he glanced over his shoulder before he whispered, "choir."

"I don't know," Tyler said with a shrug. "My dad is trying to get me to see a specialist about reconstructive surgery, but I am *not* seeing that redneck psycho." Tyler motioned with his good arm, pointing in the general direction of the school. "You see what that nutjob did to his zombie kid? I'm not letting him near me."

"Yeah," Relic said with a nod. "I'd definitely stay away." Unbidden, a crazy idea returned to him then, one that he laughed off last time—but now maybe it made more sense. "You know," Relic said, stepping closer to Tyler, "if you really want to stick it to your dad, and since your schedule is opening up a bit...my band could really use a singer."

Relic regretted the words even as they left his mouth. Time seemed to stop as he imagined all the different embarrassing outcomes: Tyler laughing in his face, getting pissed at even the idea of playing music with Relic, or really even just saying no. However, nothing prepared Relic for Tyler's reaction—which was nothing.

The former star quarterback just stared through Relic, silently pondering. After what seemed like far too long, Tyler nodded slightly and said, "Yeah, that'd really set him off. Honestly," he continued, his eyes refocusing and looking back into Relic's, "sounds more fun than choir."

"Seriously?" Relic couldn't hide the doubt in his voice. *Did I just find us a singer?*

"What are we called?" Tyler asked.

The use of "we" made Relic question how the hell he wound up in this position. "Altar Stone," he replied, on autopilot mode now.

If Tyler liked the name, he gave no indication. He simply gave another curt nod. "Cool."

"Sweet," Relic said as he turned toward the door, not quite sure if that was his cue to leave.

"Hey, Relic." Tyler's voice changed then, growing soft. "Sorry I called you fat, man."

Relic felt his eyes tingle, but whether it was because he was touched by the sentiment or angry at even being reminded of Tyler's bullying, he couldn't be too sure. Regardless, he faked a nonchalant smile and shrugged. "It's alright, I guess I am kind of fat."

Tyler shook his head. "No, that's...that's something my dad would say." Looking directly into Relic's eyes, he added, "And I'm not my dad."

Relic nodded and turned to leave again.

"Oh. What'd you do to the dog?" Tyler asked in a dismissive tone that implied he didn't actually care.

Relic faced him. "How'd you know about that?"

"After that overgrown corpse blasted my arm," Tyler said, "I couldn't roll over to see him try to kill the entire team. I heard the shouting, but I had to just lay there, staring at some huge dog running toward the school. Saw someone chasing after it. When you came walking from that way later, figured it was you." He looked distantly at the ground. "Only...it was weird...you look a lot smaller when you're running.

"And where'd you get those cool knives?"

Relic barely remembered the ride home, and when Bree asked if he wanted to hang out at her place, he declined—something he never did, and Bree would certainly suspect something was wrong. Fortunately, she couldn't really press him in front of his mom and Calvin.

Once home, he retreated to the basement and immediately dialed Delilah's number. Having no clue what he'd actually say to her—"Oh, hey, Delilah. Are you secretly the Widow, or maybe a ninja who killed a dog with an alien dagger at the homecoming game?"—he was more than relieved to get her answering machine. He hung up, staring at the empty spot where his drums used to be while he considered how everything that was happening was somehow connected.

Relic could no longer ignore the fact that nearly everything he had thought to be an urban legend in this town was actually very real. His dad's band somehow managed to open a portal to a hellish dimension where the ghost of a serial killer from the 19th century was somehow trapped, and now his dad was stuck there in some weird drum solo time loop and only Relic could get him out. And it turns out Relic might actually be dating the Widow, if she could somehow take human form.

Wouldn't the new girl in town be the perfect guise for a spectral murderer?

How do I know Delilah was who Tyler even saw? Relic wondered. *Because, you moron, she disappeared right when it all happened and then reappeared after*, his reasonable self told the doubtful self.

He'd have to talk this over with Gate on Monday. Tomorrow was the homecoming dance, and Relic knew he would have a busy day trying to figure out if he was going on a double date with Cecily Moreau, the Widow or Delilah Crane, the Werewolf Stalker. Maybe both. He laid down on the couch and rubbed his eyes, not wanting to have to worry about any of this right now.

It wasn't long before he fell asleep.

Steven Meyers once again provided the soundtrack to Relic's dream, and once again Relic wasn't himself. This time, however, he knew exactly whose eyes he looked through.

As he stared down at Delilah's hands, it was a surreal experience not having control of them. Similar to his experience in Larry's body while buying the copy of "Alternus" from Natalie, he was merely an observer. But he recognized Delilah's black-nailed fingers, even now that they were wrapped in black leather fingerless gloves.

Beyond her flexing fingers, there was a round table adorned with burning candles, all surrounding a familiar cassette tape in the center.

"Are you sure about this?" a man asked. Relic thought he recognized the voice, but he couldn't put a face to it.

Delilah looked up from her hands to see a robed figure with a hood pacing in the darkness beyond the candles.

"I'm not sure about anything in this place," Delilah said, watching the man. "But whatever is killing these people is clearly following this tape. And now I know it's not Relic."

What?! Relic thought, shocked that his girlfriend thought he was a murderer. Then again...hadn't he just considered she was the Widow?

"I know enough about the Meyers family to know any trouble in Laramie can be traced back to them," the man said, stepping closer to the table with his hood still hiding his face, "one way or another."

Delilah scoffed. "Whatever Relic's dad did can't be worse than what you've done, Daddy."

Marshall Crane lowered his hood then, the scowl on his face made all the more sinister by the candlelight below him.

"That's the last time you call me that," he warned, raising a finger. "This arrangement is purely temporary. Once we've set things right, this charade," he motioned to both of them with his finger, "will have run its course."

"You going to have me killed?" Delilah asked in a nasty tone. "Stick me back in the system?"

"More like pull you out of the system," Marshall said, turning to grab a book off a shadowed shelf behind him. "The company will have plenty of use for someone of your...capabilities. Once the cult regains control of the Rothen Corps, you'll join their ranks and retreat from public life."

"Fun," Delilah said. "I'm sick of homework anyway."

Marshall walked to a lectern that overlooked the table, placing the book upon it and taking position behind it. "Get ready."

Relic watched through Delilah's eyes as she reached below the table, pulling out a belt with two knife sheaths, one of which was empty. Wondering if Delilah could feel him blushing as he gave her low cut shirt an ungentlemanly stare, Relic watched her put the belt on and adjust it.

She rested a hand on the hilt of the arcane knife that affirmed his suspicion that she was indeed some sort of monster hunter.

But who—or what—is Marshall? Relic wondered.

As if in response, Marshall began speaking in a deep, ceremonial voice. "Our unfathomable Lord Adratheon, Harbinger of Gracious Afflictions and Maladies, I call for your guidance through the vast ways of Alternus."

Delilah cracked her knuckles, tilting her head to either side as she loosened up for whatever awfulness approached. She moved away from the table into the consuming shadows, watching the cassette wreathed in candlelight.

"Call your wayward spawn toward this artifact that binds her to our realm," Marshall continued, the light seeming to gather around him as his voice raised a terror within Relic. "Show us the path to realign the stars, returning balance to our ancient accord."

The flames on each of the candles swayed then, as if a gentle breeze had been summoned in response to Marshall's bizarre incantation.

"She's here," Delilah said, drawing a knife. She spun it flawlessly in her hand, and Relic fell in love all over again.

"I feel it," Marshall said in a whisper before raising his hands and continuing his ceremony in a full-bodied yell. "Mighty Adratheon, show us the way! Lend us your wrath and let us punish this traitorous one! Banish her to the oblivion!"

The Widow emerged from the shadows, a terrible ghostly presence that wore the rotting visage of a pale woman who was once probably beautiful, but now was a horror to look upon.

Delilah didn't blink, holding her knife at the ready. She stared at the specter of Cecily Moreau, and Relic felt every ounce of deadly hate that Delilah reserved for this creature.

"Now!" Marshall slammed the book shut, putting out the candles on the lectern.

The Widow shrieked as if the man had fatally wounded her, and Delilah leapt like a tigress, her knife's blade trailing a poisonous green light as it was driven straight for the Widow's heart.

But at the last moment, Steven Meyers shouted from the darkness beyond. "Noooooo!" His rhythm—the drums that always accompanied Relic's dreams—stopped then.

The Widow dissipated with the ceasing of the music, and Delilah crashed into the table, her knife driving into the cassette tape and shattering it.

Marshall Crane screamed in pain, as if Delilah had just stabbed him in the heart, and the Widow's shriek sounded almost like laughter as she faded into the sounds of Steven Meyers resuming his rhythms of ruin.

Chapter 23

R elic only remembered enough of his dream to know that the homecoming dance was going to be...complicated. He woke up covered in sweat,
unsure if the nocturnal visions he had about Delilah were good or bad. But
when it came to his girlfriend, those lines seemed to be blurring too often.

He still couldn't be a hundred percent sure that his date to the dance wasn't
the Widow, but he supposed there was only one way to find out.

Bree came over late in the morning so they could finalize their plans for the
evening.

"We should try to cut out as early as possible," Bree suggested. "We could
probably practice a little down in the basement and no one would even hear us
with the dance going on."

Relic loved the idea, but he was struggling with how to tell Bree about his
concerns with Delilah. He felt like he had to say something before the dance.
However, every time Bree mentioned homecoming, he thought about how
much he wasn't looking forward to seeing her with Nick. He could barely keep
a straight thought, much less plan some sort of intervention for his date.

They agreed to ride together to dinner at Grayson's, which was across the
street from the school. That way they could just walk to the dance and get
picked up by Bree's dad afterward. As they discussed post-dance activities, Relic
kept thinking about Delilah's "until homecoming" deadline for the brakes they
put on their physical relationship. There was a significant chance that either he
would die or his virginity would, and he really wasn't prepared for either event.

After Bree called Nick to relay their plans, Relic reluctantly dialed Delilah's
number. However, all his fears and concerns felt like paranoia when he heard

her voice. She sounded so infectiously excited about the dance, that when he hung up the phone, his nightmares were shoved to the back of his mind.

Now he was just concerned about what to wear.

Bree helped him piece something together, consisting of his old black blazer from when his mom made him get confirmed at the local Presbyterian church—it still fit, just a little snug—along with some black slacks and his nicest Iron Maiden shirt.

"Just be glad you don't have to wear a dress," Bree grumbled, admiring his wardrobe.

"I thought you wanted to go," Relic said, taking off the jacket.

Bree shrugged. "Eh, I know we had fun at the middle school dances, but mostly we just sat around and watched Howie try to do the robot to every song."

Relic chuckled at the memory.

"Why don't we just not go?" Relic asked, but even as the suggestion came out, he couldn't imagine making that call to Delilah.

Shaking her head, Bree got up off his bed. "No, Nick really needs this."

The way she said that, Relic could tell that his friend had feelings for their bass player. While she was a kind person, she was not shy about stating her own preferences over the comfort of others—it was a quality that Relic always appreciated about her. If she didn't want to go to the dance, but would attend anyway for someone else, that meant something.

While the familiar jealousy turned his stomach at the moment, he still tried hard to be happy for his friend.

"I'm gonna head home for a bit," she said. "See you at five."

Relic gently smacked her upheld hand, noticing that she grabbed it and held on longer than usual as she moved to the door.

He heard the words "release me" then, but he didn't let go until she did.

That afternoon, after reluctantly posing with his mom for a quick photo shoot while Calvin snapped way too many pictures, Relic walked over to the Thompkins' house and knocked on the door. His mood was mixed, but when Bree opened the door, his entire world narrowed in, and a painful realization hit him.

Breanne Thompkins was the love of his life.

The girl who used to have fart competitions with him stood in the repaired doorway of her family home wearing an emerald green dress that fit her body like a glove. Her red hair was done up in a tight bun with a few strands on the right side hanging loosely on her cheek. She stood leaning on one leg with an arm on her hip, a worried look on her face.

"Do I look weird?"

Relic was absolutely speechless. He felt like a bloated creep standing there gawking at her, but his brain just refused to function at the moment.

Bree shifted, stepping away from the door to let Relic in. She smoothed the dress out around her torso, pulling it down slightly. "Mom says it's supposed to fit this way, but it feels too tight." After shutting the door, she asked again, "Does it look weird?"

Relic finally blinked as he stepped backward into the living room, unable to take his eyes off her. "It looks awesome," was all he could manage. "Super green."

She laughed. "Yeah, I feel kind of dumb wearing school colors, but I figured I'd match your drums...can be our band color. Plus, mom says it goes with my eyes."

Relic smiled.

"Hey, who's this stud?!" Russ came walking into the living room with his camera. Lydia followed him with a glass of wine in one hand and a tissue in the other, clearly struggling with the emotions of the event.

I feel you, Mrs. Thompkins, he thought, wishing suddenly that he was old enough to drink.

"Let's get a picture of you two," Russ said, motioning for them to come into the living room.

Relic would never forget the night of the break-in, but with the replaced furniture, repaired door, and the kitchen cleaned up, he had an easier time dealing with the fact that a werewolf had invaded the home and was slain just twelve feet from where he stood.

"Get closer," Lydia said, looking over Russ' shoulder as Bree and Relic stood in front of the stairway banister. "Relic, put your arm around her. And Bree you have to put your hand on his."

The teens did as instructed, and Relic felt like he was about to float out of his body as he touched Bree. He had obviously touched her plenty before, but now it felt different—it was electrical and surreal. And he noticed when Bree leaned her head against his shoulder without her mother's instruction. For a brief moment, it felt like they were taking each other to the dance, and nothing and no one else mattered.

But when Bree said, "Come on, Mom, Nick's waiting for us," the storm gathered once more in Relic's mind.

Tonight was going to suuuuuuuck.

Grayson's was packed, as predicted, but Nick had reserved them a table and was waiting for Bree and Relic near the front door. Still limping slightly from last night's game, Nick wore a very simple tux that looked like it was probably his dad's from the 70s. He complimented Bree, whispering something in her ear that made her laugh, and then joked with Relic about him choosing to go "casual" for the event.

While Delilah's arrival didn't have quite the same impact on Relic as Bree's reveal, she still stunned him and made him feel entirely out of his element. As he watched her walk toward the group, her pale skin accented by an elegant black dress with lacy sleeves, black fingerless gloves, and fishnet stockings, Relic couldn't stop asking himself how the hell he wound up in this situation.

Any thoughts of last night's dreams were too distant to even make sense of at this point. He followed the group to their table as if he were in a trance. But he was jolted back to reality when he saw Tyler and Miranda nearby, both looking like Hollywood's version of teens going to a dance, sitting with Tammy Beck and some guy that Relic didn't recognize.

Relic saw Miranda and Tammy whisper something and then look toward his table, but Tyler leaned over to Miranda and whatever he said killed the mirth the two girls were sharing. Tyler gave Relic an extremely subtle nod before a waiter stepped up to the group's table and blocked Relic's view.

"Are you alright?" Delilah asked him quietly, as Relic pulled a chair out for her.

Relic took a seat next to her, across from Bree, and nodded. He thought of a quick excuse for his detachment. "Just...last night was a lot."

"Tell me about it," Nick said. "I'm actually surprised they didn't cancel the dance or something after all that."

"That probably would have caused more problems," Bree offered. "Anyway, since when did this town ever acknowledge the weird shit that goes on?"

Relic wanted to offer his own theory, but managed to hold his tongue, taking a long drink of water as the conversation drifted to more trivial matters. Dinner was a blur for him. Between trying to act normal for Delilah and watching every interaction between Nick and Bree, he felt mentally exhausted by the time they left Grayson's to walk to the dance.

For some reason, Nick seemed entirely preoccupied with what Tyler's group was doing, and he kept stealing looks at their table during dinner. Now as both parties walked through the dark parking lot toward the school lights, Nick seemed to quicken his own group's pace to follow. Secretly, Relic feared that Nick was trying to merge their parties. He wasn't ready to tell the band that Tyler was their new singer, and he also didn't want to spend the dance around Miranda or Tammy.

Fortunately, when they arrived at the dance, Relic's quartet split off from the popular kids, and Delilah led them toward Sebastian and his date, another guy that Relic didn't recognize.

"This is Trent," Sebastian said, motioning to the muscular arm he was latched onto. "He goes to Fortland High." Trent gave them all a nod, but seemed particularly interested in Relic, if his lingering gaze was any indication. "We met in a chat room," Sebastian told Delilah.

Trent wore a black vest (with nothing underneath) and had shoulder-length hair framing an emotionless face that sported a five o'clock shadow. Relic was no expert, but he was fairly certain this guy wasn't in high school. He looked more like a professional wrestler.

Nick leaned over and whispered something to Bree, who looked out onto the dance floor. She nodded and turned to Delilah. "We're going to go dance. You guys coming?"

Relic dreaded this moment, but he was both relieved and surprised when Delilah shook her head. She turned to Relic, "I have to talk to Sebastian. Can you and Trent wait for us here?"

"Unless you guys want to come dance with us?" Nick asked Relic and his new silent companion. Savage Garden kicked on at just that moment.

Relic looked at Trent, who gave him a grin. "I'm alright," Relic told Nick. "I have to run to the restroom anyway."

Relic watched his band members holding hands as they went out to the dance floor. Bree's smile was dazzling, and it hurt Relic's heart, so he let his eyes wander away from her as he walked toward the Little Chamber. He saw Tyler and Miranda kissing near the gym's bleachers, her hand gently moving up and down his restrained arm as if she had some sort of mystical healing powers.

Looking back at Nick and Bree, Relic saw them laughing and dancing, Nick's eyes constantly glancing past Bree where Tammy Beck danced with the guy who Relic still didn't recognize.

After leaving the gym, Relic walked past the restrooms, his hands in his pockets and his head hanging. The music and laughter of the dance faded behind him. He didn't look where he was going, but something guided him to the stairs, and eventually he was walking through the darkened basement halls. Before long, he was standing at the entrance of the maintenance room, Gate sitting in that lone chair in the middle of the room.

"You're lookin' sharp," he said, his voice thick as if he had just woken up.

Relic took off his jacket and threw it on the table with the old coffee maker. He crossed his arms and leaned in the doorway. "You ever have to go to these things?"

Gate laughed. "Nah, man. Your dad and I usually just hung out in my basement playing *Dungeons & Dragons* or watching scary movies." He leaned back in his chair, and it was then Relic saw the knife in his hand.

Seeing the blade triggered a crippling sense of déjà vu, and bits of last night's dream came flooding back. Before Relic could even say anything, he saw Gate's eyes latch onto something behind him.

"This yours, then?"

Relic spun around and saw Delilah standing there, her right arm crossed over her waist, holding her left elbow—an innocent stance that contrasted heavily with the memories he now recalled of her from the nightmare duel with the Widow.

"Can I have it back?" Delilah asked Gate, as if Relic weren't standing right between them.

Of the thousand questions racking around his brain at the moment, Relic could only think to ask, "What is it?"

Delilah looked from the knife to Relic, her expression softening. "I wanted to tell you, but...there's a lot you don't know, Relic."

Gate stood up. "I cleaned it off—figured you didn't want all that wolf blood on it." Holding it by its strange blade, Gate extended the knife to Delilah as he approached the door. She stepped forward to take it, and Gate looked to Relic. "You guys probably have some stuff to talk about. I'm gonna go have a smoke."

After Gate left, Delilah and Relic sat in the maintenance room for a long time before either of them spoke. Leaning against the wall, Delilah stared at her knife while Relic sat in the chair and replayed all the pieces of his dream that had finally come back to him.

He finally broke the silence. "Is your name really Delilah Crane?"

Without hesitating, Delilah said, "No. It's Delilah Valentine." She paused before adding, "Your dad killed my father."

Guy Valentine, Relic thought, remembering the video from the show. He stared at her knife. "Does that mean you're here to kill me?"

"No," Delilah said again. "My dad was a monster." She tucked the knife behind her and stepped toward Relic. "In every sense of the word. Those things that your pops set free, they made my dad a vampire. Just like they made that Jason guy a werewolf, and Cecily Moreau a murdering ghost."

Relic didn't have to mentally wrestle with what she told him, as it explained a lot—except for how she knew all this. "So, are you like half-vampire or something then?"

"Dhampir, they call it," Delilah said, not smiling despite the joking tone in Relic's voice. "One of those Alternians possessed my dad, made him believe he was a vampire—either out of fear or desire—and eventually turned him into one." She must have seen the skeptical look on Relic's face. "You know all the weird stories from around here? Those werewolves? Ghosts, zombies, whatever. They're Alternians broken free by the Widow, feeding off human fear and creativity to make our nightmares real."

Not entirely shocked to hear any of this, Relic just nodded. "And you're like...what? Delilah Crane the Alternian Slayer?"

Delilah crossed her arms. "My dad killed a lot of people—probably more than the Widow—so, yeah. If I can kill any of those things, I will. But we have no clue how many escaped and are still out there." She stepped closer to Relic. "But what we do know, is that they were all being drawn back here after you played that tape. And only by getting the Widow can we really figure out how to put an end to this."

"Who's we?" Relic asked.

That broke Delilah's confident facade. She looked to the ground and shifted her feet before looking back up into his eyes. "I need you to keep what I'm about to tell you a secret, because it could get you or your friends killed. Okay?"

It was a tall order, but Relic nodded, his curiosity piqued.

She lowered her voice, "Marshall Crane—my adopted father—is a High Warden in the Cult of Alternus. In 1794, Gustave Moreau became a member of the cult and eventually betrayed the order so he could use the cult's knowledge of Alternian hexes to afflict his wife out of his own superstition and fear. He discovered that the cult was behind the Curse of the Ninth. No one in the order actually knows how he did what he did, but his actions stripped the cult of their power."

"What power?"

Delilah shook her head. "Marshall says they once had influence over the entire world from the shadows, using curses and afflictions, blackmailing important people to do their bidding. They dealt in fear."

Relic scoffed. "Sounds like Gustave did the world a favor if he took their power then."

"Maybe," Delilah said, "but the cult had control over the powers they wielded. It wasn't until the Widow did something to break the balance that things got really messed up. Then, when the cult managed to seal her away in Alternus, their full power never returned and the cult slowly diminished.

"Marshall is the only remaining High Warden now," she continued, "and he wants to restore the cult by ridding the world of Alternians—he is certain their presence here is what has tipped the scales."

"So you're helping him?" Relic asked, standing up. "That's why you stole my tape?"

She looked down again, stepping so close to Relic that their heads almost touched. "I'm sorry about that, but I had to try to draw her out. When I found out the Widow was killing anyone who had the tape, I thought maybe she was coming for you."

Relic felt a sudden clenching in his chest. "So that's why you became my girlfriend? To see if I got murdered?"

She looked up with a grin. "I'm your girlfriend?"

"No," Relic said, not in the mood for jokes.

"I wouldn't have let her kill you," Delilah said, "But, yeah, I had to be sure."

Relic turned toward the door, but Delilah caught his arm.

"Relic, wait. You don't understand what this is like. I have part of these monsters inside me—it's in my blood. It revolts me, but it also gives me the power to stop them from hurting other people." She let go of his arm as he turned back to her. "I'm sorry I had to lie to you, but I was trying to protect you."

"I get it," he said, more sad than angry. It's not like he hadn't been lying to just about everyone since school started anyway. "So what do we do now?"

"Now, we figure out how we can help each other. But first," she grabbed his hand, "you should dance with me. Because this will be easier if everyone still thinks I'm your girlfriend."

Feeling sort of numb, Relic grabbed his jacket and let her lead him back to the dance. When they got to the gym, some Backstreet Boys ballad was playing, and he saw Bree slow dancing with Nick. Her head was on his shoulder, just like it had been on Relic's earlier, and Relic thought he might just crumble into dust. But he let Delilah guide his arms around her waist, while she put hers on his neck, caressing him with her wicked fingers.

For the rest of the night, they played the part of happy high school kids, hiding their dark secrets.

Chapter 24

The weeks that followed homecoming allowed Relic to focus more on his band. Bree helped him keep up with school, because they were in most of the same classes (despite not having them at the same time, unfortunately). Studying and practicing with her were good distractions from focusing on how heartbroken he was seeing her dance with Nick. Although, strangely, Nick and Bree hadn't since shown that same affection for each other as they had at homecoming. Relic wondered if that was for his sake, hiding their relationship so he wouldn't feel uncomfortable.

Part of Relic was grateful for that, but a louder part found it insulting; that is, until he would remind himself that he was partaking in a sham relationship with Delilah just so she could have an excuse to stay close to him while maintaining her cover as a normal, teenage human girl—he had no room to judge.

His home life had drastically improved since summer, with his mom in a consistently better mood than he ever remembered. Calvin was around more often, but Relic found he didn't mind as much as he used to. It made him feel slightly guilty, secretly planning on finding his dad while also allowing this man to pretend to take his place, but he tried to remind himself that even if his parents reunited, there was probably no way they would be like they were.

It was a sad reality, but one he figured would be better to accept than being blindsided by it later on. He just wanted his dad back, in whatever capacity.

September slipped into October, and by the time Halloween rolled around, Altar Stone had begun playing "Alternus" in its entirety, if slightly sloppily. Tyler had easily slid into the band as if he and Relic had never butted heads all through middle school. Nick and Bree only offered slight hesitations about his joining the band, but after hearing him sing Skid Row's "Youth Gone Wild," all doubts were put to rest.

School became much more bearable to Relic as well, with Tyler even acknowledging him in front of his popular friends on occasion. While the former star quarterback didn't go around bragging about singing for a metal band—partly because Relic made it clear to him that they didn't want to advertise their rehearsal space in the maintenance room—he also didn't pretend to not know his bandmates even if they didn't belong to the same social circles.

As for his relationship with Delilah, it had remained complicated, reaching a tipping point on Halloween.

At school, the two had kept up their charade, holding hands in the hallway, even going so far as to kiss occasionally when seen off school grounds. Delilah made sure to kiss Relic in front of Bree whenever possible, which irritated Relic, but he remembered Delilah's warning to keep the truth of her identity from his friends—he wouldn't do anything to risk Bree's safety, so he swallowed his misgivings. Besides, she was probably kissing Nick behind his back.

On Halloween, Bree and Relic always used to watch horror movies in the Meyers' basement, pigging out on candy—bought from the store, as opposed to knocking on doors in costume—while seeing how many slasher flicks they could get through before the sugar wore off. But Delilah pulled Relic aside at school that day, giggling as she took his hand and led him to an empty classroom between periods. When they were alone, her mood shifted immediately.

"Have you played the tape?"

Relic had told her about the last copy of the tape Gate had, and he knew the janitor wouldn't have played it on his own. He shook his head. "Not since before homecoming. Why?"

"Well something's happening," she said in a low voice. "I found two bodies this week, all chewed up, human teeth marks." She bared her dazzling white teeth for effect.

"I didn't hear anything about that," Relic said skeptically. He didn't think Delilah would lie to him, necessarily, but this was a dhampir who had tried to seduce him so she could steal a cursed cassette tape from his room—nothing was entirely off the table.

"Yeah, because I cleaned it up," she looked over her shoulder to ensure that they were still alone in the room. Kids walked past the door completely ignoring a vacant classroom with the lights off. Looking back at Relic, she added, "I need you to come out with me tonight."

"I can't," Relic said, "I have plans."

"Look, Relic. I know Altar Stone has been learning that song, alright."

He hadn't told her that.

"Which means it's not just the tape," she continued. "Your dad's band played that song live and started all of this, so your band playing it live now is doing something. So I need you to come out with me so we can find out what it is."

"Why do you need me?" Relic asked, refusing to abandon Bree during their spooky movie fest. "I'm not a damp-hair or whatever."

"She didn't come after you," Delilah whispered, pointing a black-nailed finger at him. "That tape left a trail of bodies, but you and that janitor hold onto it just fine. You're connected somehow. I need you with me to see if whatever is being drawn toward the music comes after you."

"So I'm bait?!" Relic snapped, startling her with his raised voice. "I almost got killed by those Dirge hounds, so let me assure you: they do indeed come after me!"

She kept a level gaze. "Relic, do you want to find your father or not?"

He seethed, but nodded.

"Alright, well Marshall needs some more information if we want to figure out how to recreate whatever ritual Unknown Oath performed. I have to bring one of these things back alive. So are you going to come out with me or not?"

Resigned, Relic agreed to go out monster hunting with his annoying "girl-friend."

After making plans to meet up at Murdock Woods near the Oakridge Ceme-tery where Delilah had found the bodies, they made their way toward the door.

"Oh," Delilah said, grabbing his arm as the bell to next period rang. "Remember what you told me about the attack at Bree's? When you hummed that rhythm?" Relic nodded. "Bring your drumsticks."

Relic felt like one of those dweeb drummers in movies or shows that carries their drumsticks in their back pockets just so people knew they play drums. But at least there weren't a lot of onlookers walking down Creasy Lane to judge him. Most of the neighborhoods drawing trick-or-treaters were a block in either direction, leaving him the sidewalk mostly to himself.

He tucked his fists into his jacket, bracing himself against the autumn wind. In Indiana, you were just as likely to have a seventy-degree summer evening on Halloween as you were to have a snowstorm, and right now it felt like somewhere in between. Relic tried not to think about the disappointment he had heard in Bree's voice when he canceled their annual plans. It was almost worse when she acted happy for Relic when he told her he had a date with Delilah.

Replaying the exchange in his head, Relic blew an angry breath between his chattering teeth.

"We can just do our Halloween another night," Bree said in a nonchalant tone that Relic sensed was forced. "You guys go have fun."

Fun, Relic thought miserably. He was walking toward a cemetery so his half-vampire fake girlfriend could use him as monster bait on a chilly Halloween night. *Super fun.* But he reminded himself that his dad needed him, and Delilah was right: they still had to know more about the circumstances of Unknown Oath's fateful battle of the bands if they hoped to recreate it.

As he approached Murdock Woods, Relic saw Delilah leaning against a tree, draped in a black cloak.

"I didn't know we were wearing costumes," Relic said, climbing up the small grassy hill where she stood sentinel. "I would have dressed up as a giant worm on a hook."

"Cute," Delilah said, not sounding impressed. She pulled her cape back to reveal her knives at her waist. "Easier to hide in plain sight." Motioning across the street, she added, "I found one of the bodies just outside the cemetery. Like some pedestrian just got jumped. But whatever did the jumping wasn't clever enough to clean up after themselves."

"More dogs?" Relic asked, pulling out his drumsticks and spinning them through his fingers so his hands had something to do.

"I'm thinking ghouls," Delilah said, her gaze drifting to Relic's twirling sticks. "If we can find them, I want you to try to do the same thing you did with the werewolf. Hum, tap, whatever, just see if you can keep their focus while I incapacitate them."

"You mean kill them?"

Delilah closed her cloak and stepped down from her post. "Only if we have to. I mean, if there's more than one, then yeah. But I need to bring one back to Marshall alive." She nodded to his drumsticks. "That's why I want to see if you can distract them."

Relic followed her across the street. "So you think they just live in the cemetery?"

"Where else do ghouls hang out?" Delilah whispered, motioning for Relic to keep his voice down.

"I don't know," Relic hissed. "In Stephen King novels?" He followed her along the outer gates of the Oakridge Cemetery, stopping at a side entrance. He watched her reach into her cloak and then begin fiddling with the gate's handle. There was a click, and Delilah pushed the gate open enough for them to slip through. "So you're like a burglar, too? Busting open safes and cemetery gates."

Delilah peered over her shoulder and gave him a wink, motioning for him to follow. He tried to keep as low as her, but Delilah was like a graceful cat, and he felt like a lumpy baboon. They weaved their way through headstones toward the center of the graveyard. Relic wasn't sure where they were heading, but soon they were outside the pools of light provided by the lamps along the pathways.

Relic nearly bowled Delilah over when she suddenly stopped, holding up her hand. After recovering from Relic colliding with her, she motioned toward a bench near the cemetery's fountain. There were two figures sitting there; Relic could only see their silhouettes blocking the light from a distant lamp.

"Those aren't ghouls," Relic whispered.

Delilah held a finger to her lips, scowling at him. "Listen," she whispered.

Relic heard the two figures on the bench laughing, a girl and guy, probably his age. They were whispering things between themselves, the girl restraining laughter as the guy leaned over and kissed her neck. But Relic heard something else to the left; the rustling of bushes. He followed Delilah's hand as it motioned that way, and three hunched figures emerged.

The ghouls.

Well that was fast, Relic thought, gripping his drumsticks as if they were some sort of weapons. The idea almost made him laugh. Delilah melted into the shadows, moving toward the gangly creatures that crept toward the bench. Relic tried to follow, but in order to move silently, he had to move much slower than Delilah. Seeing how fast the ghouls moved toward the unknowing prey, Relic knew he wouldn't reach the couple in time.

Having to make a split-second decision, Relic broke into a run toward the bench. He saw Delilah out of the corner of his eyes draw her knives and move in the opposite direction.

"Look out," Relic warned, trying to reach the bench before the cannibalistic creatures did. The two teenagers on the bench jolted to their feet, and Relic saw the ghouls scamper toward their now alert dinner. As Relic reached the two by the bench, he nearly tripped. *Nick?!*

Relic's bass player gave him a shocked look as Tammy Beck let out a blood-curdling scream. Relic turned to see the three ghouls race across the pool of lamplight, running on all fours toward their living snacks.

"Get back!" Relic warned, stepping on the back of the bench and jumping between the teens and the monsters.

"Relic, what the hell?!" Nick shouted, falling onto his ass when he saw what Relic faced.

"Do it!" Delilah shouted.

Suddenly remembering his drumsticks, Relic sidestepped one of the creature's claws as it tried to trip him and lunged toward the bench. He knelt down and started playing the wooden seat as if it were a set of rack toms: *tap-ta-ta-tap-ta-ta-ta-tap-tap.* He hummed out the sounds that his drums would normally make as he played the intro of "Alternus." He could see that Delilah's plan had worked. All three ghouls were frozen, watching his sticks as they tapped out the song that had birthed them.

It was then that Relic could see how grotesque these things were. Pallid, nearly translucent rotting skin was stretched across the emaciated forms of the ghouls, each one with a skull-like face adorned with crooked fangs and pale red eyes. They watched Relic in angry fascination, their mouths salivating for living flesh despite their inability to devour it.

Tammy shrieked again, but Relic could see Nick on the edges of his vision move to protect the terrified girl, wrapping his arms around her. *Was the creep on a date?!* Relic couldn't help wondering while he kept the ghouls distracted. *You're supposed to be with my best friend!*

Delilah appeared from the darkness then, knives trailing that arcane green glow as they were dragged through the night by their wielder. The first ghoul let out a horrid scream as she buried one of the knives into the back of its neck; it crumpled lifelessly as Delilah landed, rolled, and slashed with her other knife at the next ghoul. Dark blood sprayed across the dark grass as Tammy screeched again.

The last ghoul finally managed to break its trance, blinking its red eyes and resuming its scramble toward fresh meat. This time, it came for Relic. As Delilah slammed both of her knives into the earth where it once stood, the wretched creature leapt away and now sailed through the air toward Relic.

Time slowed, and Relic heard his father. "Release me!"

Relic spun his sticks away from the bench and turned toward the oncoming foe. He felt something inside him then, similar to the presence of the Widow in his dreams, and he felt a chill touch move through his arms and into his hands. His sticks began to glow with the same energy enchanting Delilah's knives, and he spun them again as the ghoul's claws reached for him. Relic swiped his sticks as if they were blades, rotating them inwards like green disks of light and severing the ghouls hands in one more spray of blood.

Tammy and the ghoul shrieked once more—this time almost harmonizing in their shared horror—and Delilah moved over to smack the ghoul on the back of the head with the butt of one of her knives. She looked up at Relic's sticks, her mouth hanging open in amazement.

"Dude, what the fuck?!" Nick asked Relic, his arms wrapped around Tammy. "How'd you do that? And what are those things?!"

Relic stared at his sticks, still glowing with a strange spectral energy. He wished he had answers for all three of Nick's questions, but he only had a question of his own. "What are you doing here with her?" Relic pointed at Tammy with one of his glowing sticks and the girl cowered away from him.

"Relic," Delilah said, grunting as she lifted the ghoul and threw it over her shoulder as if it were nothing but a bag of laundry. "We have to go."

Ignoring her, Relic pulled Nick aside. "What are you doing, man? I thought you were with Bree."

Nick gave him a confused look. "Bree said she was hanging out with you tonight. Besides, she'd be stoked for me, man." He lowered his voice, leaning in. "She's been helping me make Tammy jealous ever since the dance, so she'd ditch that turd from Benton Central." Despite the current circumstances, Nick laughed quietly as he hooked a thumb toward Tammy. "After she saw us at the dance, she dumped him, and we've been dating ever since." He leaned closer. "But don't tell anyone...she's weird about it."

This stunned Relic more than cutting off a set of ghoul hands with a pair of magic drumsticks. "I won't, as long as you don't tell anyone what you saw here tonight."

Nick surveyed the slaughter. "Trust me, man, I'll be pretending I never saw this for the rest of my life..."

"Dude!" Delilah called from the distance. "Help me!"

"Get her out of here," Relic told Nick. "I'll see you at practice tomorrow."

Nick didn't argue, and Tammy was more than eager to leave the cemetery. Relic tied up the unconscious ghoul while Delilah disposed of the other two bodies—Relic didn't ask how—and together they loaded their captive into a black Hummer near the back of the cemetery.

"Take us to the site," Delilah told the mysterious driver, who wore a hood and sunglasses even though it was pitch black out.

"What site?" Relic asked, feeling like he had no choice but to get in the vehicle with her.

Delilah pulled the door shut behind him and the Hummer sped off.

Relic was understandably distracted during the short drive from the cemetery to Delilah's house. Having never been to her home, he only assumed that's where they had arrived. The vehicle pulled down a private drive, which wrapped around a massive house on a hill overlooking the appropriately named neighborhood: Sanctuary.

"You didn't tell me you could do that," Delilah said, but Relic was only half-listening. His eyes were fixed on the bound, unconscious ghoul in the vehicle's trunk, and his mind was still wrestling with the deception Bree and Nick had played. While he was obviously relieved that Bree's apparent affection for Nick was all for show, he was confused why Bree hadn't said anything to him.

When Delilah laid a soft hand on Relic's arm, he turned to her and realized *she* was most likely why Bree kept it to herself. If there was any chance Bree had similar feelings for Relic, she probably wouldn't have minded making him jealous in the process as well.

"How long have you known?" Delilah asked.

"Known what?"

She let go of his arm. "That you were an Alternian."

The Hummer pulled to a stop, just like Relic's heart.

Chapter 25

Before Relic could respond to Delilah's accusation of him being an inter-dimensional being, Marshall Crane pulled the Hummer's door open and stood staring at the teens, a surprisingly bored look on his face.

"What's he doing here?" The man wore a dark crimson dinner jacket that was decorated with black floral patterns. His silky black shirt was unbuttoned to the chest, revealing a strange amulet hanging by a silver chain.

"Inside," Delilah said from the back of the vehicle, dragging the limp ghoul toward the house, "before it wakes up."

Relic hadn't realized how foul the creature smelled until he stepped into its wake. As he plugged his nose and walked toward the rear of the car, he was unsure if he should follow Delilah and Marshall to the house. But when the driver—whose face was still concealed by a dark hood—closed the back door, got back in, and drove away, Relic supposed he had no other choice.

He caught up to Delilah and Marshall as they entered a back door near a pool house. When Relic followed them inside, he heard a click around the corner. Turning that way, he stepped into a small study just in time to see a bookshelf slide away to reveal a stone staircase lit by a series of sconces. Even before seeing where they were going, he knew he was descending into the chamber from his dream, where Delilah had tried to slay the Widow.

Father and daughter lugged the ghoul between them as they silently descended the stairs. Relic stayed a few steps behind. The stairs ended in a cool, dark basement, with smooth wooden floors, decorative rugs, shelves of books, and that large round table in the center of the room. Looking up, Relic couldn't see a ceiling, only darkness beyond the soft light of the candles and lanterns that illuminated the place; it was almost as if there was no ceiling, just some fathomless void that separated them from the world above.

"Relic," Delilah said, pulling his gaze from the hanging abyss. She jerked her head toward the table. "Can you move those candles so we can put this thing on the table?"

Having no logical reason to refuse, he did as he was asked, pushing the burning candles away to create an opening for Marshall and Delilah to place the ghoul on the table. Marshall moved the candles back into place afterwards, casting Relic the occasional glance as the newcomer backed away.

After watching Delilah and Marshall restrain the ghoul to the table using the ropes they had secured it with at the cemetery along with strange black chains that Marshall had produced from a nearby chest, Relic just wanted to leave.

His mind kept wandering back to what Nick had said earlier, about him and Bree just trying to make Tammy jealous; it just seemed so absurd—although he was currently in a secret cult lair watching a dhampir restrain a ghoul to a table.

"What have you told him?" Marshall asked Delilah, as if Relic weren't even there.

"Enough," Delilah said, wiping sweat from her brow as she stepped back from their work. She looked at Relic and then back at Marshall. "He needs to know. He's like me."

Marshall looked at Relic, his bored expression now more interested. "So, your dad figured out how to bang a ghost, did he?"

"Rude," Delilah said, moving toward Relic. "It's more likely that the Widow possessed his mother when she first broke free of her banishment, weakened from the bindings."

Relic's mind spun out of control.

"Perhaps," Marshall said, now turning to a bookshelf and looking for something. "And how can you be sure he's not just similarly possessed by one of them?"

"Well," Delilah said in an annoyed voice, "besides the fact that the Widow hasn't killed him when he had the tape, he's able to neutralize them with that song." She motioned to the drumsticks that Relic held in one hand. "He also cut off this sucker's hands with a pair of glowing drumsticks."

Marshall turned around to glance at Relic again, a heavy tome in his hand. "That does indeed sound quite different than our typical tropes."

Relic was still mentally reeling when Delilah turned to him. "All these monsters are inspired by known fears—all the Hollywood classics and folktales. We call them tropes," she motioned to the ghoul, "like this guy."

"Delilah's father was a trope," Marshall said, placing the book on the lectern overlooking the table. "But we discovered that while she is technically an Alternian, she is not merely possessed by one like her father was. She's a hybrid, if you will, born of this dimension and thus belongs here. But tropes do not belong here and must be sent back." He focused on the ghoul, whose limbs suddenly shifted. "And death is the only way."

Relic noticed Delilah hang her head then, as if the mention of her father brought some kind of shame or sadness.

So many questions surged through Relic's mind, but one overpowered the others. "Are you saying my mother is a trope? Some kind of monster?" He looked at Delilah. "Your dad was a vampire, but my mom is...just a person."

"It seems you may have two mothers," Marshall said, opening the large book and flipping through pages. "Cecily Moreau could have possessed your mother—spirits are known to do that—and after you were born, an exorcism must have occurred. Elsewise the Widow would have consumed Dina Meyers."

The ghoul moaned then, waking up.

"So you're saying, what?" Relic asked, stepping toward the table. "I'm like...half ghost or something?"

"Call it what you will," Marshall said, motioning to Delilah without looking up from the book. "Watch our guest, oh sweet child of mine; he will likely be peckish when he wakes."

Delilah moved to the table, her knives drawn. "We don't know all the rules," she told Relic. "But that power—the way you made your sticks glow—that's Alternian magic." Her own knives began to glow, as if to show him.

The ghoul shrieked, flailing its limbs as it realized it had been trapped.

"You may go now," Marshall said, still scanning the book for a particular passage. "This is a family matter. Thank you for your assistance."

Relic looked from the man to Delilah. She looked at him over her shoulder, giving him a faint smile and a nod. "See you at school."

Not wanting to hear those inhuman cries anymore, Relic turned toward the stairs and slowly made his way to the world above.

It was a long walk home, but he had plenty to think about.

The week following Halloween was probably the most uncomfortable Relic had ever been while hanging around Bree, not knowing how to act or what they should even speak about. She began noticing almost immediately, and he knew he had to make something up.

Having to juggle so many deceptions and separate lives, he concocted a way that he could share bits of the truth with her without laying everything bare. When she would ask what was wrong, he'd tell her that he and Delilah had been fighting, or that he had been having weird dreams about his mom being a murderer.

When she'd accepted his reasons, it made him feel almost more guilty, as if it would have been better if he had just straight up lied. Only giving her these half-truths made the deceptions feel that much worse. But he kept hearing Delilah's warnings echo in his mind whenever he saw Bree. Also, Relic hadn't forgotten that when he told Bree about the werewolves, they almost got killed; he wouldn't risk her safety again.

It's only until the battle of the bands, he kept telling himself, trying to believe that once he got his dad back, everything else would fall right into place.

Well...maybe not the part about him being a normal human being.

"I feel like I should be more weirded out by it," he told Delilah as they patrolled along Kossuth Street on a cold evening the week before Thanksgiving break. He spun one of his drumsticks, still unsure if he could turn anything into a weapon—like Gambit's kinetic powers in *X-Men* comics—but preferring the feel of his trusty Vic Firths.

"It's hard to feel weird about the nature of yourself," Delilah said, adjusting the furry collar of her coat. Her eyes were fixed on the group of teens they had been following, suspecting that they were being hunted by the tropes that Relic had dreamed of two nights ago. "When I found out what I was, it made so much sense that it was more like a relief to finally have answers."

Relic felt the truth of that. Finding out that the Widow was sort of like a second mother to him helped explain why he had been having such weird, spectral dreams. It also explained why the Widow hadn't killed him for having the tape.

"You really think these things are going to hunt around here?" Delilah asked, looking up into the clear night sky. There were only stars overhead, with a few falling snowflakes. "Shouldn't they be, I don't know...perching somewhere?"

"I don't know what to think," Relic said with a shrug. "This is your territory. I just told you what happened in the dream."

"Well," she said, "I guess they could be wrong sometimes, yeah? I mean, it seems like Altar Stone has really only been drawing the ghouls out since we got the last werewolf. Maybe it's like Marshall said: you guys have to play in front of some people...get that whole ritualistic aspect going."

"Again," Relic said, motioning to her, "this is you guys' territory."

They followed the teens around two more blocks, keeping their distance to blend in with the occasional pedestrians. Relic's feet were going numb, and he wanted to get home to see if Bree wanted to watch *Son in Law* for the fourth time—another holiday tradition for them leading up to Thanksgiving.

"Hey, D," Relic said, wondering for the hundredth time how to broach this subject in a different way, "I had an idea... What if you joined Altar Stone as our keyboardist?"

She glanced toward him. "Why? I barely have time to practice with Sebastian. We're trying to keep our covers consistent, remember?"

"Well, I mean do you *have* to be in Autumnal Fall? If you were in Altar Stone, we wouldn't have to keep pretending we're dating. We could just be bandmates, and you could keep up with everything on the frontline, help us get ready for the battle."

"Is this about Bree?"

Relic felt a rush of anger. "Of course it is! I'm getting sick of having to wait to talk to her about stuff. I can't keep lying to my best friend like this."

Delilah sighed. "I told you this is to protect her. While the Widow's still out, there's something going on with these tropes. It's like they're feeding off the fear people have of them, making them more powerful." She motioned to the kids up ahead. "When you dreamed of Mark Baxter getting attacked, he probably told all those friends of his about the incident, and now they're all afraid of—"

There was a sudden gust of wind then as both Relic and Delilah ducked below a pair of huge leathery wings. A gargoyle flew over the trees above them and barreled toward Mark and his friends nearly a block away.

"That!" Delilah shouted, scrambling forward as she drew her knives. Relic could never match her pace, but he clomped along right behind her. A car swerved ahead as the gargoyle descended, crashing into a fence near Laramie's First Credit Union as it tried to avoid the shadowy form. Delilah rushed across the street, stepping on a trash can and launching herself up after the gargoyle.

Relic watched in amazement as Delilah side-armed one of her knives toward the gargoyle, looking like an action movie star. But the disc of emerald energy spun just over the creature's head as the gargoyle descended faster, claws stretched out to snatch its prey.

Following his partner's lead, Relic also hurled one of his sticks, choosing not to try leaping in the air beforehand. His green disc spun vertically, end-over-end, and connected cleanly in the back of the gargoyle's head. Dark blood sprayed as the creature sagged and fell in a heap just behind a fence where Mark and his friends couldn't see.

Delilah and Relic stopped near where the gargoyle fell, both of them wheezing for breath and waving awkwardly to the other kids.

"Weirdos," Mark said, waving his crew to follow him toward the movie theater, more distracted by the wrecked car than the two whack-jobs running around in the street.

Relic and Delilah shared a quick chuckle as they moved to dispose of the gargoyle. The black Hummer—driven by someone Relic now knew only as Quentin—came as scheduled and transported the beast back to the Crane residence. Delilah stayed behind to walk Relic home after they found her stray knife.

"Look, about Bree," Delilah said, "I get it. But I don't think me being in the band will fix it. The thing is," she motioned back to where they had just defeated a gargoyle, "I need your help out here. We need an excuse to be alone together, away from our friends, so we can take care of these things. We can't tell them 'Oh, hey, we're going to go fight some monsters. But they feed off your fear, so don't believe in them!' It just wouldn't work."

Relic knew she had a point.

"We need to thin these tropes down," Delilah said. "The more you guys play that song, the more will be drawn back here. Which is good! But they'll try to stop the ritual, so we need to take out as many as we can before the battle."

"Alright," Relic said with a nod. "I'll keep playing along. But please, do me a favor. Stop kissing me in front of Bree?"

Delilah laughed, "Will do." She gave him that devilish grin, "Just thought I'd give you some practice."

CHAPTER 26

Christmas was creeping up and Relic still had no idea what to get Bree. They always got each other two gifts—one joke gift and one real one. Relic hadn't even found a joke gift yet, which was usually the easiest. Between hunting tropes with Delilah, Altar Stone practice, and keeping up with homework, he wasn't even sure when he'd find the time to shop this year.

But after screwing up their Halloween, he would not flake out on their Christmas.

"Relic!"

"Huh?" Relic shook his head, looking at Bree who was scowling at him from across the maintenance room.

"You going to count it off or what?"

"Actually," Nick said, looking at his watch, "I gotta bail. We can all practice tomorrow, right?"

Gate smashed a beer can under his boot as he got up. "I think you're the only one who still needs to practice, bud. You're still missing the chokes after the breakdown."

"I know, man," Nick said, taking off his bass and putting it in his case. "I'll practice tonight. Can I borrow the tape to play along to?"

"No!" Bree and Relic snapped simultaneously.

"Dude," Tyler said, leaning his head against the mic as if it were an ice pack, "I swear you never listen to anyone here."

"Okay, okay," Nick said, "I'll figure it out. Let's pick it up tomorrow. I'm supposed to meet Tammy at her place." He shuffled out of the room before they could hassle him anymore.

"Check your priorities, Nick," Bree called after him as she took off her guitar. She looked at Relic, "Actually, we should go, too. Buffy night."

"You guys still watch that crap?" Tyler asked, rubbing his still-healing shoulder. "Second season any better?"

"Yeah," Gate said from the other side of the room, "except for Buffy; she's still annoying. Matter of fact, I'm going to go watch tonight's episode, too." He smacked his hands together. "So get out."

Relic and his bandmates made their way through the basement hall, chatting about local news.

"Your mom hear anything about that psycho Lavenza?" Tyler asked Bree, still rubbing his shoulder. "They said he was on some Rothen drugs after his surgery."

Bree shook her head. "They make her sign some sort of NDA so she can't discuss work stuff." She looked at Relic, "Unless we get dad drunk again on old fashioneds and get him yacking."

Relic laughed, then turned to Tyler. "How's the shoulder?"

"Still feels weird," he said, rotating it like he was warming up for a game, "but at least I can move it."

"Think your dad will come cheer you on at the battle of the bands?" Bree asked sarcastically.

Tyler scoffed. "Good one. Dude barely even talks to me now. I'm pretty much dead to him."

As sad as that was, Relic was glad to see Tyler in better spirits. While it still seemed wild that one of the most popular guys in their grade had been so miserable, it felt rewarding to help Tyler find his own identity away from his father's oppressive wishes.

Once they got to the main entrance, Tyler's ride was already there waiting for him. His mom waved eagerly to the bandmates from behind the wheel of her Mercedes. When Relic and Bree were left alone to wait for her dad, she took off her backpack and began rummaging around in it.

"I got your Christmas present," she said.

"What? It's not even Christmas break yet. What's the rush?" He would obviously take an early present, but he hadn't gotten hers yet.

She pulled out a small, flat item wrapped in green and red wrapping paper. "I have to go to Maine to spend Christmas at my uncle's this year. They're having a big reunion thing since he just beat cancer, so I have to leave on Friday."

Relic apprehensively took the gift. "I don't have yours, though."

She waved that away. "Don't worry about it, let's not make it a huge deal this year since I won't be here. I just wanted to make sure you had this—I didn't get a joke gift this time though, sorry, it's just this one." She sounded truly remorseful.

Relic felt immensely sad, having not gotten her anything yet. "I'll wait to open it then, until you get back."

"No!" Bree said. "Come on, open it! Really hope you like it." She gave him her crooked, reluctant smile.

Relic tore it open and was greeted by an album called *Legendary Tales* by the band Rhapsody. The cover featured a shirtless medieval warrior riding a unicorn, facing down a deadly dragon that swooped down over a majestic cityscape.

"I read that anyone who likes HammerFall would probably like these guys," Bree said, raising her eyebrows as if she wasn't sure what kind of reaction to expect. "They're from Italy, I guess."

Relic flipped the album over, feeling an immediate sense of escapism and adventure emanating from the CD. The tracks on the back bore names like "Warrior of Ice," "Forest of Unicorns," and "Land of Immortals," and each one promised a story that Relic couldn't wait to get sucked into.

"This looks awesome," Relic said in genuine wonder. He flipped it back over to see a sticker on the cover. "I don't know what 'Symphonic Epic Power Metal' is, but I'm stoked to find out!" He looked up to Bree and he thought he might start crying like some idiot. The look on her face—a strange mix of pride and vicarious wonder—made him embrace her in a huge hug. "Thank you." She returned it.

He thought back to that night Bree had returned from summer camp—before Delilah really entered their lives, before the murders, before all of it—and he really did start to cry, wanting everything back the way it was.

As usual, Bree was on cue. "I know the unicorn is a bit much, but you don't have to cry about it. I'll take it back."

By the time Russ Thompkins pulled up, Bree and Relic were both laughing and crying.

The next day, before going out with Delilah to look into the recent wendigo sightings near the Wabash River, Relic convinced his mom to take him shopping for Bree's Christmas present. Calvin was at the house at the time, so he offered to drive them and take them out for dinner—the man certainly knew the way to Relic's heart.

"What's she into now?" Relic's mom asked as they wandered the mall.

Relic could go on for hours on that topic, but it wouldn't help him figure out what to get her. Most of Bree's interests didn't require material things, which made shopping for her infuriating. Short of buying her a new guitar, he was basically at square one. "I kind of want to get her something she doesn't expect," he decided to answer. "She got me an awesome album that I'd never heard of—it'd be cool if I could surprise her like that."

"Believe it or not," Dina said, motioning to Veronica Jay's, a popular jewelry store, "but all girls secretly like shiny things."

"Let's steer clear of there, then," Calvin joked, earning a light smack from Dina. Relic wanted to barf.

Relic pointed to a quirky hipster novelty shop called Rebel gifts and said, "I'm going to check in there real quick."

"Okay," Dina said. "We're going to grab some coffees next door."

Happy to be alone to think, Relic perused the store's collection of flatulent joke products and sexually suggestive paraphernalia. There was lots of funny stuff, but nothing that felt appropriately "Bree" enough.

Until he came across a rack of boxer shorts.

Having to cough to cover his sudden, snorting laugh, Relic grabbed a hangar that held the perfect joke gift, as if placed upon his path by some higher power. He quickly paid for them and walked over to show his glorious finding to his mom.

"That's what you want to give her for Christmas?" Dina asked, skeptically staring over her coffee cup at the boxer shorts with a pattern of pizza slices printed across them. "I thought you liked the gift she got you."

Relic smirked. "Yeah, this is the joke gift."

"I have to know," Calvin said with a raised eyebrow. "What's the joke?"

Laughing, Relic shook his head and returned his prize to its bag. Remembering how Calvin had reacted to Bree's frank discussion about her period, he added, "No, you don't want to know."

The hunt for Bree's real gift continued, but after taking a lap of the mall, Relic felt like it might be a lost cause. They still needed to get dinner, and he had to meet up with Delilah at seven.

"Let's just go," Relic said, defeated. "I'll figure something out tomorrow."

Dina rubbed his shoulder. "We can come back before Bree leaves. Just give it some thought."

When they got near the mall exit, Calvin stopped them. "Can you both wait here a minute? I just need to use the restroom."

Once Calvin had turned the corner and was out of sight, Dina sat down on a nearby bench, motioning Relic to join her. "I wanted to talk to you about something." He sat down next to her. "You know that I've been seeing Calvin for a while now, and...well, things are going well."

Please, no, Relic thought, *not now.*

"I know this can't be easy for you," Dina continued, staring at her coffee cup as if it had the right words printed on it somewhere. "It's definitely not been easy for me."

Just give me a few more months, he begged her telepathically, knowing for sure he was on the right path to find his dad. Relic still knew how unlikely the chances were of his parents reconciling, but he still felt like his mom needed to know the truth before she made any drastic decisions.

"The thing is, Relic," she said, looking up at him now, "I've felt like I've had my life on pause since your dad left. I won't burden you with telling you how bad things got before you were born, but I went through so much for your father—even after he left us, I felt like I owed him..." Dina took a deep, trembling breath.

Images flashed through Relic's mind of a younger version of his mother, screaming as something took root inside of her. He couldn't be sure if what he saw were actual memories that the Widow somehow imparted on him, but it was a reminder of what his mother had endured.

"But that's not the point," she continued. "I just want you to know that I think things might...move forward with Calvin. I know you're not one for mushy stuff, but I love him."

"I know," Relic said, thinking of how he felt about Bree. Seeing his mom so happy these last few months, the last thing he wanted to do was deny her that joy, like his current situation had blocked him from being with Bree. "I can tell."

She smiled. "So, you're alright with that? I'm not saying Calvin will be proposing to me anytime soon, but I am saying that I'm open to that possibility. Are you?"

What if Dad came back? Relic wanted to ask. *Would you be alright with that?* But he knew he couldn't say anything. If his mom knew anything about what was happening, she would try to stop Relic from getting involved. If she knew he and Delilah were out killing monsters, she'd pack up their house and move somewhere far away from Laramie.

And far away from Bree.

Relic nodded. "Calvin's alright. And he makes you happy, so I won't bust his balls too much."

Dina laughed, putting an arm around her son. "We'll both bust his balls."

"Gross, Mom!"

"Hey," Calvin said from behind them, "sorry that took so long."

Relic was about to make a killer poop joke, but when he got off the bench, he saw that Calvin had a small jewelry box in his hand. *Oh shit,* Relic thought, not expecting for all of this to happen right now.

Calvin noticed Relic staring at the box, and he held it out for him. "I thought Bree might like this. But you're the expert."

Relic took the box and opened it to see a gleaming silver guitar pick pendant engraved with the words "Altar Stone" with two purple gems dangling on either side of the silver chain.

"I got the idea when your mom asked what Bree was into," Calvin said. "Seems like her favorite thing in the world is playing music with you, so this should hit the spot, yeah?"

"Calvin," Dina gasped, "that's beautiful! Oh, Relic, she will adore that."

Relic felt a massive lump in his throat. His mom was right, this was perfect for Bree. He wasn't sure how to adequately thank Calvin, but he tried. "This is awesome. Thanks, Calvin."

His smile showed Relic how much that meant to him. "You bet, man. But just so we're all clear, this was your idea. I just picked it up for you."

Smiling, Relic nodded, thinking that he'd be pretty alright if the bulge in Calvin's pocket was an engagement ring for his mom.

Much to Relic's delight, he and Delilah managed to find the wendigo only a few miles outside of town that evening. Quentin had driven them to the Happy Hollow campgrounds—which were pretty dormant this time of year—and they tracked the thing to a nearby cave. It was a rather uneventful encounter, with Delilah taking the lead and Relic just freezing his balls off as he covered her approach.

His fingers were going numb—since he refused to wear gloves while handling his drumsticks—and he was having trouble keeping his breathing as steady as Delilah's. But as they came up on the small rocky alcove where the tracks in the snow led, he felt a familiar unease, similar to the feeling he got during his dreams of the Widow's murders.

Fortunately, he didn't hear his dad's drums, and no one asked for release, so Relic shook off the feeling and watched Delilah do her work. The thing—whatever a wendigo was—looked like an elk or something, with a skinless skull for a head and a sludgy tar-like substance caked around where its gnarly fur met its gruesome neck. It tried to charge Delilah when it finally sensed intruders, but she easily rolled away and raked the entire side of its body with both of her daggers.

The wounds on the thing glowed with the same eldritch energy that coated her blades, and it stumbled out into the snow, dying with a pathetic snarl.

Once the monster from another dimension was dead, killed by a dhampir that Relic had to pretend to be dating, things started to get weird.

"Release me," the voice said in Relic's mind. Having not heard that voice in weeks, he froze, his eyes pulled to the dead creature. The greenish glow coming off the beast slowly turned into a ghostly blue aura, and a misty silhouette of the wendigo was pulled away from its physical form like smoke from a candle.

The drums began pounding, once again only for him.

"Uh, that's new," Delilah said, her tone not suggesting she was anywhere near as shocked as Relic. The creature's body disappeared before their eyes, its essence drifting away in a trail of blue smoke. She turned to Relic. "I guess we don't have to clean them up anymore."

Relic was at a total loss, trying to ignore his dad's drumming. "You're not concerned about this?"

Delilah raised an eyebrow at him as she made to leave. "Am I concerned about the dead monster disappearing or the fact that there are, in fact, monsters running around?" She motioned to the skeletal trees around them. "I'm concerned, Relic, but I don't want to freeze my tits off out here thinking about it. Let's go."

On the way back to the Hummer, Relic offered his opinion. "I haven't heard my dad's voice in a while, and I just heard it before that thing disappeared. Can't be a coincidence."

"What'd he say?"

"Same thing he always says," Relic snapped. "Release me. He wants out. I would too if I had to play the same damn drum beat for, like, four years in some hellscape."

"Well," Delilah wondered aloud, "you said you guys got the song down. And we've been seeing more and more of these tropes showing up lately." She pushed her gloved hands together, her fingers intertwining. "Maybe there's a concentration of Alternian energy or something."

"Or maybe you've meddled too much."

Relic and Delilah both spun around, drawing their weapons. The Widow stood before them, Cecily Moreau's face partially formed by a strip of pale, rotting flesh that was splayed across her spectral skull. Delilah's knife flew through the ghostly form, causing a smile to spread across the Widow's half-formed lips as her body shifted from smoke back to a billowing blue shroud.

"Still think I'm here, don't you?" Her voice was an echo in Relic's mind, and he heard it as if from a dream. She turned to him, her smile fading. "I've asked you to release me, son. Why do you wait?"

From the edges of his vision, Relic saw Delilah turn to him, but he had no answer for either of them.

"It was you," was all he could offer. *Release me, son.* It was always her, calling out to her child. *She thinks I'm her son.*

Cecily smiled, gliding toward them. "Don't you know your mother's voice?"

"You are not my mother!"

The Widow laughed, easily dodging Delilah's second knife as the green disc flew past her incorporeal form to bury itself in the snow.

"How did I feel your father inside me, then?" The Widow asked, her phantom fingers rising to brush Relic's cheek, but he drew away at the last moment. He held his drumsticks between them, their green glow more powerful than ever. "You are both just like the rest of them," she said with a soft laugh.

"Adratheon's wretched thralls. Don't you know your lord is dead? I killed him because he tried to keep me, and I don't belong there." She spun around to face the trees. "I belong here."

Relic was frozen in fear, but Delilah quickly grabbed one of his drumsticks and drove it into the back of the Widow's skull. "Ah!" Delilah cursed, grabbing her hand as if the drumstick had burnt it. Cecily turned around slowly as her form began to dissipate.

"Release me, son," the Widow said, her skin melting into the same smoke it was formed from. "I'll be waiting."

The drive back to town was morose. Neither Relic nor Delilah had much to offer in the way of theories about what just happened. As they approached Greenbriar, Delilah finally said, "We need to meet with Marshall. He's still in Milan until the new year, but we need to tell him about this and figure out what to do."

"What do you mean?" Relic asked. "We know what to do. We free my dad and kill that bitch."

"But what if we can kill her now?" Delilah asked. "You saw that back there, she's getting bolder, which probably means she's getting stronger, too. It's like she's gaining power from the tropes we kill, and I don't know how."

Relic remembered something that Gate had said, about the werewolves, and he couldn't believe he hadn't thought about it until now. "It's because we knew about the wendigo."

Delilah just stared at him.

"Look," Relic said, turning toward her, "most of the tropes we've found either through my dreams or your dad's connections. We heard about the wendigo from everywhere, and not just as a wild urban legend. People truly believed they saw it. That fear made it more powerful, and the Widow was about to latch onto it, to steal its essence."

Nodding, Delilah rubbed her chin. "That could explain why the cult lost all its power. If the Widow was in Alternus sucking up all of Adratheon's power, then when they locked her away, they essentially gave her an all-you-can-eat buffet."

"I don't care about that, or about the cult," Relic said. "I just want my dad back."

"Relic," Delilah said softly, "I never wanted to float this, but what if your dad isn't there? What if the Widow is just fucking with you? As we just saw, all she can do on this side is toy with you. For whatever reason, she can't or won't hurt you or your friends."

"He's there," Relic said, giving her a look that dared her to disagree. "I know it."

"I'm just saying," Delilah pushed, "if we can find a way to kill her here and now—"

"No!" Relic punched the back of the passenger seat. "He's there! I need to save him!" But even as he said it, part of him wondered if she might be right.

They rode the rest of the way in silence, and Relic exited the Hummer without saying a word. It was almost ten o'clock, and his mom was in the living room watching TV with Calvin. He waved to them, went to his room to get his gifts, and then walked to Bree's.

It didn't look like anyone was up when he approached the dark house, but he knocked softly anyway. Bree's bedroom light flicked on, and he heard her come to the door.

"Dude, it's late," she said, crossing her arms over her pajama shirt, "and freezing. Get in here."

Relic slipped through the door and presented her gifts, each one simply wrapped in Christmas tree-patterned paper. As Bree took them with a smile, he unleashed on her.

"So, last night I listened to that CD you got me...and," he felt that lump in his throat, "it's like the best gift anyone's ever gotten me. I put it on, and all

I could think about was when we used to play *HeroQuest* or build those Lego castles and have our knights hunt monsters." He felt tears coming to his eyes, but this was Bree, so he felt safe crying. "I thought of my dad...and how even though he wasn't here, he was creating escapism for people, and that's what I needed—that's what you gave me. I needed Rhapsody, and I didn't even know it, but you did." He was running out of breath. "I wanted to make sure you knew that."

She was beaming, holding the two gifts. "I'm glad you liked it, man."

He let out a laugh, his eyes watering. "Alright, go. Open."

The boxers were first, and Bree had to cover her mouth to keep from waking her parents up with her laughter. "You dick," she whispered through a snorting laugh. But when she opened the other box, the mood shifted into something much more serious.

"Whoa..."

Relic's stomach twisted in knots then, worried he might have overstepped or something. "I...uh, I know you don't wear a lot of jewelry, and it's kind of...I dunno, girly? But I got the band name on it, so that's kind of cool, right?"

She stared at it in silence, one of her fingers reaching slowly into the box to touch the necklace as if it might explode.

"It's alright if you don't like it, I just—"

Bree closed the gap between them and kissed him forcefully, but when their lips touched, it was a soft collision. It was like nothing he had ever experienced. Visions flashed through his mind, not of the Widow or his father or some tropes causing mayhem, but of him and Bree laughing together, smiling for pictures before homecoming in this very living room, and being happy together for most of their collective lives.

Relic wrapped his arms around her waist as she threw hers around his neck.

He never wanted to leave.

Chapter 27

R elic chewed on Bree's words for days after their kiss.

"I guess it's a good thing I'm leaving for a while," she had said, with that half-smile she liked to hide her true feelings behind.

They both had laughed softly afterward, but Relic felt there was some truth behind those words, as if they had both crossed a line. He hoped it was only because Delilah was still in the picture, and not something deeper. He had to believe they felt the same way about each other at this point.

He was able to distract himself during Bree's absence over the holiday by focusing on the ritual they needed to organize for the battle of the bands. Relic and Delilah had spoken to Marshall on the phone just before Christmas, and through the combination of whatever mystical interrogation techniques her adopted father used on that ghoul and his research in Milan, Marshall found the crucial details they needed.

"We know how the cult originally sealed Cecily away," Marshall said, his voice slightly distorted on the speaker phone in the Cranes' underground lair. "They tracked her to the old music hall that once stood where Chambers High now resides. That was the nexus—where she was created when Gustave lured Adratheon's imprisoned daughter, Valaina, to possess his wife in exchange for breaking the curse." Marshall's voice grew tense. "I still can't figure out how the bastard did it, but it accounts for how Adratheon's power waned."

Relic couldn't keep track of all these names. It reminded him of his father's story for the Unknown Oath concept album, *The Rest of the Wicked*—far too convoluted. "What do we need to do?"

"I'm getting to that," Marshall replied, unbothered by Relic's impatience. "The circumstances of Cecily's original curse were rooted in music. Gustave had her bound in the basement during his ninth symphony, surrounded by whatever cryptic markings were necessary to bargain with Valaina. As an Alternian, she was easily drawn to the music, interfering with Adratheon's traditional Curse of the Ninth, and then claiming Cecily's body. Valaina's overwhelming power that she stole from Adratheon eventually turned Cecily into the monster we know as the Widow."

"So, that's how my dad summoned her back?" Relic asked, eager to get to the point.

"Chill out," Delilah hissed at him with a scowl.

"Eventually, yes," Marshall continued, "and that's the part on which I've found more specific details. After the cult sealed the Widow away, they documented the process, and I have gathered all the scattered pieces needed to understand their method.

"It all comes back to music," Marshall said, as if that explained it all. "The cult used Gustave's ninth symphony—which was apparently called 'Offerings to Alternus,' but since the music did not survive, I can't speak to its relation to your father's song—to ensnare the Widow during one of her brief times of hibernation."

"Hibernation?" Delilah asked.

"Yes," Marshall replied. "The cult said they battled the Widow on several occasions, but she was always too powerful. She would have to return to this nexus—where she entered our world—to regain her power. That must be why she seems compelled to return to Laramie. Anyway, the cult recruited enough musicians to perform Gustave's ninth symphony in the basement of the ruined music hall.

"However, the first time they attempted to seal her away was a failure. The music only seemed to embolden her. It wasn't until the second time, when one of the cultists—a musician, in fact, named Claudia Ranald—suggested playing Gustave's seventh symphony, which was dedicated to his wife Cecily."

"They played a different song than the one that got her killed?" Relic asked.

"Indeed," Marshall confirmed. "Claudia's reasoning was because Valaina is a being of hatred and rage. She's incapable of any of the creative forces humans possess. So even if Valaina was drawn toward the music that spawned the Widow, once Cecily's body returned to the place of their union, the positive emotions were too much for Valaina to endure, so she was driven back—by whatever remained of Cecily in her body—to the only place she could find refuge from it."

"Alternus," Delilah said.

"Precisely," Marshall replied, the sound of ice clinking in a glass as he took a drink.

Relic was connecting the dots. "So we need to play 'Alternus' to open the nexus, let my dad out, and then have that song somehow ready to play afterwards to drive the Widow back in there. But where are we going to get some super old symphony? Is there a recording of it or something?"

"That's what I've been working on finding," Marshall said. "Pieces of the music were scattered throughout the States, but I couldn't find the complete score. The only full copies were in the music hall when it was burned following the Widow's imprisonment. However, the final sheets I needed were here in Milan, and I've been working with a local symphony to make a recording of it."

"So we could run it through the PA system after Altar Stone plays their set," Delilah interjected. "Is there anything else?"

Marshall took another drink. "Because we don't have all the specifics of what role your father played in the Widow's return, Delilah, I think it may be important for you to be near this nexus. Relic's attunement to his parents makes me suspect that you might experience a similar connection to your father. I believe he is the key to all of this. Perhaps you should begin attending the band's rehearsals?"

Relic signed inwardly. *Just what I need,* he thought, *my fake girlfriend hanging around the girl that I actually want to be my girlfriend after we secretly kissed. Beautiful.*

"I doubt that dead asshole will want to talk to me," Delilah said, although without the usual sarcasm in her tone. She sounded almost...mournful. "But sure, I'll drop in on practice."

"Good," Marshall said, followed by the sound of rustling paper. "I'll be back in a week. Keep up the patrols, and if there are any more encounters with the Widow, it's probably best to avoid engaging her. I'm sure she would like to expedite our plans, because it's her only shot at freedom, but we do not want her to fully understand each of your capabilities."

Too late, Relic thought, remembering their last fight. The Widow had to know she was more powerful than them. Relic only hoped that his dad—when freed—would be able to help them truly seal the deal.

He had to know what to do.

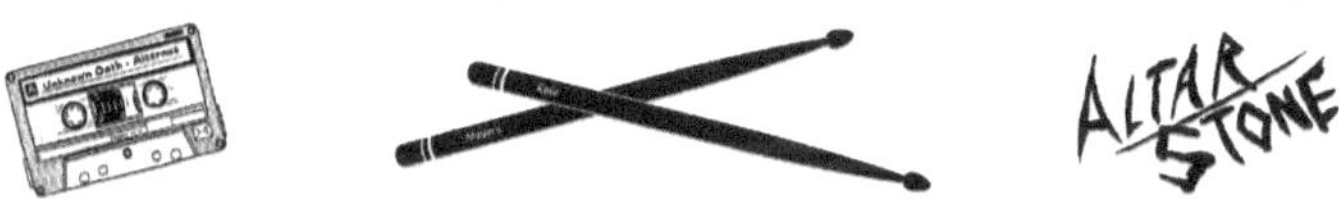

Bree's return felt very anticlimactic for Relic, but in a relieving sort of way.

He had expected some level of awkwardness or discomfort, but when she came over to his house on New Year's Day, she immediately pulled him down to the basement so they could watch *The Fifth Element* that she had just gotten on DVD for Christmas. Relic had told her on the phone about the DVD player his mom and Calvin had gotten him, and it was all hooked up and ready to go.

During the movie, they didn't have to talk much, so there was no discussion about their big kiss. Relic didn't want to be the one to broach it, so a sort of understanding was built on that first day back: life would return to normal, as if it hadn't happened. But he was certain it was at the forefront of both their minds, even if they didn't act like it.

The battle of the bands couldn't come soon enough.

Altar Stone's first practice of 1998 was awkward, to say the least.

Not only had Relic brought Delilah along—as instructed by Marshall—but when Tyler showed up, he had Miranda Cartwright with him.

"Full house?" Gate asked from his seat behind the crude desk that occupied the corner of the room. He was playing a game of solitaire with an actual deck of cards, which Relic didn't know people actually did.

Delilah assumed her bashful goth persona, sitting cross-legged against the wall near Relic's drums. Relic and Bree gave each other an annoyed look, but after their eyes met, Relic couldn't help but notice when Bree's gaze shifted to Delilah behind him before she returned her attention to her guitar.

Just what I need, Relic thought.

"You guys alright if Miranda hangs out?" Tyler asked, walking over to the mic while Miranda gave the room a clearly disgusted observation. "We're going to a movie afterwards."

As Nick tried to say he didn't mind, Bree cranked her volume knob and pretended to tune her guitar, turning her back toward Miranda.

"It's fine," Relic shouted, motioning for Tyler to get on the mic.

Wanting to get this over with, Relic counted off "Alternus" immediately, sloshing his hi-hats with one, two, three...

The rhythm began as it always did, with Bree's fading-in guitar chord playing beneath it. Nick's bassline followed Relic's tom work, now locked in after weeks of practicing—the song's intro was naturally the first thing they'd all perfected as a band.

As he spun his sticks out of habit, Relic noticed Miranda reacting with surprise. He knew that she thought he was just some fat loser, an insignificant speck on the Chambers High social radar. But she was in his domain now, and he was part of a heavy metal legacy that gave him a sudden, overwhelming sense of pride.

Feeding off the energy, Relic tried out a new fill, rolling all the way across his four rack toms with perfectly timed triplet accents. Out of the corner of his eye, he saw Delilah's eyes widen, but he was focusing on Bree who smiled brightly as she added her own new flourish with a squealing lead at the tail end of Tyler's clean vocal entry.

"The curse has come," Tyler sang, "from far beyond."

Relic looked over his drums and saw Gate bobbing his head, sitting up in his chair—a new reaction from the janitor. *We must finally be nailing this thing,* Relic thought, doing another fill as they transitioned into the first verse.

"A price to be paid," Tyler bellowed, channeling Ricky's dynamic range, "for the masterpiece made."

Relic let his hi-hats slosh open a little more during the verse, adding more weight to the song. He closed his eyes and lost himself to the music, gnashing his teeth and banging his head. His father's form appeared almost immediately once he closed his vision to the world.

Steven Meyers played every beat in lock with Relic, moving like a mirror image.

"Dad," Relic said, without speaking. They communicated through the song they played together.

"You can't do this," his dad said, "not after everything I've done." His dad's eyes glared at him from behind a shaggy beard and a frame of wild hair showing the effects of half a decade of headbanging.

"We can get you out, Dad!" Relic felt himself speeding up the tempo, feeling the urgency to convince his father that he could do it.

"—will get out again," Steven said, his own tempo increasing in turn. "—kill again." His cymbal crashes cut off some of his father's words, but Relic was sure he was talking about the Widow.

"Wake up, Dad!" Relic began hitting his drums harder. "Haven't you seen?! She *is* out again, and definitely killing!"

"No, Relic," Steven said, with a desperation in his voice.

"I can do it, Dad! I can save you!"

"Relic!"

The tension exploded, and Relic slipped into a massive fill that fell out of the pocket, pulling him back to the maintenance room. "Alternus" fell away into a distorted guitar hum as Bree cocked her head and gave him a questioning look as he finished the impromptu drum solo that quickly lost its energy as the rest of the band stopped playing.

"Was it supposed to sound like that?" Miranda asked when the noise faded.

"Babe," Tyler said, annoyed. "Come on."

"My bad," Relic began, but was interrupted by Bree.

"You know, Miranda, you can take a walk outside and hum whatever boy band songs you want while we practice."

Shit, Relic thought, knowing how easily this could escalate. But he followed Nick's gaze to see Delilah to his left, crouching low and looking like a rabid dog.

"She alright?" Nick asked.

Relic couldn't say. He slowly got off his drum throne. "Delilah?"

She didn't respond. Crouched low with her hand braced on the ground, she stared at each of them with her mouth hanging open. Relic couldn't be positive, but he thought he saw fangs.

"Get out," Gate said, slipping out from behind his desk. "Now!" He moved quickly to put himself between the dhampir and the kids.

Relic motioned for Bree to get the rest of the band out. When Delilah leapt toward Gate, Relic heard the maintenance door close, but then he heard Bree's gasp. He turned from the fight to see Bree in the room with her back against the doors, blocking anyone else from coming in.

Dammit! Relic thought, hoping he wouldn't have to explain all this.

"Why didn't you tell me?!" Gate hissed through his teeth as he tried to keep Delilah's fangs from his neck. "You're dating a vampire?!"

Relic didn't have time to explain. He grabbed his drumsticks and spun them, unable to hide his abilities now, and knowing that Bree would have learned about them eventually. The green energy from Alternus flared to life, and he raced toward Delilah.

The dhampir hissed like a feral cat as Relic wrapped an arm around her waist, pulling her from Gate. He managed to put a stick to her throat as a threat, and the girl recoiled as if it were a burning brand. Relic fell back as Delilah released Gate, and together they hit the ground with Relic's legs wrapping around her.

"Do I stake her?" Gate asked, his voice low and calm.

"No!" Relic said, struggling to keep Delilah still. "Just hold her!"

Gate knelt down and helped Relic keep the girl's limbs restrained as her heavy breathing began to slow. Relic managed to turn toward Bree to see her staring at them from the door, but whether she was more shocked to see Relic's powers or Delilah's true nature, he couldn't say.

Finally, Delilah's breathing returned to normal, and she said in a thick voice, "I'm fine."

Together, they got to their feet.

"What the hell was that?" Relic asked.

Delilah shook her head, looking from Bree to Gate, clearly realizing her cover was slightly blown. "I...I don't know. Usually, I can ignore those times when I think I hear my dad's voice. But this time...I couldn't turn him off." She looked to Relic. "I think the song has a little power over me as well."

Bree walked over to them, staring at the now mundane sticks in Relic's hands. "What the hell was *that*?" she asked.

Relic took a deep breath, looking to Delilah, who nodded as she turned away to give them a moment. Gate followed Delilah, keeping a close eye on her.

Relic told Bree everything—summarizing as much as he could before the rest of the band came back in. While Relic could explain away Delilah's behavior to the rest of Altar Stone as some sort of medical condition, he had to be much more brutally honest with Bree.

As she listened, Bree reached up to grasp the Christmas gift that dangled from her neck, as if it was suddenly choking her.

Chapter 28

After that practice, Relic and Bree became distant. They still hung out and—now that Bree knew there was no real romance involved—things were much less uncomfortable when Delilah happened to be around.

But things had changed, and Relic didn't know how to fix it. He kept getting the sense that Bree didn't want to talk about all the secrets he had to keep, so he wouldn't bring it up. The energy between them made Relic feel like their kiss had never happened—like it was one of his cruel dreams.

Part of him knew this was just the hand he was dealt. Lots of kids would kill to have some sort of magical ability to fight monsters—even if they didn't fully understand it—and maybe not having the girl of his dreams was part of the price he had to pay.

But that was too high a price for him, and Relic even began to wonder if everything they had worked toward—the battle of the bands, saving his dad, keeping the town from being devoured by monsters—was worth it if he couldn't have Bree.

On Valentine's Day, he made his decision.

Calvin had invited Dina and Relic out to dinner for the occasion, and Relic was allowed to bring a date. Since Delilah was still technically his girlfriend—as far as most of the world was concerned—it was assumed he would invite her.

"Won't your girlfriend get jealous?" Dina asked when Relic said who he was bringing. "Delilah seems like such a sweet girl, and you get to hang out with Bree pretty much every day."

"You said I could invite whoever I wanted," Relic reminded her.

"Absolutely," Calvin butted in, and for once Relic welcomed the intrusion.

They picked up Bree that evening, and Relic—running up to her door alone—was stunned by her attire.

He hadn't specifically dressed up for the occasion, but she wore a very flattering, loose-fitting red blouse tucked into tight slacks with high-top sneakers. Her shirt was unbuttoned just enough to make Relic blush, and her Christmas present sparkled proudly against her freckled chest.

"You look incredible," Relic said honestly, and for the first time in weeks Bree looked at him with unreserved affection. It wasn't the sort of compliment he was used to giving, usually relying on sarcasm or back-handed offerings to make himself feel less vulnerable. But he was tired of hiding things from this girl—trying to do so was weakening him.

Bree's look turned into a rueful smirk as she grabbed her coat and stepped out into the cold with him. "Wish I could say the same, but you wore that to school, chump."

Relic laughed, and for the first time since they knew each other, she reached out and held his hand as they walked back to the car.

From there, the night felt perfect. They went to Archie's, a local pizza place that was oddly famous for their salads and sandwiches. Dinner was like falling back into a comfy couch, with lighthearted conversations about funny memories, recent movies, and school happenings.

Halfway through dinner, Dina got up to use the restroom. As Relic and Bree joked about the shape of one of the breadsticks, Calvin leaned over the table.

"Hey, Relic, I wanted to run something by you."

The seriousness in his voice brought the levity down at the table. "Yeah?"

Calvin placed a ring box on the table. "I wanted to know if you would be alright with me asking your mom to marry me."

There was a sudden knife in Relic's gut, twisting and refusing to let him breathe. He stared at the box as his mouth went dry, trying to figure out what to say. But out of the corner of his eye, he saw Bree react with genuine joy and eagerness, lifting the weight that he had felt pushing down on him.

He was reminded that he had prepared for this possibility. Calvin made his mom happy, and his dad—whether he was actually alive or if he would even be able to come back—had left this life a long time ago.

This was a chance to move on.

Underneath the table, Relic grabbed Bree's hand. Her face didn't change, glued to the box and waiting for Relic's response. But she squeezed his fingers in return, giving him the strength he needed.

Relic nodded. "Yeah," he said with an honest smirk. "I think that'd be cool."

Calvin looked close to tears as he returned the box under the table just as Dina returned from the restroom. They finished their dinner while trying to act as if everything would proceed as normal for the rest of the evening.

The proposal happened outside of Archie's, in the busy parking lot where plenty of Valentine's celebrators were able to witness a classic scene of romance. Despite the frigid temperature, there was tangible warmth in the air.

Dina obviously said yes—after casting Relic a quick, reassuring look—and embraced Calvin in a squealing hug as the onlookers broke into applause. Bree put a hand on Relic's shoulder then, and whispered in his ear, "You did a real good thing, man."

He turned and kissed her. It wasn't as earth-shattering as their first one, but he felt her kiss him back just before he pulled away. She smiled at him.

"We don't have to play the battle of the bands, Bree. I don't even know if our plan would work, but I just...I want you to know, we don't have to do it." He looked down at his callused hands. "I don't have to do *that* anymore, with the sticks. I don't even know how I do it, really. But I'm sorry I kept it all from you—just too many secrets—and I just want...you." He looked up at her. "I love you, Bree."

It felt like the most honest thing he had ever said in his entire life.

"You guys coming?" Dina called from where they had been celebrating their big moment, the onlookers now scattering.

Bree grabbed his hand so Dina and Calvin could clearly see. "Come on," she said, giving him her crooked smile. "I only caught, like, half of that, so we'll need to talk a little more in your basement."

Laughing, Relic let himself be pulled back to Calvin's Jeep.

The drive home from Archie's was pure bliss for Relic. Calvin had his favorite band, Foreigner, on the stereo, his mom was admiring her engagement ring, and Bree leaned her head on Relic's shoulder. He wasn't sure it could get much better than that.

"Release me, son," his dad decided to say then. Although, now Relic couldn't be sure if that voice was his father or the Widow. The monster that Cecily had become had deluded herself into believing that Relic was truly her offspring.

"No," Relic said, refusing the plea for the first time.

"Huh?" Bree said, turning her head up toward Relic.

"What the hell is that?" Calvin asked.

There was sinister laughter in Relic's mind and Calvin began slowing the car. Relic peered around the driver's headrest and saw a familiar figure out the window.

"Drive!" Relic shouted. "Go now!"

"Relic, what the hell?" Dina began, but when she looked out the windshield, she joined in Relic's cries. "Oh god, Calvin, drive! Go! Go!"

The Widow glided toward the car from the tree line, a nearly translucent specter of faint blue energy that resembled the decayed form of Cecily Moreau.

"Don't release me, son," Steven Meyers whispered to him, his voice clearer now.

Calvin accelerated, but it was too late. The Widow closed the distance to the Jeep and shattered the driver's side glass with a piercing shriek. Blood sprayed across the interior dash as the Widow raked her elongated fingers across Calvin's exposed flesh. He screamed as the car lost control and burst through the guardrail, sending them down an incline.

The Jeep slowed to a roll at the base of the hill and came to a not-so-jolting stop when it bumped into a tree.

"Oh my god, Calvin?!" Dina scrambled for the door handle so she could get out and check on her fiancé.

"Are you alright?" Relic asked Bree, carefully running his hands over her arms and neck.

She nodded, looking at Calvin with wide eyes. "I'm fine." She turned to him. "You?"

He nodded and got out to join his mom, looking back up the hill to make sure there was no sign of the Widow. All he saw were swaying trees and the lights from the nearby Denny's.

"Honey, can you go call an ambulance?" Dina asked, taking off her coat to cover Calvin. "Run up the hill to that diner and call 911. Please hurry!"

Bree joined him as they clambered up the snowy hill. Within four minutes, Calvin was loaded into an ambulance, and Relic accompanied his mom and Bree to the hospital in a police car.

The wait was excruciating, and Relic felt like he couldn't leave his mom's side. But Bree made the perfect excuse for them to go find her some coffee so they could have a quick word.

"You knew something was going to happen, didn't you?" she asked Relic when they were alone in the vending area. "Before that thing showed up?"

Relic remembered everything that Gate and Delilah had told him, about how telling people about the Alternians was like painting a target on them. He pictured Bree getting slashed by the Widow just like Calvin had been, and decided lying was the only way to keep her safe.

He shook his head. "What do you mean?"

She stared at him in shock, but the fear of seeing her hurt or killed made Relic continue playing dumb.

Bree sighed, looking away from him. "You know, maybe you were right before. It might be smarter if we wait until after the battle..." She looked at him, and Relic could tell she was hiding sadness behind her crooked smile as she motioned between them. "...before we have that chat in your basement. Yeah?"

Relic wanted to scream, "No!" and run toward her like in the movies, suffocating her with a kiss. But he couldn't stop seeing that blood spray across Calvin's dash. "I don't want to," Relic began.

"Until you're ready to open up to me," she interrupted, moving toward the coffee machine, "let's just wait." She slotted in three quarters and pressed the coffee dispenser button before turning back to Relic. "You know how much I hate half-assing shit." This time, her half-smile was more genuine.

As they made their way back to the waiting room, Relic reflected on how much he didn't deserve someone like Bree, and how he couldn't help thinking he had let her down. But he refused to endanger her any more than he stupidly already had.

Dina was talking to a doctor when they came back. From her reaction, Relic couldn't tell if it was good news or bad. But when she turned to him and rushed over to hug him, he knew it was positive.

"He was awake, but they had to put him under for surgery," Dina told them, taking the coffee gratefully. "Red, would you mind calling your parents and seeing if they wouldn't mind picking you two up? I'm going to wait here, but you two should get home and rest. It's getting late."

Russ made it there in record time, and Relic was dropped off back at his house. While the evening had taken a drastic downhill turn after the accident, Bree still cupped his face and kissed his cheek before he got out of the car. "See you tomorrow," she whispered, and her voice lingered in his ear as he went to bed in a seriously conflicted mood.

When he dreamed of his dad again that night, Steven Meyers looked like he was turning into some kind of monster.

CHAPTER 29

The day of the battle of the bands arrived, and the weeks leading up to it had allowed Relic to fall back into a relatively normal rhythm. Calvin had recovered from the attack, and his mother was in an amazing mood as she planned their wedding, involving Bree in many of the decisions. Altar Stone had damn near perfected "Alternus" (without Delilah observing any more practices), and Relic was surprised that there had been a significant decrease of tropes during his patrols.

If the Widow was somehow feeding off the fallen tropes, at least he and Delilah weren't giving her too much to eat before their big showdown.

Now that the big day had arrived, he felt almost like a normal kid with stage fright. The school day had dragged on, and Relic couldn't concentrate on anything. But there was an electricity in the halls of Chambers High, with almost everyone talking about going to the competition and who they were supporting.

Actually winning the battle of the bands hadn't been something Relic had concerned himself with up until this point, but a competitive edge began to emerge inside of him when he heard people talking about how they were sure Bag of Sax would win, or that Autumnal Fall was going to clinch it. There was even a new ska band called Malnormality that Relic hadn't even heard about until now.

After school, Altar Stone moved their gear up from their convenient basement rehearsal space to the auditorium. The fact that the janitor was helping them move Relic's huge drum set drew more than a few eyes and whispers. After their gear had been situated to the side of the stage, Relic snuck away to meet Howie, who nervously waited by the auditorium's sound booth.

"You sure you're good to do this?" Relic asked him, reaching into his pocket to pull out the CD. "This is super important."

Howie looked at the disc in a blank white sleeve that just said "Cecily" in block letters. "Why, again?"

Relic sighed. "It's part of the song, man. Once we finish playing, you just need to have the sound guys cue that up. Like, right when we finish."

He took it, placing it atop the huge *Warhammer* rulebook he cradled in his arm. "Alright, I'll do it. Just don't forget," he slapped his book, "you're coming over to play next weekend. You can use Alvin's army; he's got a ton of orc miniatures collecting dust."

"You bet," Relic said, hoping he survived the ordeal to do so. There were steeper prices to pay for favors from the AV club than playing toy soldiers with his buddy.

Relic turned to see Bree making her way down the aisle toward them. "We've got a problem," she said, motioning back toward backstage. "Tyler is freaking out."

"About what?"

They made their way backstage and Nick was calmly seated on a chair warming up on his bass, but Tyler was pacing around with his hands on the back of his head. It looked like he was talking to himself.

Relic pulled him aside as other bands arranged their gear and mingled amongst the competition. "What's going on, dude?"

"I don't know if I can do this," Tyler said, looking over his shoulder at the student audience that had already begun filing in. "I've never performed on stage before."

Aside from playing trumpet in 6th grade band, Relic just now realized he hadn't either. "So what, man? You've played, like, every sport in front of dozens of people. And you're, like, the most popular guy in the freshman class."

Tyler looked at him, genuine fear in his eyes. "That's different. Singing? In front of all these people?!" He shook his head. "I guess I kept thinking: I'm in a band, and we're just practicing in front of people. But I'm the singer. Everyone will know when the singer fucks up."

Normally, Relic would have trouble empathizing with this outburst. He would have considered it a joke, given what they had been working for these past months and what was at stake.

If you had asked Relic yesterday, he couldn't have cared less about how the crowd might respond to their performance, he just wanted to give his dad a chance to come home. But now, seeing Tyler's stage fright and feeling the energy carried into the auditorium by the excited crowd, his own stomach began twisting into knots as well.

He looked to Bree who also stared at the crowd, nervously flexing her fingers. Nick had joined them, his eyes wide as he watched the crowd come in. Relic knew he had to keep them together; if he didn't, and they didn't nail the performance like Unknown Oath had, all of this might have been in vain.

"Look," he said to them, trying to assume a commanding tone while keeping his voice just audible enough for the band to hear, "what happens before or after we play doesn't really matter. Once we get out on stage, every single person out there is entirely dependent on what we do.

"They came here for us," he said. "They are like little sparks looking to latch onto a flame, and all we have to do is light the fire. We go out there, we are gods—the creators of what they need. There's no way we can fuck it up, because we are going out there to give them what they don't even *know* they need."

As corny as he felt—like Emilio Estevez trying to rile up the Mighty Ducks—his words resonated with Altar Stone, each one of their faces turning from concern to enthusiasm. And it was infectious—Relic couldn't wait to get out there now.

"We kind of need one of these now, right?" Bree said, putting her hand out between them. Relic was the first one to put his own on top of hers, followed by Nick. Tyler gave Relic a skeptical smile before putting his hand on top.

"Let's knock 'em dead," Tyler said.

The first band to perform—by request—was Autumnal Fall, because a member of their band had to guard the nexus to another dimension when Altar Stone took the stage. Delilah and Sebastian both played keyboards and a sophomore named Harper VanHorn sang extremely off-key (though Relic was no vocal expert).

While Relic wasn't the target audience of their music, he applauded their performance with most of the other bandmembers hanging out in the wings. The curtains closed, and the goth-clad trio removed their instruments as Bag of Sax began setting up.

Delilah pulled Relic aside. "I'll be downstairs keeping an eye out," she said. "I brought headphones so I can listen to something else while you guys play so I don't freak out again. And Marshall is getting the nexus ready." She looked into his eyes and put her hands on his shoulders. "You can do this, Relic. We're counting on you."

Worried that she might try to kiss him—he could never tell with Delilah—he turned away and patted her shoulder in return, assuring her they would do their part.

Relic stood next to Bree as they watched Bag of Sax cover a Green Day song. Altar Stone was next on the set list, and Relic was starting to feel the nerves creep through his body like a swarm of skittering parasites. He couldn't stop twitching his feet, tapping out the double bass patterns of "Alternus" while trying to keep his arms from shaking.

Toward the end of Bag of Sax's set, Relic felt Bree's arm against his as she moved closer, wrapping her fingers through his. She was subtle enough that no one else could probably tell they held hands, but her touch let his entire body breathe a cleansing breath, purging the anxiety that was building up.

"We got this, man," she said, just loud enough for Relic to hear as the punks of Bag of Sax let their final chord ring out. The crowd exploded, much more exuberantly than they had for Delilah's band.

That made Relic's nerves return slightly, but at least he was able to move now, scrambling to help Bag of Sax get their drums out of the way so he'd have time to arrange his. The downside to being an egotistical metal drummer is that it took much longer to get a seven-piece, double bass drum kit properly set up than it did a traditional three- or five-piece kit with a single bass drum.

But Relic told himself he'd always make the sacrifice to appease the metal gods.

Within a few minutes, Relic was sitting behind his drum set arranging the cymbals and toms to make sure they were as close to normal as possible. Nick and Bree quickly checked their tuning while Tyler stood there with his back to Relic, clenching and unclenching his fists as he stared into the folds of the curtains.

But when those curtains were pulled back, and time froze as Relic closed his eyes and took a deep breath, sending a message to his father.

I don't care if you want me to bring you back, he said in his mind. *You're coming back today, Dad. And then we kill the Widow together.*

Relic counted them off, the first hit of his hi-hats transporting him from that stage to the misty oblivion of his dreams. When he began the rhythm, he saw his father's drum set, but there was no sign of Steven Meyers.

Unfazed, Relic played the song as closely as possible to what was recorded on that cursed tape, careful not to get too carried away like he did during that first practice of the year. All the tension inside him melted away as he felt Nick's bassline settle right under his rhythm, with Bree's guitar accompanying them perfectly. Tyler was flawless, and even though Relic couldn't see the spectators with his eyes closed—his consciousness swept away to another dimension—he could feel the energy of the crowd.

And it was swelling.

Unbidden, Delilah came into his visions, wearing her black-hooded sweatshirt as she stalked the ethereal basement halls below. He could see the bulge of big headphones under her hood, blocking out the arcane energy that Altar Stone was summoning. As Relic performed the fill leading into the verse, a shape melted away from the shadows in a classroom, but Delilah didn't notice it. The form took shape and became a crooked, limping scarecrow, moving as if it were in some stop-motion animation, following the girl through the halls.

Relic tried to scream at Delilah, but his vision suddenly shifted to a different scene, and Steven Meyers was reaching for him, being pulled into the mists by contorted hands with long, sharp fingers. Once more, Relic wanted to cry out, but he kept playing his part, feeling something grow within him.

"No," Steven Meyers whispered, "don't do it, son."

The sensation was similar to when Relic first channeled the energy to fight with his drumsticks, the feeling he also got when he first started playing drums and would accidently fall into the pocket, not really knowing how he got there or how to remain in its comforting embrace.

A light pierced Relic's waking dream, and the mists that obscured his father were parted. The hands still groped him, but they pulled him into the light. Relic felt immense release as he performed another fill into the song's breakdown, which fell back into the iconic rhythm from the intro. As the energy of the song flattened, the light intensified, and a figure stepped in front of Steven Meyers' struggling form.

Cecily Moreau—her face twisted with scars and protruding bone spurs—turned to look at Relic, giving him a wink as she walked toward the light. Relic knew in that moment that the nexus was opened, and anything trapped on the other side—Steven Meyers included—could come into their world. Their work was almost done.

Relic followed Bree's lead as she transitioned back into the final chorus, opening his eyes to see glimpses of an astonished crowd through the blinding stage lights. Bree and Nick were thrashing their upper bodies back and forth to the rhythm as Tyler held out the last piercing wail of the song.

Now, Howie, Relic thought, waiting for Cecily's song to kick on, to drive her back into Alternus. *Now!*

As Relic washed the cymbals over Bree's final chord, the crowd was beginning to cheer. *No,* Relic thought, *not yet!* He needed their energy for the next part of the ritual. He could feel the power coming off the crowd in waves, and the piece of Alternus within him assured Relic that he would need that energy for the next part of their plan to work. *Come on, Howard!*

There was nothing coming over the sound system, and panic rose within him. But it was hard for Relic to not get distracted by the wall of applause that his band currently basked in.

Knowing he only had one shot at this, Relic got up from behind his drums and raced to the front of the stage, sliding across the slick surface toward the edge. As he started to run up the aisle amidst a flurry of laughs and questions from the crowd, the door to the sound booth was thrown open and Howie tumbled down the stairs into the aisle.

The noise from the stage died away as a figure descended the sound booth stairs, holding the CD that Relic had given to Howie containing the final piece of the ritual.

"You thought I'd actually let you do this," Delilah said with a smile that wasn't hers. She waved the CD back and forth, tauntingly. "You play this, the crowd goes wild, and you and I just go back to being normal?"

"Delilah, we have to hurry," Relic said, looking at the crowd. All eyes were on him, including the faculty and staff, apparently convinced that this was part of the show or something. "Give Howie the CD. Hurry!"

With a quick motion, Delilah snapped the CD in half, sending pieces of plastic flying in all directions.

"No!" Relic yelled, reaching out as if he could somehow repair the thing.

Delilah laughed and her eyes were pale white orbs that no longer belonged to her. Whether it was the Widow or Guy Valentine, someone had taken over the dhampir's mind.

Relic reached for his back pocket where he kept his sticks during his patrols, but they were up on stage sitting atop his snare drum. His mind raced as he imagined his father being torn apart by Alternians while the Widow ushered her legions into their world through the nexus they had just opened.

"I should thank you," Delilah said. "My daughter wouldn't listen to me, but you followed in your daddy's footsteps like a good little boy."

"Valentine," Relic said between clenched teeth.

In response, Delilah launched toward him, her knives left in their sheaths as she reached out with both hands in a feral attack. Relic heard the entire crowd gasp, but he braced himself for her and managed to keep his footing even as she collided with him.

"Delilah," Relic said, struggling to keep her fangs from his neck, "I know you can hear me."

"Alright, that's quite enough," an adult called from near the stage. "Break that up back there."

"You broke the seal," Delilah hissed. Despite her familiar voice, she spoke with her father's words. "You set us free, and we're not going back."

Relic broke free of her grasp, pushing her away. He imagined his dad down in the basement, struggling against the Alternians trying to flee into his world. He hoped Gate would be able to help him.

"Relic!"

Turning just in time, Relic saw Bree toss him his drumsticks. Even before they were in his hands, they began glowing that sickly green color and spun in midair as if they were magnetically pulled toward his hands. He snatched them out of the air and turned back to Delilah who hissed and recoiled. He dove on her, eliciting another gasp from the crowd.

Once atop her, Relic heard more shouts from behind him to "break it up," but he was only focused on Delilah, watching for any recognition in her eyes. After a moment of being pinned by his arcane sticks, her pupils returned, and he could tell the real Delilah looked back up at him.

"I'm sorry," she mouthed, her expression twisted in shame. "They knocked my headphones off."

Relic got off her and helped her up. But when he looked around, he saw that the crowd was nowhere near as riled up as they should be, and several faculty members were moving toward them.

They had failed. He pictured his father being torn apart and the entire town being overrun by the Alternians now pouring through the nexus, looking for hosts to turn into blood-thirsty monsters.

Sorry, Dad, Relic thought miserably.

But that was when he heard Bree.

"Watch out," she whispered into the mic, before strumming her guitar to a clean version of Madonna's "Open Your Heart."

A hush washed over the crowd, and the adults moving to put an end to this whole scene turned back to the stage to watch Bree play guitar.

Bree stepped back up to the mic to sing to Relic, about how she saw him walk by on the street. Immediately, Relic felt the same embarrassment that crippled him in history class the time Miranda played that video of him dancing to this very song. Looking around, he saw several students turn back to him expectantly—they could have just been enjoying the song, waiting to see what his part in it was, but in Relic's mind, they were mocking him.

Nick started playing the bassline along to Bree's slow version of the tune, but it began to pick up pace. Bree begged Relic to give her half a chance, mimicking the moves that Madonna had made in her famous music video, and suddenly all the shame the song had conjured up a moment before melted away and Relic couldn't help smiling at his friend's performance.

As Bree sang the part about not resisting her, Relic was infected by the energy now surging amongst the crowd (who were now woo hoo-ing and singing along), and he broke into a sprint for the stage. Almost as if this was all a dream, the crowd began cheering him on. He ran up the stairs near the side, dodging a confused teacher, and made his way to his drums just in time to hit the chorus with the band.

The auditorium exploded when both Relic and Tyler joined in, filling the place with a much different energy than what "Alternus" had brought forth. Relic forgot about the ritual and Delilah's interference—for a moment, he was just the drummer of Altar Stone playing in front of a riveted audience.

With Tyler taking over lead vocals, Bree came back to play guitar facing Relic, mouthing every word of the song to him as he sang back at her. Complete joy overwhelmed Relic as he spun his sticks and did something with his band that none of the vile Alternians could do.

They created real magic.

CHAPTER 30

After Altar Stone's extended set, Relic more or less shoved his drums to the other side of the stage and raced down to the basement. Bree and Delilah accompanied him while Nick and Tyler were caught up reveling in the aftermath of their performance, but Relic didn't wait. He felt something change within him, and he knew their plan had worked.

It *had* to have worked.

Relic still heard the crowd's distant applause continuing as his feet slammed down the stairs to the basement. It was exhilarating, and it gave him the energy to push his body harder than normal. He jump-kicked through the stairway doors like Chuck Norris and turned the final corner toward the maintenance room.

That's when he saw Guy Valentine near the open doors with one arm holding Gate up by his neck, pinning the janitor to the wall. The vampire wore a black trench coat and hand long, oily hair hanging like seaweed from his skeletal head. He smiled when Delilah stepped into view.

"Well," he said, his voice like bark being pulled from a tree, "you're quite the disappointment, young lady."

There were flashing lights from within the maintenance room and an echoing cry as if someone were falling through a massive hole.

"Delilah, don't listen to him!" Marshall yelled from within. "I need your help!"

"No, Delilah," Guy said wickedly, tilting his head as his eyes focused unnaturally on her. "Maybe listen to your old man just a little…"

Relic snapped his head around just in time to see Delilah bare her fangs. With bloodlust in her eyes, she grabbed Bree from behind.

"Bree!" Relic leapt in her direction as the dhampir sank her teeth into his friend's neck. Guy cackled as Relic—overcome by rage and desperate concern for Bree—drove one of his glowing drumsticks into Delilah's chest.

The dhampir threw her head back, her bloody mouth open wide in shocked agony. She let go of Bree, falling to the floor with Relic's drumstick still shoved into her breast, trailing that sickening green magic.

"No," Relic said, suddenly realizing what he had done.

Guy laughed maniacally.

Bree knelt down next to the dhampir, holding her own neck that bled from the bite. "Delilah!"

Overcome with blinding fury, Relic turned toward the vampire that held Gate and threw every ounce of his body weight toward him. Guy still cackled even as the collision knocked Gate free.

"Someone get in here!" Marshall was screaming. "I can't hold this much longer! Meyers is going to die!"

Relic raised his other glowing drumstick to drive it into Guy Valentine's heart, but the vampire just laid there with wide expectant eyes as if this were exactly what he wanted.

"Don't!" Delilah screamed, her voice breaking as if it took everything she had to even speak. "We need him..."

"What?!" Relic asked incredulously, his weapon still raised and his eyes still on the smiling lunatic beneath him. "He can control you!"

"No," Delilah said, coughing and spitting. "I'm not hungry anymore."

"Get them in here!" Marshall shouted. "Both of them! Now!"

Relic spun the drumstick and started to get off the vampire.

"Just a pussy like your old man," Guy began, but before he finished his next thought, Relic spun his stick again and drove it into the man's leg. "Ahhhh!!"

The vampire rolled around in agony as the enchanted stick did its work. Relic helped Gate up before going to check on Delilah.

"You alright?" Relic asked.

Delilah tried to laugh, coughing again and spitting up more blood. "No."

"Relic!" This time it wasn't Marshall shouting from within the maintenance room; it was Steven Meyers.

As Gate dragged the squirming vampire into the room, Relic and Bree helped Delilah through the door. Lights still flashed from within, and smoke billowed out as if they were entering a Kiss concert. It took a minute for Relic to see anything as they entered the haze, but soon the arcane circle of glowing light in the center of the room illuminated a horrific scene.

Relic had never imagined a reunion with his father playing out like this. His dad looked just like he had from the dreams, wildly overgrown hair and beard obscured a face that was twisted in agony. He wore a ripped Unknown Oath shirt, revealing an emaciated body riddled with scratches and bruises. He was restrained to the undulating floor as misshapen, blackened hands clutched at him, trying to pull him back into whatever substance it was they emerged from.

In that shifting mass of strange shapes, Relic saw something that froze him in place. Cecily Moreau looked up at him, her rotting face contorted and twisted into something demonic, which Relic could only assume was Valaina's true visage. The face disappeared back into the roiling sludge, and Relic's focus was jolted back to the task at hand by the High Warden's voice.

"By my side!" Marshall Crane shouted. He was dressed in full cult regalia, with a yellow robe adorned with a crimson stole hanging over his shoulders. He clutched a book desperately with both hands as some unnatural wind tried to pull it into the nexus at the center of the arcane markings. "Delilah! Bring her here!"

Stunned by what he saw, Relic obeyed. He felt the energy from the nexus try to pull him in as well, and he had trouble taking his eyes off his father, even though it was agonizing to see him in such a state. He felt like he had to physically go and help him, but he had no idea the complexities of what Marshall was trying to orchestrate. His only hope was to obey.

"Oh my fucking god," Bree said, the blood from her neck wound and staining her shirt as she observed the chaos of the room. Together, she and Relic managed to get Delilah into position next to her adopted father.

"You!" Marshall shouted to Gate. "Bring Valentine here! Hurry! We need to close this!"

Gate deposited the writhing vampire next to Marshall. The cultist read something from his book aloud, but between his dad's screams and the fact that the language was probably Alternian, Relic had no clue what it meant. Whatever it was, Guy Valentine and Delilah both did not care for it, and their wails of pain joined Steven's. The energy from the nexus began swirling like a concentrated tornado in the room.

Relic reached for Bree, holding her as the wind threatened to pull them into another dimension. They clung to each other while Marshall shouted out the rest of his incantation. Just as the energy seemed like it was reaching its climax, Marshall reached out and grabbed both of Relic's drumsticks: the one stabbed into Delilah's chest and the other in Guy's leg. Both vampire and dhampir screamed in pain and the world exploded in a brilliant white light.

Relic opened his eyes to see Bree looking down over him, blood all over her cheek, chin, neck, and shirt.

"I need a Band-aid," she said weakly, giving him a desperate, bloody kiss before helping him sit up.

Despite the debris left from the mystical storm, the room looked like it had returned back to normal. Several bodies littered the ground, and some began to move. Gate began sitting up next to a motionless Guy Valentine, and Marshall Crane rolled to his side moaning as he clutched his hands together. Delilah laid still like her father, and at the center of a circular pattern drawn on the ground in chalk...

"Dad!" Relic saw Steven Meyers lying unconscious on the floor, which was no longer undulating or birthing strange appendages. Using Bree's support, Relic got to his knees and scrambled over to his father.

"Careful, man," Gate said from nearby. "He kind of tried to kill me when he first came out of there…"

"Dad," Relic said, approaching more cautiously. His dad's eyelids fluttered open. "Dad! It's me, Relic!"

Steven Meyers parted his lips, a weak moan escaping.

"I'm going to go get some help," Bree said, struggling to her feet. "Be right back."

"Dad, are you alright?" It was a stupid question to which Relic knew the answer, but he had no idea what else to say.

"Son," Steven said weakly, blinking very slowly and trying to wet his lips with a dry tongue. "I…tried…to warn you…"

Relic grabbed his dad's callused hand, which felt completely limp and lifeless in his, feeling tears streaming down his face. "I know, Dad. I heard…I'm sorry, but I had to get you out of there. I couldn't leave you!"

Marshall groaned loudly as he sat up. "He fought me to stay down there." Marshall stared at his burned hands, blackened from where he'd touched Relic's drumsticks. "Once the song opened the nexus, I reached out to him using Adratheon's power…but he wouldn't accept our help…"

"Why?" Relic asked, staring at his dad through hot tears. "Why would he want to stay there?"

"Because," Marshall said, getting to his feet, the man's normally stoic face looking very concerned, "apparently he was the only thing holding Adratheon back from entering our world."

Altar Stone won the battle of the bands by a unanimous vote, but only Tyler and Nick were available to accept the cash reward because the rest of their band had disappeared. The celebration, however, was cut short by the arrival of the police and paramedics, summoned by Bree's 911 call.

Relic and Bree held each other's hands during the ensuing chaos, which involved Gate orchestrating a small fire in the maintenance room to cover up their ritual, Marshall hauling away the unconscious Valentines with the help of his driver, and finally the paramedics tending to the found missing person, Steven Meyers.

Dina found her son at the hospital later, waiting just outside the exam room where several doctors were examining Unknown Oath's estranged drummer. Nearly in hysterics, Relic's mother held him and sobbed. She didn't ask what had happened or any particulars about the battle of the bands, and Calvin hung back in the main lobby, giving the family time to process.

"Did you see the show?" Relic asked.

Dina laughed. "Yes, you guys were incredible. I got Calvin to record it, so we can watch Bree sing to you again and go 'awww' while you two blush."

Relic laughed, looking forward to that.

Much later, Relic and Dina went into the room to visit Steven.

"Hey, Dad," Relic said, still feeling like he was in one of his dreams. "Feeling any better?"

The nurses had shaved away most of Steven's beard, and his hair was trimmed up slightly but still long as ever. The smile on Steven Meyers' face made Relic feel like he had never been gone—it was unsettling, in a way. "Much better, man, thanks to you." Steven's eyes went to Dina's, but Relic noticed that they lingered on her hand where it rested on Relic's shoulder, probably noticing the new engagement ring replacing the old wedding band. "Hey, Dina. Sorry I've been late with the checks."

Dina let out a choked laugh. "We thought you were dead, Steve." She stepped around Relic, putting a shaking hand on the bed's railing. "What happened?"

Steven's eyes fell on Relic, and he reached a hand out to his son. "It's a long story, but," Relic took his dad's extended hand, "maybe one for another time."

For a moment, Dina laid her hand on top of theirs—the hand with Calvin's ring on it—but she drew it back and said, "I'll let you two catch up." She walked toward the door, but turned around before leaving to add, "I'm glad you're alright, Steve."

"Thanks, Dina," Steven said, and Relic saw the tear in his dad's eye before Steven reached up to rub his face as Dina left the room. "I tell you what, Relic," his voice thick with emotion, "I'm pretty upset with you."

Relic pulled his hand away, worried that his dad would be angry at him for going against his warnings.

But Steven just smiled at him. "Where do you get off passing up your old man on drums? Altar Stone tore that stage up, man!"

Father and son laughed, and Relic barely even heard the howls outside.

Epilogue

Steven Meyers punched out at 4:58 PM, putting his card back in the rack right between Ralph Lipton's and Susie Neff's timecards. It was the last Friday of May, and he wasn't going to be late to his son's birthday festivities. He walked swiftly out of the factory toward the back of the lot where he always parked Gate's junky Cavalier.

"Meyers," someone shouted, "we're grabbing some beers at Robin's. You in?"

"Sorry, Tommy," Steven shouted. "I got plans. Raincheck, buddy!"

He beat the flow of traffic out of Tippecanoe National—where most of the Midwest's trailers were manufactured—reflecting on how there was a time in his life when he probably would have detested the idea of working a nine-to-five job like some corporate zombie. But as he drove down Sagamore Parkway with his windows down, blaring Mötley Crüe on his way to hang out with his son, he thought this life might not be too bad.

About a block from the factory, Steven stopped at a red light. A ringing payphone in the nearby parking lot of a Village Pantry drew his attention. Looking at it, Steven was reminded of another payphone from a decade ago. When it rang again, he thought of Dina and the life they once shared, which now felt like some old half-remembered dream. The third ring took on a different sound, and Adratheon whispered something on the edges of his hearing.

A car honked behind him, and Steven shook away the somber thoughts, continuing toward Greenbriar.

The old neighborhood was a lot like he remembered, though there were some areas that looked a little more haggard than others. Overall, it was a pleasant drive to his old home.

A nice red Jeep sat in the driveway as he pulled up to the house, parking the Cavalier out front along the curb. He got out and approached the porch, but before he could even get there, Relic burst through the door.

"Hey, Dad!"

"My man!" Steven shouted with delight. "We playing here or what?"

Relic shook his head, his long hair flopping around like a true little metalhead. "Over at Bree's. Her dad picked up Gate on the way back."

"Awesome, let's do this," Steven said. But his mood damped slightly when he saw Dina come to the door. "Oh, hey! Just here for the birthday boy. Is it alright if I park here?"

"Of course," Dina said as Calvin Green stepped up behind her.

"Hey, Steven!" Calvin said, pushing open the storm door. "How you feeling, man?" He approached, holding out a hand for Steven to shake.

A variety of emotions coursed through Steven, but a quick glance at Relic's anxious face steeled his resolve. He took Calvin's hand and gave it a firm shake. "I can't complain too much, dude. One day at a time, you know?"

Calvin gave him a genuine smile. "Well, you guys don't get in too much trouble, alright? We'll hang out here if you want to grab a drink later or something."

Steven looked from Calvin to Dina, feeling oddly content. "Yeah, I'd like that, man." He turned to Relic. "But we got shit to do, right?"

"Yeah," Relic said, turning to lead Steven toward Bree's.

"Russell!" Steven shouted when his old acquaintance-turned-new-gaming-pal answered the door.

"There they are!" Russ opened the door and led father and son toward the kitchen.

"Dude, aren't you, like, Altar Stone's drummer?!" Russ' daughter came barreling around the corner to embrace Relic, who laughed and kissed her eagerly.

Steven couldn't help but smile as he watched his son interact with his girlfriend, Bree. It reminded him of how he and Dina used to be in high school. The thought made him slightly sad.

"Don't worry," Russ said, setting a beer down on the table near Steven, "he's not allowed to sleep over anymore."

"Dad!" Bree said, repulsed.

"Good call," Steven said, winking at Relic. "Where's Gate?"

"Working," he called from the other room, "on stuff you pesky adventurers don't need to know about."

Bree and Relic took their seats next to each other at the table. In front of them was a collection of dice and their own *Dungeons & Dragons* books. Steven cracked his beer and claimed his own seat next to the yellow dice Russell kept for him.

After a few moments of catching up and snacking on chips, Gate finally emerged from the den with his notebook and dungeon master's paraphernalia. "So, are you guys ready to see if the birthday boy can survive the lair of harpies you got lost in last time?"

"Let's do it," Russ said excitedly.

"Well," Lydia said from the other end of the kitchen, "I guess I won't make dinner."

"Honey," Russ said teasingly, "you know it's Relic's birthday. We got pizzas coming in about an hour."

"Right, right," she said with a smile, sipping her glass of wine. "Oh, Steven, could you come here a sec?"

Casting a curious glance at Russ, Steven frowned. "Sure?" The look Russ gave him was one of resignation, like at least it wasn't *him* getting called away. Steven got up and followed Lydia out of the kitchen, down the hall, and into her office. She shut the door behind them.

"Have you considered our offer?"

Steven looked over his shoulder to make sure no one else was peering into the office. Satisfied they were alone, he said, "Look, Lydia, I feel like I just got back, alright? The kids are just starting summer…I mean, can I get some time to consider?"

She narrowed her eyes. "You like working at the factory? What do you make, like ten bucks an hour?"

Shaking his head, Steven tried not to reflect on the crappy one bedroom apartment that waited for him, or the rent he could barely afford, or the only miserable job he could find. Instead, he tried to think only of Relic as he said, "This isn't about the money—you know that. I just…give me a little time with him. Please?"

Taking a sip of her wine, she nodded. "Two weeks. Make 'em count, alright?"

Steven nodded, leaving the office and taking a deep breath before returning to the revelry. As he made his way back to his seat to take on the role of Krobble the dwarf barbarian, Steven watched his son laugh at something Bree said before nuzzling her neck and making her squeal. He stopped in the middle of the kitchen, wondering if he could sacrifice this for some stupid corporate interest—no matter how many digits the salary had.

"You coming, Dad?" Relic asked, nodding to the seat next to him.

A payphone rang in his mind then. *You coming, Stick?* Adratheon asked him. *You gotta answer some day.*

Despite the dread Adratheon filled him with, Steven smiled at his son.

There was no guarantee that him joining the Rothen Corps would do anything to stop Adratheon from eventually interfering in his life. But like he told Lydia, he just wanted a little more time.

Taking his seat, Steven picked up his polyhedral dice and rattled them around in his hand.

"Alright, sorry about that." He looked at Relic, satisfied. "I'm back now."

His son's smile quieted Adratheon's echoing laughter.

Please consider writing a review for

Scan to Review

www.bradyjsadler.com

SOPHOMORE YEAR
BEGINS NOW

RELIC MEYERS
& THE HARMONY OF HEXES

www.bradyjsadler.com

ABOUT THE AUTHOR

Brady J. Sadler is the drummer and founder of the Indiana-based fantasy metal band, Lorenguard. Since abandoning the not-so-prestigious life of a mediocre percussionist for an amazing band—playing an obscure style of music in America—Brady has become a prolific tabletop game designer and author.

He lives in Indiana with his loving family and a couple hateful cats.

You can keep up with him at www.bradyjsadler.com.